She Can Tell

Also By Melinda Leigh

She Can Run
Midnight Exposure

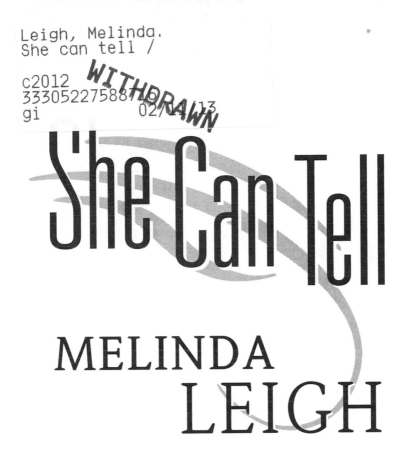

She Can Tell

MELINDA LEIGH

Montlake
Romance

Published by Montlake
P.O. Box 400818
Las Vegas, NV 89140

ISBN-13:1612185657
ISBN-10: 9781612185651

This book is dedicated to my kids, Annie and Tom. You were right. Bandit was a great addition to the book. Love you.

Prologue

Twenty-five years ago

He liked to watch.

To see the secret, private things people did when they thought they were alone.

From the moon shadow of an evergreen, he stared across the weedy backyard at the dilapidated rancher. Harry was inside. The Watcher's breath steamed out into the crisp winter air. Twenty yards of crabgrass was all that separated him from retribution.

Harry had to die.

It was the only way to make things right.

Impulsive responses, while satisfying, were rarely successful in the long term. Discipline was the key. He'd buried his rage and weighed all the options. Harry's life against his actions. His future against the impact of what he'd done. Ultimately, it was what Harry intended to do that made the difference.

Don't worry. Just come with me. I'll take care of you. I promise.

An hour of standing on the frozen ground, waiting for the house to go quiet and dark, had left the Watcher's toes with a numb ache. Fiery tingles shot through the balls of his feet as he crept toward a dark window cracked an inch for ventilation. The ground was too frozen for his boots to leave prints, but the crunch of dead grass echoed in the otherwise silent night. He crouched under the window, then peered over the sill. No sound. No light. No movement. He raised the sash and climbed through into the living room. Lacquer fumes and sawdust stung his nostrils. Heat rattled from a baseboard register as the aged furnace tried to raise the temperature above meat locker.

The Watcher had never been in Harry's house, though the carpenter had invited him over a few times to watch hockey games. They were both Flyers fans. They had other things in common too, but they wouldn't be friends. Not ever. Not after what the Watcher had seen—and what he'd heard—the other night.

Don't worry. Just come with me. I'll take care of you. I promise.

Betrayal sliced into him like the drop point of his knife through a deer's belly.

Silver moonlight gleamed through bare windows. In the far corner, a drop cloth shrouded a battered recliner. The gutted house had a hollow, unfinished feel that matched the empty space in the middle of his chest.

The house was in mid-renovation. Harry planned to flip it in the spring. The oak floor in the living room had been sanded down to raw wood, but the kitchen was still old and ugly. On the worn vinyl tiles, a four-by-eight sheet of plywood spanned two sawhorses as a makeshift table. The Watcher scanned the assortment of woodworking supplies. Flammable liquids. Newspapers. Rags. Check.

It was a small house with a simple floor plan. Living room, kitchen, and dining area grouped at one end. A short hall led to the single bath and three tiny bedrooms. The door to the master was ajar. He touched it with one finger, and it swung open a few more inches. Single guys don't think much about things like curtains. Enough moonlight filtered through the blinds for the Watcher to see Harry sprawled on his back under a thick comforter, one arm thrown over his head, snoring. His posture was childlike. Innocent.

The guy was anything but. Anger, hot and sour, rose into the back of the Watcher's throat. He swallowed, backed away, and clenched his freezing knuckles until they screamed. The pain focused him. He drew a chilling, chemical-laden breath into his nose and exhaled slowly. In the kitchen, he stretched a hand to the ceiling and disconnected the 9-volt in the smoke alarm. He moved to the sawhorse table. Paint thinner would do the job.

"What're you doing?"

He whirled. Harry shivered bare-chested in the doorway, hands tucked under crossed arms, face wrinkled with sleepy confusion. The prelude to a middle-aged paunch hung over his low-riding sweats. Now what? Harry was awake. The plan was fucked.

The Watcher bowed his head to hide his eyes. They burned with frustration. Couldn't let Harry see. The Watcher needed to say something. Something to throw Harry off. Something that would make him comfortable with a middle-of-the-night intruder.

"I need some help, Harry." The plea choked him on its way out. His fingers crawled past the matches in his pocket to his hunting knife. He palmed the weapon alongside the back of his thigh, out of Harry's line of sight, and opened the blade one-handed. "I'm sorry for scaring you."

The Watcher knew he should wait it out. Come back another time with another plan. His arm even contracted to return the knife to his pocket.

"It's OK. You're always welcome here." Harry was a sap. He stepped closer, rested a cold hand on the Watcher's shoulder, and gave it a compassionate squeeze. "Let me get a sweatshirt. Then we can talk."

The sympathetic touch and gentle words short-circuited something in the Watcher's brain. Harry's voice played in his head again.

Don't worry. Just come with me. I'll take care of you. I promise.

The Watcher's vision went red. He lunged at the carpenter. The knifepoint pierced Harry's belly. Blood seeped around the hilt and ran hot over frozen-stiff fingers. He yanked upward, as if gutting a deer, splitting Harry open from navel to breastbone with a moist rip. The Watcher wriggled the knife loose and stepped back. The frigid air filled with the metallic, raw scents of blood and freshly slaughtered game. Harry's eyes bugged. His hands clutched his belly as if to keep his insides…well, inside.

"Why?" Blood gurgled from his open lips as his body went limp, sliding to the floor as if the bones had melted.

At the Watcher's feet, dark liquid spread in a thick puddle on the raw wood. He stepped back before it reached his shoes. Sweat dripped down his back, and his heart knocked around his chest like a pinball.

Harry was supposed to die in the fire. There's no way anyone would think *this* was an accident. Now what? The house was a mile outside town. No other buildings in sight. How long would the place burn before the fire department arrived? Would the fire destroy the body? Too many unanswered questions.

Harry's limbs twitched and went still. His torso deflated; gray eyes glassed over.

The Watcher whipped the canvas drop cloth from the recliner and spread it out on the floor. At five-foot-nine,

Harry was smaller than the big buck the Watcher had bagged last autumn, but dead limbs flopped and tangled as he rolled everything in the cloth, deli-wrap style. He dragged the body to the back door. After covering the kitchen floor with lacquer, newspapers, and rags, he tossed a lit match into the center. Fire sprinted across the hardwood with a *whoosh*. He flipped up his hood and hauled the bundle out. Using the three-foot elevation of the back stoop, he squatted and heaved the body onto his shoulders. He wasn't small, but he staggered under the dead weight. Brittle-cold air and smoke clogged his lungs as he stumbled for the detached garage behind the house.

Discipline was the key. Lesson learned. He wouldn't forget it again.

But at that moment, all he could think about was how to make Harry disappear.

Chapter One

Present day

Leave town or die, you fucking whore.

Not the most original statement, but it sure got the point across.

Rachel raised the portable lantern over her head and scanned the side of her barn. In the artificial light, the blood-red words slashed across the white paint like fresh wounds. Every letter was still billboard clear despite hours of cleaning.

She rolled her aching shoulder and shut off the pressure washer still chugging at her feet. Silence fell abruptly on the too-warm, wet October night. It was no use. The graffiti wasn't coming off. Fresh coats of primer and paint would have to wait until the weather cleared.

Someone was not happy she'd returned to Northeastern Pennsylvania. *Troy?* Who else would bother? Didn't matter. She wasn't leaving, no matter how difficult her brother-in-law made her life.

Exhaustion weighted her quivering muscles as she half-dragged her equipment to the detached garage. On the way out, she secured the outbuilding with a thick padlock. No sense in tempting fate—or her vandal. The soggy grass squished under her boots as she crossed the lawn to her back door. After slipping off her boots in the mudroom and making sure her new deadbolt clicked securely into place, she padded into her empty kitchen.

The rumble of her stomach reminded her she hadn't had time for a grocery store run—or dinner. She yanked open the ancient refrigerator door and let the cool air waft over her sweaty skin. One lonely yogurt huddled next to a nearly empty quart of skim milk. Rachel poked a green and furry package in the bottom of the vegetable bin. When had she bought broccoli? And why? She picked the plastic bag up by the corner with her forefinger and thumb, and gingerly transferred it to the garbage can. It hit the bottom with a wet squish. She snatched a box from the counter, shook out the last strawberry Pop-Tart, and washed it down with water.

A damp breeze and the patter of light rain drew her gaze to the window. Through it, the barn sprawled behind the house. Pride expanded her chest. She had ten horses boarded, not bad considering the number of setbacks the barn renovation project had suffered. Come winter, New Hope Farm would welcome its very first foal. Was it possible the black cloud that had dogged her for the past thirty-one years had decided to move on?

Don't jinx it. The pot of gold at the end of your rainbow has a way of turning into a pile of crap.

As evidenced by the return of her vandal last night.

Rachel's cell phone burst into its digital rendition of the "William Tell Overture" from its charging cradle on the kitchen counter. She reached for the phone. The tiny screen displayed her sister's name. Rachel's heart fumbled a beat as she flipped open the cover. "Sarah?"

"I'm sorry for calling so late." Sarah's apology trembled.

Rachel's heart squeezed. "It's OK. What's wrong?"

"It's Troy."

Wasn't it always? Sarah's husband was the lowest form of life Rachel could imagine, at least two rungs below amoeba on the evolutionary ladder. Chimpanzees would be appalled to learn they shared ninety-eight percent of their DNA with Troy Mitchell. He was the main suspect for her vandalism—and the reason Rachel had returned to sink every single nickel into the rundown family farm.

Six years Rachel's junior, Sarah had her reasons for marrying young, but surely she could have done better than him.

Rachel heard banging in the background, then Troy's voice yelling for Sarah.

"Sarah? Are you OK?" Sarah didn't answer. "Do you want me to call the police?"

"No." Sarah blurted out her answer too quickly.

"No, you're not OK, or no, you don't want me to call the police?"

All Rachel heard was Sarah's ragged breathing for one long moment.

"Could you please just come and get me and the girls? Troy and I had an argument earlier, and now he's back. He's drunk and he's really mad. Please, Rachel, just until he sleeps it off."

"OK. I'll be there in ten minutes. Stay on the line with me." Rachel stomped into a pair of battered tennis shoes, snagged her keys from the bowl on the counter, and bolted into the drizzle. Behind her the door closed with a resounding *thwack.* With her cell phone still pressed against her ear, she sprinted toward her truck. "Sarah?"

Sarah didn't respond, but Troy's voice came through, louder this time. "Gimme the damn phone!"

A muffled smack and a thud sounded over the open line as Rachel slid behind the wheel. Her heart thumped in her throat. "Sarah, are you OK?"

Nothing.

Rachel's truck engine roared as she took off down her rutted dirt driveway. Her tires screeched as took the turn onto the paved rural road too fast. Raindrops blurred her windshield. She flipped on the wipers. "Sarah, are you there?"

She lifted the receiver from her ear and glanced down at the display.

Call ended.

"Shit!" She smacked the steering wheel. Possibilities reeled through her mind. None of them good. Did Sarah hang up to call the police? Or did Troy take the phone? Should Rachel call the cops? She debated for a nanosecond before dialing 911. She described the situation and gave Sarah's address to the dispatcher, who assured her that a patrol car was en route.

The next five minutes stretched out in slow motion marked by the steady drip of sweat down Rachel's spine and the rhythmic thud of her heart against her breastbone. Shiny pavement stretched out in front of her headlights like an endless black ribbon. Wipers swished on wet glass, arcing like dual metronomes.

Each second that ticked by was an opportunity for Troy to commit an act of violence against her sister.

Rachel turned the truck into Sarah's tidy middle-class neighborhood. The sidewalks were edged, the shrubs trimmed. Minivans, SUVs, and basketball nets lined the gently curving streets, but the wholesome suburban scene was an illusion. Nothing was ever exactly what it seemed.

She pulled up to the curb in front of Sarah's house and jerked the gearshift into park. Except for the weak amber glare cast by streetlights, the neighborhood was dark, the street empty. No police yet. She was on her own.

Rachel shoved open the truck door and jumped down to the curb. The rain intensified, filtering through the leaves of the mature oak and dripping on her head. She brushed a droplet of water off her cheek with a forefinger and turned to face Sarah's deceptively quaint house. The furious yaps of Sarah's little mutt came from around back.

"You lying bitch!" Troy's expletive carried through the open living room window and burst the neighborhood's peaceful bubble. Next door, a light in the second-floor window blinked on. The dog yapped louder.

A female scream sliced through the humidity.

Rachel sprinted across the wet lawn and flew up the cement steps to the front stoop. Heart hammering, she pushed the unlocked door open. Her sister lay crumpled at the bottom of the stairs, one arm twisted behind her body at a grotesque angle. Red-faced and sweaty, Troy stood over her in the narrow foyer.

As Rachel stepped across the threshold, Troy's booted foot connected with her sister's unconscious body with a sickening thud. Limp, Sarah slid a few inches on the polished oak floor. Rachel's lungs sucked in a reflexive gasp before she could stop them. Troy's head swiveled toward her. Under a shock of sweaty brown hair, green eyes glittering with unnatural, rabid excitement. "What do I have to do to get rid of you?"

Shock paralyzed her for a few seconds. He swung. Rachel slipped sideways, but her reaction was slow, and the sloppy hook glanced off her cheek. Pain, bright and sharp, burst through her face with a kaleidoscope of colors. She stumbled sideways. One hand caught the banister and kept her upright.

Rachel shook her head. A glance at her sister's broken body jolted her into movement. The pain in her face evaporated as Troy moved closer. She raised her hands, twisted her torso, and plowed an uppercut into Troy's soft solar plexus. He grunted. An exhalation of stale whiskey passed over Rachel's face. She brought her arm up to block a looping right, and then looked for a groin opening. No shot.

Swinging wildly, Troy stumbled forward. Rachel moved away until her back hit the wall. Troy grabbed for her throat. Her ears strained for sirens as she shoved the heel of her palm under his chin. Troy's head snapped back, the movement taking his body with it.

His eyes shone with malice. He lunged unsteadily for the hall closet and pulled out an aluminum baseball bat. Rachel's heart rammed against the inside of her chest as if it wanted out. She stepped in front of her sister. Running wasn't an option. She'd never leave Sarah. Nor could she abandon the little girls that she knew were upstairs somewhere, terrified. But if Troy managed to hit her with that bat, it was game over. Sarah would be alone. Just like when Rachel had abandoned her little sister all those years ago.

Where were the damned cops?

Troy raised the bat over his right shoulder in a two-fisted batter's grasp as he weaved toward Rachel. His face contorted with hate as he swung at her head.

Chapter Two

Rachel vaguely registered approaching sirens as she ducked under the bat's arc, catching Troy's arm on the backswing. Her right hand grabbed Troy's wrist while the other forearm slammed into the back of his elbow, hyperextending the joint.

"I'm gonna fucking kill you!" Troy lifted a work boot to stomp on her foot. Rachel sank her weight into the arm-bar, bending Troy hard at the waist and bringing her knee up to meet his face. Her peripheral vision caught strobe lights in the open doorway just as bone crunched and blood spurted onto the hardwood. The bat dropped to the floor with a metallic clunk. Rachel pulled her gaze off the red liquid.

"Police!" A hulking figure stepped over the threshold. The cavalry.

About freaking time.

Rachel maintained her hold on Troy and lifted her gaze to the huge cop in the doorway. Though he was dressed in jeans and a button-down shirt instead of a uniform, Rachel recognized the massive shoulders and red hair of Westbury's chief of police, Mike O'Connell. Her eyes locked on his for a second—just long enough for her to be surprised at the soft shade of baby blue—before Troy's flailing and cursing broke the strange connection between them.

"Little help here?" Rachel adjusted her grip on Troy's sweaty wrist.

The chief blinked. He holstered his weapon, cleared his throat, and moved toward her, calling out over his shoulder to the uniformed officer who had joined him in the doorway. Rachel recognized the young cop as the one who'd handled her vandalism complaints. She couldn't remember his name, but his black hair and nice manners were distinctive. "Ethan, call for an ambulance."

"Yes, sir." Ethan turned around and disappeared. Flashing red and blue lights reflected disco-ball-style off Sarah's freshly painted front door.

Rachel released Troy and stepped back. The chief brushed past her. They'd never met, but she'd seen him around town. Always from a distance though. He was way bigger up close. Way, way bigger. Though not particularly tall at about six-foot, his linebacker body exuded raw power. He handled skinny Troy like a toy, spinning him around and cuffing his hands behind his back in a few deft movements. "You're under arrest."

With Troy restrained and the police chief's giant body as a barrier, Rachel was suddenly aware that her heart was racing and she couldn't suck in enough oxygen. The flowered wallpaper closed in on her. She took a step back, away from the chief and Troy. Her sneaker slid a couple of inches. She glanced down at the smear of red left by her shoe. *Blood.* The foyer tilted. Blackness encroached on the edges of her vision, and a rushing sound echoed in her head. She averted her eyes from the spatter, planted both hands on her knees, and gulped moist air.

"You OK?" The police chief's baby blues zeroed in on Rachel.

With no air to spare for words, she nodded. Her eyes locked onto his. With vague discomfort, her brain registered this was the first time in her life she'd been tempted to hide behind someone else instead of facing risk head-on.

She did the deep-breathing Zen-ish thing her martial arts instructor had attempted to teach her.

From behind a blood veil, Troy narrowed drunken, piggish eyes at her. "That bitch assaulted me."

She forced another breath through her clenched teeth. Those mediation lessons never really sank in, but then no amount of training could prepare her for Troy. The Dalai Lama would lose his cool with Troy.

The chief didn't respond, but Troy rose onto his toes as if the chief exerted force on the arm chicken-winged behind the cuffed man's back. O'Connell passed Troy off to Ethan as soon as the younger officer poked his head through the doorway. "Read him his rights and drive him to the ER. Get them to run a blood alcohol level on him too."

Rachel's sight cleared as Ethan frog-marched Troy toward the front door. On the way out, her brother-in-law shot her an I'll-get-even-with-you glare over his shoulder, and a tremor slid along Rachel's spine. She'd always thought he was a bullying asshole, but tonight she'd seen the true dark side of Troy, the out-of-control brute buried under a boys-will-be-boys façade. She was number one on his to-screw list. Not a good place to be.

Sarah groaned and Rachel turned. Her adrenaline-loaded system was less steady than she realized. Her knees buckled as she stumbled to her sister's side.

"Easy." Next to her, Chief O'Connell steadied her with a firm grip on her elbow. His hand was warm, solid, and strong as he dropped to a knee, lowering her down to the floor with him. Side by side, his telephone pole of a thigh made hers look like a matchstick. When his hand left her arm, she felt the acute lack of support.

"Can you find a blanket?" he asked without taking his gaze off Sarah. The chief put two fingers to the wrist of her sister's unbroken arm. With his other hand, he lifted the hair from Sarah's temple and winced at her injuries. The bruises on Sarah's pretty face were the deep red of raw meat.

Rachel's eyes misted as she watched him treat Sarah with the gentleness she deserved. Sarah was the kind one, the considerate one, the polite one. And what did her sister get for being such a damned nice person? A fist in the face.

Rachel swallowed hard and ducked into the living room to whip an afghan from the back of the sofa. She used those few seconds, and the white-hot surge of anger, to tighten the rein on her emotions. With the need to put some distance between her and the cop, she knelt on the opposite side of her sister.

Her voice barely cracked. "How is she?"

"Her pulse and respiration are steady. Who are you?"

"Rachel Parker. I'm Sarah's sister."

He nodded and helped her spread the blanket over Sarah. He glanced up at Rachel, his eyes locking on her hers again. An invisible frequency, like a Bluetooth link, hovered in the air between them. He opened his mouth to say something, but the movement of Sarah's head distracted him. "Don't move, Mrs. Mitchell."

Sarah's eyes opened, passed over the chief, and focused on Rachel. Her voice was a tight rasp forced through a split lip. "Rachel, please take care of the kids. They're hiding…"

Rachel jumped up, her feet already heading toward the steps. "I'll find them."

"Wait," the chief called.

Rachel turned back. The police chief frowned. "You're bleeding." He pointed to his own cheekbone. "You might want to clean that cut first so you don't scare them."

Cut? Rachel probed the corresponding spot on her face. The wet, sticky film and underlying gash were a surprise, as was the lick of pain when she prodded it. Troy's high school ring must have caught her skin on that first punch.

"There's a first aid kit—"

Rachel barely heard him as she used her sleeve to wipe her face. "Better?"

He grimaced and shook his head. "I guess. Not quite what I had in mind."

Rachel jogged up the stairs. She stepped into the girls' room, wall-to-wall Hello Kitty and pink ruffles. "It's OK, girls. It's Aunt Rachel."

A sniff drew Rachel to the closet. She slowly folded the louvered door. Both girls, ages three and five, huddled in the dark.

"It's safe. Come on out."

They hurled their tiny bodies at her. Rachel caught them, lowered them all onto the floor, and gathered the sobbing children into her arms.

"Shhh. I've got you now."

"Mommy told us to hide," Emma whispered into Rachel's breast. "We didn't hide very good. Next time we'll do better."

"You did just fine." She held them, she rocked them, she stroked their hair, but she didn't promise them everything would be all right.

⤍

Mike entered the hospital through the big sliding doors of the ER. The glaring overhead lights stabbed his eyeballs. Disinfectant stung his nostrils and camouflaged other, nastier odors. God, he hated this place. Sweat dampened his forehead, and the fire in his gut flared as he scanned the waiting area.

At the end of the hall, just past the nurses' station, Troy Mitchell slumped in a plastic chair. Troy had been the star of the baseball team in high school, but now his once lean body was just scrawny. Dried blood caked his face and stained the front of his white undershirt. In the last hour, his nose had swelled to twice its normal size. "I need a doctor. I've been waiting a long time."

Next to Troy, Ethan stood ramrod straight, clenching and unclenching his square jaw as if he were chewing gravel. "Be. Quiet."

Troy's beady, bloodshot eyes locked on Mike, and his chest inflated with the self-righteous belligerence only a drunk could muster. "I want to file a complaint against Sarah's sister."

Ethan tensed. Before he could respond, Mike caught his eye and silently signaled him to relax. Troy's daddy was a town councilman. Vince Mitchell owned Mitchell's Sporting Goods, one of the largest and most successful businesses in town. The mayor lived to kiss Vince's rich butt. "Calm down, Troy. You'll get to make your statement. Where's Mrs. Mitchell?"

"The stupid cow's in there," Troy interrupted, cocking his head toward one of the closed exam room doors. A smug look crossed his face. "Clumsy bitch fell down the stairs."

The vein in Ethan's temple throbbed, bulging out like a kinked hose with the water on full. He spoke through gritted teeth. "Dr. Wilson's in there with her."

The ER doors behind Mike whooshed open. Miss Parker, still clad in ripped, blood-stained jeans and a T-shirt, stalked through the opening and hesitated. She scanned the cramped space. Mike lifted his gaze to her face, getting his first good look at her in bright light and without a medical emergency in front of him. Five-three, one-fifteen, trim athletic build. She was older than he'd thought, somewhere just past thirty. Brown didn't do justice to the color of her eyes, which were the color of polished amber. Long, brown hair was scooped up in a messy ponytail. Damp tendrils clung to her face and neck. Blood still oozed from the cut on her cheekbone. Her face was more interesting than beautiful. But the determined set to her jaw and the fire in her eyes were captivating. Mike couldn't take his eyes off her.

Her upper lip curled as she glared at Troy.

"There's the bitch! Why isn't she under arrest? She assaulted me," Troy whined as she drew closer. "This is all your fault. Things were fine until you moved here, you interfering whore."

The lines around her eyes deepened. Her body vibrated with barely contained energy as she shifted her gaze to Mike. "How's Sarah?"

"This way, please." Mike gestured down the hall. There was a small, private waiting room at the end where he could interview Miss Parker—and let her calm down.

But Troy just couldn't keep his mouth shut. "I knew this was gonna happen when you moved back. You turned your sister into a lying bitch."

She catapulted herself across the gray linoleum toward him.

Holy—! Mike sprang forward. He planted his bulk in her path and caught her around the middle with one arm. Absorbing the impact of her small body, he swung her around and braced her back against his chest. She twisted. Her feet kicked as they stretched toward the floor. He wrapped his other arm around her squirming body. *Ow.* A sharp pain radiated up his leg as one sneakered heel connected with his shin.

Hefting her a few inches higher, Mike walked quickly down the hall and ducked into the lounge. He shouldered the door open and tapped it closed with his foot. Though half his size, she was difficult to restrain. Her feet dangled and kicked around his ankles. "Take it easy, Miss Parker. Don't let him set you off like this. That's what he wants."

She stopped struggling abruptly, as if he'd pulled her plug, but Mike didn't set her down until he felt her body go limp. Even then he loosened his grip slowly, letting her slide to the floor. He ignored the faint flicker of physical awareness as her body rubbed against his, and he stayed between the woman and the door just in case she went ballistic again.

She faced him. The scattering of freckles across her nose didn't fit the hard-ass attitude. Since Mike had seen her wrapped around the little Mitchell girls, he suspected the tough act was just a veneer. Up close, her face was even more striking. Florescent lights paled her already fair skin, highlighting the cut and darkening bruise on her cheek. Her hair was a rich sable, and her eyes were flecked with every warm shade from gold to brown. And staring into them was probably rude.

"I'm Police Chief Mike O'Connell, Miss Parker." He held out a hand. "We were never formally introduced."

Her grip was strong, but her fingers were cold. Though heavily callused, her hand was small and fine boned, nearly disappearing in his big palm. He'd seen her take on a man with a fifty-pound advantage, yet the only word that ran through Mike's head was *fragile*.

"I know who you are." She scowled down at their joined hands as if the awareness that buzzed between them annoyed her. Her cheek was swelling, making the cut gape.

The prospect of a scar on her smooth skin gave him a dull ache in the middle of his chest. "That needs to be stitched."

"It's not that bad. It can wait. How's Sarah?" She shrugged off his concern—and his hand—which bugged him more than it should.

"I don't know. She's still with the doctor. Why don't you tell me what happened while we wait for Dr. Wilson to finish examining your sister?" Mike took a notebook and pen from his pocket and waited as she began to pace.

She took a deep breath and shoved a few straggling pieces of damp hair off her forehead. "Sarah called me a little after midnight..." Her strides steadied as she reconstructed the events in a logical sequence, but her body remained in constant motion, propelling itself back and forth across the small space like the Energizer Bunny strung out on amphetamines. "Then you were there."

Mike nodded and appraised her again with respect. He'd seen her arm-bar Troy, but he'd missed the toe-to-toe action. She was a lot stronger than she looked. There was a lean, lithe body—which he shouldn't be thinking about—under that oversized clothing. She'd had some martial arts training somewhere along the line too. But even with all that, she'd put herself at great risk. Troy could've killed her with that bat. The ache in Mike's gut amplified. She should have waited for the police—for him.

She rubbed her side absently.

"Did I hurt you?" Guilt flooded Mike. His arms were almost as big around as her waist. After her brawl with Troy, she was probably sprouting quite a few bruises under those ragged clothes. She could have cracked ribs or internal injuries if Troy had hit her hard enough. Adrenaline could mask pain for a short time.

"No. I'm OK. He was too close and too drunk to do any real damage." Distracted by his question, she stopped moving. Without her vigorous pacing, she suddenly looked tired and vulnerable. The creamy white, utterly feminine shoulder that poked out of the neck opening of her shirt stirred up protective instincts in Mike that had nothing to do with his badge. They were primitive, Neanderthal-like feelings that came from deep inside and made him want to teach Troy what it was like to be beaten to a pulp by someone much larger. He herded her toward the door.

"Let's see if Dr. Wilson's finished with your sister." Though he knew there would certainly be a resident available to examine her, he would feel better if the head of the ER, Dr. Quinn Wilson, looked her over personally. Quinn would make sure she was really OK. Mike suspected Miss Parker would be a difficult patient. He suspected Miss Parker would be difficult, period.

Relief filled him as he caught sight of Quinn's green-scrubbed form at the nurses' station. Mike caught his eye and nodded toward Rachel. After one glance at her face, Quinn steered them toward the main triage area. Three patient bays were divided by sliding curtains. The first was empty and open.

"How's Mrs. Mitchell?" Mike followed them in and introduced Rachel to Quinn.

The doctor gestured toward the exam table and washed his hands, the overhead lights glinting off the silver threads in his blond hair.

"Mrs. Mitchell's in X-ray. She has a broken arm and a concussion. I don't think her cheekbone's fractured, but we'll make sure." Quinn snapped on a pair of gloves and probed the cut on Rachel's left cheek, while she stared over the doctor's shoulder at the opposite wall. She didn't flinch as the antiseptic passed over the wound, but the hand that gripped the edge of the table went white at the knuckles. "I'd like to get the plastic surgeon down here to stitch this. Anything else hurt?" Quinn handed her a cold pack.

"No." She raised the ice to her cheek.

"She was holding her side a few minutes ago, Quinn." The gaze she turned on Mike could've melted steel. He avoided direct eye contact and backed toward the door. "I'll just wait outside."

It was for her own good. He could tell she was hurting much more than she wanted to admit. Someone had to make sure her injuries weren't serious. Thankfully, that was Quinn's job, not Mike's.

Quinn exited a couple of minutes later. Mike fell into step beside him.

The doctor talked while he walked, his running shoes squeaking on the waxed linoleum. "She refused X-rays, but I don't think anything is broken, just a couple of bruised ribs. Miss Parker can go as soon as she's stitched up. I'm keeping her sister overnight. Mrs. Mitchell's sedated, so if you want a coherent statement, it'll have to wait until tomorrow." He paused with one hand on a closed door. "And Mike? Get some sleep. You look like shit."

Mike found Ethan and his prisoner in an exam cubicle. Ethan had removed the cuffs from one of Troy's wrists and snapped the metallic bracelet onto the bedrail. Troy's swollen nose was bandaged over the bridge. Wads of cotton protruded from his nostrils walrus-style. The sockets of both eyes were rapidly blackening as he glared at Mike.

Nice shot, Miss Parker.

A young resident scribbled on a chart. "He'll live. Nose is broken. He doesn't need to stay, just make sure he has ice."

Mike turned to Ethan. "You get his statement?"

"Yes, sir." Ethan's disgusted eye roll told Mike what the officer thought of Troy's statement.

"Sarah fell down the stairs. I tried to catch her. Then Rachel burst in and attacked me. She's been trying to turn Sarah against me for months, since she moved back here. She broke my nose." Troy pounded his untethered fist on the bedrail. "You should be arresting her, not me! Wait 'til my father hears about the way I've been treated."

Troy leaned forward and Mike silently wished he'd take a swing at him. No such luck. Troy shifted back and abruptly found the bedrail fascinating.

"When you get to the station, Officer Hale can fill out those forms for you. But at this time, the only person under arrest is you."

"My father will be calling you, Chief O'Connell." Troy spat out the words with contempt, and Mike was perversely pleased to see a little more blood. "And the mayor."

"No doubt." A headache rapped on the back of Mike's eyeballs. He turned to Ethan. "When he's done here, take him in."

Mike left the room and drew his keys from his pocket. As he stepped out into the warm rain, his thoughts strayed to the inexplicable—and inconvenient—pull he'd felt toward Rachel Parker.

He had to keep his interactions with her entirely professional. The clash between her and Troy wasn't over, and any attraction to her was a conflict of interest with his job. Plus, he couldn't ignore the uncanny resemblance she bore to the young woman who'd been murdered just a short while ago. The woman whose dead body Mike saw every night when he closed his eyes. The woman Mike had failed to save. Whatever the cause, the tight ball in the center of his chest told him Rachel would be like quicksand. Under her seemingly solid surface was a boggy pool of complexity. His instincts were screaming that once he waded in, he'd be mired neck-deep.

⁀

Rachel turned her truck into her neighbor's driveway. The porch light glowed through the rain like a beacon and summoned her aching body from the cab. She rapped lightly on the sidelight. Sarah's little mutt, Bandit, popped up on the other side of the glass pane and yapped.

"Hush." A robe-clad Mrs. Holloway scooped the dog up in one arm as she opened the door to usher Rachel into the warm, dry foyer. "Come inside. You're getting soaked."

Rachel slipped off her soggy canvas shoes and left them by the door.

Over her clear eyes, Mrs. Holloway's forehead crinkled like crepe paper as she reached up to cup Rachel's jaw. Mrs. Holloway turned Rachel's face to get a better look at the bruise and bandage on her cheek. "Does that hurt? Do you want some ice or aspirin?"

"No, ma'am." Rachel reached over to stroke the dog's long silky ears. Liquid brown eyes stared at her from a masked face. "He hasn't been any trouble, has he?" Bandit was slow to warm up to strangers, and he didn't get his name from his markings alone.

"No. He's been a comfort to the girls." Mrs. Holloway set the dog down on the floor. "Be a good boy. Go back to the girls." She used the same firm voice that had kept fourth graders in line for decades. The dog trotted obediently down the hall. "How's Sarah?"

"They're keeping her overnight, but she'll be OK." Rachel blinked back fresh tears. Fatigue had left her emotions raw. "If only I'd been there for her after Mom died. She wouldn't have married Troy. But no, I was on the first plane back to Europe." Too bad turning the clock back seven years wasn't an option.

"Honey, none of this is your fault." Mrs. Holloway wrapped an arm around her and rubbed her back.

"Sure it is. She eloped with him barely two months later." Rachel let herself lean on the older woman.

"Troy wasn't so bad back then. Sarah seemed happy enough."

"She was only eighteen."

Mrs. Holloway sighed. "Rachel, your mother's illness took a toll on everyone around her, including you."

Rachel shut down the childhood memories before they flooded her. She couldn't handle them on a good night. She straightened, pulling out of the embrace. "Anyway, I thought I might as well come and get Bandit and the girls out of your hair."

"Absolutely not. You will not wake those children. Took me a full hour to get them calmed down enough to sleep. They're exhausted. Leave them be." Mrs. Holloway crossed her bony arms over her chest.

"OK." Rachel didn't argue, even though the retired schoolteacher wasn't even five feet tall, and that measurement included her sprayed-solid iron-gray curls. Rachel was too tired to debate anyway. Dawn was only a few hours away. It was a relief to have someone she trusted share the burden for a couple of hours. Here, she didn't have to explain or pretend or hide behind a brave front. Her neighbor already knew all the dirty details from Rachel's childhood.

Mrs. Holloway cupped Rachel's elbow and steered her into the living room. "Sit down, Rachel, before you fall down."

Rachel glanced at the dried blood on her jeans and hovered over the couch. "I'm filthy."

"You're fine. Sit. I'll make you a cup of chamomile tea."

The words were spoken with authority, and Rachel eased her butt down on Mrs. Holloway's soft, flowered sofa. Her shoulder throbbed, and she felt every spot on her body where Troy had managed to land a blow. There were more than she remembered.

"That's not..." Rachel began, but Mrs. Holloway turned back and stared her down. "Tea would be great." And warm. Rachel flexed her toes to restore blood flow. Fiery pinpricks spread through both feet.

"You certainly didn't need this after what happened yesterday," Mrs. Holloway called over her shoulder as she disappeared through the doorway to her kitchen. A few seconds later Rachel heard cabinet doors opening and closing, then the tap running.

She pushed the thoughts of obscene threats and vandalism out of her mind and rested her head against the back of the sofa. All she wanted to do was close her eyes for few minutes. She doubted she'd sleep, but her eyelids felt like they weighed twenty pounds apiece.

Her thoughts lingered on the police chief. In his early forties and comic-book-hero big, he wasn't exactly handsome. His nose had seen a few fists, and he had a weirdly deformed ear. She wasn't into pretty boys anyway, but she couldn't believe the quiver in her stomach when his hand had so gently enveloped hers. What was her deal? In the middle of tonight's horror and chaos, her brain decided to go all female?

Still, it was hard to ignore O'Connell's man-next-door appeal. His steady, imperturbable demeanor was more attractive than any Hollywood hunk. Even with all those huge muscles—he probably bench-pressed tractors—he'd been careful not to hurt her. The chief was in complete control over all that brawn. He hadn't lost his cool with Troy. Nor had the cop gotten angry when she'd inadvertently kicked him in the shin. Rachel's face heated. Troy was scum, but that didn't excuse her behavior.

Enough about Troy. Sarah had married the bastard and that was that. Rachel did not allow herself to criticize her little sister. Sarah's bad choices were partially Rachel's fault—and Rachel would be there to help deal with the consequences.

Why couldn't Sarah have found someone sweet? Like that black-haired young cop with the nice manners and chivalrous attitude.

Marriage was an antiquated institution. Love and children created vulnerability. Both ways. Men could be equally damaged. Rachel's father had certainly paid the price for falling for the wrong woman. Love had destroyed him.

How could people trust others enough to open themselves up like that? This incident with Troy was far from over. With his daddy's help, he'd be out of jail in no time. Once Troy was on the loose, he'd be looking for his wife and kids—and taking aim at the only person standing in his way—Rachel.

Chapter Three

"Here are the reports on the Mitchell case, Chief."

Mike yanked his gaze off his computer screen as a manila file hit his in-bin. "Thanks, Ethan. Did you include copies of Miss Parker's previous vandalism complaints?"

"It's all in there. You need anything else before I take off?" Ethan yawned. "I could run by the Parker place and get the statements signed."

Mike glanced at the clock. Eight o'clock already? "No. You better clock out. I'll take care of it. Good work last night."

"OK. Pete's already here for his shift." Ethan ducked out into the Sunday-morning-quiet police station.

A minute later, Mike's second in command, Lt. Pete Winters, stuck his bulldog face through the doorway. "I'm headed out on patrol. Anything special?"

"Yeah. Ride by the Lost Lake development every couple of hours."

"More vandalism?"

"Yesterday somebody slashed some bulldozer tires."

"OK. Want me to check on the Parker woman?"

Yes is what Mike should've said. "No. I'll take care of it."

"OK."

After Pete left, Mike picked up the Parker file and flipped through it. Something felt off about the whole Mitchell-Parker mess, but he couldn't nail it down. Maybe if he'd actually shut his eyes last night, his brain cells would be functioning. He turned his attention back to the article that had popped up in his Google search on Rachel Parker. Her background check had been clean, but Mike wanted details. He wanted to know everything about her. More than the facts in his reports. She was thirty-one, never married, and, until six months ago, was employed as a rider and horse trainer by Rising Star Farms. Several news articles had linked Rachel romantically to the stable's owner, Blake Webb, a richer-than-rich blueblood with nothing better to do with his life than play with horses and sailboats.

A tall shadow filled his office doorway. "Don't you ever go home?"

Sean Wilson, the ER doctor's younger brother and Mike's best friend since grade school, set a take-out bag and a cardboard drink tray on the desk.

The smell of fresh coffee filled his nose, and Mike leaned toward the pair of steaming cups. "Sorry I had to cancel breakfast with you and Jack this morning. I have a man out on disability. I'm swamped." In addition to the Mitchell domestic, a brawl at the local dive bar, three drunk drivers, and a burglary had rounded out the weekend.

"You bailed on the last two poker games at Jack's too. My cousin is starting to think you don't like him." Sean slumped into one of the chairs that faced Mike's desk.

In fact, Sean's cousin, Jack, was a former cop and an all-around good guy. But Mike's failure to catch a serial killer six weeks ago had almost cost Jack his fiancée. Mike couldn't help but wonder if Jack blamed him as much as he blamed himself.

"And we haven't sparred in weeks," Sean griped.

"There are plenty of other guys at the gym. Maybe if you didn't fight so dirty some of them would spar with you."

"Bunch of pussies. No such thing as rules in a real fight." Sean handed Mike his coffee. "Never stopped you from taking me on."

"Criminals fight dirty too. I consider sparring with you good practice." But Mike didn't blame anyone for turning Sean down. The six-foot-four former Army Ranger turned security consultant sparred to keep his hand-to-hand combat skills sharp, not to score match points.

"Now you're comparing me to criminals?" Sean opened a small box of doughnuts out of the bag and offered it to Mike.

"I'm just saying it wouldn't kill you to follow a rule now and then." He waved off the sugar-fest.

"Yeah, I know. Your body's a temple and all that crap." Sean lifted a foil container out of the bag and handed it to Mike. "Western omelet and whole wheat toast."

"Thanks." Mike lifted the lid. The smells of sautéed onions and peppers wafted out, and his empty stomach growled in approval.

Sean gestured with a Boston cream. "Just like it wouldn't kill you to break a rule occasionally. Admit it. You like the chance to let loose in the ring with me. You're so uptight the rest of the time."

Since Mike had long ago accepted his uptightedness, he dug into the omelet. "Don't you have a wife to bother this morning?"

"Already did that." Sean grinned. "Seriously, you can't be the chief and a full-time patrol officer."

"Until Matt Dexter's broken ankle heals, I'm exactly that. I don't have enough bodies to cover shifts, and there's no room in the budget for overtime." Mike washed down a corner of toast with his coffee. "I don't send officers into domestic disputes alone."

"Just make sure you take the same care with your own safety." Sean shot him a pointed look. "And take an occasional day off."

"Doesn't matter. Sleep isn't exactly coming easy these days." Not without nightmares anyway.

"Mike, you can't take responsibility for what happened. The FBI couldn't find the Riverside Killer, and they were working that case a lot longer than you."

"I'm supposed to protect the people of this town. I failed." One of them had died. An innocent young woman. The vision of her abused and bloated body would haunt him forever. Jack's fiancée had also been abducted by the serial killer. Beth had barely survived, something Mike was reminded of every time he went to Jack's house. Mike could've made the last poker game if he'd tried. "Doesn't matter. It's all over now. On to other crimes."

But there was no moving on for him. Though the Riverside Killer was dead, neither Mike nor the town would ever be the same. His quaint little hamlet bore the permanent stain of murder.

Doubt lurked in Sean's eyes, but he let it go. "Heard about that cluster at the Mitchell place last night. Troy's such an asswipe. Is he really going to press charges against his sister-in-law?"

"I have to wait until he sobers up to find out. When I called over to the jail this morning, he was painting the concrete with last night's Wild Turkey."

"Nice."

"Probably the only thing that'll keep him in jail today. No lawyer wants to put a puking defendant before a judge, even if the judge plays golf with the defendant's daddy."

"They prefer their courtrooms hurl-free."

Mike finished the toast and pushed the container away. "Thanks for the food."

"Somebody has to take care of you. And on that note, we're having a barbecue this afternoon and Amanda—"

"Sean." Mike cut him off. "I'm sorry. I just don't have the time."

Sean sighed. "Amanda's worried about you. She'd like to see you relax and get a real meal."

"Just had one." Mike pressed a hand to his solar plexus, where it felt like the onions were bursting into flames.

"You cannot work twenty-four-seven."

Mike's gaze drifted to his computer screen and the *Philadelphia Times* article. From the back of a huge stallion, Rachel Parker squinted out from under a black riding cap. Those eyes were intense, even in black and white. The snug riding pants and tall black boots showcased that tight, athletic body. But getting turned on by the memory of it rubbing against him was totally inappropriate. Mike's chair squeaked as he shifted his weight.

The caption below the photo read, *Local Rider Takes Silver at the Pan American Games.* Miss Parker wasn't just a horse trainer. She and her mount, Fleet O' Feet, were former members of the US Equestrian Team. "Besides, I have to pay Sarah Mitchell's sister a call today."

Sean reached over and swiveled Mike's screen so he could see it. "That her?"

"Yeah."

Sean gave him the once-over. "You should shower and shave first. She's hot."

"This is not a date." Mike rolled his eyes. "She's involved in an active case. Totally off-limits. Plus, she's the complicated type, and I've had enough of that kind of complication."

"You're not exactly Mr. Simple. You have enough baggage to fill a fucking freighter."

Mike ignored Sean's uncomfortably accurate comment. "Look, Vince Mitchell is pissed enough that I had the audacity to arrest Troy last night. He doesn't care that his son knocked his wife down a flight of stairs and broke her arm. You can bet he's already working on the rest of the town council. I'm surprised the mayor hasn't paid me a visit yet to convince me to make the charges magically disappear. They're gonna be on my ass like a pair of tighty-whities. I need to walk the line here. One slipup and I'm history."

Mike pulled an economy-sized bottle of antacids from his drawer and shook out three.

"Buying those things in bulk now?"

"They were on sale." Mike tossed them back and chewed, then used the last of his coffee to wash the chalky taste from his mouth.

"You're chronically overworked and underpaid. You look like crap. Tell the town council to kiss your Wonder-Bread-white ass. You know you always have a job in private security with me. I've only been trying to hire you for years."

"Look, I hate small-town politics, but I like my job. Or at least I did before Vince Mitchell got elected to council last year." Mike's exhaustion made his friend's offer more tempting than usual, but he wasn't ready to quit on his town. This job had pulled him out of a deep, dark place ten years ago, and the place he was headed now wasn't exactly bright and cheery. Free time to ponder his failures would be the equivalent of swallowing gasoline and a lit match. "Besides, if I get fired there'll be no one to look out for Sarah Mitchell and her sister or anyone else."

"Mike, working nonstop won't keep another killer from finding this town." As usual, his friend cut through the bullshit like a power saw. Sean's eyes dropped to the papers on Mike's desk. "Awfully thick file for one night."

"Somebody's been hassling Rachel Parker for months. Three incidents of nasty graffiti." Mike flipped through half a dozen reports. "Tires slit on heavy equipment. Damaged construction materials. Stolen materials."

Sean rounded the desk and looked over Mike's shoulder. "Seems like a lot of work for Troy. He's drunk most of the time and lazy all of the time."

"That's exactly what I was thinking. Try as I might, I can't believe that Troy orchestrated all this."

"Nope," Sean said. "Not by himself."

"So, either Troy had help or someone else is trying to hurt Rachel Parker."

The last time Mike's instincts had waved a red flag, a woman had been murdered.

⌒

Rachel removed a nail from between her teeth, held it in place, and raised the hammer. That pain-in-the-butt gray horse picked the wrong day to bust through the fence.

"Miss Parker?"

She jumped. The hammer slipped and smashed her thumb. Pain shot through her hand. "Shit." Rachel gave her throbbing fist a shake, then tapped the last nail into the new top rail and turned to face the chief of police. He had a file tucked under his arm.

"I'm sorry." Chief O'Connell's ruddy face creased with concern. "I didn't mean to startle you."

She scanned the back lawn, where Emma and Alex played in a large cardboard box. Tied to a nearby tree, Bandit took a break from digging and barked. Mud obscured his black and tan coat. Above it all, a sky of unbroken gray threatened to dump more rain on her swampy pastures.

"I have a lot on my mind." Rachel tested the board. It held. She looked at him. His hair was still damp, his face freshly shaven, but he could've packed for the weekend in the bags under his eyes. She'd managed a two-hour nap on Mrs. Holloway's sofa. O'Connell looked like he hadn't even blinked. Even puffy with lack of sleep, those baby blues over-loaded her brain's circuit board. A He-Manly man shouldn't have eyes that soft and beautiful. A girly squeal floated across the yard, and Rachel seized the chance to glance back at her nieces. No more of this locking gazes bullshit.

"I guess you do." O'Connell's eyes shifted to the barn. His mouth tightened. Rachel followed his gaze. In the unforgiving light of day, the side of her barn might as well be a profane marquis. "The threats seemed…personal. And nasty."

"They do. My nieces can't read yet, but covering that up is on my to-do list." She lifted a heavy shoulder. The ache in the injured joint reminded her that failure and pain were part of life.

"You've had a lot of vandalism since you moved here. Are you sure it was all Troy?"

"Why?" Rachel froze. A damp chill crept up her arms. "Who else would it be?"

"I don't know. When you put it all together, it seems awfully well organized for Troy. Are you sure no one else has a grudge against you?"

Tough question. "I can't think of anyone else who'd go to that much effort to get rid of me." She jerked a thumb toward the barn. "That graffiti sounds just like him."

The chief just stared at her for a minute in silence, as if contemplating her comment. Then he nodded at the girls on the back lawn. "How are they?"

"Better than I would have predicted. Kids are resilient." She tried to shrug off the comment, but her insides knotted.

Rachel headed to the barn. One of the barn cats snaked around her ankles as she heaved at the sliding double doors. A wide dirt aisle separated two rows of stalls. She had a clear view of Alex and Emma while she worked. She led Lady from her stall and snapped the mare onto the cross-ties in the aisle. O'Connell tagged along. His huge body moved with controlled grace that suggested athletic prowess. He leaned a shoulder against the wooden wall like he needed the support. He scanned the pasture in the distance, as if searching for a way to say what was on his mind. She doubted he'd driven over just to check on the girls.

Rachel waited a few seconds, and when he didn't show any sign of spilling his news, she went to work with a soft brush. As she swept it across Lady's gleaming side, the slight swell shifted. Rachel splayed her hand against the mare's belly. The lump moved under her palm. Fleet's baby. Hope budded in her chest. She jerked her hand from the mare's side before optimism could take root. She couldn't get too attached. Fate had the nasty habit of yanking happiness away from her every time it dangled within reach.

"When's she due?"

Rachel swallowed the lump in her throat. "February."

Denim rustled behind her as O'Connell moved closer, invading her space. When she looked over her shoulder, he was right behind her, stroking Lady's neck. His broad hand slid down to caress the mare's shoulder. "She's beautiful."

His fresh musky aftershave tingled in her nostrils—among other places. The soft cotton of his button-down stretched across the heavy muscles of his torso. Which she should *not* be staring at like a horny teen. But damn, he liked horses and everything.

She ripped her gaze off the chief's impressive chest and patted a gleaming coppery haunch. "This baby's our first, isn't it, girl?"

Lady's ears flickered. Usually a little of the horse's quiet contentedness rubbed off on Rachel, filling her with the peace she imagined other people got from an hour of yoga or a massage. But not today.

O'Connell's face spread into a sad half smile that recategorized him from man-next-door attractive to edible. Rachel's heart did that fluttery thing again, like it wanted to bat its eyelashes at him. Ridiculous.

Rachel sidestepped to the grooming box and selected a stiff brush for Lady's tail. "So, you like horses?"

"I had one when I was a kid." His voice roughened. When Rachel glanced back at him, the smile had slipped from his face and his eyes were clouded as the sky. How could a man that big have a vulnerable streak? And why was he more attractive because of it? He cleared his throat. "You inherited this place from your grandfather more than ten years ago. Why did you just move out here six months ago?"

"I was riding competitively, traveled most of the time." Until one slip of a hoof ended her career—and Fleet's.

He looped an arm over Lady's neck and rested his forehead on her arched crest. Lady bent her graceful neck into an elegant curve and nuzzled the waistband of his jeans. *Shameless hussy.* But Rachel was a teensy bit jealous.

"So, you retired?" he asked.

A twinge ran through the scar tissue in her shoulder. "Yeah. You could say that."

"Are all these horses yours?"

"I wish. Just Lady. The others are here for training." She moved her eyes from the cop to check on the girls. Two pairs of feet protruded from the box. Muffled childish chatter drifted through the humidity. OK. Enough pretending she had an ounce of patience. "So, what brings you out here this morning, Chief O'Connell?"

"Call me Mike." A sigh heaved through his chest. Muscles bunched and released. "Please?"

"OK, it's Rachel, then. Mike, what brought you out here?"

"I have papers for you to sign." He raised his hand and pressed the palm to his eye. "And we need to talk. Can you take a break?"

Discomfort lodged in her belly. Without asking, she knew it was bad news, like a vague message from the doctor's office requesting a callback. "Sure. Give me a minute."

She led the horse back into her stall. Across the aisle, she pulled out her pocketknife, sliced through the baling twine, and tossed a fresh section of hay into Lady's stall. She folded the knife and returned it to the pocket of her jeans.

"If you want to talk, come up to the house. I need coffee."

He followed her as she left the barnyard and strode across the grass. Bandit barked and growled as Mike approached. Emma and Alex crawled out of the soggy box as they approached. Their jeans were soaked from the knees down. The dog's paws were encased in mud.

"We're hungry." As usual, Alex spoke for both of them.

"Keep it down, Bandit." Rachel untied the bristling dog but kept a firm hold on his leash. "How about lunch?"

Bandit led the charge as the girls skipped to the back door of the house, where Rachel toweled off the mutt's paws and belly before letting them all into the kitchen. The dog squirmed in her arms, and she lost her grip on his sausage-like body. He hit the floor and headed for the cop. Shit. Growling, the dog approached Mike on stiff legs.

"Look out." Rachel made a grab for his furry body, but the dog ducked her hand. He sniffed suspiciously at Mike's feet, then slunk back to sit by the girls' feet. Rachel stopped midlunge.

"Little defensive?" Mike set his file on the table.

"Just a little." Keeping a doubtful eye on the dog, Rachel pulled a chair over to the sink and turned on the faucet. Bandit liked his visitors in small, juicy bites.

Five-year-old Alex scrambled up, squirted soap into her palm, and lathered up. "Bandit's par-ti-cu-lar." She drew out the word, enunciating carefully. "He bit Daddy."

Emma moved her fist toward her face. Rachel took her tiny hand and squeezed it gently before the filthy thumb made it into the child's mouth.

Mike squatted down and held a hand out. Bandit curled a lip. "What kind of dog is he?"

"The rescue kind," Rachel said. "Sarah got him at the animal shelter. He must be part hunting dog of some sort though. That nose of his can find a single potato chip crumb buried under the sofa cushions."

Alex climbed down and dried her clean hands on her dirty jeans before Rachel could stop her. Rachel lifted the younger Emma onto the chair and washed the smaller child's hands between her own. In her peripheral vision, she watched Alex wrap an arm around the small dog's neck. Bandit turned his head and licked her chin.

"Daddy says he's a useless mutt." Alex's lip trembled. "He won't let Bandit in the house. Sometimes it's cold outside."

Rachel's chest tightened as she set Emma down. Mike's gaze caught Rachel's. Too much sympathy there. Her eyes burned, and she turned away to collect herself. Behind her, she heard Mike soothing her niece. "Bandit has lots of fur to keep him warm."

She blocked out his deep voice before it completely melted her resolve. Rachel slapped two peanut-butter-and-jelly sandwiches together, handed the dog a chew, and led all three into the den. She switched on the old TV before retreating back to the kitchen. The swinging door closed, muffling SpongeBob's squeaky voice.

"Kids are tough. They're going to be OK."

Mike's voice startled her. She looked at him. The understanding in his eyes made her feel trapped. Something about him tempted her to let go, to let him in, to let her guard down. Her spine stiffened. One weak moment could lead to more. Then where would she be? Dependent. Emotional. *Vulnerable.*

Not gonna happen.

"How about you?" Mike took a step toward her. The room shrunk, the space contracting around them.

"Fine." Her bruised face throbbed, and she reached for a bottle of ibuprofen in the cabinet. After swallowing two tablets, she turned her back on him, measured coffee into the basket, and filled the reservoir with water. She flipped the on switch. The machine gurgled.

When she turned around, he was there, just an arm's length away. Close enough to touch her. Close enough to feel the heat emanating from his body and smell that damned aftershave.

He reached out and lifted her chin with one finger. His gentle touch sent a shiver straight down to her toes. The buzz amplified. "How's it feel?"

Her face ached, but her girl parts were singing "It's Raining Men." Not that she was going to tell him that. It wasn't bad enough that this man was all sexy muscles and gorgeous blue eyes. He had to be über nice too. She was in deep trouble.

Rachel jerked her chin away and took two hurried steps back. "It's not bad." He-Man was dangerous.

He raised a brow in disbelief. "Looks like it hurts."

She had to stay away from this man. He did something to her. Not only did he seem to see right through her, he made her feel things she had no interest in.

Rachel retreated to the coffeepot to pour two cups. Steam heated her face. Yeah, right. It was the steam. Cripes, she should've brewed decaf. She handed him his cup. He was still giving her a seriously toe-curling sexy look. She snatched a Pop-Tarts box off the counter and thrust it toward him. He shook his head. "That's disgusting."

"To each his own." Pastry in one hand, coffee in the other, she backed up to lean a hip on the kitchen table. The Pop-Tart went down in three bites. As Mike watched, disgust replaced the smolder in his eyes. Thank God. She braced herself for the bad news she was sure he'd come to share. "Let's get down to business. You said you needed to talk to me."

His expressive blue eyes filled with regret. "Troy'll be out on bail tomorrow."

Rachel's legs went limp. She braced her weight with a palm on the table and sank into a kitchen chair. She didn't know why she was so surprised. She'd known this was coming, but the reality of the entire situation swept her knees out from under her. "I knew his father wouldn't waste any time, but I'd hoped…"

For what? A miracle? No such thing. Not for you.

"If he'd been in any condition to go in front of a judge today, he'd be out already." Mike dropped his gaze to his coffee. His face sagged with guilt. "I wish I could keep him locked up, but he has no *official* record of violence."

Rachel gave her head a slow shake. "It's not your fault. He's always been a loudmouthed bully, but to my knowledge he's never hit her before." The coffeepot hissed and Rachel stared at it, numb. She wrapped both hands around her cup, grateful to feel the warmth spread into her palms. She lifted her chin. "I can handle Troy."

He shot her that look again, the one she now recognized as the we-both-know-you're-full-of-shit look. He opened the file on the table. "I need you to sign your statement, and I brought copies of the police reports." He gave her instructions on filing for a temporary restraining order and recommended Sarah get a good lawyer ASAP.

Rachel barely heard him. Last night Troy'd been drunk. She'd taken him by surprise. That wouldn't happen again. Her fingers touched the bandage on her cheek. Bravado aside, she had no idea how she was going to protect Sarah and the girls.

And what if Mike was right and all her troubles hadn't been caused by Troy? What if someone else was out to get her? Mike's words echoed in her mind. *Are you sure no one else has a grudge against you?*

If only she could've answered yes.

⟾

Mike set his cup on the counter. No more women were going to get hurt on his watch. He could barely live with the one he'd failed.

Rachel's courage, although admirable, wasn't going to keep them all safe. Not from Troy or anyone else who was willing to go to such considerable lengths to cause her harm.

Mike crossed the room and opened her door. The shiny new deadbolt and hardware were all heavy duty, as was the sturdy old door. No glass panes. But crowbar marks scarred the jamb. "Is this where he tried to break in?"

"Yeah. About a week after I moved in, I heard a noise in the middle of the night. He took off when I came downstairs. All I saw was a shadow. I called it in, but he was long gone before the officer got here." She frowned. "Good thing I'd already installed that new deadbolt."

He'd read the report, but seeing the evidence of the attempted entry—and how close the prowler had come to getting in undetected—demonstrated that Rachel's farm was too remote for Mike's comfort. The lock operated smoothly when he turned it. "Top of the line. You were expecting trouble?"

"Troy was pretty clear how he felt from the beginning. He made some threats."

Locks would barely slow down a determined man.

"Look, you've done your best to make this place secure, but windows can be broken, by Troy or someone else. You really need an alarm system."

Her eyes narrowed, that attractive spark of annoyance returning. "It's on my wish list."

The situation was unacceptable. Mike had to *do* something. He couldn't leave her—them—this exposed. He pivoted, striding through the kitchen and down the hall, past dented trim and hanging strips of faded wallpaper, toward the front of the house. Except for investing in new locks, Rachel had obviously put all her resources into renovating the barn. The old farmhouse needed to be completely gutted.

He turned and nearly bumped into Rachel as she stood, arms crossed over her chest, in the center of the hall. "Where are you going?"

He looked down at her. Why was the fiery flash of anger in her eyes so damned hot? The last temperamental woman he'd fallen for had filleted his heart like a trout.

"I just want to check your front door." He brushed past her and walked out onto the wide front porch. Protected by the overhang, the door was solid, with no visible rot or glass. The deadbolt was new here as well. Mike pulled out a notebook and made a few notes on the general layout of her house as he walked back toward the kitchen.

She bristled, stiff-legged. Her face flushed as she barred his path with a rigid arm. "What are you doing?"

Mike stared down at the arm across his chest. Did she have any idea how small she was? Or how vulnerable? He raised his gaze to her face. She did. Over the stubborn jaw and bandaged, bruised cheek, doubt lurked behind the fire in her eyes. And maybe some well-suppressed fear. He sighed. She still wasn't going to make this easy on either one of them.

"Look, you really need a security system. I know a guy who'll give you a good deal. Rachel, let me help. Just a little." He tilted his head toward the den. "For their sake. Please."

Her inner battled waged across her face. If it weren't for her sister and nieces, she'd probably tell him where he could stuff his assistance. But for the girls' protection, he knew she'd cave. He'd only known her one day, and he was already certain she'd put their needs above her own desires.

"One condition. All the bills come to me. I don't do charity or personal debt."

"OK," Mike agreed. Sean would do the job regardless of how or when she paid him. Women and kids were his super-tough friend's weakness. He'd give her a great deal. Some of the invoices would likely get lost.

"Let me make the call."

"Fine." She exhaled hard and met his gaze. The defeat in her expression made something in Mike's gut ache even more. He preferred those brown eyes all feisty. "Thank you."

He knew he should say something, acknowledge her gratitude, but all he could manage was an awkward nod. Something about this woman pulled at him, and it wasn't just the way her threadbare jeans hugged an incredibly tight butt. No, it was her fierce loyalty and courage that was reel-ing him in, along with her willingness to humble herself for her family's benefit.

Then there was that other little issue. Every time their eyes met, like now, a heavy sensation filled his chest. Massaging his sternum, Mike broke eye contact. Probably just his twenty-four-seven work schedule catching up with him. His concern was justified. Troy would be out on bail tomorrow, and Mike's instincts were sure that her case was more complicated than Troy's revenge. There was someone else involved. Mike wouldn't be able to sleep unless they were as safe as possible. There didn't have to be anything more to it than that.

But *call me Mike?* What had he been thinking? And he could excuse the shower and shave, but the aftershave? Pathetic.

He could not afford to get personally involved. He needed to get back to the station—away from Rachel. Before he was tempted to do more than help her secure her house. Before he acted on the scorching heat that had filled her eyes when he touched her chin.

But it was Rachel who moved away from him. She poked her head into the den and called out, "Girls, it's time to go."

The kids and dog trooped in. Rachel lifted Emma onto her lap and wiggled the muddy sneakers onto the little girl's foot. Alex dropped to the floor and chewed on her bottom lip as she concentrated on tying the laces.

Mike backed away from the wholesome family scene that was threatening to bore a hole right through his heart. He'd wanted kids. His ex-wife hadn't wanted to be tied down or risk her figure. Considering how things had turned out between them, he *should* be glad. "I'll get my friend out here as soon as possible. His name is Sean Wilson in case he calls."

Rachel leaned a cheek on the top of Emma's head and stared at Mike. "You don't have to do all this."

But he did. "It's my job to make sure you're safe." He pulled out a business card and a pen, printed his cell number on it, and set it on the table. "Call me if you need me."

His interest was purely professional.

Mike left by the back door. The aroma of manure and wet grass hit his nose as he walked to his truck, which was parked alongside the barn. He climbed behind the wheel. His eyes settled on the side of the building. The graffiti practically had Troy's tag on it, but the rest? Even bolstered by anger and alcohol, Troy was hardly the industrious type.

But as she'd said, who else would go to this much trouble to get rid of her? Though she hadn't really answered his question, had she?

As Mike fished a roll of antacids from his center console, he glanced back at the old farmhouse. Two stories of solid Pennsylvania fieldstone towered over the rural landscape. He knew the white trim and black shutters needed replacement, as did the roof. But from a distance, the peeling paint and missing shingles weren't visible. The house was impressive, its weaknesses not discernible until closer inspection.

Like its owner.

He pulled out onto the country road. There was a whole lot of nothing in every direction. Heavy woods provided cover on three sides of her cleared acreage. No. Sturdy doors and locks weren't enough. Even an alarm was only a warning. The itch on the back of Mike's neck was telling him this farm was too isolated—and, behind her tough façade, Rachel was far too vulnerable.

He wouldn't let another woman get hurt on his watch if he had to work twenty-four hours a day.

His phone buzzed on his hip. He glanced at the display. His gut clenched as he turned his truck around and stomped on the gas pedal.

Chapter Four

The Watcher leaned out from behind a fat oak at the edge of the trees. The ankle-deep stream at the edge of the property swirled around his waterproof boots. He raised the binoculars to the opening of his camouflage hood and adjusted the focus. Rachel carried the small child to her pickup and secured her in the rear of the extended cab. Another child followed, climbing into the truck on her own. Rachel stopped and scanned the woods. Her posture stiffened.

He lowered his field glasses and backed against the tree. She couldn't see him. It wasn't possible. Not at that distance. Not dressed head to toe in his best autumn forest camo.

She returned to her task, and he relaxed. But he'd never forget the fact that she, and she alone, could tie him to a murder.

He'd only killed one person in his life. Though he could still feel the burn of betrayal down to his soul, he regretted his reaction to this day. Getting rid of the body and destroying the evidence had been a hassle. Frankly, he'd panicked and botched the whole thing. He'd been lucky. The cops had assumed Harry had taken off. There'd been no evidence of a crime. But now that *she* was back, there could be.

She could ruin everything.

He turned to stare at the old farmhouse. What would it take to get rid of her? A lot, apparently. Troy Mitchell sure wasn't going to get the job done. He was too lazy and undisciplined to be useful as anything except a pawn.

The Watcher focused his binoculars on the barn with disgust. Graffiti was the best Troy could do? Really? What an amateur.

Clearly, more of the Watcher's assistance was necessary. He'd leave the juvenile tactics to Troy, while the Watcher took care of the serious business. Rachel had proven more resourceful than he'd expected. Both of his early attempts to break into the house had failed. With more time, he'd have managed it, but Rachel was never gone long enough. If he did get inside, he'd need a few hours to do what needed to be done. He couldn't take the chance of being caught in the act.

So, unless he figured out another way to get in, he needed Rachel to move out. But how?

Nothing he'd done so far had convinced her that she was engaged in a losing battle. The stubborn bitch was a pain in the ass. He'd worked hard to put that night behind him. He wouldn't let her ruin everything. It was time to take the plan to the next level, from mere inconvenience and financial hardship to real fear, which was easier than most people would think. Rachel wasn't as tough as she appeared. Some personal terrors ran soul-deep.

He knew all about Rachel's phobias. He'd been watching her a long time. He thought about breaking in when she was home, of standing over her bed while she slept, unaware of his presence. His groin tightened. The sight of him in her room would terrify her. She'd scream. He'd have to silence her before anyone heard her. Before she could tell.

Anticipation kindled at the thought of an eternal solution to his current problem, of acting instead of only watching. He could wrap his hands around her throat. The memory of that one and only kill rushed back. The blood. The power. The thrill. He hadn't expected it to feel so…good. Addictive. As if he'd been numb until the act had flooded him with feeling. Cold until he'd felt the hot rush of blood over his skin. Nothing in his life had come close to the few, tantalizing seconds when he'd watched the light, the soul, drain out of a man's eyes. He'd felt more in that moment than in his entire life. Killing had fueled something inside him. A yearning that watching would never quite satisfy.

But he was still paying the price for that ancient momentary thrill. Disposing of Harry's body had been more difficult than he'd imagined. It had taken a long time before he stopped waking in a cold sweat, waiting for the police to show up at the door. One moment of pleasure hadn't been worth years of anxiety. If he'd learned anything from that experience, it was the importance of sticking to his plan. Discipline was the key.

His immediate goal was to get Rachel to leave.

The rain picked up, echoing off the inside of his hood. For now, watching was his only release. But he'd do a lot more if she showed any signs of remembering what he'd done.

Her truck disappeared down the narrow country lane.

He hoisted the bag of tools over his shoulder and strode across the wet lawn. A decent tracker would see his trail, but the grass and weeds were too thick for his boots to leave discernible prints. He eyed the lock on the door. No problem. He had just the tool for the job. He reached into the bag. His gloved hand closed on his kit.

Chapter Five

"You're sure the girls are OK?"

Rachel settled her sister on the sofa in the den. Sarah's voice barely slurred, despite her swollen lip. Her arm was in a sling, and the bruises on her face had colored to a rainbow of purples. Physically she looked beaten, but the stubborn set of her jaw and the glint in her soft brown eyes gave Rachel hope that Sarah had finally had enough of Troy.

"Yeah. They love Mrs. Holloway. They'll be home soon anyway. The movie ended at three." Rachel straightened. "Hungry?"

"Not really, but I'll eat anyway."

"That's the spirit. Soup?" Despite her sister's new tenacity, chewing solid food would be challenging for the next few days.

"OK." Sarah shifted on the couch. "Rachel, I'm sorry. About everything."

"I told you. It's gonna be all right. I'll take care of everything."

"But I don't want you to take care of everything." Moisture glittered in Sarah's eyes. She looked away. "Marrying Troy was my mistake. He was always temperamental, but I thought when he got away from his father, he'd change. I could make him happy. I used to go to all his baseball games. In the beginning it was OK. It was way better than Mom and Dad's marriage. But then he got cut from the minor leagues. I'd just had Emma. His dream was gone. He had a wife and two babies to support. He started going to the bar instead of coming home at night. The more he drank, the meaner he got." Sarah turned back, a spark of anger in her eyes. "But he never hit me before this time. I wouldn't have stayed with him if he had."

"I know."

A breath heaved through Sarah's thin frame as she rested her head on the back of the couch. Whatever resolve she'd bolstered for the drive home deflated. "I promise I'll pay you back every cent."

"And I'll hold you to it." Rachel wouldn't, but Sarah needed the self-respect.

In the kitchen, Rachel selected a can of chicken noodle from her meager pantry. She dumped the condensed blob into a saucepan.

Sarah needed a high-powered attorney. Troy's daddy's money could buy a hell of a lawyer. And the bastard wouldn't do it because he wanted the girls. He'd only try to take them to hurt and control Sarah. None of that mattered. Sarah had to keep her children. Whatever the cost.

With a sick feeling in the pit of her stomach, she picked up her cell phone. Blake's number was still on speed dial, as if she could still call him at any time for advice or just to talk. So much for her being over what had happened between them.

"Rachel?" Surprise colored Blake's voice.

She couldn't do polite banter, not with Blake. She didn't want to give him false hope, but she needed his help. She blurted out, "I need a favor."

What was wrong with her? She couldn't even manage a simple *hi, how are you?*

"What's going on, Rachel?" Blake's tone sharpened. "I haven't heard from you in six months."

"I know. I'm sorry. For everything." Exhaustion smoothed her voice. "Let me start again. How—"

"I miss you." Visceral emotion filled those three words.

She closed her eyes and rested the phone against her forehead for a few seconds. She missed him too, but she couldn't say that. He'd misunderstand, and she didn't have the energy to fight with him. "I need your help. It's for Sarah and the girls, or I wouldn't ask."

"Yeah. God forbid you actually need anything from me."

"Blake, please. Don't go there."

"You just don't get it." He sighed. "I know you can't believe it, but I'll always be here for you. You can trust me."

"My leaving had nothing to do with trust." And everything to do with things she wasn't capable of feeling. She'd loved him in her own way, but it wasn't enough. She couldn't match the intense emotions he had felt for her. Marrying Blake would have set them up to repeat the disaster that was her parents' marriage.

The line went silent for a few long seconds. "Just tell me what you want."

They made the arrangements with a few brisk and businesslike exchanges that fed the ache in Rachel's heart. Her fingers tightened on the edge of the counter. Alex and Emma were more important than any of her dreams. She'd do whatever was necessary.

Rachel turned to the sink with the empty soup can. She lifted the handle on the faucet. Nothing came out. What now? She checked the valve under the sink. No problem there. She ducked into the den. Sarah's head lolled back on the sofa. Her eyes were closed.

Rachel grabbed a flashlight. Maybe it was a blown fuse or something else with a simple fix. *Yeah, right.* When was it ever something simple? After locking the door securely behind her, she headed across the weedy yard to the far corner, where the well house hid behind the detached garage.

A cold twinge curled in the pit of her belly. She wasn't alone. Goose bumps broke out on her arms. Stopping in the middle of the lawn, she rubbed her biceps. She scanned the buildings and trees ahead. Everything looked the same. A pair of blue jays burst from the underbrush at the edge of the trees a dozen yards away. Rachel started, and then forced herself to breathe. Birds. Just birds.

She was losing it. Big time.

She swallowed her paranoia and resumed her stride. Clearly, her imagination had paid attention to Mike's warnings. Memories rushed at her, video clips of various arguments she'd had over the past year all spliced together, a montage of her disagreeable nature. There were quite a few. Blake's were the longest—and the most bitter. Someday, she'd learn to think first and open her mouth second. Hanging around with the unflappable He-Man could be good for her. She paused midstride. Where did that thought come from?

The building was small, roughly measuring eight by ten feet. Though built of solid Pennsylvania fieldstone to match the main house, the outbuildings hadn't been maintained as well over the centuries. Mortar crumbled and ivy climbed the patchwork of brown and gray rocks.

The weather-beaten door moved in the breeze with a squeak of old hinges. The padlock she'd installed lay in the grass next to the stoop. *Oh no.* Not the well. Panic swept her hesitation out of the way.

Rachel pushed the door open and stepped inside. Her gaze fell on the debris strewn across the dirt floor. She gasped. Before she could move, a shove between her shoulder blades sent her flying forward. Her hands instinctively shot out in front of her to brace her fall. Pain sang up her forearms as her palms hit the dirt floor. Something slammed behind her, and everything went dark.

⌒

Mike bounced along the gravel lane that led to Lost Lake and approached the turnoff for the controversial vacation home development project. Thanks to last week's rock blasting, the construction entrance was flanked by die-hard picketers, even on a dreary Sunday. The protestors were too spread out to capture with his dashboard camera. He grabbed his cell phone camera from the passenger seat and switched the camera function to video. Slowing the truck to a crawl, he steered around a bearded guy toting a hand-lettered STOP OVERDEVELOPMENT sign and navigated the muddy ruts left by heavy equipment. As he passed through the crowd, he held up the phone and recorded the crowd on both sides of his vehicle. He now had two dozen vandalism suspects.

The rutted entrance opened to a cleared space littered with puddles and construction debris. Mike's tires crunched on the gravel of a temporary parking area. He stopped his vehicle facing the lake. Beyond the scarred clearing and the weedy shoreline, water rippled in the late afternoon breeze.

Scenic, despite the bulldozer that was parked in the lake's shallows, the top half of its yellow form visible above the surface of the water.

To his left, a twenty-foot section of chain-link fence surrounding construction equipment was flattened to the ground. In a wooded area next to the enclosure, two mangled port-a-johns lay on their sides, crushed like tin cans. Blue-tinted sewage spilled from gaping holes. A group of construction workers clustered around a guy Mike labeled as the foreman from his in-charge posture.

On his right, three men in their late fifties huddled in a conspiratorial cluster: Mayor Fred Collins, Vince, and a tall, thin guy dressed in the latest ruggedly expensive outdoor apparel.

Mike's hands twitched on the wheel. He could turn around and drive away, let them fire him, but he didn't want to give Vince the satisfaction of winning. Though why Vince wanted to get rid of Mike was a mystery. Vince had had it out for Mike since the first day of the new council term. Plus, there was the heavy load of responsibility Mike felt toward the residents of his hometown. He'd let them down once. He didn't want to do it again.

With irritation pooling, Mike stepped out of his SUV. Protestors' chants of "Save our lake!" competed with the tweeting of birds and breezy rustle of foliage.

Mayor Fred picked his way around a puddle. His off-the-rack gray suit and wingtips were splattered with mud. Vince was dressed more practically in jeans and work boots. He hung back, crossed his arms over his chest, and glared at Mike. Vince wholeheartedly supported the Lost Lake project. Vacationers equaled more business. The rest of the town was divided. Residents who would benefit from the development, especially the large unemployed construction workforce, were cheering it on. Environmental concerns were a luxury for those with stable employment.

"You have to do something about this." Vince waved a wiry arm. "These pranks are costing the developer time and money."

"Easy, Vince." Fred gestured toward Moneybags. "Mike, this is Lawrence Harmon, owner of Harmon Properties."

Well, that explained the expensive duds. As the Coming Soon sign out front clearly stated, Harmon Properties owned Lost Lake Realty.

Harmon held out a hand. Mike shook it.

"As Vince pointed out, Chief O'Connell, this type of activity is costing my company a great deal. We've already lost several weeks, and the project is still in its early stages."

Mike scanned the wooded shoreline. Lost Lake had been little more than a deep, muddy hole until developers had run out of waterfront property on more-accessible lakes in the area. In the past six months, neatly spaced lots had been bulldozed free of trees and awaited construction of oversized vacation McCabins. Periodic blasting took care of rocky areas. An underwater survey was in progress to dredge the swampy lake for boating and fishing. Part of the shore was being cleared. Sand would be hauled in to make pretty, fake beaches for city people who wanted weekend nature retreats without all the mess and fuss of actual nature. Westbury was less than two hours from both Philadelphia and New York. Plus, Harmon Properties had recently announced its desire to build a hotel and resort on the south shore of the lake. The developer was scheduled to make a presentation at Tuesday's town council meeting, which Mike expected to be a total mess.

He drew in a deep breath. The scents of decaying leaves, moist soil, and pine were decimated by the nasty odors emanating from the flattened port-a-johns. "Mr. Harmon, I understand your frustration, but I've pointed out several times, the township police force isn't equipped to provide twenty-four-hour security to private businesses."

Vince's thin face flushed deep red to the roots of his receding hairline. "We've never needed outside security in the past. When Bart Howell was chief, we never had crime like this."

"Things have changed over the last decade," Mike said. "In light of the recent increase in crime, I would suggest we expand our police force. A few more officers would go a long way toward providing better coverage."

Population-wise, Westbury was a small community, but the township encompassed a large chunk of rural acreage. Mike's five-member force, currently reduced to four officers, was inadequate without the problems at Lost Lake. Their backup, state and county law enforcement, was spread equally thin.

"You know that's not in the budget, Mike," Fred clucked. "And raising taxes isn't an option."

The mayor's condescending tone made Mike's teeth ache.

Harmon tilted a lean face. "This project is a boost to the local economy. We're employing construction workers and administrative staff. We're paying property taxes. The sales of these units will increase the taxpayer base and increase revenues for local businesses. I'd hate to see it all fall through."

"Can't afford to lose the jobs, Mike." Fred's head bobbed like bobblehead doll.

Mike put on his serious, neutral face. "Look, I'd love to help you out, Mr. Harmon, but I don't have the manpower. I've suggested several times that your company hire outside security." Mike turned to the mayor. "Fred, if you have a suggestion about how to cover this amount of territory with five officers and no overtime, I'm happy to listen."

"There's always one officer on patrol, right?" Fred asked.

"Yes." Mike tensed.

"I don't see why that officer can't park on this road during his overnight shift."

"We have a few thousand other residents to protect," Mike said. "Harmon Properties can't monopolize the police force."

Harmon crossed his arms over his chest and raised an eyebrow at Vince, not Fred, Mike noted. And the look that passed between the two men suggested they were keeping something important out of the conversation. A full background check on Lawrence Harmon went on Mike's to-do list.

Mike's phone buzzed. He pulled it from his pocket. "Excuse me. I need to answer this." He turned his back on them and strode toward his truck.

"You're on shaky ground, O'Connell," Vince called out. "Watch your step."

Mike pivoted. He stared at Fred. The mayor shifted his gaze away from Mike's to study the submerged bulldozer. Hmm. Did that mean Fred was indecisive as usual or that he was going to backstab Mike? The council was split down the middle on most matters, and Fred's deciding vote wavered with public opinion.

Mike cell phone buzzed again, sparing him the necessity of a response. He glanced at the display. Sean, returning Mike's earlier call.

Mike retreated to his vehicle before punching the talk button.

"You called?" Sean asked.

"Yeah. I need a favor—"

"Says the guy who turned down my invite to a barbecue and pissed off my wife," Sean interrupted.

"Come on, Sean. I really need your help. I'm serious."

"So am I. You need a favor? Get your lame ass over here and ask me in person. While you're here, you can score a decent meal and convince my wife you're alive. Then I'll think about this favor you so desperately need."

"You suck." Mike started the engine. "I don't have time to party this afternoon."

"What can I say? Happy wife, happy life. If you hurry up, we can talk before everyone else gets here." Sean clicked off.

Mike tossed his phone on the passenger seat and suppressed a primal scream. Did everybody have him by the short hairs?

⤳

Terror rose in Rachel's throat. Sarah was alone up at the house, and Mrs. Holloway was due back with the girls at any moment. Rachel rose onto her knees. Pain burst through her head as she banged it on a piece of pipe. Scant light filtered in through a narrow window high on one wall. Using a chink in the mortar as a foothold, she hoisted herself up to peer out the window. A dark shape disappeared into the woods.

Thank God he'd run away instead of going up to the house.

She picked up her flashlight from the floor where she'd dropped it and switched it on. The beam shone on the brown body of a wild rabbit stretched out on the dirt floor. A six-inch metal spike protruded from the middle of its body. The pool of blood seeping into the earth around it seemed way too large for such a small creature.

Lightheaded, she looked away. Tiny stars swam in front of her eyes as she surveyed the inside of her well house.

She swept the light around the dim interior; a few broken pipes and some ripped-out electrical wires littered the floor, but the storage tank in the corner was merely dinged. It appeared that she'd interrupted her vandal before he completely destroyed the larger equipment.

On the wall, words were painted in a dark red substance she doubted was paint.

Roses are red.

Violets are blue.

You're a nosy whore,

And I'm going to kill you.

An image sliced through the haze; a hulking silhouette covered in blood. Her knees wobbled. Straightening, she walked to the door, twisted the knob, and pushed. It was stuck. She pushed harder. No give.

She was locked in.

Trapped.

She closed her eyes and breathed. Composure, control, and a calm mind were the keys to defeating her fears. Everything would be fine.

She patted her back pocket. Empty. Her cell phone was in the kitchen. Rachel looked toward the small window. Dust motes swirled in the light angling through the dirty glass. Even if she could climb up there, she'd never be able to squeeze through. The door was the only exit.

Relax. Sarah or Mrs. Holloway would miss her eventually. Someone would come looking for her. But the white walls seemed like they were getting closer, the air thicker.

She tried to insert the blade of her pocketknife between the door and the jamb in the approximate location of the door handle. Too tight. The wood was swollen from the recent rains. Rachel wiggled the blade, her chest constricting as the point refused to go in.

"Rachel?" Mrs. Holloway's voice was muffled through the door.

"In here," Rachel yelled. She banged on the door with the butt of the flashlight. A few minutes later, the door rattled.

"Give me a minute," Mrs. Holloway shouted.

Seconds ticked by in silence, followed by a bang, some scraping, and the creaking sound of wood being pried apart. The door opened. Fresh air blew in, along with Mrs. Holloway. She clenched a crowbar in one arthritic hand. The older woman was flushed and out of breath. "Goodness."

Behind Mrs. Holloway, a thick board lay on the grass. "That was nailed across the door. What happened?"

"Someone locked me in here. After he did this." Rachel stepped aside.

Mrs. Holloway peered into the building. She scanned the damage. Her eyes widened as she read the threatening poem. She pressed a palm to the center of her frail chest. "Oh, my. Just now?"

"I'm not sure how long ago." It felt like hours since Rachel had been locked in. She tilted her head to read Mrs. Holloway's watch. Time did not fly during a panic attack. "Less than twenty minutes."

"That's even worse that the last one." The flush on her neighbor's face paled. "I thought Troy was still in jail."

"He is."

"Oh." Mrs. Holloway wiped a hand on dark jeans ironed to a sharp crease. "So you don't know who did this?"

"No. I didn't get a look at him either."

Mrs. Holloway cast a nervous glance at the tree line, now thick, impenetrable with early evening shadows. "We should get back to the house."

And lock the door.

Rachel's foot slipped on a patch of wet grass. Mrs. Holloway righted her with a hand on her forearm. In her other hand, she still held the crowbar. "Are you all right?"

"I'm fine." Rachel pasted a smile on her face. But from her neighbor's suspicious frown, Rachel doubted she was fooling Mrs. Holloway any more than she was kidding herself. Sweat was pooling at her lower back, and her heart was hammering like it'd been cast as a lead in *Stomp*. She had no idea who was behind today's prank. Troy she could predict to a certain extent, but this...

How could she rate a danger she couldn't identify?

Mrs. Holloway tugged on Rachel's arm. "Don't touch anything. He may have left fingerprints or DNA evidence."

Her sweet neighbor was a rabid crime show fan. The bloodier the better. Rachel followed obediently as she was led toward the house.

"And we'll call Michael," Mrs. Holloway said.

"Michael?"

"The chief of police."

Oh. Right. *Him.* Rachel's pulse did a quick rat-a-tat-tat. Cripes. She needed to get a grip.

"That's not necessary. I'll just call the station," Rachel protested. The chief of police already had way too much interest in her. The last thing she needed right now was the laser focus of his blue eyes slicing through her I-can-handle-it charade.

"Nonsense. I have his cell number. I've known him since he was in my fourth grade class. I'm positive he'll want to handle this personally." Mrs. Holloway guided Rachel across the grass to the back stoop. The grip of her crooked fingers was surprisingly strong. "You should write the details down before you forget anything."

Rachel suppressed a shudder. No matter how hard she tried, there were some things she would never forget.

Chapter Six

Steeling himself for the inevitable third degree, Mike pulled up to Sean's house, a modern cedar-sided two-story built on five acres of wooded mountainside. A bright gold and red collage of turning foliage framed the structure. Quinn's minivan was parked out front. Not in the mood for the doctor's scrutiny, Mike bypassed the front door. The faint whir of discreet security cameras shadowed him as he followed the smell of grilling meat around to the back deck.

"There you are." Sean lifted the lid on a cooler and pulled out a dripping bottle. "Beer?"

"No thanks."

Twisting the cap off his beer, Sean gave Mike the fish eye. "Don't tell me you're still working."

"I'm not." Not officially anyway. He helped himself to an iced tea from a glass pitcher on the table.

"Bullshit. You're dressed in police chief casual." His friend frowned as he lifted the lid of his enormous grill to baste three racks of ribs. "When was the last time you took a vacation?"

The smoky scent of meat and barbecue sauce wafted across the deck. Mike's stomach growled. "I have no idea."

"You look like you've been mostly dead all day. You'd better take some time off soon, or I'm siccing Quinn on you." Sean emphasized his point with giant tongs.

"My ears are ringing over here." Quinn stepped through the slider onto the deck. The door closed, muffling the sounds of kids and commotion inside. He handed his brother a plate of raw hamburgers and headed for the cooler.

Both brothers were tall and blond, but Quinn was merely runner fit, while Sean looked like he could still fastrope off a helicopter with a hundred pounds of gear on his back.

"Just commenting on Mike's overall crappy appearance." Sean moved food around on the grill.

Twisting the cap off a Bud Light, Quinn gave Mike the once-over. "You do look like shit."

"Gee, thanks." Mike grabbed a pretzel.

"I mean it. You are dead-fish pasty. I know I'm usually ragging on you to ease up on the weightlifting, but not today. You've lost weight. On the bright side, it's probably the first time in years you've been able to fasten the neck on that shirt." Quinn crossed his arms over his chest. "You used to be Mr. Disgustingly Healthy. What the hell happened?"

Neither the pretzel, the iced tea, nor his friends' nagging was helping the burn that was working its way up into Mike's chest. "Christ. Are you two going to tag-team me? I have enough stress."

Quinn's eyes zeroed in on the hand Mike was unconsciously pressing to his sternum. *Shit.* Mike shoved his hand into his pocket. Truth was, it was getting bad enough he'd actually considered calling Quinn last week, and that was before Troy Mitchell went ape-shit.

Quinn lowered his voice. "I haven't forgotten your, uhm, *aversion* to the hospital. I'll see you in Claire's office, and we'll arrange the test in an offsite facility. You trust me, right?"

Mike squirmed. He was only slightly less phobic about going to Quinn's wife's family practice.

"I'll get him there if I have to ambush and drug him," Sean volunteered with a feral smile that indicated that he'd enjoy a kidnapping.

"This week." Quinn gave his younger brother a nod before turning back to Mike. "In the meantime, lay off the coffee, eat regular meals, and try to close your eyes at some point."

Mike's sigh was his admission of defeat. Neither Quinn nor Sean would give up. They were a pain in the butt that way. The Wilson brothers were also the closest thing he had to family.

A woman called Quinn's name, and he went back into the house, leaving Mike and Sean alone on the deck. A breeze rustled through the trees. Leaves tumbled along the back lawn.

"Now tell me about this favor," Sean said.

"I need you to put in a security system for Rachel Parker."

"No problem." Sean sipped his beer.

"I don't think she has any money."

Sean shrugged. "Also not a problem. We'll work something out."

"And Troy's bail hearing is tomorrow. He'll be out by lunch."

"Then I'll shift some things around in the morning and be at her house in the afternoon. We can get a basic system up and running in a couple of days."

"Thanks."

The sound of a car door slamming signaled the arrival of another guest.

"Who else is coming?" Mike asked.

"Just Jack and Beth and the kids."

Guilt flooded Mike. Through the sliders, he watched the happy chaos as Jack and his new family entered. Jack's fiancée, Beth, rose up on her toes to kiss Quinn on the cheek. She was small and delicate, her pregnancy barely showing on her tiny frame. The thought of her in a killer's hands was a shaft of guilt that skewered Mike like a shish kebab.

Jack looked up, saw Mike and Sean, and headed for the deck. As he opened the door, his German shepherd, Henry, bolted through the opening. The big dog greeted Mike with the usual slobbery enthusiasm before turning his attention to the smells emanating from the grill.

"Don't even think about it, Henry," Scan warned, closing the grill lid.

Leaning on his cane, Jack limped over and sank into a patio chair with a grimace. "How've you been, Mike?"

"Finc. You?" Before Jack could respond, Mike reached into his pocket. "Excuse me." He pulled out his not-vibrating phone. Pretending to read the display, hc backed away. "I have to go. Sorry."

"Hey, you didn't eat yet," Sean yelled, but Mike was already jogging back to his truck. What he needed was a few hours of solid sleep, not the living reminder of how his failure to catch the Riverside Killer had almost cost Beth her life. But he'd just turned onto the main road that led toward his small house in town when his phone vibrated for real. He glanced at the display. Alarm rushed through him. Lying had its price, and fate was going to make him pay up.

Rachel shivered in the damp evening air. All business, Mike finished writing her statement in his notepad. Had she misread him that morning? God knew her people skills could use some work. Kids and animals were so much simpler.

She rubbed her arms, then lifted her chin and straightened her spine. "He took me totally by surprise." *Which shouldn't have happened.* But she'd never expected anyone to be in the building. Not when Troy was still in jail. Sure, Mike had suspected another person was involved all along, but Rachel hadn't wanted to believe it. No getting around the truth now.

Someone besides her brother-in-law hated her enough to go to some serious effort to hurt her. Sarah's theory was that Rachel had been attacked by one of Troy's friends. He had a whole contingent of low-life drinking buddies to pick from. On top of the immediate property damage, Troy could claim his daughters weren't safe at Rachel's place. It was a perfect setup.

Mike squinted at his notes. "Let me get this straight. You saw that the lock had been cut, you went in anyway, and then you were surprised that someone was in there?"

Rachel didn't miss the edge in the big cop's voice. His emotions were ruthlessly controlled, but she sensed the anger simmering beneath his calm façade. He paced the grass in the fading twilight. His body was stiff, and his movements lacked their usual athletic grace. And really, could she blame him for being frustrated with her? She was frustrated with herself. Rushing into the well house had been dumber than dumb. "In hindsight, it wasn't my best decision."

Mike stopped pacing, crossed his arms over his chest, and glared at her. Seemed the big cop wasn't as imperturbable as she'd originally thought. She'd been able to provoke his temper. But then, she was especially skilled in that area.

A flash went off inside the well house, where Ethan was collecting evidence and taking pictures. White halogen silhouetted Mike's face, adding stark shadows beneath his exhausted eyes. A pang of concern tweaked through her. The cop needed more sleep and less aggravation. In short, he needed less of her. She and her rabid impulsiveness had added to his workload again tonight.

"If you called us instead of rushing in there, we might have caught him," he pointed out.

And didn't that sting? She rubbed her throbbing forehead. "I know."

"You're sure you're all right?" His eyes zeroed in on hers. "Maybe you should go to the ER."

Rachel dropped her hand. Her headache had diminished to a dull thrum. "It's just a bump. Trust me. My head is the hardest part of my body."

His mouth quivered for a second before he went back to being Mr. Serious.

Ethan poked his head out the door. "This rabbit didn't die right away, but there's an awful lot of blood in here. You want me to sample it?"

"Yes," Mike answered without turning away from her. A muscle in his jaw quivered, and the emotion in his eyes intensified, like he could see her distress—which made it worse. How was she going to keep all her issues and angst buried nice and deep where they belonged if he was going to look at her like that?

She swallowed hard and ripped her gaze away. His ability to read her—and her inability to hide her feelings from him—made her feel too exposed.

Rachel shoved a stray piece of hair behind her ear. As Ethan left the shed, she caught another glimpse of the blood puddle. A rushing sound echoed in her ears, and stars danced in her vision. She ripped her eyes away. One hand on the trunk of a tree steadied her, hopefully before Mike noticed. She had already made herself look like a fool in front of him today. Several times.

"You should go inside and sit down."

Damn. He'd noticed. But he didn't make any move toward her. Why wasn't he invading her space the way he had this morning? Was it because they weren't alone? The bright light swept the ground as the other officer searched the area around her well house.

Rachel looked down at her filthy jeans. She looked like a horror film extra, but the night before she'd been a wreck too, and that hadn't stopped him from looking and acting interested. It was him. Something was different about him tonight. Maybe he'd finally figured out she was hopeless. Also impulsive and borderline self-destructive, according to that therapist she'd let Blake talk her into seeing. Once. A single visit to her psyche had been more than enough.

"You can't think of anyone besides Troy who has a grudge against you?" Disbelief laced Mike's sharp tone. "This guy is going to a lot of effort to cause trouble."

"Look, I'm not the easiest person to get along with, but I'm not exactly a social butterfly. I keep to myself. Frankly, there aren't that many people involved with my life."

"Rachel, I need more if I'm going to help you." She didn't have to see Mike's face in the darkness to picture his exasperated expression. "An ex-boyfriend? Disgruntled business associates? Did you cut someone off on the turn-pike? There has to be someone you've annoyed other than Troy in the recent past."

Rachel hesitated, thinking. She shook her head. "Nothing serious enough for all this."

"What about this property? Does it have any value?"

"I doubt it. There are quite a few farms on the market that haven't sold despite reductions in asking prices. Overall, real estate up here is cheap. Property values have been dropping, not rising. Besides, this place sat empty for years. No one showed any interest in it."

He was quiet for a minute or so, then sighed heavily. "Next time anything strange happens, lock the doors and call the police. Do not investigate anything by yourself. Sean will be here tomorrow to start installing the alarm system."

Rachel nodded, uncomfortable with his scrutiny. She shifted her gaze to the barn's hulking shadow on the other side of the yard. A breeze brushed over her skin. Clouds parted and moonlight shone through onto the white clapboards, highlighting the threatening graffiti. Goose bumps rose on her arms. She glanced over her shoulder at the forest behind the well house where shadows threatened from its dark depths.

"Not finding anything out here, Chief." Ethan switched off the halogen lamp.

Rachel's throat tightened. The cops would be gone soon. She was definitely on her own. That said, time to cut the self-pity act short and clean up. "Can I clean this up?"

"Yes." Mike glared at her.

She fetched a shovel, scooped the rabbit up, and buried it behind the building. A few more turns of her shovel took care of the bloody stain on the dirt floor. With that nasty chore out of the way, she felt rejuvenated. No more whining. She could take care of herself just fine. So why, with three extra people living in her house, did she feel more lonely than ever?

Mike shoved his hands in his pockets to keep them from wrestling the shovel out of Rachel's hands. Though she didn't flinch from the task, he could read her like a billboard. She radiated with pain that had nothing to do with the bump on her head.

As she tamped the dirt flat, he glanced back at the well house. How did her assailant get here? Mike doubted the creep had parked in the lot. Nor had the guy gotten lucky that Rachel hadn't been home. More likely he'd watched and waited for his opportunity. But from where?

Mike scanned the area. Roughly ten acres had been cleared for the farm compound and pastures. Woods surrounded the property on three sides. The road provided the fourth leg of the rectangle. Behind the outbuildings, an ankle-deep creek edged the cleared land and disappeared into the forest. An itch started between Mike's shoulder blades. Those woods were dark and thick. They'd provide perfect cover.

He played the beam of his flashlight on the ground between the well house and the trees. Nothing. He walked toward the woods, beyond the perimeter established by the crime scene techs. A narrow game trail led away from the shed and toward the creek that meandered into the woods.

Rachel tossed the shovel aside and followed him. "Where are you going?"

"Just checking something." He frowned at the woods and then down at her. "You should go back up to the house."

"Like hell." Her response wasn't much of a surprise. "This is my place and my problem. I want to know what's going on."

Mike clenched his teeth. "If you're going to follow me, at least walk behind me so we leave one trail."

"Oh, right." She hesitated midstride, then fell into step behind him. As they approached the creek, the foliage thinned. The light fell on a faint impression. Footprint?

"Stop," he said, but not fast enough. Rachel bumped into him, or more accurately, her much smaller body bounced off of his.

"Oof. Sorry." She stumbled.

Mike reached out, but she caught herself by grabbing his shoulder.

Her small hand generated more heat than it should, and he liked her leaning on him way too much. If he were going to keep their relationship professional, there could be no more touching. She regained her balance and let go of his arm. He bent to examine the print. No visible tread. Too shallow and smudged to cast. Mike called for Ethan to photograph and measure the mark. From the length of the mark, it was left by a large man.

He straightened. "Don't move."

"But—" Rachel protested.

"Please."

She grumbled and crossed her arms over her chest, but she stayed put while he walked a path parallel to the intruder's trail. He swept the light back and forth across the weedy area that led to the creek's bank. Under a nearby tree, a three-by-three patch of tall grass was crushed.

Mike's itch graduated to paranoia. The dark pressed in on them. He tuned in to the night sounds. Insects buzzed. Frogs croaked in the nearby creek. A few bats flew overhead with a whisper of sound. Nothing unusual, but Rachel needed to know how dangerous her situation had become. No amount of bullheadedness was going to make her safe.

The woods, the creek, the danger. All were the stuff of his nightmares.

He shined the light on her face and watched it pale as she realized what she had just seen.

"That's where he stood and watched you." When she didn't respond, Mike continued. "I'm not sure you understand the severity of the situation. Your vandal has graduated to stalking and assault, and the only thing we know about him is that he likes to watch things suffer."

Chapter Seven

In a lucky spell of moonlight, the Watcher navigated the tributary that connected the Blue River that flowed near Rachel's farm with Lost Lake. He crossed the calm lake, secured his aluminum boat, and hurried up the dock to his cabin. Everything was fine. Rachel hadn't even gotten a glimpse of him. Even if she had turned around in time, the shadow under his brimmed camouflage hood concealed all his features. Planning things down to the smallest detail was essential.

She didn't know it was him.

Nerves humming, he cleaned his boots with the hose before walking into the mudroom. He shucked his light-weight coveralls, folded them, and stored them with his other hunting gear. His bag of tools went on a shelf with his other tools.

He wanted to check his feeds, but first things first. Discipline was the key.

Only after he'd showered and donned clean clothes did he lock up the cabin and drive to his small house in town. The ten-minute drive into town was agonizingly slow. He parked in the driveway and hurried up the walk. Once inside, he closed the blinds for the night and beelined to his home office. His weight settled into his favorite chair. This jittery feeling had been compounding since the episode at Rachel's farm. His computer booted at the push of a button. Nerves rushed through him. She'd surprised him, coming home much faster than he'd expected.

The screen flickered to life. He entered his password and clicked on a small icon on the bottom of the screen. A second login box popped up. One couldn't have too many layers of security. Not considering what he was doing on this computer. A thrill bubbled through him as the direct feeds appeared on his screen. Movement attracted his attention. Camera number two. The shower. His favorite. He enlarged the window to full screen and turned on the audio.

A person walked into the camera's path. Tanya. Sweet Tanya. His erection pulsed. She reached into the shower and turned on the spray, closing the door while the water heated. The patter of water on tiles sounded over the Watcher's speakers.

He clicked *record*. His palm was already sweating on the mouse.

Her hands moved to the buttons of her snug shirt. One by one she opened them, revealing the bare skin of her chest, her flat belly, the silver ring in her navel. Her nipples showed through the sheer lace of her bra. She dropped the shirt into a wicker hamper. Reaching around with both hands, she unhooked the bra and bared her breasts. The Watcher's breaths came faster and his pulse quickened as she unsnapped her slacks. The silky fabric slid down her toned legs. Her panties were a lace thong, her buttocks smooth and round.

She was perfect.

The Watcher leaned back in his chair and unzipped his pants. His cock sprang free, as if it too had been watching and waiting.

The woman stepped into the shower. Through the steamy glass, her blond hair darkened as she leaned back to soak it thoroughly. Water sluiced down her perfectly engineered breasts. She squeezed liquid body soap into a palm and lathered them. Was it his imagination, or did she spend extra time rubbing those pink nipples clean? She soaped her legs, propped one foot on a small teak stool, and bent over to shave her legs.

The wide-angle lens had been an excellent choice.

His imagination and Tanya's unsuspecting innocence brought him to release in seconds. Tension rushed from his body.

She rinsed, then leaned back on the tiles. A tear ran down her face. She wiped it away, but more followed. A few sobs sounded under the rush of the shower. Several minutes passed before she was able to shake off her melancholy. The blond turned off the water and toweled her body dry. She didn't leave the shower until her game face, a sunny smile, was firmly in place.

He was certain she only cried in the shower, only let her true emotions show when no one could see her. Or so she thought. These moments with Tanya were precious. Only he shared her pain, her vulnerability. Intimate secrets were so exciting. He learned so much from watching people in their most private spaces.

Like he'd watched another woman cry many years ago.

Tanya moved out of view. The bathroom went dark. He moved the cursor over the *end recording* button when the bathroom light turned back on. Looking for *her*, the Watcher focused his attention on the monitor. Tanya's old man, Vince, entered the picture, a cell phone pressed against his ear. Vince checked the hall secretively, then closed and locked the door. He flipped a switch on the wall. The ventilation fan whirred. The Watcher turned up the volume. Vince was up to something, and the Watcher didn't want to miss a word of it.

"I told you not to call me," Vince hissed into the phone. "No. I didn't say anything, but this goes way beyond our agreement. You'd better hope no one else knows what was stolen, and you'd better hire some security. We can't afford any other disasters." Vince paused and listened. Sweat glistened on his forehead. He picked up a hand towel from the granite counter and wiped his face. "Don't worry. I'll take care of O'Connell."

Chapter Eight

Muffled thumps floated through a haze of sleep. She surfaced to a still-dark room. Not morning yet. Closing her eyes, she burrowed deeper into her pillow and waited for slumber. But sleep would not come. Heat built under the heavy quilt. She pushed the covers away and rose from her bed, clutching her favorite stuffed bear under one arm. Cool air caressed the hot, damp skin of her face, but the shock of her bare feet hitting the cold hardwood sent a shiver through her limbs. She anchored a lock of sweaty hair behind one ear as she moved toward the door.

Something scraped outside her window. Her arms sprouted goose bumps as she turned, her eyes wide, searching the darkness beyond the glass for the source. Another scrape. A branch?

Dread and curiosity twisted her insides. Her throat tightened, the breaths rasping in and out like sandpaper. She swallowed painfully in a dry throat. She had to know. As soon as she saw that it was nothing, she'd be able to go back to sleep.

She put on her robe and slippers, then tiptoed out of her bedroom, down the hall, to the kitchen door. The door eased open with a faint squeak. Her breaths fogged in and out, the cold-crisp air

soothing her throat and feverish skin. Snowflakes drifted in the still,
pretty night. Everything was fine. She'd had a bad dream.

She opened her mouth to catch one on her tongue and froze when
she heard the scrape of a boot on frozen earth. Her jaw slammed
shut, and her head swiveled toward the noise.

A hooded form stood across the icy yard. Something dark and
red dropped from a large, gloved hand. Thick as cherry Jell-O, it fell
in a wet lump to the white-dusted grass next to his boot. Wet, dark
stains the color of rust dotted the ground around him.

She froze, paralyzed except for trembling legs that threatened to
collapse. The scream clawed its way out of her chest and lodged in
her throat, choking her.

The man's head swiveled toward her. Instead of eyes, a black
hole stared back. She couldn't see his eyes, but she knew *he was*
watching her, sensed it with the same primitive knowledge that
warned a rabbit of a wolf's hungry glare.

Pain zinged through Rachel's knees as she hit the wood
floor. She straightened her fingers, still clenched around
the edges of the sheets she'd dragged off the bed with her.
One hand pushed her damp hair off her face as her heart
pounded. She inhaled and held her breath for a few seconds to gain control. She glanced at the window. A hint of
dawn hovered on the horizon.

Her own personal boogeyman hadn't visited her dreams
in a decade. Last night's nasty incident in her well house
must have triggered a spin-off of her childhood nightmares.

But damn. He was still as terrifying as he'd been when
she was six.

She headed for a hot shower in a pathetic attempt to
wash all evidence of the foul dream away. She reached in
and turned the faucet before the lack of spray reminded
her that she had no water. Last night, after Mike had left,
she'd showered at Mrs. Holloway's house and gratefully

accepted her neighbor's emergency stash of bottled water.

She crossed her fingers that the well repairman came as early as he promised and that he could fix the pump on the spot.

She brewed a pot of coffee. Bandit zoomed into the kitchen and went into his impression of a furry pogo stick. She grabbed his collar and opened the back door. She drew back. In her driveway, Mike was getting out of his SUV.

What the—?

Bandit wiggled out of her grip and tore across the yard.

Mike stood still as the dog skidded to a stop a few feet away. Head low, Bandit approached him slowly and sniffed his shoes. Satisfied the dog wasn't going to rip a small hole in his ankle, Rachel poured him a cup of coffee before walking out into the cool morning. Predawn mist floated over the surrounding meadows, a strange blend of eerie and peaceful.

He held a hand out to the pup and waited patiently as the dog put his paws on Mike's knee and stretched out his nose. The dog was licking his hand when she handed him the coffee. He was unruffled by the dog spit bath, which made him even more attractive. Dammit. But his face looked even more haggard than it had been the night before. "Guess I pass."

"Looks like."

Mike gave the dog a scratch behind his ears. Bandit wagged his tail, then sniffed his way toward the big tree in the center of her back lawn. He lifted a hind leg.

Rachel kept one eye on the dog, but her other eye was busy watching Mike stretch his shoulders. Just because she couldn't get involved with him didn't mean she couldn't enjoy the show. No uniform this morning. Instead, a navy blue T-shirt outlined the heavy muscles of his broad shoulders and chest. He rubbed the back of his neck and winced as if it were stiff.

"Have you been here all night?"

A flush spread across his stubbled jaw as he looked away, avoiding both her question and her gaze. "I was concerned about your house's lack of security."

So, despite his irritation with her last night, he was worried about her. Rachel's heart thudded. "So, you slept in my driveway?"

He lifted the mug to his lips and drank, no doubt stalling while he tried to formulate an appropriate answer. The police chief was a careful man who gave his words as much thought as his actions. Unlike Rachel, *he* was not prone to acting on impulse and regretting it later. A moment passed before he met her eyes, the resignation in his face a sign that he couldn't think of a way to evade her question. "Well, I wasn't here *all* night, and I didn't actually sleep."

"That wasn't necessary." Although maybe if she'd known he was here, acting as sentinel, the boogeyman wouldn't have popped by for a visit. She eyeballed his bulging muscles. He certainly looked...*hot?* Ack, no. Capable. Keep it professional. The cop's hotness was not in question. Because it was indisputable? This mental discussion was not going the way she wanted. God, she needed more caffeine. "But thank you."

"Thanks for the coffee." Shadows rimmed his eyes from two nights with little rest, two nights of sleep he'd lost protecting her and her family. A heavy sigh purred through his wide chest as he swallowed.

"It's the least I could do."

He leaned closer. A flash of desire cut through the exhaustion in those beautiful eyes. Rachel felt her own body being pulled in as their gazes met. Warmth rushed south. *Whoa, Nellie.* He smelled good.

His gaze dropped to her lips. If she moved just a few inches forward, he'd kiss her. Then she could press her whole body against all that brawn. He'd wrap those beefy arms around her. Those big hands were as gentle as they were strong. She'd feel more than blazing sexual contact. She'd feel safe—and she'd be tempted to stay there. She ripped her focus away. Barely.

Displeasure flashed on his face before he pulled back and pokered up.

He stirred up too many feelings inside her for a fling. Plus, those eyes were just too serious. Mike wasn't a one-nighter kind of guy, and Rachel was not up to another relationship. Especially with a man who couldn't make up his mind. Granted, she fully realized she was a giant pain in the ass and could easily drive the bravest of men far away, but still. Last night he'd been all annoyed and distant, and this morning he was ready to kiss her. What was up with that?

Rachel turned toward the barn. The horses needed to be fed. No time to deal with the hot cop. She whistled for Bandit. The little dog trotted to her side, then raced ahead. "You should go home, He-Man. Even superheroes need sleep."

She glanced over her shoulder and was rewarded by a sexy smile. She looked away as her face heated. A few other body parts got on board.

Behind her, his engine started, and she heard his vehicle bouncing down her disaster of a driveway. She lifted her chin. Her gaze locked on the barn, and her jaw dropped. Black tarpaulin covered every inch of graffiti. The cop hadn't just sat in her drive all night. He'd saved her hours of work this morning.

She was in big, big trouble. Not only did He-Man make her girl parts hum, he made her feel all warm and fuzzy inside. A few hot, sweaty bouts of sex she could handle, but Rachel did not do warm and fuzzy. It just wasn't worth the risk. Generally, people let her down when she needed them the most.

A jingling sound snapped her out of her musing. Bandit streaked out from behind the garage. Dirt covered his forelegs, and a muddy, dead rabbit dangled from his muzzle.

"Bandit!" Rachel started to sprint after him. The dog lowered his chest to the ground. Butt in the air, his feathery tail swept back and forth in a come-and-get-me wag.

"Bandit, be a good boy." Rachel skidded to a stop and inched toward the dog slowly. "Drop it. I'll give you a treat."

Enjoying the game, Bandit pranced backward a few feet.

"Come on, boy," Rachel said in a low, quiet voice. She stepped forward. The dog shot off around the barn, ears flapping and short legs churning in a brown blur. Rachel darted after him, trying to cut him off by looping around the other side of the building, but Bandit proved too quick to be caught. He faked a left and tore off in the opposite direction. Rachel circled. She hid behind the door and waited. Bandit sensed her presence, gave her a wide berth, and zoomed joyfully around the barnyard. Rachel stopped, hands on hips, and blew out a hard breath.

This was ridiculous. She had zero chance of catching the little bugger.

Hoping he'd get bored, she went to work. Friendly nickers and snorts greeted her as she entered the barn. She stopped at Lady's stall and slipped a carrot from her pocket. The mare crunched placidly while Rachel stroked her neck.

Keeping one eye on the exit, she flipped on the lights and started measuring grain. Bandit's head, complete with dangling, decaying animal, peeked around the door frame. Rachel ignored him. He set the rabbit down and woofed. She moved from stall to stall dumping grain into feed buckets. Every time she passed within a couple of feet of him, he snatched the body and danced away. By the time she'd finished feeding the horses, the little dog lay in a dejected heap next to his disgusting prize. She walked past him out the door. Dog tags jingled at her heels. She glanced down. Empty mouthed, the dog trotted at her side. Could a dog look disappointed?

"Oh, no you don't." Rachel made a quick grab for his collar on the stoop. There wasn't a square inch of fur that wasn't dripping with mud. She tied him to the tree. "You're a mess. And no way am I letting you lick any faces until I brush your teeth."

He looked up at her. His ears drooped, and he made full use of his sad spaniel eyes.

"But I promise we'll have a game of fetch later." Rachel patted him on the head and put *bathe Bandit* on her to-do list. And she'd have to rebury the rabbit before the girls saw it. In a much deeper hole.

⤳

With a carefully schooled expression, Mike crossed the tiled lobby of the small county courthouse. Inside, anger was burning a hole through his gut. He turned down the hallway that led to the rear parking lot only to see Rachel Parker pacing outside the Family Court Administration Office.

Yowza.

Her usual uniform of worn jeans and ponytail were sexy enough, but since their dawn encounter, she'd changed into a slim skirt, a cotton blouse, and low heels. Mike's gaze dropped to her bare legs. Big mistake. They were as tight and toned as he'd suspected. He reluctantly lifted his eyes to her face. She'd downsized the Band-Aid on her cheek, and the bruise under it was faint. And her mouth… Her lips looked soft and ripe and tasty.

Her brows lifted and a slight smile pulled at one corner of her mouth. "Do I clean up OK?"

Mike blinked and cleared his throat. "Er, how did it go? Did she get the temporary order?"

"Don't know yet. She's been in there awhile. She wanted to do this solo." Rachel raised her chin as if she were proud of that. "I assume he's out on bail?"

"Troy was released on his own recognizance."

Rachel's jaw tightened. The humor slid from her face.

"No history of violence, close ties to the community, etcetera," Mike said, disturbed that he had to work to keep his voice level. Yeah, he was annoyed with the judge, but he never had trouble with emotional control. Ever. Until he'd met Rachel.

"Damn. I don't know why this is a surprise. I should've counted on Vince to play dirty." She scowled, and the temper that lit her eyes made her sexier. What was wrong with him?

"He has to join Alcoholics Anonymous, attend twice-weekly meetings, and generally keep his nose clean until the next hearing."

Rachel's disgusted snort echoed Mike's opinion. The conditions were simply a cover-your-ass move for the judge so it didn't look like he was just letting the scumbag go to please an old crony friend, which was exactly what he was doing.

Rachel chewed her lip in silence. Mike searched her face. Something about her totally threw him off. He'd spent half the night stapling tarps over the graffiti on her barn. Had to be a reason. Was it the way emotion played so transparently across her face? She was incapable of deception. Or the way her dark hair fell in loose, shining waves around her shoulders? It smelled like...He leaned a little closer. Her eyes widened, but she didn't back down. No, she would never back down. Her eyes blazed with that sexy fire. Mike inhaled. Lemons. She smelled like lemons, all fresh and clean. The scent of her hair made him think of other body parts he'd like to sniff.

Footsteps sounded in the hall behind Mike. He turned his head. Vince Mitchell was coming down the hall, his trophy wife hanging off his arm. In her sky-high heels, the beautiful young woman on his arm was taller than her wiry, gray-haired husband. Tanya Mitchell had restrained her long platinum blond hair in a conservative bun, but her suit was too tight for her to pull off the suburban wife image. With overly enhanced breasts straining the buttons of her silk blouse, the pearls and pumps getup made her look like Donna Reed's slutty alter ego. Her heavy makeup contrasted with Rachel's clean, fresh face.

Vince guided Tanya past. One arm slid around his wife's body. His hand gave her hip a possessive squeeze, but his beady eyes darted back and forth between Mike and Rachel. Mike realized too late that he was standing closer to her than professional interest would dictate. Hell, his face was only a few inches from her head. Yes, he'd actually sniffed her hair in the hallway of the municipal building—in full view of the town councilman who'd been trying to fire him for the past year.

Suspicion lit Vince's thin face. His mouth twisted in an evil, satisfied smile. Mike gritted his teeth. He'd known all along his interest in Rachel was going to come back and bite him on the ass. Now that Vince knew about it, it was only a matter of time.

☙

Rachel felt his withdrawal. Mike's body was still close enough that she could smell his damned aftershave and feel the heat his body emanated. But his attention was riveted on the blond bimbo's retreating butt. Yup. Vince's wife had it all going on. Legs, butt, boobs, all *Sports Illustrated* Swimsuit Issue perfect. Oh well. Rachel couldn't take it personally.

Mike's eyes closed as he moved a step away from her. "I can't believe I just did that."

"Did what? Got an eyeful of Tayna's booty?" Rachel patted his forearm. "Give yourself a break. Mightier men have fallen."

Mike's brow creased. "No. It's not that. I can't believe Vince saw...*that*." He motioned between them with one hand.

"Is that a problem?"

"Yes." He paced a few feet away and back. "You're a key part of an active case. Professional ethics dictate that I cannot be involved with you."

"Oh." Disappointment settled over Rachel like freezing drizzle. She pushed it away and lifted her chin. "I wasn't aware that we were involved."

Mike pinched the bridge of his nose.

"Your face is getting all red," Rachel said. "Have you had your blood pressure checked lately?"

"I never did anything like this before I met you." His voice was clipped, and his jaw muscles moved like he was grinding his teeth. "You're distracting."

"Distracting?" Rachel felt her mouth gape. *She* was distracting. Women like Tanya were distracting. Not Rachel.

"You destroy my objectivity."

"Gee, sorry."

Mike's eyes blazed. "Nothing can happen between us."

"OK by me." Rachel folded her arms across her chest. "You're the one who's having a stroke about it."

"Stroke?" he choked, eyes bulging.

The door behind her opened, and Sarah walked out, her eyes bright behind the bruises.

"Any problems?" Mike's tone shifted back to super-polite.

"No," Sarah answered, then stared at Rachel and frowned. "Is everything all right?"

"Fine." Rachel forced a smile on the protesting muscles of her face. "All done?"

Sarah nodded. "Yes. It wasn't too bad. Troy can't come near me or the girls until the hearing, which will be in ten days. I'll need a lawyer for that."

"Already working on it." Rachel pushed away from the wall and started down the hall. "Let's talk about it at home."

"All right." Sarah followed with a confused glance at Mike.

Rachel tried to resist, but her eyes were pulled to him, damn them. Traitors.

Thankfully, he was looking at Sarah. "If you have any trouble, don't hesitate to call. Please don't try to handle things on your own." He shot Rachel a disapproving frown.

Rachel embraced the dig and glared back. Anger welled, hot, familiar, and definitely preferable to self-pity. She pivoted on her heel. A few long strides later the door opened to the smack of her palm. A damp breeze cooled her face. Holding the door open, she waited for Sarah.

"Thanks for everything, Chief O'Connell." Sarah's kitten heels tapped on the tile floor as she hurried to catch up.

"You're welcome."

Rachel didn't look back as he responded. That deep voice was as devastating as his eyes. She let the door swing shut. In the parking lot, Rachel didn't allow herself to run for the truck. Her sister was still walking stiffly and would have trouble keeping up. Plus, pride wouldn't let her admit how much his snub had affected her. She slammed the door of the pickup harder than necessary and shoved the key into the ignition.

Sarah eased her body into the passenger seat. "Is there something going on between you and Chief O'Connell?"

"No."

"You're sure? Because he looks at you like you're a juicy rib eye and he's been eating vegan for a long time."

Rachel jerked the gearshift into drive. "That was your mother-in-law who had him drooling on the floor. He's just perpetually pissed off at me."

"Really? That's not the impression I had." Sarah rested her head on the back of the seat. "Well, he's out of luck there. Tanya isn't leaving Vince, at least not as long as he's still buying her everything she wants. She isn't giving up the cash flow anytime soon. She's not as dumb as she looks."

"She couldn't be and still be able to dress herself."

"Rachel, that's mean." But Sarah laughed as she protested.

"Yeah, well, I'm not as nice as you are."

Sarah flexed the fingers of her casted arm and winced. "I still think the police chief is interested in you."

"No way. I'm telling you he was staring at Tanya. Maybe there's something going on between them. She wouldn't have to leave Vince, you know. People cheat all the time."

As she well knew. Her throat clogged with the memory of Blake's betrayal. No. She wasn't going to dwell on the past. She'd rejected him, and he'd turned to someone else. End of story.

With a deep, cleansing breath, Rachel turned onto Main Street. She depressed the gas pedal, and the pickup sputtered and then roared ahead. "I drive O'Connell crazy. I drive most people crazy, which is why I like being alone."

"That's because you don't let anyone see the real you."

Exactly. She'd briefly let her guard down with Blake, and look how that had turned out.

Rachel stopped at the traffic light. "Enough about Mike already. There is nothing going on between us."

Sarah's eyebrows shot up. "Mike? You're on a first-name basis with the police chief?"

"I'm not talking about that anymore." Rachel's cheeks warmed. She glanced at her sister.

Sarah was clearly biting back a grin. "Whatever."

Time for a change of subject. Though it was nice to see her sister's long-forgotten sense of humor. "I've been thinking about something. What if this vandal guy isn't out to get me? What if he's out to get the farm? I never had any trouble until I moved there, and most of his efforts have been aimed at the business."

She'd been thinking about Mike's questions. Frankly, she'd be thrilled if the threats weren't a personal attack.

Sarah frowned. "I don't know. The place is a disaster. Except for your new barn, nothing else has been renovated since the fifties."

"I was thinking maybe there was something about the place we don't know."

"What, you think there's an oil field under the meadow?" Sarah started humming the *Beverly Hillbillies* theme.

"Something like that. Though there aren't many oil rigs in the Poconos." Rachel laughed, and the tension in her chest loosened. "It was Chief O'Connell's idea."

"Don't you mean Mike?" Sarah teased. Her grin spread across her face. She cupped her bruised cheek. "Don't make me laugh. It hurts my face."

Rachel turned down a small side street. "We have some time before Mrs. Holloway brings the girls home from school, and the alarm guy isn't coming until after lunch. Mind if I make a quick stop at the library?"

Sarah stopped laughing abruptly. "Not as long as you don't make me go inside."

In the parking lot, Sarah slid down in the passenger seat and hid her bruised face with one hand. Rachel checked out four books from the local history section at rapid speed. Sarah didn't sit up again until the truck was in motion.

Ten minutes later, Rachel turned into her driveway. Down by the barn, the Johnson's Well Service truck was still parked in the same place it had sat when they'd left for the courthouse. But Rachel was staring at the large commercial van that occupied the parking area in front of the house. Ladders were mounted on the roof. A huge man leaned against the vehicle. As they approached, he turned to face them. David Gunner. A small bubble of long-buried anger surfaced. And the past she'd worked so hard to suppress came rushing back, a barrage images that left her as battered and bruised as any of Troy's blows.

Sarah gawked out the window.

Rachel swallowed the bitter taste a lifetime of jealousy had left in her mouth. None of what happened had been David's fault. Not directly, anyway.

Chapter Nine

"What is he doing here?" Rachel eyed the large man with suspicion.

Sarah squinted out the windshield. "I don't know. He did some work for Vince awhile back, but I haven't seen him lately."

"I haven't seen him since Dad sold him the company." Right after their mother's funeral. Of course, Neil Parker hadn't offered the family business to either of his daughters No, he'd practically adopted the neighbor's kid instead.

"Daddy needed to retire," Sarah said in a sad voice. "He couldn't function after Mom died."

"Retire? Is that what you call sitting in a recliner and drinking twenty-four-seven?"

"You can't hold that against David," Sarah answered in a sad voice. "He isn't responsible for Daddy's actions. Mom dying like she did took a huge toll on him."

On her daughters too.

"I know." Rachel took two slow, deliberate breaths. Didn't help. "Also wasn't David's fault that Dad wanted boys, and all he got was us."

Or that their unstable mother had dragged their father into her emotional wreck long before she got ripping drunk and drove her car into a tree.

Sarah didn't respond, and Rachel wondered how much a decades-old wound could bleed. Dad's decision hadn't been David's fault, but he hadn't exactly turned the company down, had he?

Rachel parked alongside Sarah's minivan, which Mrs. Holloway had helped Rachel retrieve early that morning. David's van, still emblazoned with the Parker Construction logo, sat a few yards away. He hadn't even changed the name of the company. One more indication of how David had insinuated himself into their family. She shoved open her door and hopped out of the cab, then reached into the truck for the hefty pile of library books. Old hinges squealed as she used a hip to shut the truck door.

"David." She stretched her face into a smile. The skin of her cheeks felt tight enough to crack, and the armload of books was a convenient excuse to not shake his outstretched hand. "I haven't seen you for years."

David shoved his hands into the front pockets of his jeans. "I know. I heard you two were having trouble." In his early forties, his body had thickened with age but he hadn't gone to fat. His towering frame was packed solid. Close-cropped brown hair showed just a few strands of gray.

Sarah walked past Rachel and stood on her toes to give David a one-armed hug. "It's good to see you."

Rachel suppressed a scowl. Sarah was the better person. No question.

David's weathered face flushed, and he stiffened. One beefy arm lifted as if he didn't know what to do with it. A few seconds passed before he awkwardly lowered it to return her embrace. "Thanks, Sarah."

Sarah stepped back. "Why don't we go inside?"

Sure, let's extend this awkward-fest. Ugh. Did Sarah have to be *that* nice?

David dug the toe of his work boot into the mud, echoing Rachel's discomfort. Guilt wormed into her. She was always thinking she should be more pleasant, more like Sarah. Here was a chance to practice. "Come on in. I'll make coffee."

She picked her way across the rear lawn to the back door. David and Sarah followed. Bandit barked and leapt at the door. A bee hovered above the stoop. Rachel froze. Anaphylactic shock wouldn't be a good way to round out her day.

"Watch out." Sarah moved in front of Rachel until the insect buzzed away. "You still carry your EpiPen, right?"

"Always. Wish it would just get cold out already." Rachel unlocked the door. She turned to David and dumped the pile of books in his arms. "You take these. I'll get the killer dog." She grabbed Bandit and clamped a hand over his growling muzzle as she bundled him outside and tied him to the tree. Bandit continued to protest while she returned to the kitchen. "I'm sorry about that, David. Bandit has no manners."

Sarah was already filling the coffeepot from a gallon jug on the counter. "It's been hard to get him used to people. Troy wouldn't let him in the house."

Thankful that she had no close neighbors, Rachel shut the door on his furious yapping. "Bad case of small dog's disease."

"That's all right." David slid the armload of books onto the counter. "Studying?"

Sarah set mugs, cream, and sugar out at the table, then gestured for David to sit. "Rachel and I are researching the history of the house."

"Oh. Sounds interesting." But David's tone said *not.* He lowered his bulk into a chair. Sarah sat next to him. Rachel stayed on her feet but leaned against the counter. She'd start with polite and work her way up to friendly.

The chair squeaked as David shifted to face Rachel. "Look, I know you don't like me much. Some of that is my fault. Back then, I let your father treat me better than he did you and Sarah. I knew it, and I let it happen anyway."

The knot inside Rachel's chest loosened. "You were just a kid."

"No, you and Sarah were kids. I was old enough to know what was going on. I chose to ignore it because…" He grimaced as if the words were going to hurt when he spit them out. "Because my life was horrible, and I needed something to keep me going. After my dad's accident…" David looked at the window, but Rachel knew he wasn't admiring the serene meadow view. Sarah poured him a cup of coffee and set it on the table, but he ignored it.

David had gone from teenager to adult in the amount of time it had taken a tractor trailer to squash his father's car—and spine. Another bit of pressure eased inside her. Was it time to let go of some of her childhood issues? Could it actually feel good?

"He needed round-the-clock care. We couldn't afford the mortgage, let alone nursing. Me and Mom did everything. She worked nights. I worked days. Your dad paid me decently too, and we were strapped for cash back then. Medicine. Supplies. Hospital bills. You have no idea how much stuff a quadriplegic needs." David turned back to her. "But that's no excuse. I took your father to replace mine. Wasn't fair to you or Sarah."

"You can't take something we never had." Rachel's gaze dropped to David's giant, work-scarred hands. "Our father wasn't interested in us long before you started working for him. It isn't your fault. He wasn't going to give either one of us his company. If you hadn't bought it, he would have sold it to someone else."

Tension slid from Rachel's neck. This forgiveness thing wasn't so bad. The smile that spread across her face wasn't forced. See, she could interact with other people in a mature fashion. "Look, David, all that happened a long time ago. We're all adults now. No reason we can't put that behind us."

David perked up.

Beside her, Sarah beamed. "Is that all that brought you out here today, David?"

"No. I was having breakfast at the diner. Heard about the trouble you've been having." David's intense eyes pierced Rachel's.

Rachel stiffened and crossed her arms over her chest. Just because she let one past issue go didn't mean she wanted to share anything else with him. Baby steps with this whole emotional wellness, anger management thing. "Just some juvenile vandalism."

"That's not what I heard." David's eyes stayed locked on her face. Concern? Or something else?

Scrutinized like a pinned butterfly, Rachel fought the urge to squirm. "Well, the gossipmongers must have exaggerated, as usual. The diner isn't exactly CNN."

David stood and moved toward the counter. He loomed over her as he leaned forward to place his empty mug in the sink. "I have to meet with a client. Thanks for listening. And understanding." He turned his burly frame. At the kitchen door, he paused and looked at Sarah, his expression gentled. "And if you ever need help, just call. I'd be happy to have a *talk* with Troy for you."

Sarah stared at the floor for a few heartbeats. She raised her head. "I need to handle this myself, but thanks anyway."

"The offer stands." He nodded his approval as he stepped outside.

"I'll bring Bandit in." Rachel followed him onto the stoop and closed the door behind her. "Do you know Troy well?"

"Just enough to know he's an ass. Sarah deserves better." David paused and squinted at her sideways. "You know, you look a lot like your mother."

The tension that had eased in Rachel's chest rewound like a spring.

He tilted his head. "That bothers you?"

"My mother had problems." Her mother's mental illness was a stain on her childhood memories. *And I have enough emotional overflow to worry that the condition is genetic.*

"She was beautiful, and she wasn't always that way."

Their families had been next-door neighbors since Rachel was born. Older, David would remember her mom when she was much younger. Before Sarah's birth escalated her mental illness. Rachel didn't have many of those memories since she'd only been six at the time. All she had was a mental onslaught of sobbing and screaming and *don't-upset-your-mother.* "That's good to know. Thank you."

They stood side by side in a minute of not-too-uncomfortable silence. A flapping sound drew their attention to the barn. One of the tarps had loosened. A corner flapped in the breeze, revealing a choice verb.

David gestured toward the barn. "How about I paint that for you? The next few days are supposed to be dry, and I have some downtime before my next job starts up."

Rachel bristled automatically. "That's not necessary. I'll get to it eventually."

"Come on, Rachel. I have the equipment to make it quick work. And I owe you."

She forced herself to relax. She'd sworn she was going to think things through. No more impulsive decisions, and this time she meant it. He had ladders and stuff. The job would take him a couple of hours. She'd be at it for days. He was only trying to be nice. There was absolutely no reason not to let him do this for her. People did not always have ulterior motives.

"OK." Rachel stepped back. He couldn't help being so tall, but she hated being loomed over. "And thank you."

David smiled and looked very pleased with himself, like a barn cat that had devoured a tasty field mouse. The breeze shifted, turning cool and damp. Goose bumps rippled up Rachel's arms.

She opened her mouth to tell him she'd changed her mind, then stopped. She was being paranoid and ridiculous. What motive could David possibly have for giving up an afternoon to paint her barn?

Putting aside her second thoughts about accepting David's help, Rachel grabbed the dog and returned to the kitchen to finish her coffee.

At the table, Sarah leaned over one of the volumes from the library.

Rachel's stomach growled. She reached into the cabinet and pulled out a box of Pop-Tarts. "Any luck?"

"No mention of the farm just yet, but I've only started."

The kitchen door opened, and Mrs. Holloway ushered the girls inside. A fresh round of happy barking ensued.

Alex held up a small paper bag with cartoon characters stenciled on the outside. "Mrs. Holloway got us kids' meals. Mine came with a race car. Emma got a dinosaur puppet."

"How was school?" Sarah asked.

"Dumb. I'm too old for preschool." Alex scowled. She'd missed the cutoff date for kindergarten by a week.

Sarah sighed, obviously not up to having that conversation again. "Let's see those toys."

Alex sulked to a kitchen chair. Emma set her bag on the table and climbed up onto her mother's lap. She held up her forefinger and wiggled the top half of a miniature Tyrannosaurus.

"I hope you don't mind." Mrs. Holloway closed the door and hung her jacket on a wall peg. She held up a larger bag. Enticing, greasy scents wafted across the kitchen. "I thought we could all use some indulgence today."

"I don't mind at all. Thank you." Sarah opened the bag. "That's smells gross and incredible at the same time."

"Gross? It smells fantastic." Rachel inhaled deeply, tossed aside the Pop-Tarts, and fetched napkins. "Sarah and I were discussing the history of the farm. Do you think it could have some value that we don't know about?"

Mrs. Holloway passed out burgers and cartons of fries. "According to your grandfather, the house was built by your Quaker ancestors in the early nineteenth century. I forget the date, but he had papers, books, and diaries on the subject."

"The only papers in his desk were bank statements, ledgers, stuff like that."

"Did you search the attic and basement?" Mrs. Holloway asked.

Salivating, Rachel unfolded her burger. "For the most part I've avoided both. They're packed with trunks and boxes and furniture. Going through it all will be a project."

Sarah gestured with her casted arm. "I can get started on that during naptimes and preschool. I need to get a job too, but that'll have to wait a few weeks."

"You should check with Edna Kaiser." Mrs. Holloway reached for the ketchup. "She's been the township clerk forever. She might point you toward land surveys or tax records. The township could have some pretty old documents archived somewhere."

"I've already been to the library." A car door slammed outside. Rachel jumped to her feet and crossed to the window. A Mercedes sedan was parked by the barn. "Shoot. My riding lesson's here early. I have to change."

She paused. The well serviceman was walking up the back lawn. Rachel lifted the handle on the kitchen faucet. A few seconds passed, air sputtered, water spattered and then flowed. Hallelujah.

"Sarah, can you take care of the well guy? Tell him I'll send him a check tomorrow."

"Sure," Sarah said. "But where are you going to get the money?"

"Don't worry. I have it all worked out." Rachel shoved the rest of her burger into her mouth as she jogged up the stairs barefoot, shoes dangling from her fingertips. A small lump of discomfort lodged in her throat, and not just in response to her source of cash flow.

She loved her students, but some of the parents were hell, especially this domineering father. As she slid out of her skirt and blouse, she mentally steeled herself for the inevitable confrontation.

Chapter Ten

Mike parked next to Rachel's barn beside a long, sleek Mercedes sedan. Dark window tinting obscured the interior. He made a note of the license plate number as Sean pulled his mammoth SUV in the next spot. The sound of voices and thud of hoofbeats drew them to the other side of the barn, where a horse and rider were cantering around the perimeter of a fenced riding ring. Rachel stood in the center, attention fixed on the school-aged girl and her dappled gray mount. Rachel shouted instructions, pivoting as the horse circled the ring.

Sweet Jesus. Those riding pants were tight.

Even as Mike's mouth watered, he noted that her leather knee patches were worn nearly through, as were the tall black boots. In contrast, everything about her student was new, shiny, and expensive.

The gray horse turned toward one of the wooden jumps placed in the ring. The rails were set about three feet high. Mike glanced at the sole observer, a lean, dark man in his late thirties. Dressed in slim black trousers and shirt, he rested his tanned forearms on the fence.

"Weight back," Rachel called out. "Heels down. Drive him forward." Her voice rose and sharpened with each command. The horse's head bobbed and its eyes rolled as it galloped right to the base of the jump, then ducked around the obstacle. The gray took advantage of the girl's precarious balance, threw its head down, and bolted. Its rider hauled back on the reins until the animal slid to a stop at the gate. The girl pitched forward onto its neck.

Rachel strode to the animal's side and spoke to the girl in low tones. The child's face had paled, and Mike could see her hands trembling from across the ring. Rachel was whispering, and the girl was shaking her head.

"OK." Rachel held the reins while her student dismounted.

The man leaning on the fence straightened and tensed. "You were supposed to train that animal to jump properly," he shouted, stabbing the air at Rachel with a forefinger.

Mike stepped up to the fence. Sean veered off and took a spot several feet away on the man's opposite side. The visitor took them both in with suspicious sideways glances.

Without a word, Rachel took her student's cap and jammed it on her own head. She mounted the gray in one fluid movement, picking up stirrups and reins as the horse trotted off. Her body was quiet and still as she made two laps around the ring, easing the gray into a fluid gallop. Mike's muscles went taut as she turned toward the same jump the horse had just refused, but the gray showed no hesitation. It took the obstacle in one smooth motion. They landed and galloped off. Rachel's head swiveled. Mike followed her line of sight toward another obstacle, this one four or five feet high. The horse's ears pricked and its stride lengthened as it approached the jump. Rachel's body stretched along the animal's neck as they soared over the top rail.

The girl slumped as Rachel slowed the horse and walked to her side. Rachel dismounted and handed the girl the reins. "Cool him out."

With a hard look at Mike and Sean, the slim man moved to the entrance. He focused intently on Rachel as she opened the gate. After the girl and horse passed through and headed for the barn, the man stepped up behind Rachel.

"You were supposed to train the horse so that my daughter can ride it," he said quietly. His voice was accented with a South American inflection and a threatening undertone. "She needs to master that animal."

"We've been over this before." Rachel turned. Her eyes flashed. "The horse is too much for her. She needs a calmer, more forgiving mount. No amount of training is going to make that horse docile."

The man's mouth tightened. "That animal cost a great deal of money. It is the best. My daughter deserves only the best. Perhaps she isn't trying hard enough." The man's black eyes narrowed. His lips compressed as the girl and horse disappeared into the barn.

"She's going to get hurt. Lucia simply doesn't have the experience to handle that horse yet, and the animal knows it. You are welcome to find someone else to train them both."

"I don't want anyone else to teach them," he said. "Lucia will learn."

Rachel's jaw clenched as if she were biting back an impolite retort. "I'm going to try him in a stronger bit."

"As you wish." He inclined his head, a glimmer of triumph in his eyes.

Rachel turned her back on him and stalked away, her frustration evident in the stiffness of her posture.

Rachel caught Mike's eye and tilted her head toward the house. Mike followed her across the back lawn.

Sean fell into step next to him and leaned close. "I really like her."

"She could be a little less abrasive." Mike glanced back at the South American, who was glaring at Rachel's back. Had she crossed tempers with anyone else lately?

Rachel strode across the lawn. She'd talk to the cop and his blond buddy as soon as she cooled off. Her shoulder throbbed from the effort of putting the gray over the jumps. So much for her earlier vow against impulsive decisions.

Angering Lucia's father again hadn't been wise either. Yes, Cristan Rojas was an arrogant jerk, but he was a rich arrogant jerk. She couldn't afford to annoy him. Not with the kind of money he was paying her to coach his daughter and train that unruly horse. Though why he was willing pay her considerable training fees was a mystery. The man wigged out every time she gave him her opinion or answered a question.

Rachel gnashed her teeth. Didn't matter. She had to speak her mind. As she well knew, riding was a dangerous sport. She'd hate to see the young girl get seriously hurt. Plus, Lucia would enjoy herself and progress must faster on a more appropriate mount. Impulsive or not, Rachel had made the right decision telling Lucia's father the truth, although she could work on her delivery. Sarah would've been able to get the point across without a confrontation.

Rachel stopped short as she approached the back of the house. Sarah stood at the door. A spark of anger lurked behind her shiner.

Uh-oh. Sarah had been watching. Bandit yapped and darted out to greet Rachel. She grabbed him before he spotted Rojas down by the barn. A bitten ankle wouldn't improve her client's mood.

"Rachel, you promised." Sarah blocked the door with her body. "No more jumping."

"I know. I'm sorry." Rachel halted on the stoop. "I didn't know what else to do. That guy needed to be taught a lesson."

"What if you fell?" Sarah propped her good hand on her hip.

Yeah. Unfortunately, that possibility had never crossed Rachel's mind. Consequences rarely did. "I didn't."

"But what if you did? You almost died last time. You know what the doctor said. If you fall again…" Sarah's eyes didn't waver as she paused for a breath.

Rachel didn't respond. She was freaking Humpty Dumpty. All the king's horses and so on.

"You're not supposed to ride at all. I know you'll never agree to that, but jumping is just plain stupid. You have to put yourself before those horses. I can't sit in another ICU wondering if you're going to live. You want me to leave Troy so I don't get hurt, but you're not willing to take the same care of yourself."

Guilt sat like a sandbag in Rachel's belly. "You're right. I won't forget again." Sarah didn't need another worry. She'd been in such a good mood at lunch, and Rachel had botched it. Not to mention the fact that Rachel had provoked anger in the most even-tempered person on earth.

Sarah's eyes flickered over Rachel's shoulder. Rachel froze. They'd just treated the cop and his buddy to a ringside view of a private family argument.

Sarah moved aside to let them all into the kitchen. Bandit leapt out of Rachel's arms, growled at the blond guy, then spotted Mike and went all wags and snuffles. He even had the dog charmed. Rachel turned to face the men.

She gave Mike a cold and silent nod as he introduced her to the super-buff blond. "Sean is going to give you an estimate on an alarm system."

"Nice to meet you." Sean held out a hand. A fist-sized emblem on the chest of his white polo shirt read *Wilson Security*. The guy was lean as an Olympic decathlete, and behind the friendly smile was a sharp, predatory gleam. She'd bet Sean didn't learn about security from an online course.

"I appreciate you fitting us in so quickly." Rachel shook his hand. "How long do you need?"

"Couple of hours." Sean's serious eyes gave the room a critical scan. "Old houses can be a challenge."

"Rachel, can you afford this?" Sarah filled a sandwich bag with ice.

"Yes, don't worry about it."

Doubt invaded Sarah's new bossy attitude. "I don't want you to go into debt because of us."

Rachel touched Sarah's arm. "I have it covered. I'm not going into debt, I promise." She faced Sean. "I want my family safe. So, whatever it takes."

Sean gave her an approving nod. Rachel popped a couple of painkillers and took the ice pack from Sarah. Bandit raced Rachel to the door. She blocked him with her foot. "Oh no. Not without a leash. Not after this morning."

Mike followed her outside. The security guy was right behind him.

Mike caught up with her in a couple of strides. "Your student's father seemed angry."

She pressed the ice pack to her shoulder. Ahhh. "He isn't used to anyone standing up to him."

His eyes dropped to the cold pack. "You all right?"

"Fine. Old injury."

"You should be more careful. What do you know about him?"

Rachel stopped. "Oh, don't even go there. Cristan Rojas wouldn't stoop to writing dirty words on my barn."

"Still, making people mad isn't a smart thing to do."

"Probably not," Rachel agreed. "But just because he's South American doesn't make him a drug lord."

"Maybe not, but how well do you know him?"

"Not that well," she admitted. She doubted Rojas was dangerous, but Mike's words gave her a twinge of doubt. Someone was out to get her. Could she be wrong about Rojas?

Mike stopped her with a hand on her good arm. "You're not involved with him, are you?"

"What do you mean *involved?*" Rachel narrowed her eyes at his hand. His grip was gentle but firm enough to withstand her tug.

"Dating him. Flirting with him." Mike's eyes went flat. "Sleeping with him."

"Look, He-Man. You and I need to get something straight. I'm not flirting, dating, or sleeping with *anyone.*" She rotated her arm to break his hold, then stabbed him in the center of his chest with a forefinger. "And even if I were, it wouldn't be any of your business."

"I'm just trying to eliminate possible suspects."

"Sure you are." Holding the ice firmly against her shoulder again, she whirled and stomped toward the barn.

Behind her, she heard Sean say, "Did I mention how much I like her?"

⏥

"Shut up." The short laugh that Mike couldn't quite stifle took the heat out of his retort. He watched Rachel enter the barn, toss her bag of ice into the trash, and lead her pretty mare into the aisle. She leaned on the horse's neck, her shoulders collapsing forward as if she were seeking comfort. Had he been too harsh with her? No. Wait. *She* was the one who'd chewed *him* out.

Sean went to work. Mike turned at the rumble of a large engine. A white horse van bumped up the rutted drive and parked next to the barn. A slim, silvery-blond man in breeches, boots, and a red polo jumped out of the shotgun seat and strode toward Rachel, still in the barn aisle with her horse. The driver alighted, going to the side of the vehicle, unhooking latches, and lowering a ramp.

New horses arriving?

On the way to his vehicle, Mike glanced at Rachel. Her face had gone to stone as she led the mare forward to meet the blond. He opened his door, then paused, listening. Something was up.

Rachel stopped a few feet from the guy. "Thanks for coming, Blake."

Blake Webb? As in her former boss and the owner of Fleet O' Feet?

Her former boss compressed the color from his lips. Oh, yeah. Blake Webb had more than a former employer's interest in Rachel. Looked like the tabloids were right. The tension that gathered in Mike's gut had nothing to do with a medical condition. It was jealousy, pure and simple, roaring through his blood in a way he'd never before experienced. He beat it back with common sense. Nothing was going to happen between Rachel and him anyway. So what did it matter if Blake Webb had a thing for her?

Mike's heart did a quick flip when Rachel's expression showed no returning interest. But her face was tight and alarmingly pale. Something was wrong. He closed the car door.

"You don't have to do this, Rachel. I'll give you the money," Blake said.

Tightlipped, Rachel gave her head a quick shake. "No, thanks."

Everything clicked into place, and with a sick realization, Mike knew why Blake Webb was here.

Chapter Eleven

Rachel handed Blake the rope, and with that single act, the bright future she'd envisioned six months ago dimmed. She'd gone over her finances a dozen times. There wasn't any other way. Lady was the only asset on her balance sheet worth enough money to make a difference. Bedsides, Blake would take good care of her. He loved horses as much as she did, which was one of the reasons their friendship had meant so much to her. And why losing it had hurt so much. Eyes burning, she turned her face toward the meadow.

"Rachel. Don't do this. I'll loan you the money if you won't just take it," Blake said.

Business transaction or not, sadness sealed her throat, choking off any response.

"Come on. You love this horse. I don't want you to give her up because you're helping your sister."

Lady nudged her arm. Rachel took a step back. No farewell pat. This was business, just business.

"We both know she's not just a horse to you."

"I don't have a choice, Blake. For those of us without a billion-dollar trust fund, the world's a rough place." The verbal jab was low, and throwing it at him compounded her misery. Her head ached, and her throat was clogged.

Blake's face flushed. He handed the horse off to the driver. Anger flared in his eyes as he pulled an envelope from his pocket and handed it to her. "I didn't mean to hurt you."

"Likewise. But we did a damn fine job of it anyway." She closed her fingers around the envelope and waited to feel some relief. This money was going to keep her out of debt and ensure Sarah didn't lose her kids. But the pressure didn't abate. It swelled, expanding from her throat into her chest until she could barely breathe. She had to get away. From the future she was handing over. From Blake and the feelings he still had for her. From the past she couldn't leave behind no matter how hard she tried. Rachel spun on one heel and headed toward the barn. He caught up with her in a few long strides.

"Rachel. Stop. Please." He tapped her left shoulder. Pain sang through her arm. She winced, welcoming the ability of the white-hot sting to override her emotions. She spun around to face him.

Blake frowned. "That shouldn't have hurt. What have you been doing to yourself?" Worry replaced anger in his tone. Shit. She hated it when she was a bitch and people were nice to her anyway.

"Leave me alone, Blake." Rachel pivoted and continued to walk away.

"Goddamn it, Rachel." Blake jogged after her. "I told you this would be too much work for you."

"I didn't ask you for your opinion," she said without turning around.

"Did you at least hire some help to do the heavy stuff?" He lowered his voice. "I'm worried about you."

If she looked at his face and saw the emotion that she knew would still be there, even after everything that had passed between them, the pressure cooker inside her was going to blow. Rachel stared at the mud on her boots for a few seconds while Blake's gaze seared her face.

"Lady will be at my place when you come to your senses." He sounded disgusted. "And when you pick her up, you could visit Fleet. He's missed you."

She lifted her chin and watched him stride back to the van and climb into the back to check on the horse before securing the ramp and door.

Rachel turned back to the barn. She'd give Lady up, but watching her horse's departure was too much. She stepped into the cool shade of the barn.

"Did you really have to do that?"

She stiffened. Mike. He was still here? Fan-frigging-tastic. She jerked her chin up and sniffed. "Sarah needs a lawyer yesterday. Troy can't get custody of those kids."

Troy shouldn't be allowed to keep pets or barnyard animals, let alone children. Why did loving people so frequently require ripping one's soul completely open?

Her gaze shifted to the empty stall. She walked inside and stood in the center. Her heart felt empty, as if its center had been carved out and tossed aside like a pumpkin.

The heat from his body wafted across the humid fall air, the smell of his aftershave cutting through the hay dust, the tug of her hollowed-out heart toward something that could mend it.

His hands were on her waist. Gently, carefully avoiding her sore shoulder, he eased her closer. Her back hit the hard muscles of his abdomen and chest. His arms folded around her. Her body went stiff for a few seconds, automatically protesting the confinement. Warmth seeped through her T-shirt into her skin. She turned and pressed her face into his chest. A shudder passed through her, then a single sob, muffled by his shirt. She breathed him—and an unsettling peace—in.

His chin dropped onto the top of her head. His palms flexed on her back muscles, stroking and soothing. He pulled her closer. This time she yielded immediately and leaned against him, letting him support some of her weight. Something eased deep in her chest. The power in the sensation was unfamiliar, addictive—and disturbing. She could stay right there for a long time.

Panic sluiced over her like a cold hose. She froze and pushed off his abs with one hand.

⌒

"I can't do this. I'm sorry."

Mike let her go. His empty arms dropped to his sides. "OK."

She swiped a hand across her face, as if wiping away the evidence of whatever had just transpired. In three steps, she left the stall and what had passed between them behind. "Blake'll tell you. I'm not capable of…" She waved a hand back and forth between them. "This."

For a few seconds, he stood dumbstruck. He'd expected the punch of lust when she was in his arms, but the tenderness she evoked from him was shocking. Selling that horse was breaking her heart, and he felt every fissure as if it were happening to him.

Mike stepped into the aisle. His gaze fell to the envelope in her clenched fist. She'd crushed it. Rachel blinked at the crumpled paper. A muscle in her jaw jumped as she smoothed it out with her fingers and opened it.

Mike caught a glimpse of the check. Webb had paid her thirty thousand dollars for that horse. On top of the check was a business card for Rising Star Farms. A name and number were handwritten across the bottom. He put aside the uncomfortable stuff churning in his gut. Her personal and financial situations weren't his concern. Nor was her emotional state. His job was to find her stalker and protect her. That's it. If she could ignore the connection between them, so could he. Really. "What's the story with Webb?"

"Blake used to be my boss and my friend." Her voice was quiet and lacked its usual hard edge.

"He seemed like more than a friend." Which still bugged him.

She stared at her boots. "We were together for a while."

The way she said "together" irritated him even more. "What happened between you?"

"He wanted more than I could give." Rachel shifted her weight and focused on the wall over his shoulder. Clearly, she hadn't told him the whole story. Was her ex angry or desperate enough to try to make Rachel's farm fail, thinking she'd have nowhere else to go but back to him? How badly did Webb want her back?

"What did you do?" An angry voice drew their attention to the doorway. Sarah walked into the barn. She glanced over her shoulder at the retreating horse van. Her face locked in horror. "You didn't sell that horse, did you?"

Rachel's gaze jerked away from her sister, an obvious admission that she had. "Buying and selling horses is part of the business."

Sarah blanched. "Oh my God!" Her voice rose, full of anger and insult. "You did. Why didn't you talk to me first?"

"I didn't want you to feel pressured to find the money elsewhere." Rachel reached into her back pocket and pulled out the business card. "Here's the lawyer Blake recommended. Call him."

"Damn it, Rachel. I know I'm in a bind, but you can't just ruin your life to fix everything in mine. I won't let you," Sarah protested. But she snatched the card from Rachel's hand before stomping out of the barn.

Rachel stood completely still for a full minute, then turned and faced Mike. "Did you need anything else? I have to go to the bank."

He shook his head, and she retreated to the house.

Mike drove back to the station and locked himself in his office to deal with paperwork, but as he reviewed reports and signed forms, his mind was fixated on Rachel. She claimed to be incapable of loving anyone. Her relationship with her sister and nieces said otherwise, as did her willingness to give everything she had for her family. She was quick tempered but held her deeper emotions in check. Except for that one moment, when she'd let him in. That brief surrender, those few seconds when she'd allowed him to comfort her, had lodged under his skin.

She'd rejected the bond between them, but it had been there. He'd felt it, but he didn't blame her for running. It terrified him too.

Chapter Twelve

As usual, Rachel woke Tuesday morning long before the alarm went off. Without turning on the light, she stepped into a pair of jeans and a sweatshirt, then moved to the window. She tugged one broken slat of the mini blind down with her forefinger.

Yep. In the middle of the predawn autumn fog, Mike's SUV sat in her driveway.

Confusion clogged Rachel's throat. She backed away from the window and sat on the edge of the bed.

Dammit, she wanted coffee and a Pop-Tart. But if she went downstairs, Bandit would wake. He'd want his breakfast, and then he'd need to go outside. Once she opened the door, she'd have to face Mike and what had happened between them the day before.

When she'd blubbered all over him. She'd lowered her guard. She'd been tempted to drop her walls entirely and let the peace of that moment in his arms take over.

Unfortunately, there was only so much she could stuff under her emotional rug. Warmth flooded her belly at the memory of the cop's arms wrapped around her. As hard as his body had been, his embrace was gentle, and the sincerity behind the gesture had touched her more profoundly than the physical contact. For that minute, she hadn't been alone. He'd willingly shared her pain and offered to help her shoulder the burden. So, of course, she'd pushed him away. But how could she have opened herself up like that? Even for a second? Damn, it had felt good, though. Too good. This must be what crack cocaine felt like. One hug and she was an addict.

Instead of feeding her caffeine and sugar addiction, she went into the bathroom, splashed cold water on her face, and changed the Band-Aid on her cheek. Other than the tiny row of stitches and a faint yellowing bruise, her face looked normal. On the inside, though, everything churning inside her was alien, like her body was suddenly fluent in a foreign language that her brain hadn't learned yet.

When she emerged, her bedroom had lightened with the gray of early dawn. She crossed back to the window and watched until the dark SUV started up and drove away. Grabbing a pair of socks, she tiptoed down the stairs. The jingle of dog tags alerted her to Bandit's entrance. The dog stopped for a pat on the head before crossing to the door. He lifted a paw and scratched at the molding. Once his leash was clipped to his collar, she opened the door. They stepped out onto the stoop into the chilly morning.

Bandit scanned the driveway. His tail abruptly stopped wagging as he looked up at her.

"I'm sorry. He's gone. We shouldn't get too accustomed to having him around."

The dog walked into the grass and lifted a stubby leg over a tall weed. On his way back into the kitchen, he shot her an accusing look from sad spaniel eyes.

"It'll be better for us in the long run. I know it doesn't feel that way, but you have to trust me on this one." Rachel added a scoop of kibble to his bowl and all was forgiven.

But the dog was right. No doubt about it. She was a coward.

From the weedy shore of Lost Lake, Mike stood with the hydrographic survey team and watched two divers emerge from the murky water. The late morning sun glowed on the still water. Ethan headed toward him, while the fireman who'd accompanied him into the lake moved toward his own crew. Behind Mike, a few dozen sign-toting protestors shouted, "Save Lost Lake!"

Ethan dropped his underwater flashlight on the tall grass and shed his tank.

Mike ignored the crowd. "Well?"

Water dripped from Ethan's back. "Can't see a thing down there. All I can tell is that it's an SUV of some kind."

"How long has it been underwater?"

"Long time." Ethan peeled the shorty wet suit down to his waist. "Lot of accumulated sediment. Vegetation's thick all around it."

"Anything inside?" Mike caught his eye.

"Don't think so." Ethan shook his head. "But visibility is for shit, so I could be wrong."

"May as well haul it out, then." Mike walked over to the crowd and motioned for the protestors to retreat. "I need everyone to back up to the road. Let's give them some room to work."

"Don't you mean, let's give them room to destroy our lake!" A short, balding man shook his fist. The sign he held over his head read STOP OVERDEVELOPMENT.

Mike eyeballed the heckler. "Just move back, everyone. A rusty old car in the water certainly isn't doing the environment any good. It isn't your lake anyway. You're trespassing on private property."

Shorty flushed to the roots of his receding hairline. Murmuring, the crown receded. Mike signaled to the tow truck driver. The cable Ethan had attached to the submerged vehicle began to retract.

The winch whirred. Leaving Ethan to supervise, Mike returned to his official SUV and reached through the open window for the deli bag that sat on the passenger seat. His stomach rumbled as he unwrapped his combination late breakfast early lunch, a free-range chicken breast and tomato on rye.

"Mike, I've been looking for you."

With a sigh, he lowered his sandwich and gave Mayor Fred Collins his full attention.

"Are you sure all this is necessary?" The mayor tilted his gray-streaked head toward the tow truck and its groaning winch. "The team needs to finish mapping the bottom of the lake so it can be dredged."

"Well, we can't just leave a car in the lake. Some tourist on a ski-doo could run into it and sue the township."

"I guess." Fred frowned at his wingtips. "But let's not make a big deal out of it, OK? There's a lot of money tied up in this project." Fred meant Lawrence Harmon, Vince, and Vince's pal, fellow town councilman Lee Jenkins, wouldn't be happy with the discovery of anything illicit in the lake. Not only might a crime investigation turn buyers off, but the project could be delayed. Heaven forbid.

Mike made a vague, noncommittal sound.

"The council is still angry about all the vandalism out here. You need to do more to protect this project," Fred insisted. "Like get rid of them." He gestured toward the protestors, now waving their signs from the roadside.

"The road is public. They've every right to be there unless they cause a disturbance. We've increased the frequency of drive-bys, but we been over this repeatedly, Fred. The town doesn't have the manpower for an officer to babysit this place all night, unless you can find room in the budget for some whopping overtime. Harmon Properties should hire private security, as I suggested the other day."

Fred didn't answer. Clearly, he knew Mike was right. The mayor just didn't want to admit it. "Well, there's one more thing we need to discuss."

And here it comes.

"I had breakfast with Vince this morning."

Bingo.

"Vince claims you have a personal interest in Rachel Parker, and it's influenced your decision to harass Troy."

"Harass?" Mike gave the mayor a pointed stare. "Troy was drunk and violent. His wife was unconscious. He attacked a woman with a baseball bat. The arrest was justified."

"Allegedly attacked a woman with a baseball bat."

"I saw him with the bat, Fred." Mike hadn't seen Troy take a swing at Rachel but saw no need to point that out to the mayor. "Plus, his wife was in bad shape."

Fred swallowed and looked away. "Troy had a perfectly good explanation for his wife's injuries, and he said his sister-in-law attacked him first."

"You're kidding me, right? Troy's blood alcohol was two-point-three. He was still half-loaded and puking his brains out the next morning. His statement isn't worth anything, and you know it. And for the record, I had never met Rachel Parker before Saturday night."

Fred had the decency to flush. "Just watch yourself. Vince's gunning for you. If he gets the rest of the council on his side, I won't be able to stop him. Vince also said you should think about parking your car out here at night instead of at Miss Parker's house."

Well, shit. "What I do when I'm off duty is my business."

"The vehicle belongs to the township. If you continue to show Miss Parker preferential treatment, I won't be able to help you."

Like you'd try anyway.

A metallic groan and squeal interrupted the conversation.

No longer hungry, Mike rewrapped his lunch and tossed the bag onto his passenger seat. The tow truck winch dragged the rusted carcass of an old Jeep Cherokee onto the lake bank. The windows were open. Water drained from the vehicle.

Fred hovered as Mike joined Ethan next to the old Jeep and peered inside. The only occupant was a dead perch. "It's empty."

Visibly relieved, Fred backed away. "Well, then, I'll be on my way. See you at the meeting tonight. Think about what I said."

Mike waved the mayor off.

Ethan crossed his arms over his bare chest. "Let me guess. Vince Mitchell already got to the mayor."

Mike sighed and pointed at the rusted Jeep.

Ethan took the hint and refocused on the vehicle. "It has to be twenty years old. Maybe more. No license plates."

"Try to find out who it was last registered to." Mike strode back toward his SUV. As he settled in the driver's seat, he took a bite of his sandwich, which did nothing to ease his churning stomach. He set it aside.

Vandalism and a submerged Jeep at Lost Lake. More vandalism, poetic threats, and an assault at Rachel's farm. Vince Mitchell was keeping tabs on Mike. Which of these events were related and which were random crimes?

Chapter Thirteen

The Watcher glanced both ways down the hall. He was alone. Using the hem of his shirt, he opened the door and slipped into the basement of town hall. He closed the heavy metal door behind him, muffling the sounds of the growing crowd on the first floor. The basement of town hall was dusty, dim—and empty, but he didn't risk switching on a light. Instead, he pulled a small flashlight from his pocket and picked the lock to the police storage room in seconds. Inside, filing cabinets were lined up in rows like soldiers.

Old municipal records were stored down here, including the ones he didn't want any curious cops to reread. Not after all these years. Who knew what Rachel's research would uncover? If he were lucky, he could destroy all the township historical records of her house along with the old police records. Rachel's house had secrets it should keep.

He fished a pair of latex gloves from his pocket and pulled them on. Just in case. He scanned the labels on cabinet fronts until he found the section that housed records from twenty-five years ago. There were more than he'd expected. Way too many to search. He rattled the top drawer of the closest cabinet. Locked. He pulled out a pocketknife and jammed it into the key slot. A quick turn of the handle busted the mechanism. Working quickly and quietly, he littered the floor with paper, then moved to the next few cabinets and dumped hundreds of manila files.

He retreated to the main room and perused the janitor's cart in the corner. After selecting a few flammable cleaning agents, he poured them liberally over the strewn papers. On his way out, he struck a match and tossed it in the center.

His pulse kicked up at the familiar *whoosh.*

He paused at the top of the steps, listened, and then cracked the door to make sure the hall was empty before strolling out.

⤡

Rachel ripped open the box of Pop-Tarts in the parking lot of the Stop 'N Shop. She shook a pastry out of the foil pouch and took a bite. Fake strawberry jam and frosting competed for top billing in her mouth. She stowed the rest of her groceries behind the seat. The Pop-Tarts rode shotgun. Before starting the car, she reached around and fished a can of soda from the brown bag.

Five minutes later, the sugar from three toaster pastries hadn't restored her depleted energy. The events of the last few days had drained her. In a very short period of time, she'd lost her horse and managed to anger Blake, Sarah, *and* Mike.

Sarah still hadn't forgiven her for selling Lady, and the day had been full of angry glances and uncomfortable tension. Sticking with her cowardice trend, Rachel had stayed in the barn as much as possible. On the bright side, she was ahead on her weekly chores. Missing lunch was the down-side. She popped the last bite into her mouth and washed it down with the rest of the cola. An ache rolled through her shoulder. The extra work had taxed her, but busy didn't give her time to continue to dissect anything that had happened or her reaction to it.

She glanced at the dashboard. She had another hour to kill until feed time. At four o'clock the township clerk's office should still be open. If she brought home some inter-esting tidbit about the house's history, maybe a land survey or an aerial map, Sarah might forgive her. Rachel put the truck in gear and drove onto Main Street in the direction of town hall.

The municipal lot was full, as was the lot of the strip center next door. A car in the front row pulled out, and Rachel zipped into the empty space. Inside, the lobby was teaming with people. Harsh gestures and raised voices underscored the tension. A black-lettered notice board indicated that the town council meeting would start at six, which explained all the commotion. Tonight some big shot real estate executive was supposed to talk about a proposed hotel and resort out on Lost Lake. Since the vacation home development under construction was already a local hot button, tonight's meeting could result in a brawl or three. Standing on her toes, she scanned the crowd. Mike would likely be here given the uproar. Not that she was looking for him.

The assembly room and council members' offices were on the ground floor, with the administrative departments located upstairs. She elbowed her way through the throng toward the stairwell. The crowd shifted around her. Bodies pressed closer. A hand closed around her left arm and yanked hard. Pain ripped through her injured shoulder.

Someone slammed into her back. Already off balance, she pitched forward onto a masculine back. Before she could right herself, another hand groped between her legs. *Ow!* She clutched the nearby biceps, sorted out her feet, and whipped around to face her assailant. All she saw were chests and shoulders as a crush of male bodies pushed her backward. What the hell?

Bodies shifted. A big hairy guy sneered at her, navy blue eyes narrowing with hostility. "Better watch your step."

Dammit. She bet he was the one who'd just copped a feel.

"Hey, back off." Rachel bristled, temper burning off the shock and humiliation. She fired a few bony elbows into nearby ribs. Men grunted. Her path cleared, and she broke free.

Assholes.

She headed toward the steps and spotted David walking across the tiled floor toward her. Though they'd parted on decent terms the day before, he didn't offer her his hand this time. "Rachel, are you all right?"

Rachel smoothed her rumpled T-shirt and jeans. "Yeah. Just crazy in here. You here for the meeting?"

"No. I'm picking up permits for a job." He nodded at the manila file he held against his chest. "I'd like to stay, but I have to meet a client. You?"

"No. I just stopped by to see what kind of historical records the town keeps."

Something buzzed in the pocket of his jacket, and he pulled out a cell phone. "I'm sorry, Rachel. I have to take this. I'll see you in the morning. Cross your fingers for another dry day." He turned away and pressed the phone to his ear.

Sweating, Rachel jogged up the stairs to the second level, where the administrative offices were located. On her way down the hall, she spotted the mayor and four council members powwowing in a conference room. A guy that Rachel didn't recognize, but looked like big bucks, was talking to them. The developer? None of the men looked very happy. Vince shot her a dirty look through the glass as she passed the closed door. Wow. Her day was just getting better and better.

Rachel headed for the clerk's office at the end of the hall. She closed the door behind her against the din rising from the first floor. Behind the waist-high counter, Edna Kaiser sat behind a desk and squinted through thick glasses at a computer screen. Rachel gave the clerk kudos for technological ability, given that she was somewhere around a hundred and fifty years old. Edna wobbled to her feet and reached for a cane as Rachel stepped up to the counter. Four and a half feet tall and pudgy, Edna could've moonlighted as a garden gnome. Rachel tapped her foot as the aged clerk snailed it to the counter. Her cane thunked and her orthopedic shoes scraped on the tile with every forward shuffle.

Edna pulled her glasses off her nose and looked up at Rachel. "Can I help you?"

"Hi. I'm looking for some background information on my house. Phyllis Holloway said I should see you."

The clerk beamed. Square white dentures flashed. "What kind of information are you looking for?"

"I'm not sure. I inherited the farm from my grandfather. He claimed it was a historical landmark."

"Who was your grandfather, dear?"

"Samuel Bishop."

"Oh. Your people have owned that farm forever. You know your ancestors were Quakers, right?"

"Yes, ma'am."

"Hmmm. If my memory serves me right, the farm was built in the early 1800s." The clerk tapped a gnarled finger on the top of her cane. Behind those rheumy eyes was a sharp mind. "It's not the oldest landmark in Westbury. We have a few buildings that date back to the 1780s. Any township records that old will likely be archived downstairs. The historical society may be of more help—"

The shrill peel of a fire alarm cut her off.

Rachel hurried to the door and cautiously opened it.

Smoke!

⁓

Mike closed the folder on his desk. Rachel was right. Cristan Rojas wasn't a drug lord, at least not officially, though his occupation was a little vague for Mike's comfort. A native Argentinean who immigrated to the US ten years before, Cristan was the CEO of Rojas Corp., a privately owned conglomerate heavily invested in real estate and coffee. Other than a general disregard for speeding and parking regulations, Mike hadn't been able to turn up anything suspicious in his background.

Blake Webb was fairly clean too, except for a few alcohol-fueled indiscretions from his fraternity years. Webb managed a whopper of a trust fund with an Ivy League degree in business. Richie Rich spent most of his time and money on Rising Star Farms.

Neither Webb nor Rojas had ever been convicted of a violent crime. That didn't mean they weren't capable of violence, though. Rich people often found ways of burying their dirty deeds.

The background check on Lawrence Harmon had yielded a few open investigations for illegal business practices, but nothing concrete or violent.

Mike needed more information than he could get through official channels. The situation was easy enough to remedy. One quick call to Sean would get Mike everything he needed. Discomfort pricked his conscience. His friend's sources were legally questionable.

Mike had been a cop for twenty years, the last ten of them here as chief, and he'd never colored outside the legal lines before. Not once. What was different about this case? His frustration? His lack of resources and manpower? Or his feelings for Rachel?

And this was why cops didn't get personally involved with cases.

His secretary, Nancy Whelan, came into his office with a handful of pink message slips. "Fred called while you were on the phone. He wanted to know where you were."

Mike flipped through the pile. Nothing urgent.

"The lab called. That sample you sent in was deer blood." Nancy set a form on his desk and pointed at the signature line. Mike dutifully signed.

"Deer blood?"

"That's what he said." She squinted at him, her crow's-feet crinkling like half-open fans. "Have you eaten? Of course you haven't. Why don't you grab something before the meeting? I can stall Fred."

After thirty years on the job, Nancy could certainly handle Fred. Under her pearls and cardigan disguise, she was Mike's watchdog. But in this case, he had to call her off. There was too much at stake. "No. I'll go over in a few minutes. Meeting's going to get ugly. "

Nancy shook her head as she turned. White feathery curls tapered to a point above her nape like the rear end of a goose. "He doesn't deserve the courtesy."

"He is the boss." Technically, it took a vote of the mayor and town council to fire Mike.

"You can't work this much forever." Nancy wagged a finger at him and shot him an I-know-best look over her shoulder on her way out.

Mike scanned the files on his desk. On the left, Rachel's various complaints were spread out next to the Lost Lake reports. What could the two possibly have in common? Nothing. Other than the distinct lack of evidence at either scene, he could find no connection between Rachel and the project or Harmon. The vandalism link must be a coincidence. A protestor was likely the culprit behind the damage to the Lost Lake project.

But who was out to hurt Rachel? Thinking of Rachel getting hurt made him turn back to his computer, this time searching *Rachel Parker, equestrian*. He scrolled through numerous articles from local papers and horse magazines. At the bottom of the first page he clicked on a YouTube link tagged with her name and *Tampa Cup crash*. The clip rolled.

Mike clicked on the link. The clip showed a big chestnut with a small woman aboard. He couldn't see Rachel's face from the distance and angle of the camera, but the stubborn set of the chin under the black velvet helmet was all her. A commentator confirmed her identity, remarking on the exceptional promise of the young horse and rider team. The pair popped over a jump as big as a minivan with ease. Bits of mud flew from the animal's hooves as Rachel steered him through a turn. Mike held his breath as they soared over a shallow pool of water in one huge leap. The horse galloped toward a huge, he hoped fake, brick wall. One slip of a foreleg in the mud and the pair went into a nauseating somersault, crashing through the faux brick blocks and coming to rest in a tangle of debris and inverted, thrashing equine limbs. With Rachel buried somewhere underneath. The commentator and the crowd gasped in unison.

The horse squirmed, twisted, and righted itself, limping off with reins trailing across the deathly still human form sprawled in the dirt like a broken doll. The screen went blank just as officials rushed in. The video ended, frozen on Rachel lying in the mud, motionless.

The horse's injuries proved career-ending as well. Did Webb bear a grudge against Rachel? A horse like Fleet O' Feet had to be worth serious coin. Yet Webb had employed Rachel for more than two years after the accident. Why?

Queasiness had Mike reaching for the antacid he'd stashed in his drawer. He gave it a shake and swigged directly from the bottle.

"Gee. Glad to see you're feeling better." Sean stood in the doorway.

Mike sighed and recapped the bottle. "Give me a break. It's been a long, crappy day, and it isn't over yet."

Sean dropped into a chair and nodded at the computer monitor. "What're you watching?"

Mike replayed the video.

Sean whistled. "She's lucky to be alive."

Mike swallowed. The sight of her on the ground, still and lifeless, made his gut churn harder. Still and lifeless was an unnatural state for Rachel.

"You are in big trouble with her."

"Nothing is going to happen between us."

Sean snorted. "Dude, the pressure building between you two is like the eye of a category one hurricane."

"Doesn't matter."

"Why the hell not?"

"Vince already suspects something is going on between us. He must be following me because he knew I parked in her driveway the last two nights."

Sean held up a hand. "You did what?"

"I had to make sure they were safe."

"Mike, you can't personally guard every resident of Westbury who is the victim of a crime, even if you do have personal feelings for her, which I can totally understand."

Mike ignored his friend's interruption. "She is not my type. I need someone simple, normal. *Sane.*"

"Admit it. You have it bad for her."

"I do not."

"Mike, you slept in her driveway." Sean grinned.

Despite his irritation, Mike laughed. "I don't have time to argue with you. I have to go to the town council meeting."

"Municipal building's packed already."

Mike tossed the bottle of antacid back in his desk. "I'm headed over there in case somebody decides to be stupid."

"Don't you mean when?" Sean crossed his arms over his chest. "This used to be such a quiet town."

"Didn't it? Meeting's going to get nasty. What do you know about Lawrence Harmon?"

Sean raised an eyebrow. "CEO of Harmon Properties?"

"Yeah."

"Not much, why?"

"His official records are clean enough, but he's too rich for those to be accurate. Same with Cristan Rojas and Blake Webb."

"Want me to see if I can dig up any skeletons?" Sean wiggled an eyebrow.

"Would you?"

Sean stared, openmouthed.

"What?"

"You're serious? You're tossing the Scout handbook out?" Sean asked. "Aren't you afraid they'll take away a merit badge or something?"

Mike rubbed his temple, where his heartbeat throbbed. "Please, Sean."

"Hey. No problem. Unlike you, I love playing in the dirt." Sean pulled out his cell and tapped out a quick text. "I'll put one of my tech guys on it. Have info to you in a day or two."

"I appreciate it."

"Always glad to help."

Outside, horns honked. Someone yelled. Mike stood. Nancy burst through his office door, eyes wide. "Town hall's on fire."

"Call everyone in," Mike yelled over his shoulder as he and Sean raced out the door. The police station was only half a block from the municipal building. Sirens howled. People shouted. They reached the scene just as the volunteer fire department turned its rig into the lot. Smoke and people poured out the front doors. Mike ran through the parking lot. He slowed as he passed a beat-up black pickup. He glanced in the window. It looked like a box of Pop-Tarts had exploded on the passenger seat.

Shit. Shit. Shit.

It figured. Wherever trouble brewed, Rachel was in the thick of it.

Mike held his breath as he scanned the coughing, hacking crowd, milling in shock around the parking lot. No familiar brunette.

Heart pounding, Mike pushed past the last few stragglers exiting the building. A white-haired man burst through the glass doors and fell to his knees on the concrete apron. Mike grabbed him and shoved him at Sean. Another set of sirens filled the air. "EMTs are here." He nodded toward the approaching vehicle.

Sean took the old guy and reached for Mike's shoulder with his free hand. "Hey, the firemen are here too. Let them handle the search."

"Can't. I think Rachel's inside." Mike shrugged off his friend's grip and plunged into the smoke-filled lobby.

Chapter Fourteen

At the top of the steps, Rachel adjusted her grip on Edna's arm. Smoke funneled up the stairwell, but so far, no visible flames or heat. Rachel strained her ears for crackling or, please God, sirens, but she heard only the muffled sounds of commotion outside. The building was eerily quiet.

Thunk, scrape. Thunk, scrape.

"Can we go a little faster, Edna?"

The clerk's frame trembled as Rachel tried to move faster than a crawl.

Sirens sounded outside. Edna tapped her cane on the floor. "You just go on and leave me here." *Wheeze. Thunk, scrape.* "The firemen will be along in a few minutes."

"Not gonna happen, Edna." Rachel coughed. The smoke was thickening. Edna might not last a few more minutes. Her pallor was rapidly fading, and she moved slower with each labored breath. "But how about you lean on me a little more? We'll get out of here in no time."

Edna bobbed her head in agreement.

Rachel ducked under Edna's arm and draped it over her shoulders. She wrapped her other arm around the old woman's waist. Her shoulder screamed as she half-carried the clerk down the stairs. The position was awkward, and Edna seriously needed to lay off the dumplings and gravy.

Sagging, her body got heavier as they hit the lobby. Rachel tried to pick up the pace. She'd drag the old woman the last few yards if necessary. A huge shadow appeared in the smoke. Fireman? No. it was Mike.

Relief flooded Rachel. It didn't matter who was there to help her, but she was glad to see him.

He lifted the clerk out from under Rachel's arm. "Did you see anyone else still inside?"

Rachel shook her head and choked. Mostly carrying Edna, Mike herded Rachel out into the parking lot. "EMTs are to your right."

The fresh air hit her lungs and set off a round of hacking. Nasty things vaulted into her mouth. Edna, on the other hand, was way too quiet as Mike carried her toward the waiting rescue personnel.

Rachel stopped, leaned on her knees, and gasped. Her throat was clogged with soot and smoke. The world tilted as she was scooped off her feet and whisked across the asphalt. Her hand settled on a huge, tanned forearm. She looked up. "David?"

He set her on the back of a truck and crouched next to her. "I came back to help when I saw the fire trucks."

An EMT placed an oxygen mask over her face. Rachel inhaled. And coughed some more. A shadow fell over David. Mike was standing behind him. In the background, paramedics were working on Edna. David stood up, turning around as Mike held out a hand and introduced himself.

"David Gunner." David accepted the handshake.

"How do you know Rachel?" Mike waved off the offer of a mask. He-Man wasn't even breathing hard. But then, he'd only be in the building for a few seconds. Rushing billion-year-old Edna had been like flogging a tortoise. Rachel sucked oxygen. Someone handed her a bottle of water. She rinsed out her mouth, tilted her head, and poured cool liquid over her face.

"Old friends," David said. "I've known Rachel since we were kids."

Something flickered in Mike's eyes. Or maybe they were just irritated from the smoke. He squatted in front of Rachel. "You all right?"

Tears ran down her cheeks, and her eyes burned. She poured more water over her face and dried it on her sleeve. "Peachy."

His face was serious, but his eyes brightened. "Were you here for the meeting?"

She shook her head. "No. Just stopped by to see Edna."

He digested her answer, then gently replaced the mask on her face. His fingers slid behind her head as he adjusted the elastic band. God help her, she wanted to lean into him and let him comfort her the way he had the day before. She could practically feel the strength and warmth of his body.

"I have to go." He stood. His head swiveled as he scanned the chaotic scene. Strobe lights swirled on emergency vehicles. Firemen hustled with equipment. The soot-streaked crowd huddled in groups on the periphery. Water, smoke, and debris littered the parking lot. Mike turned to David. "Can you stay with her?"

"Sure," David agreed.

Mike disappeared into the crowd. The EMT brought more water and then suggested she go to the hospital to get checked over. Rachel declined.

"You're sure?" David looked doubtful. "You don't look so good."

"Gee. Thanks." Rachel rinsed her mouth again. "I want to go home. It's nearly time for the horses to be fed, and I would kill for a shower."

"At least let me drive you."

"No. I need my truck." Rachel tipped the bottle and chugged the remaining liquid, but her throat still felt like someone had rubbed it raw with charcoal briquettes.

David sighed. "I'll follow you home."

Rachel took a few more hits of oxygen before testing her legs. "I'm ready."

A twinge of nerves stroked along her spine. Leftover adrenaline?

She looked over the scene. Smoke still flowed from the brick building. The sirens had been turned off. Radios chattered. Firemen were going in and out of the building with hoses and other equipment. Two EMT units assessed a few black-smudged people. A few state police cars had joined the slew of rescue vehicles.

On the other side of the lot, the stocky man from the foyer crowd stood in the same group of rough-looking guys that had crushed her in the municipal lobby. His navy blue eyes locked on Rachel, and his sneer sent a fresh wave of nausea rolling through her stomach. She coughed and covered her mouth.

"Rachel?" David supported her elbow.

"Who is that?" She nodded toward the motley group. "Black hair, dark blue eyes."

David's head swiveled. "In the black T-shirt?"

"Yes."

"That's Will Martin. You want to stay away from him. He's friends with Troy, and he's dangerous."

⌒

Sarah looked through the kitchen window. Rachel and David walked across the lawn from the barn to the house. She could hear their muffled voices but couldn't make out the words. At Sarah's feet, Bandit bristled. His body tensed. Not wanting him to wake the girls she'd just put to bed, she grabbed a chew and locked him in the den with it.

Rachel's face was smudged with soot and her eyes were red-rimmed. "I'm going to shower for the next half hour. Thanks for helping me, David. I know you're not a horse guy."

"No problem." David shuffled his feet and stared at his work boots. "Doesn't take much skill to dump grain in buckets."

Did David have a thing for Rachel? She couldn't blame him if he did. Her sister was amazing, while Sarah was a weak imitation. Why couldn't she be half as strong as Rachel?

"I appreciate the help anyway." Rachel squeezed her eyes shut tightly and reopened them. A few tears ran down her cheeks. They were likely just watery from smoke irritation, but it looked shockingly as if Rachel had been crying. Sarah couldn't remember the last time she'd seen her sister cry. Their mother's funeral maybe? Rachel's inner warrior didn't let down her guard very often.

"Go shower." Sarah opened the refrigerator. "I'll make you something to eat."

"I'm not hungry." Rachel headed for the hall. A few seconds later, the wooden stairs creaked and the shower turned on with a squeal of old pipes.

Sarah pulled out the casserole she'd made the girls for dinner.

Boots scraped on the kitchen floor. She looked over at David. With his size, how could she have forgotten he was in the room? "Hungry, David?"

"Ah. Sure. Thanks."

"Have a seat." Sarah scooped out a large portion of noodles and chicken and popped the plate into the microwave.

David crossed to the sink and lathered up his hands and forearms. "She's tough. She'll be OK."

"Someone has to look out for her. God knows she won't take care of herself." Only Sarah and Mrs. Holloway knew the fragile heart of the person underneath that prickly exterior. Well, maybe David did too. "Thanks for helping her tonight."

"I did as much as she'd let me." He sat down in a bulky captain's chair. Her sister wasn't much of a decorator. The table, a worn dark pine monstrosity leftover from the early seventies, was equally hideous. But Rachel didn't give appearances priority. Whatever Granddad had left was good enough for her.

Sarah thought about the pretty kitchen she'd left behind. Ruffled curtains and polished furniture hadn't covered the ugly truth. She'd married Troy to escape her parents' house. He'd said he loved her. Really, he just wanted to sleep with her. She'd refused until they were married. Coming from a publically dysfunctional family, she'd strived to be the good girl. She always did what would seem right to others. Now she was left with the fallout.

The microwave dinged. Sarah pulled out the steaming plate and set it down in front of David. He looked surprised when she set silverware and a napkin by his plate.

"Do you have a girlfriend, David?"

He lowered the forkful of food that had been on its way to his mouth and stared at his plate. "Not at the moment."

Oh no. Wrong question. She'd made him more uncomfortable. Trying to think of a new conversation topic, she moved toward the counter. "Coffee?"

David had resumed eating. He nodded midchew and swallowed. "This is incredible."

"It's not much. The girls like simple food." She brought down a mug, set it on the counter, and poured, every task taking longer one-handed. Which reminded her. "Would you mind carrying an old trunk down from the attic when you're finished?"

"Not at all." David scraped the last bit of food from his plate. "Let's go now. Coffee's not done yet anyway."

He followed her upstairs. On the second floor, Sarah paused to listen at Rachel's bedroom door for a few seconds. The rushing sound of water was muffled by the closed door. The narrow flight of steps to the attic was at the end of the hall. Except for the cleared landing and a center aisle, furniture, boxes, and other odds and ends were haphazardly piled to the seven-foot ceiling.

"This one?" He pointed to the small black trunk at the top of the steps.

"That's it. I think that's the one my grandfather used to keep in the den." Sarah touched the filthy, tattered black leather. "Can you manage it by yourself? The handles have rotted through."

"I've got it." David lifted the trunk in his arms with a grunt. "It's not too heavy."

It had felt heavy when Sarah had been pushing it through the maze of clutter. But then, David was at least twice her size and didn't have a broken arm.

Downstairs, David asked, "Where do you want it?"

"In the living room."

He made a left and set the box down in the old parlor in the front of the house, empty except for a couple of end tables. The upholstered furniture hadn't survived the house's years of neglect. Sarah switched on the only lamp.

David fingered the lock. "I don't want to break it. The trunk itself looks like an antique. Do you have a small screwdriver?"

Sarah fetched one from the kitchen, then retreated to collect two mugs of coffee, which she brought in one at a time. David popped the lock and raised the lid.

Inside was a jumble of yellowed papers and books. Perching on the edge of a table, Sarah lifted a leatherbound journal from atop the pile. The binding creaked as she opened it. The faded script would need more light than the one meager lamp at her elbow.

David sifted through some of the papers and came up with a modern manila envelope. He slid some papers from inside and scanned them. "This says the farm is listed on the National Registry of Historic Places."

"Let me see."

With an odd expression David handed her the pages. "Does it seem weird your grandfather never mentioned it to you?"

"My grandmother was the one who filled out the forms. She died before I was born. Guess it wasn't important to Granddad." Sarah scanned the pages. "Oh, it says here that the house was part of the Underground Railroad."

"How can a railroad drive under the ground?" Alex's sleepy voice came from the stairs. She sat on the bottom step, blanket under her arm, peering through the spindles.

Their footsteps must have woken her.

"Excuse me, David. Let me put her back to bed. Help yourself to more coffee." Sarah rose to herd the child back upstairs.

"That's OK. I should get going. Thanks for dinner."

"Wait right here, sweets." Sarah patted Alex on the cheek, then followed David to the kitchen door. "Thanks for bringing my sister home safe."

"You're welcome. Good night." He ducked out.

Sarah locked the door behind him and returned to herd her daughter up the steps. Knowing Alex wouldn't let an issue go any easier than Bandit would relinquish a bone, Sarah answered the child's question. "It wasn't a real railroad. A long time ago, during the Civil War, runaway slaves used to hide here."

However much of the explanation the little girl understood, the child's nod was too serious for her age. Sarah's heart squeezed. She should've left Troy a long time ago, but she'd kept hoping he'd grow up.

"Where did they hide?"

Wishing she could pick her daughter up, Sarah wrapped her arm around Alex's shoulders and steered her down the hall. "I'm not sure. The attic or basement maybe. I'll have to do more research to find out."

With Alex tucked into bed, Sarah stopped at Rachel's door. She didn't hear any sounds. She turned the knob slowly and opened the door a crack. Rachel was sound asleep on the bed, facedown and wrapped only in a towel. Sarah tiptoed in and covered her sister with a blanket.

Sarah leaned closer. Rachel was breathing easily, but she looked more battle scarred than Sarah. Rachel hadn't covered the stitches on her cheek, and the puckered scars on her shoulder and arm were deep red after what must have been a long, blistering shower. The angry color would fade, just as the cut on her cheek would knit. Rachel was a warrior at heart. Her strength wasn't in question. She would cope with her physical injuries.

But the scars on her sister's soul were a different story.

Chapter Fifteen

On the edge of town, the Watcher turned left in a small, exclusive development. The road curved gracefully between stately homes. Intermittent streetlights illuminated extra-large lots with diffuse amber circles. He looked ahead. The tall brick colonial at the end of the street was dark.

Strange. Tanya usually kept the porch light on all night, especially when she was alone. The Watcher slowed. Something was off. He cruised to the curb and cut the lights.

A few seconds later something moved behind the trimmed shrubs that edged the front lawn. A woman emerged. Even in the hooded jacket, he recognized her by the way she moved. Tanya. Tiptoeing in sky-high heels, she jogged down the sidewalk to the corner, where a truck idled.

There was only one reason a woman snuck out in the middle of the night.

The truck's brake lights glowed briefly. Running dark, the vehicle slid away from the curb. The Watcher followed at a discreet distance. Two blocks ahead, the truck's headlights blinked on as Tanya's lover made a right onto the main road.

The Watcher kept his own headlights off.

Why did he always choose women who cheated? A memory of another betrayal intruded into his thoughts.

Don't worry. Just come with me. I'll take care of you. I promise.

He shouldn't follow. He should turn around and go home. Things went bad when he acted without a plan. But he couldn't help himself. He had to see.

Tanya was going to cheat. She was going to betray her vows just like another woman had done all those years ago.

Excitement, dread, and horror mingled in his blood.

He wouldn't do anything. He would only watch. Watching was his thing, after all. He had more control now than last time.

Last time had been murder.

"Are you sure he's occupied?" Will drove behind the feed store his old man owned. After midnight, both the retail building and warehouse were dark. At the very back of the parking lot, in the deep shadow of an overhanging tree, Will shifted the truck into park and doused the lights. With the warehouse at their back, no one would see his truck unless he was looking for it.

There were two reasons he brought women here for sex. One, a dickhead cop couldn't arrest him for sex in public or indecent exposure or any other trumped-up charge because the parking lot was private property. Two, he never took women home. It was too hard to get rid of them. He had no interest in their conversation or opinions. This way, he just had to zip up and drop them back off wherever he'd picked them up. This was simple. Convenient. Like the drive-through at a fast-food joint.

He could hardly go to Tanya's house, and this was a small town. If they checked into a motel, someone would notice.

On the passenger end of the bench seat, Tanya was already stripping off her clothes. "He just called. He's going to be tied up for hours because of the fire."

Will shifted the seat all the way back. Watching her unhook her fancy bra and spring those huge titties, he cupped his growing erection with one hand. He wasn't going to need hours. Hell, if she kept jiggling around like that, he wasn't going to need minutes. "Must be hard to be married to such an important man."

"Not hard enough." She giggled. Naked, Tanya straddled his lap. "I need you to fuck me."

"No problem." Her boobs were right in his face. He grabbed them with both hands. They were huge and round and porn-star perfect. "Doesn't Vince take care of you?"

"Takes plenty care of himself." She made a face. "More than I'd like. Damn Viagra."

He sucked a nipple deep into his mouth. Tanya groaned. Her practiced hands went to his belt and zipper. She had him freed in two seconds and covered in three. That was another thing he liked about Tanya. She wasn't into foreplay. She got right down to business, like she'd spent all day thinking about his hard cock. She had no interest in anything besides fucking him.

True to form, she stood him up and slid right down his shaft to the hilt. He grabbed her ass with both hands. Tiny stars flickered in his vision. Her tits bounced in his face as she rode him hard. He barely held on until she exploded around him.

Not that he was all that concerned with her pleasure, but a well-serviced Tanya came back for more. And more. And more.

She was insatiable.

She climbed off his lap. Will removed the condom and tied it off. He had more where that came from, which was good because Tanya's face was already heading for his lap. Her breath warmed his head, and his cock tingled. It already knew what her hot mouth and tongue could do. She had talent. He had no doubt she'd blown her way into a proposal from her old man.

"Oh, baby."

Something rattled outside. Running footsteps crunched on gravel. Tanya's head shot up. "What was that?"

An engine started up and faded away.

"Omigod. Someone saw us." Eyes wide, Tanya crawled off his lap and crouched on the floor of the truck. She grabbed her sweater, holding it against her glorious tits. With the rest of her stark naked, the sight was making Will's cock throb.

"Probably just kids. Maybe we took their spot."

Tanya drew her lower lip between her teeth. Will pictured his cock there instead.

"Well, they're gone now." He grabbed her around the waist and hauled her back onto the seat. Tanya liked it risky and rough. But she also liked the shiny stuff her old husband bought her. She wasn't going to take the chance that he'd find out about their little arrangement. "Relax. It's dark. No one watching could possibly know it's you."

"But someone was watching." Excitement teased her voice.

"Does that make you hot?" He wrapped his hand in her long blond hair.

She lowered her head to his lap and breathed on his cock. "Oh yeah."

Will's hips surged. He was dying to have her again.

Mike pulled into his garage and parked. Exhaustion dragged at his limbs as he walked past the disemboweled carcass of the 1970 Mustang convertible that had been waiting for his attention since early summer. He pushed open the door leading into the house. The sound of a woman moaning roughed the hairs on the back of his neck. He pulled his gun from his hip and pressed his shoulder against the door-jamb. What the hell? What kind of intruder turned on the lights?

"For fuck's sake. Put the gun away."

"Sean?" Mike walked through into the living room. Sean lounged in the recliner in front of the TV, which was the source of all the female moaning.

"Who else would it be? You don't have anything worth stealing except the big-screen." Sean sipped from the beer bottle in his hand. "You haven't updated anything else in this place since your mom died. That was a long time ago, Mike."

Mike didn't argue. Except for converting her room into a home office, the house was pretty much the same. After dumping his keys and phone on the kitchen counter, he went into the bedroom and locked his piece in the gun safe in his nightstand. Other than sleeping, he spent little time here. He ducked into the bathroom to start the shower on the way back to the living room. "What are you complaining about? You only come here to watch your porn flicks."

"Well, I can't very well watch them at home. There are kids there," Sean said. "You don't mind, do you?"

"Nah. It's not like I'm ever here." Mike started unbuttoning his uniform shirt. "You don't even need to break in. I've offered you a key dozens of times."

"That's no fun." Sean turned the volume down on the TV, stood, and stretched. "Amanda sent you dinner. I'll stick it in the microwave."

"Thanks. I have to grab a quick shower. I smell like an ashtray." On the way, Mike scanned his house for any sign of Sean's entry. As usual, Mike saw nothing. Someday he'd figure out how his friend got in and out without leaving any trace. Tonight, he was too tired to care.

The bathroom was steaming when Mike stripped and climbed under the hot spray. The water pounded on his shoulders as he soaped up. Heat relaxed his muscles. Too much. His eyelids drooped. He'd managed exactly one sip of coffee at the scene before his stomach had let him know in no uncertain terms that wasn't a smart idea. With a shake of his head, he turned the water to cold and stuck his head under the full force. The shock of the icy spray cleared his head. He shut off the faucet and toweled off. Shivering, he stepped into a pair of sweatpants that looked reasonably clean. He really needed to scrape out an hour to do some laundry. The smell of chicken drew him back to the kitchen, T-shirt in hand. The ceramic tiles were cold under his bare feet.

Sean was pulling a bowl out of the microwave. "It's just leftover chicken and dumplings." He turned as Mike pulled his shirt over his head. "Holy crap."

"What?"

"You look like you've lost fifteen pounds."

"It's been a rough couple of weeks." Actually it'd been more like twenty, but Mike wasn't going to volunteer that bit of information.

Sean set the bowl on the counter bar that divided the cooking and dining areas. "Eat."

"Yes, Mom." Mike slid onto a wooden stool and dug in. His stomach protested the first few bites. He paused, chewing slowly, but it settled enough for him to continue at a slower pace.

Sean leaned back against the counter, arms crossed over his chest, watching. He kept his mouth shut until Mike had worked his way through most of the food.

Mike pushed his plate away. "Tell Amanda thanks."

"She's worried about you."

"I appreciate that." Mike got up, crossed to the fridge, and poured a glass of organic skim milk. He held up a beer and, hoping to distract his friend, waved it at Sean.

Didn't work. Sean picked up the TV remote from the counter and turned off his movie. Bad sign. "You can't keep this up. You need help."

"I know. That's why I asked you to do those background checks." If porn didn't sidetrack his happily married yet mildly perverted friend, nothing would. Mike gave up on the diversion. "Do you know David Gunner?"

"Vaguely. Local contractor. Mostly remodels kitchens and baths."

"I've seen him around town, but I don't remember where or when."

"He's homegrown. Why?"

"He was hanging around Rachel tonight after the fire." Mike drank some milk. Was he suspicious of David Gunner for valid reasons or because he acted familiar with Rachel?

Mike had no business being jealous. She wasn't his, but damned if that thought didn't make his chest go hollow.

"She was there? Any chance the fire was another attack on her?"

"I don't think so. She said she just stopped by the township clerk's office. Didn't sound like it was a planned trip. Hell, everybody in town was there tonight for the meeting. I may as well use the voter registration rolls for my suspect list."

"So it was definitely arson?" Sean asked.

"The state police arson investigator hasn't confirmed that yet, but that's what the fire chief thinks. Found traces of an accelerant. Point of origin was the basement, where the actual fire was contained."

"What's the damage?"

"Everything in the basement is history. Upstairs fared better. Most of the damage is from smoke and water. Structurally, the building seems intact, but we'll need an engineer to verify that."

"Could've been worse. Lucky nobody died, considering how many people were inside."

"Definitely." Mike scrubbed a hand across his face. "The state police will handle the arson investigation, but the fire has to be tied to the Lost Lake project. It can't be coincidence that an arsonist picked tonight to torch the place. The night Lawrence Harmon is scheduled to make a presentation about the proposed resort."

Sean's expression went grim. "I don't like this, Mike. This goes beyond vandalism. Setting a building on fire when it's full of people shows a disturbing lack of conscience or murderous intent."

"I know," Mike agreed. "We're either dealing with an environmental extremist or a sociopath. I don't like either of those options."

"Or someone who has a vested interest in the Lost Lake project tanking. Got any suspects for the prior vandalism complaints?"

"Shit, yes." How could he have forgotten? Mike grabbed his cell phone from the counter. He opened the video app and played the scan of the protesting crowd outside the Lost Lake project. "Damn picture is too small to identity anyone."

"Send it to me. I'll enlarge it on my computer and print stills from the individual frames."

Mike considered. Technically, the video was evidence. But the township didn't have the ability to do what Sean could. The town council was probably going to fire him anyway. Mike tapped the keys on his phone. "Here it comes."

"OK. I'll be at Rachel's early to work on her security system. You're going to get some sleep, right?"

"I don't know. I'm worried about Rachel and her sister. The fire has me thinking there's something going on I haven't figured out yet. What?"

Sean was staring at him. "I have never seen you this hung up on a woman."

Mike sighed. "I don't understand it either."

"Some things defy logic." Sean grinned. "But if I were you, I'd buy some fresh condoms. They do expire over the course of a decade."

"Mine aren't quite as old as that." But they weren't fresh by any stretch of the imagination. "And I think you're getting ahead of things. I'm not going to sleep with her."

"Sure you're not." Sean didn't sound convinced as he rinsed out his beer bottle and placed it in the recycling bin under the sink. "You trust me, right?"

Mike rolled his eyes. "Of course I do. We've been best friends since the third grade."

"I'll have a man at her house in thirty minutes."

Mike didn't know what to say.

"Before you find an argument, no one gets past my guys. Rachel and her sister will be perfectly safe. If you want, he can be invisible. They won't even know he's there."

Mike was so tired, he felt like putting his head on the counter and closing his eyes. The trek to the bedroom might not even be necessary. There was no reason not to take Sean up on his offer. Mike's weird caveman instinct toward Rachel, that he should be the one guarding her, was totally irrational. What mattered was that she—they were safe. Besides, getting behind the wheel as tired as he was right now would be dangerous and stupid. "OK."

"You aren't going to be worth shit if you don't get some sleep, and you have a crime spree to stop. Plus, Quinn is watching your sorry ass. You start looking any worse, he's coming after you." Sean stopped. His brow furrowed. "Wait a minute. Did you agree with me?"

"Yeah."

"Well, shit. You didn't even argue. You must feel worse than I thought."

Mike didn't comment.

Sean whipped out his phone and shot out a few messages. "My guy will stay until I get there to start on the security system tomorrow."

"Thanks, Sean. Lock up when you leave." Mike trudged toward the bedroom before he passed out on his feet. He collapsed facedown on top of the quilt.

"You know, there's one question you haven't asked."

Mike rolled over.

Sean stood in the doorway. "Why Vince has been gunning for you since he took office. There's only one reason I can think of for Vince's actions: guilt."

Chapter Sixteen

Rachel stripped off her barn-cleaning clothes and quickly showered off before dressing in riding pants and a clean T-shirt. Downstairs, she grabbed a Pop-Tart from the kitchen and stepped out into the overcast afternoon. Sean, the security guy, and his assistants were pulling stuff out of the back of their van. A ginormous white SUV was parked next to the commercial vehicle. Down by the barn, David was rolling his commercial paint sprayer toward his truck.

Rachel crossed the rear lawn, stopping at the tree to give the frustrated Bandit a pat and a corner of her pastry. "Sorry, buddy. Can't let you nip any of the workers."

Rachel approached the barn. Fresh white paint gleamed. "Thanks, David. I can't believe one coat covered all that, and in just a few hours."

"The right equipment helps." David blushed and held up the paint gun in his hand. "I used heavy-duty primer so the red doesn't bleed through. Top coat might have to wait, though. This morning's weather report showed more rain on the way."

Despite the prospect of an incoming storm, Rachel beamed. The absence of profanity lifted her mood. Behind her, tires crunched on the gravel of the driveway. Rachel turned as Sarah parked her minivan next to the Wilson Security truck. Her sister got out of the van and sprung the girls from their car seats. The kids ran to greet a joyously jumping and yapping Bandit.

Holding a grocery bag in her good arm, Sarah walked over to Rachel and David. Her sister's gait was smoother than the day before. "Do you have time for lunch, David?"

"Sure." David nodded. "Give me a few minutes to clean up."

"Rachel, are you hungry?" Sarah asked.

"I have to some work to do first." She'd lost too much time this morning going over the proposed alarm system with Sean. "You go ahead."

Rachel strode into the barn. A hoof banged on wood. The only horse in the barn, the obnoxious gray, stuck his head over his half door and whinnied.

"Relax. I have one thing to do. Then you and I are going to spend some quality time together." Though the horse's issue was his inexperienced rider, Rachel would do everything she could to make the animal a safer mount. Even if that meant riding it every day to burn off excess energy before Lucia arrived for her lesson.

In the feed room, she cleaned the dust from the bottom of the empty bin and grabbed a new fifty-pound bag of pellets from the raised pallet in the corner. Still sore from the previous night, old scar tissue in her shoulder ached as she dragged the bag across the floor. She stopped to rest for a minute, then squatted and hugged the bag. She stood up and hoisted the bag onto the edge of the bin.

"What the hell are you doing?" A deep, annoyed voice from the doorway startled her.

She fumbled with the bag. Mike stepped through the doorway. He took two long strides and lifted it from her grip one-handed. Under the uniform shirt, biceps bulged, but his face was flushed with anger, not effort, as he dumped the pellets into the container. "This is way too heavy for you." He moved closer, looming over her.

Rachel didn't back off. The knowledge that he was right sent a stab of irritation through her. It wasn't like she enjoyed the backbreaking manual labor. As soon as her budget allowed, she'd be more than happy to hire help of the younger, stronger variety. Until then, chores needed to be finished. "Look, He-Man, I appreciate the concern, but I have a business to run. I can't wait for a big, strong man every time there's heavy work to be done."

His expression went to that exasperated look she seemed to cultivate from him. The blue of his eyes darkened as he stared at her. Warmth radiated through her belly, almost making her forget why she'd just been annoyed at him.

"Well, you should. You're going to hurt yourself."

As much as she hated admitting weakness, her shoulder still throbbed with every beat of her heart. She blew out a hard, frustrated breath. "While you're here, can you throw another one of those bags in there?"

Mike hoisted the fifty-pound sack and filled the bin like he was pouring a bowl of cereal. Show-off.

"Thank you." Rachel crossed the aisle to the tack room, a ten-by-ten space that accumulated dust no matter how often she swept it. The sweet smells of glycerin soap and leather filled her nose as she lifted her saddle. She settled it on a rack in the aisle. A humid breeze wafted through the double doors.

Mike leaned on the wooden wall and crossed his arms across an acre of chest. "Should you really still be riding?"

Rachel couldn't answer. Her eyes burned, and her throat tightened. But it wasn't irritation from last night's smoke causing her discomfort. It was the same question she'd been struggling with for two years. If she couldn't ride, what would she do? She had no contacts outside of the horse business. She was not a social person. The only time she didn't feel like an outcast was on the back of a horse. It was where she belonged. Avoiding his gaze, she moved back into the tack room for a bridle.

"I saw the video of your fall."

Heat rushed to Rachel's face, anger and shame competing with self-pity for top emotional billing. One moment, one reflex failure was all it had taken to ruin her career and an incredible horse's legs. Stepping back into the aisle, she faced him and gritted her teeth.

"It's on YouTube."

"Wonderful."

"My point is you shouldn't be doing stuff like this. You're only going to make it worse. You should find another line of work."

She shot a finger into the center of his broad, hard chest. It was like poking a boulder. "Like what? In case you hadn't noticed, I'm not exactly a people person."

Sympathy crossed his face. Rachel closed her eyes. Mike wasn't to blame for her predicament. The fall had been her fault. She hauled back on her temper and counted to ten. He didn't interrupt, just stood there with all that damned understanding in his eyes. "Look, it's the only thing I know how to do. The only thing I ever wanted to do." Her voice faltered, and she regretted the admission of vulnerability the second it left her mouth. Think first, talk second. Such a simple concept shouldn't be this hard to implement.

Mike's eyes softened. "I wouldn't want to see you hurt like that again."

"I can handle myself."

"Tell me about last night. You're sure no one knew you would be at the municipal building?"

"I didn't even know I'd be there." Rachel gave him a quick rundown of her impromptu stop at the clerk's office.

"Where did you get those bruises?" His eyes narrowed on her forearm, where last night's groper had left angry finger marks.

She told him about the men in the crowd. To avoid his eyes, and her humiliation, when she got to the nasty grabby part, she ducked back into the tack room for a saddle pad. "David said the ringleader's name was Will Martin. I didn't actually see him do it, but I'm pretty sure it was him. Big guy, dark blue eyes, hairy, chip on his shoulder the size of Jupiter."

When she turned around, he'd followed her into the small space, his size dwarfing the room. Moving closer, close enough that she could smell his mouthwatering aftershave, he caged her against the wall and held out his empty hand, palm up. Rachel's pulse trembled. Her fingers tightened on the fleece pad in her hands. She looked up, expecting heat. But his face had gone hard, his eyes cold as a clear winter sky.

"Let me see it."

"It doesn't hurt."

He cocked his head to one side and gave her a look that said he didn't believe her. She blinked first.

"Let me see it," he repeated more deliberately.

She should protest, move, do something to put some space between them. She didn't allow anyone to corner her. But Mike overwhelmed her senses, shut off her ingrained defensive reactions. "It's no big deal."

A muscle in his jaw twitched. "Please."

She wasn't prepared for his soft request. Her arm moved all without any consultation with her brain. Surrendered without even the pretense of resistance. The saddle pad slid from her grip and landed on the floor. Mike's freakishly polite manners threw her off her stride. Rachel was more comfortable with hostility and confrontation than his calm, reasonable routine.

Mike closed his fingers around her slender wrist and examined the darkening bruises.

Rachel willed her heart to slow its manic contractions, but it defied her. Her pulse rapped against his thumb as if it were trying to get his attention. He rotated her arm to look at the marks. A featherlight fingertip caressed her skin, and her heartbeat jumped for joy.

She tugged at her arm, but he didn't give it up, managing to keep his fingers closed without exerting any additional pressure on her skin. His grip was a padded vise. Strangely, it wasn't the restraint that bugged her, but her reaction to it. Her body was waving a white flag. A strange thrill bubbled up inside her as a frightening thought passed through her mind: at this moment she'd do anything he asked. And probably like it. A lot. He'd be gentle—and patient, the kind of patient that could eat up an entire night. The shiver that sprinted down her spine and raced into her belly was all hot liquid.

The intensity and hunger on Mike's face brought a flush to Rachel's whole body. When his hand snaked out and caught her around the back of the neck, she didn't exactly fight him. He tilted her face up and crushed his mouth down on hers.

His mouth was hot and demanding. Her blood roared, and her body responded all on its own, pressing itself up against every steely inch of him. The small, dusty room vanished. He tasted like peppermint. All she could smell was the warm scent that drove her crazy. He pulled his head away, but she hadn't had enough. Not nearly enough. That kiss had been an appetizer when she was hungry for a meal. Her fingers clenched his uniform shirt lapels, and she yanked his mouth back down to hers. She wanted to wrap herself around him. She wanted him pressed against every inch of her skin. She wanted him under her, on top of her, inside of her. Skin to skin.

She wanted it all.

Mike turned his head, angling his mouth to dive deeper. His tongue slid across hers, and his hands drifted down to her body, cupping her ass and squeezing. Her palms splayed on his pectorals. She leaned even closer, until their bodies were in contact from mouth to hip and she could feel the massive erection straining the front of his pants. Oh, baby. All his body parts were in proportion. One leg hooked over his thigh, pulling that I-beam of a hard-on exactly where she wanted it. He pressed into her. *Yes. Oh, God. Yes. Right there.*

Her eyes closed, and all she could do was feel. The heat and raw power under her hands, against her body, pressuring her core, made her limbs tremble.

Liquid fire flared deep in her belly. But that wasn't the only part of her that was heating up. Mike's embrace fanned a yearning, something she'd never experienced before and would've never missed had she not felt it. Something shifted inside her as this man softened the tough shell around her heart.

What the hell just happened?

She opened her eyes. He lifted his mouth an inch from hers. He was searching her face as if he were looking for the answer to the same question.

"I don't like the thought of another man's hands on you. It makes me crazy. It makes me want to break him in pieces." He breathed the words out against her mouth. His lungs were heaving and sweat had broken out on his forehead. The blue of his eyes was nearly black with desire. He-Man's iron self-control was slipping, all because of her. "What have you done to me?"

Rachel froze. Even if the kiss hadn't left her breathless, she didn't have an answer for him. His statement had a possessive edge that was making all the melty parts of her tense up again. She let her leg slowly slide back down to the ground, patted his uniform shirt into place, and smoothed out the wrinkles. For once in her life, she was speechless. Her brain mirrored his question. What had *he* done to *her?*

His eyes locked on hers. "What is it about you? You're prickly and stubborn and reckless. Yet I can't seem to get enough." He pressed his forehead against hers in a surprising and unfamiliar gesture that highlighted the shift from sexual desire to something more intimate.

Oh no. She couldn't handle more. Look what she'd done to Blake. And what her mother had done to her father.

She leaned away. A chill swept over her at the loss of contact—and at her loss of control. Was he just one more impulse decision? Something fueled by the tension built over the last few days?

Her inability to commit to Blake had destroyed the best, the only, real friendship of her life. She couldn't go through that again. The stakes were higher this time. Mike fostered hope inside her. He filled the lonely, hollow space beneath her breast bone. But what would happen when he figured out she wasn't capable of giving the same back to him? Cold panic seeped through her skin and burrowed into her heart. Clammy sweat moistened her palms. She was breathless and lightheaded though her lungs were working like a fireplace bellows.

She needed air. She put both hands to his chest and pushed him away. "I can't do this."

The warmth in his eyes snuffed out like she'd doused a fire.

"Fair enough." Mike's voice went tight. He took a giant step back. His hands clenched once, then dropped to his sides. "My behavior was unprofessional, and I apologize."

Rachel leaned over and picked up the saddle pad. She held it in front of her like a shield. "I'm sorry. It's not you. It's me. I'm not ready for this. I'm used to losing control, letting my emotions run away with me, and regretting what happens. I don't want to regret you."

⌒

Disappointment flooded Mike. She was already thinking she'd regret him. A minute ago, he'd been poised to risk his job, his whole life, to take whatever was brewing between them to the next step.

She was used to losing control? Well, he wasn't.

Who was he kidding? Another minute or two and he would've made love to her right up against that wall. An image of her naked body wrapped around his sent a current of desire ripping through him.

Maybe she was right. He didn't understand the effect she had on him. Even after her rejection, his body still raged for her. Every time she was nearby, his carefully honed control deserted him like a coward running from battle. His divorce had left deep scars, but he'd never lost emotional control with Laura. Not once. Sure, his body had lusted after hers. His ex-wife modeled underwear. She was sin on stilettos. But his heart had never been in danger.

He stared at Rachel. She was on the verge of hyperventilating. Her eyes were wide, her face pale. The hands that gripped the saddle blanket still trembled. What happened between them had shaken her as badly as him.

She was absolutely nothing like Laura. Life with his ex-wife was full of melodrama, but it was the purposeful kind. Never once had she looked at him like he'd just rocked her body and soul with a kiss. Laura would've used him well before pushing him away, and then tried to keep him on a string.

No, Rachel wasn't manipulating him. She was terrified. More frightened than when Troy went after her with a baseball bat. She'd been damaged at some point in her life. Whatever baggage she was carrying was way heavier than his, and from her reaction, she had no interest in letting him share the burden. As different as Rachel was from Laura, the fact that he still wanted to help her despite her rejection proved that he was a doormat as far as women went.

Mike ripped his eyes from her and turned away. The ache in his chest would surely abate eventually. He adjusted his slacks and willed his raging hard-on into submission. No luck there.

Moving on…

The incident with Will Martin, the one that had made Mike want to claim Rachel in the first place, had to be addressed.

"You can't testify that it was Will who grabbed you?" He glanced over his shoulder to catch the expected shake of her head. Her eyes were dark and filled with sadness. "I need to talk to Sean."

He left her in the barn. Every step he took toward the house fueled the burn in his gut. This was ridiculous. He had no reason to feel guilty, like he was abandoning her. *She'd* rejected *him.*

But damned if he still didn't want to know what had made her this way—and if the damage was permanent.

Rachel saddled the gray and led him into the barnyard. Her knees weren't as steady as she'd like, but nothing would smooth her out faster than a good hard gallop— something the antsy horse could also use. Sensing her turbulent emotions, the gray started prancing before her foot hit the stirrup. She gathered the reins and bypassed the ring, jogging instead into the meadow that edged the road. She and the horse both needed to get out of that small, enclosed space and into some open air. The gray pulled for the bit. She kept him to a trot but pushed his stride to lengthen as they looped the large field twice as a warm-up, then worked him through some serpentines.

He collected beautifully under her seat, his supple body flexing and yielding to her cues. Maybe jumping was the wrong sport for this animal. He seemed more cooperative as she eased him through a few basic dressage maneuvers than when she'd put him over fences.

His hindquarters gave a short buck, reminding her that he was full of pent-up energy. She softened her hands. The horse responded immediately, surging forward into a canter. Rachel shifted her weight forward and let him stretch out. But not even the wind in her face or the flow of muscles beneath her could wipe out the memory of Mike's kiss. Even with her eyes open, she couldn't forget the image of the pain in his eyes as she'd pushed him away.

Fresh pressure built in her chest. Her eyes burned, and a few tears escaped.

Before she hadn't known what she was missing. But now...

A tug on the reins brought Rachel's attention back to her mount. The gray had slowed as they rounded the turn toward the barn. The horse drifted toward the barnyard. Rachel turned his head and applied pressure with her calves to maintain his forward momentum. The gray pulled harder, and Rachel's shoulder, already exhausted, cramped. She dropped the rein. With a flick of his tail, the horse swerved and ducked his shoulder.

Rachel dropped her heels and butt. "Sorry, buddy. You're not getting rid of me that easily." Seat secured, she scooped up the dangling rein and turned the horse firmly away from the barn.

Everything under her came loose. Rachel sailed from the horse's back. The grass rushed up. Her body slammed into the ground. Pain ripped through her shoulder and arm. Inside her riding helmet, her head rang at the impact with the earth.

⌒

After Mike was sure his hard-on had deflated enough for mixed company, he headed toward the house to talk to Sean. He knocked on the back door. Sarah let him in.

"I'm looking for Sean."

"He's working in the den."

Mike walked through the kitchen. At the newspaper-covered table, the girls were disemboweling a pumpkin with big plastic spoons. The guy from last night, Rachel's *old friend*, was at the sink rinsing out a mug.

"David, I'd like to ask you a few questions about last night."

"Uhm. Sure." The guy was six-four, two-fifty, and solid as a refrigerator. Brown hair and eyes. Buzz cut. No visible scars or tattoos. But the way David refused to meet Mike's gaze pricked his suspicion.

"You can use the living room." Sarah nodded toward the hall.

The room was mostly empty, except for a few small tables, one lamp, and an old trunk.

Mike pulled his notebook from his breast pocket. David frowned at the pile of aged, yellowed papers on the nearest table. "How long have you known Rachel?"

David shifted his eyes to the wall over Mike's right shoulder. "We were neighbors when we were kids."

"When was the last time you saw her before this week?"

"When she came home for her mother's funeral." David's grim expression gave Mike the impression that there was a long story behind that statement. One that Rachel wouldn't share without bright lights, thumbscrews, and waterboarding.

"And you just showed up this week to help her out?"

"Actually, I came to see Sarah." David didn't elaborate, but Mike got the picture from the bright red flush that spread across the contractor's face.

"Why were you at town hall last night?"

"I needed to pick up some building permits for a job." David's gaze dropped to the hardwood. Could the guy just be super socially awkward? Or embarrassed that he had the hots for a married woman and was jumping in at the first sign she might be available?

"So, you weren't there for the meeting?" Mike made a note to check his claim with the township construction department.

"No."

"Did you see anything unusual?"

"Place was packed. I just grabbed my permits and got out of there. I don't like crowds much." Clearly uncomfortable, David shifted his weight and clasped his hands in front of his belt buckle. "I was pulling out of the lot when I heard the alarm and stuff. I went back to see if I could help."

"What brings you here today, David?"

He crossed his arms over the hardware store logo on his chest. "I repainted the barn for Rachel."

"Did she hire you to do that?" Mike wanted to know how close David was to Rachel. For purely professional reasons. David had been at the municipal building when the place caught fire.

This had nothing to do with jealousy or with the fact that Mike couldn't get Rachel out of his head even after she'd held up the big red stop sign in front of his face. He was an idiot, thinking about that smoking kiss and the way her body felt under his hands. Her tight butt had fit perfectly in his palms. He'd wanted to lift her up and—

Forgive me, Father. When *was* his last confession? He was ringing up sins like Christmas sales at the mall.

David shook his head. "No. I got a couple days between jobs. Goes fast with the right equipment. Thought I'd help her out."

"Nice of you."

"I guess."

"Thanks for your cooperation, David. That's all for now, but I might have more questions later. Here's my card. Call me if you think of anything else." Mike snapped his notebook shut. He didn't like this guy. Was it jealousy? Stupid if it was. Mike wasn't getting anywhere with Rachel. There was nothing suspicious about an old family friend helping the sisters out.

They went back into the kitchen. David headed for the exit while Mike pushed through the swinging door into Rachel's den. Unlike the kitchen, which had been uglified sometime in the seventies, this room was an echo of the house's original beauty. The wide-planked floor underfoot was darkened and worn from two centuries of foot traffic. A huge fireplace dominated the room, its fieldstones still gorgeous despite the need for some masonry repair.

Sean was by drilling a tiny hole in the window jamb. He looked up and silenced the tool as Mike approached.

"I don't like the low windows here. Especially after Will Martin threatened Rachel last night." Mike gave Sean the lowdown on the confrontation at town hall.

"This happened right before the fire?" Sean's eyes went great white cold. "Where does Will stand on the Lost Lake project?"

"Probably for it, considering he's so buddy-buddy with Troy, whose daddy brought Harmon Properties into town in the first place."

"So, there'd be no reason for Will to set the fire."

"I sure as hell can't think of one," Mike said. "I doubt he'd burn down the entire building, stop Harmon's presentation, and risk his own neck just to get to Rachel."

"Probably not. Will's a lot smarter than the rest of Troy's crowd."

"He's definitely the most dangerous, but who knows what Troy's other low-life buddies have planned. This house needs to be a fortress."

Sean scratched his chin. "When I'm done, neither Will nor Troy will be able to get in here. Glass breaks, motion detectors, two exterior cameras."

The swinging door opened with a squeak. Sarah stuck her head through the opening. "Have you seen the girls?"

"No. Why?" Mike asked.

Sarah chewed on her lip. "I ducked into the laundry room to start a load of wash. They were in the kitchen cleaning their pumpkins. Now they're gone. I was only out of sight a minute or two."

"Then they can't have gone far." Mike scanned the backyard through the window. "Could they have gone to the barn to see Rachel?"

"I didn't hear the door open." Sarah stared through the windows that looked over the backyard.

Sean pushed past Mike. "I'll go check." He brushed past them on his way outside.

"Why don't you search upstairs again?" Mike suggested. Sarah's quick footsteps thudded on the stairs. He went into the kitchen. The table was still littered with pumpkin innards, the chairs pushed back and left that way. He leaned over and picked up a few slimy seeds from the floor. The girls had left in a rush.

But where did they go?

The door opened and Rachel walked in, still clad in riding clothes. "Any sign of them?" Her face was pale, the skin drawn tight as a drum.

Had his kiss messed her up that badly? Or was she worried about her nieces?

"No," he said.

"Sean and his guys are checking the yard and outbuildings." She brushed past him to the hallway. Mike followed, not liking the stiffness of her gait. A door at the end of the hall stood ajar.

"Where does that door go?" he asked.

"The basement." Alarm laced her voice.

He followed her to the door. On the jamb, a foot from the top of the door, a large hook dangled loose from its eye closure. An end table had been dragged across the pine floor as a makeshift ladder. So much for Rachel's child-proofing efforts.

"Smart little buggers," Mike said wryly.

"I put that lock on the door for a reason." She turned to him with eyes that were more than worried. "They could fall down those stairs and break their necks."

"True." He pulled the basement door fully open and stared down. No bodies lay at the foot of the steps. "But they didn't. Is there any other way out of there?"

"No."

"Then they're down there. We just have to find them."

"There're all kinds of tools and who knows what else stored down there." Rachel's voice cracked. "Nothing's been sorted through since my grandfather died ten years ago."

"We'll find them. It'll be OK."

Rachel grabbed a flashlight from the closet. Boards creaked underfoot as they navigated the steep and narrow staircase single-file, stepping down into a dirt-floored room that spanned the width of the house but only half its depth. She yanked on a short chain. Bare bulbs strung along overhead joists lighted the area. Exterior walls were made of rough-cut fieldstone like the house's foundation. Interior walls were a hodgepodge of plaster and brick construction. Workbenches and hanging tools lined one wall of the large main space. There wasn't anywhere to hide in the open workshop, but the rear portion of the cellar was sectioned off into multiple rooms in a rabbit-warren fashion that spoke of several generations' additions with emphasis on functionality, not aesthetics.

Mike ducked to avoid a thick beam. "How old is this house?"

They passed through the first area, shelved for long-term storage of canned goods and rarely used kitchen equipment. Mike scanned the space for the girls. No sign of them. The boxes along the walls all bore a thick, undisturbed coating of dust.

"Over two hundred years." Rachel squatted to peer behind a large box marked *Christmas Decorations* in faded block letters. "They could be anywhere down here."

"I have an idea." Mike jogged back up the stairs and out of the house. In the yard, he scooped up an ecstatic Bandit. When he returned, he set the wiggling dog down. "He has a great nose, right?"

"Sure, for food. But it's worth a try." Rachel encouraged the pup. "Where's Alex, Bandit? Where's Em?"

Bandit snuffled along the floor. Mike and Rachel followed him toward another doorway in the back of the room. Rachel darted ahead into another, smaller space crammed with junk. She pointed to a steamer trunk marked by tiny handprints on its dusty surface. "They're probably in there."

Bandit agreed, putting his nose to the crack of the trunk and wagging his tail.

Mike bent his neck to avoid the low header. The wall behind the trunk was stone, like the foundation, but it didn't look exactly the same. The proportions of the room didn't feel quite right either.

Rachel tried the lid. "It's locked." Her voice rose with nerves.

Mike moved closer. "We'll open it. Relax."

"But they can't breathe."

"Plenty of air for the five minutes they've been missing." Something moved behind the trunk. Mike leaned down. "They're not in it. They're behind it."

"Alex? Em? Please come out."

Fabric rustled and a small white face peered out from the dark space between the trunk and the wall. Breath whooshed out of Rachel, and she wobbled next to him.

"Come on, baby." Rachel knelt in the dirt and extended a hand.

The smallest child crawled out and clambered onto Rachel's lap. "I told Awex we didn't hafta hide. You'd protect us."

"From what, Em?"

"Daddy."

Mike's heart dropped into his stomach. They'd overheard his conversation with Sean.

Rachel brushed a streak of dirt from the child's cheek, then turned back to the darkness. "Where's Alex?"

Alex's head popped out of the space. "We found a good hiding place this time. Like the slaves on the underground train."

"What?" Mike asked.

"Sarah found some documents that claim the house was part of the Underground Railroad," Rachel explained. "Just come out of there, Alex."

Alex stopped halfway. Her tiny forehead crinkled. "I'm stuck."

Mike pulled at the trunk, sliding it away from the wall. The hem of Alex's jeans was caught on a protruding stone. The little girl pulled. Crumbled mortar rained down. Stones shifted.

Mike reached for her shoulders. "Don't move."

But Alex's eyes went wide and she scrambled, jerking her leg free. Mike threw his body across hers and waited for the wall to collapse on them. Nothing but a small cloud of dirt and dust descended.

The dust cleared as Mike sat up. "What the...?"

A two-foot square section of the wall had swung open toward them like a small door. After lifting the child to her feet and dusting her off, Mike crawled to the dark opening and shone the beam of the flashlight around the hidden space. In the center of the room was a long, narrow depression in the dirt, the approximate size of an old grave.

Chapter Seventeen

Rachel focused on the strange expression on Mike's face. "What is it?"

He shook his head.

"Is someone down there?" Sarah's voice came down the stairs.

"We found them," Rachel yelled back. "Why don't you two go see your mom?"

The girls scrambled to their feet. Pain rushed fresh as Rachel stood and ushered them back to the foot of the stairs. "I'll explain later," she said to her sister.

Sarah, already on her way down, hugged the children hard before herding them back up the steps. Rachel heard Sarah asking gentle questions as voices faded.

Relief at finding the girls cut into Rachel's adrenaline overload. Unsteady, she sat on the bottom step.

"You OK?"

She lifted her head. Mike was squatting in front of her. She'd have to tell him what had happened. But first… "What did you see in there?"

"I don't want to say until I check it out. Could be nothing."

Rachel squinted at him. "I don't need sheltering, He-Man."

Mike sighed. "I think there might be a grave in there."

"That's absurd."

"I could be wrong." Mike frowned and shined the flashlight on her arm. "You're bleeding. Why are you always bleeding?"

"It's just a scrape. Must've hit a rock or something when I fell."

"Fell off what?"

"The gray horse."

"You just fell off a horse?" His voice took on an urgent edge, and he started running his hands over her legs.

"My legs are fine. I walked down here, remember?"

"You're stubborn enough to walk on a broken bone."

Rachel couldn't argue with that.

His hands moved up to her hips and back. "What did you hit?"

"Landed on my back."

His fingers slid through her hair as he prodded her scalp.

Rachel brushed his hand away. "My head is fine. I was wearing my helmet."

"Good thing." Cool air played over her skin as he lifted her T-shirt and shined the flashlight over her ribs and back. "You need to go to the ER."

"Nah." She shook her head. "I'll ice it. It'll be fine."

"You already have some swelling. You could have broken something."

"I am well acquainted with what broken bones feel like. Mine are intact." But how had her Cyborg parts fared? She'd been warned that her titanium tidbits could shift, and that it wouldn't be a good thing.

"You can't even stand up."

Her knees were a little wobbly, but she could certainly stand up just fine. She started to rise.

His hand on her thigh stopped her. "For Christ's sake, that wasn't a challenge."

Footsteps on the steps above interrupted their argument. "Is it safe to come down? Or are you two…busy?"

"Would you please come down here, Sean?" Mike shouted up the steps.

"What's up?" Sean's voice went serious as his boots thudded down the wooded treads.

Mike pointed toward the back room. "There's a hidden room back there with a shallow depression that looks suspiciously like a grave, and Rachel needs a ride to the ER."

"I do not." Her shoulder hurt, sure, but not *that* much. She'd walked back to the barn and cooled out and untacked the horse before Sean's yell about the missing girls had interrupted her. But now that the kids were found and fine, her battered torso was stiffening up.

Sean was beside her, checking out her bare back in the beam of Mike's flashlight.

"Do you mind?" Rachel tugged at her T-shirt.

Sean ignored her protest. "He's right. You're a mess. What the hell happened?"

"She fell off a horse," Mike explained.

"Not exactly. And it's probably just scrapes and bruises." But she wasn't sure what exactly *did* happen. One minute she'd been secure and in control, and the next she'd been skidding on damp grass like a slip 'n slide. "Mike is overreacting."

"Uhm, Mike." Sean gestured toward the doorway that led to the back of the basement.

Rachel followed Sean's pointing finger. Bandit stood behind Mike. A long bone was clenched between his doggy jaws, his paws were caked with dirt, and his entire butt was wagging.

Mike turned. "Uh-oh."

"Don't chase him," Rachel warned. Too late. Mike was already lunging for the dog. With a joyful wag, Bandit bounced away and shot through the doorway.

"Come here, boy." Mike followed, disappearing into the next room. Rachel listened to the sounds of boxes falling and feet scraping and Mike calling after the dog. "Aw, that's not cool, Bandit."

Meanwhile, Sean walked up the steps and came back down a minute later with a slice of lunchmeat in his hand.

Bandit shot back out into the open. The little dog's ears were flapping and his stubby legs churning. Dirt flew as he drifted through a turn all *Fast and Furious.* Mike appeared in the doorway a second later. The cop was covered in dust and breathing hard.

Sean squatted down and waved the chicken. Bandit skidded to a stop in front of him and spat out his prize in exchange for the meat. The bone dropped to the hard-packed earth with a hollow *thunk.* "She told you not to chase him." He picked up the still chewing dog and looked down at the discarded bone. "Femur. Guess you were right about the grave."

"My life used to be gloriously uneventful." Mike grimaced as Sean handed Bandit over. The dog swallowed the chicken, wagged his tail, and licked Mike's face. "I have to call the medical examiner."

"I'll run her over to the hospital. Quinn's there today." Sean circled to her nonsmashed side. "Can you stand up or do we need to call an ambulance?"

In answer, Rachel pushed to her feet. "I already told the cop I'm fine."

Mike lifted her chin. "Please go with Sean."

Rachel's glare melted. The *please* did it to her every time. Weakening, she huffed. "Nothing's broken."

"So humor me. I have a lot to do, and I won't be able to concentrate if I'm worried about you."

"You're worried about me?" Maybe she was hurt more seriously than she suspected. The schoolgirl giddiness swirling in her belly was not normal.

"You have a knack for getting hurt. Your sister seems to think a fall could be dangerous."

She didn't deny the risk. "I didn't exactly fall. The saddle fell off."

She hadn't had a chance to inspect her tack, but she couldn't see how that could happen without some sort of sabotage.

☞

Mike squatted on the floor outside the secret basement room. In the windowless interior, medical examiner Dr. Gregory Campbell worked by the light of a portable lamp. With his lean body and shoulder-length hair, the young doctor looked more like a college stoner than a medical examiner. "The house's owner just discovered this house might have been a stop on the Underground Railroad."

"Sorry, Mike." Greg's excited voice echoed in the empty space. The hidden area was approximately seven feet in width and spanned the length of the house. "I know you'd like these to be Civil War–era remains, but this skeleton isn't that old."

"You can tell already?"

"The big clue is the sheet of plastic underneath." With a gloved finger, Greg brushed some dirt away from the now-exposed remains. Light reflected off a shiny surface. "I don't know the exact date clear plastic sheeting was invented, but it's clearly not Civil War material."

"Any guess how recent?" Mike asked. There was no point in speculating as to the origins of the remains until he had at least a rough time frame.

Greg sat back on his haunches and contemplated the skeleton. From the shallow grave, a skull stared back at them with mock attention, empty ocular cavities and disconnected jawbone giving it an eyes-wide-open, permanently surprised expression.

"The remains are fully skeletonized. There's some partially deteriorated clothing, looks like some kind of poly-cotton blend. More than ten years—most likely these bones have been down here longer than that. I might be able to narrow down the estimate when I get everything back to the lab, but we'll need to ship the remains to a forensic anthropologist." Greg straightened his lean frame. "Call me tomorrow."

Mike rubbed his face. Fresh cases deteriorated after forty-eight hours. These remains were likely at least a decade old. They weren't just cold; they were glacial. If he were lucky, he'd be able to identify the victim. It was a long shot that they'd ever determine the cause of death. Actually solving a case this old would take a miracle.

He left Greg to do his thing and went outside in search of air that wasn't dusty and dank. Mike passed Sean's assistants, installing something under the eaves that hung over

Rachel's back stoop. Why hadn't Sean called? Were Rachel's injuries more serious than they'd thought? Bandit stood up and put both paws on his knee. Mike stood on the back lawn, scratching the dog behind the ears and looking over the rolling green of Rachel's pastures.

Recent heavy rains had made Pennsylvania look like Ireland. Horses grazed under an overcast sky. The mountain that rose behind the farm was a dramatic backdrop. The trees that ringed the open space were turning, their leaves fiery with reds and golds. It was peaceful out here. Or at least it would be without all the vandalism. Mike could do without the skeleton too. But Rachel's farm had something that his little house in town didn't possess. Quiet. Solitude. Privacy. The knowledge that your neighbors didn't care if you put your garbage cans out before dark. The fact that no one would call, well him, if the dog were barking. This was the kind of place where dogs and kids could make as much noise as they liked. Where a comfortable chair and a cup of coffee were all he'd need in the evening.

Like the house Mike had grown up in, before his dad had died. Afterward, the small house in town had been all Mike's mom could afford. That house symbolized everything that he'd lost. It represented settling for less than he wanted. So why the hell had Mike kept it? Did he like rubbing his own nose in his misfortunes?

He had no time to lament. Instead of a relaxing evening in the country, tonight he'd be dealing with the mayor, the fire, rampant vandalism, and, just for kicks and giggles, he now had a skeleton on his hands. He'd have to squeeze in an interview with Blake Webb. Rachel's stalker was still on the loose, and he was getting more serious. Good times…

Mike headed toward the barn. An engine purred. A familiar Mercedes turned onto Rachel's driveway.

Cristan Rojas.

Mike kept walking while the Argentinean got out of the car. The tween daughter climbed out of the back and slumped unhappily toward the barn.

Rojas fell into step beside Mike. He glanced sideways, eyes scanning Mike's uniform with suspicion. "Is everything all right? Where is Miss Parker?"

"Miss Parker won't be able to teach her lesson today. She's at the hospital because she fell off *your* horse earlier." Mike waited for Rojas's reaction.

"That is preposterous," Rojas said in accented but precise English. "Miss Parker does not just fall off horses. She is one of the best riders in the world. Shadow Dancer is a challenge for my daughter, but for Miss Parker, he is nothing, a carousel pony."

The praise took Mike by surprise. "Funny, I was under the impression you didn't like her much."

Rojas laughed. Amusement flared in his black eyes. "Oh no. I like her very much."

Mike did not appreciate the way Rojas emphasized *very*. "But you were arguing with her over the training of your daughter's horse."

"Ah, yes. Fighting with Miss Parker is very stimulating. She is… How you say it?" Rojas paused, gesturing as if seeking the correct translation. Mike had a feeling the Argentinean didn't need as much help with the language as he pretended. "She is a passionate woman. Her eyes sparkle when she is angry, no?"

The fact that Mike also found her hot when she was mad was disturbing.

"Miss Parker and I disagree on how to best raise my daughter. I believe a child should be challenged so she does not become weak. Miss Parker favors a gentler approach, and she is not afraid to voice her opinion. But I highly doubt Miss Parker became such a skilled horsewoman by riding tame animals." Rojas smiled. "I want my daughter to be strong, to seek a challenge rather than take the easy path, to be the best at whatever she chooses to be. One must not be afraid to take risks."

Rachel was a risk-taker. No question.

Rojas's face went grim. "I hope that she is all right. Are her injuries serious?"

Mike's gut twisted. "I haven't heard, but she was walking on her own." Mike didn't intend for his voice to be colored with respect.

"Ah, I see." Rojas's accent deepened with understanding. Of what, Mike wasn't sure. But the guy's know-it-all tone was irritating. "That does not mean she is not hurt. She is a strong woman. Very proud. She would walk to her own deathbed."

"Yeah." Mike had been thinking the same thing, and it wasn't comforting. He checked his cell for messages from Sean. Two texts and three missed calls from the mayor, which Mike ignored. There wasn't anything from his friend. Mike pulled up Sean's number, typed a question mark, and pressed the send key.

He was probably going to get fired, but with each second that passed, Mike cared less about small-town politics and more about keeping Rachel safe. He was going to miss his job, and he couldn't imagine staying in Westbury without it. Could he leave it all behind? He'd lived in Philadelphia for a number of years when he was married to Laura, but the city had never been home.

Rojas looked ahead. His gaze fixed on the saddle hanging over the corral fence. His eyes went flat, like a cop's—or a criminal's—and Mike wondered what Sean was going to uncover in the Argentinean's background. His demeanor didn't exactly scream boring executive. Hired killer was a better possibility.

Rojas pointed at the thin straps still buckled to the girth strap that would encircle the horse's belly and hold the saddle in place. "These were cut with a very sharp knife."

Mike had suspected it all along, but seeing the evidence intensified the sick feeling in his stomach. "Why wouldn't she have seen that when she saddled the horse?"

Rojas reassembled the pieces. "Because the part that was severed was concealed under the skirt." He tucked the cut ends under the large flap of leather that comprised the side of the saddle. "She might not have noticed unless she was cleaning it."

She'd been distracted right before her fall because of their kiss. "No matter how you look at it, someone intended to hurt her."

"Only cowards attack women." Rojas's face darkened. Pain and anger replaced cool amusement.

Mike held out a business card. "Call me if you see anything or anyone suspicious while you're here."

Rojas took the card. "Tell Miss Parker to contact me if I am able to be of assistance. If you'll please excuse me, I must help my daughter." He stalked away.

Mike stashed the saddle, now evidence, in the back of his SUV. In no rush to deal with the mayor, he made a detour to the hospital on the way back to the station.

Sean was standing guard outside a glass-walled exam room in the ER. "Quinn just went in there with her X-rays."

Mike knocked on the jamb and walked through the open door. "Rachel?"

"In here," she answered.

He ducked around the floor-to-ceiling curtain. Rachel was semireclined on a gurney. She was still wearing her riding pants and boots, but a hospital johnny had replaced her grass-stained shirt.

On the other side of the cubicle, Quinn turned on a lighted box and backlit her X-rays. "This arm looks like something my boys built with their erector set. But as far as I can tell, the rod and screws are still in place, which is a medical miracle. I can't say how the soft tissue around all that hardware fared. Are you sure I can't talk you into that MRI?"

"Positive."

Mike shot her a what-the-hell look.

She gave him a squinty-eyed glare back. "Their machine is a closed tube. I don't do small spaces."

"Why not?" Mike asked.

"Because I don't." Rachel looked at the wall and took a deep breath. "When I was six, I got locked in a storage container in a game of hide-and-go-seek gone wrong." Her jaw clenched. A shudder passed through her body. "No one found me for like eighteen hours. It was the middle of summer. I almost died." Her voice broke. She squeezed her eyes shut.

His chest tightened. She'd been alone and small and scared, not much different from her current situation. Mike wished he could take her in his arms and hold her until the memory, and the pain that came with it, passed. Rachel had had far too many close calls.

Quinn's pen scratched on her chart. "Bruises should improve in a few days. If not, you should go back to the university hospital and see the orthopedic surgeon who did the original surgeries. Ice and rest that arm for the next week. Don't go anywhere just yet. We'll get those stitches out while you're here." The doctor ducked out.

Mike stepped up closer to the bed. "The girth straps of your saddle were cut."

That opened her eyes, but resignation rather than shock crossed her face. "I should've seen that."

"The cuts were all the way up at the top, under the flap. When was the last time you used that saddle?"

"With the weather and everything else, it's been a few days, but I clean it every week or so. I would've noticed if anything wasn't right."

"Do you always keep it in the tack room?" Mike asked.

"Yes."

"And the room isn't locked up at night." He already knew the answer but had to ask anyway.

"Guess it will be from now on."

"How many boarders and students have been in and out in the last few days?"

"Not that many. Less than ten."

"Can you give me a list?"

She nodded. "Sure."

"I have to go. Sean's going to take you home."

"That's not necessary. I can get Mrs. Holloway to pick me up."

"I'd feel better if you were with Sean." Mike was pretty sure Mrs. Holloway wasn't sporting a nine millimeter under her jacket.

Rachel's expression changed, as if the gravity of the situation had finally sunk in. "Someone tried to hurt me. Intentionally."

"Sean will make sure you're safe."

She looked up into his eyes and nodded. "Thanks." Along with apprehension, there was something else in her eyes. Trust. In him. His chest swelled. Her heart might be closed off, but she believed he'd keep her safe.

"I'll try to come by later, but no promises. I have a lot on my plate."

She didn't tell him not to come. On the contrary, her eyes were misty. Gratitude? He didn't dare hope for more.

Mike headed toward the door, his steps a fraction lighter.

"Hey, He-Man."

He turned back.

"I told you nothing was broken." Rachel was feeling feisty enough to smart-mouth him. Damned if that didn't make him feel better.

He walked out. Sean was hanging in the hallway.

"You mind staying with her and driving her home?"

"Not at all," Sean said. "Her alarm will be up and running tonight."

"Thanks. I appreciate everything." Mike turned away.

"Where are you headed?"

"Going out to interview Blake Webb before I get fired," Mike said over his shoulder.

"Fidiots."

Mike heard Sean's disgusted retort behind him as he strode down the hall. His pocket buzzed, and he checked his phone. There was a new voice message from Fred telling him his presence was mandatory at an emergency meeting of the council members in two hours. Mike headed toward the exit.

Quinn snagged him on his way past the desk. "Got a minute, Maalox Man?"

"Damn Sean," Mike muttered.

"My brother says you're downing that shit like a frat boy chugging beer."

Mike backed toward the door. "It's been a rough week."

Quinn gave him the hairy eyeball and pointed at him with his folded reading glasses. "Today's Wednesday. You have until the end of the week. Don't make me send Sean after you."

It was going to get shittier.

⇐

Rising Star Farms was a thirty-minute drive down the Northeast Extension. Mike turned into a mile-long driveway flanked by white-fenced pastures. On either side of the road, sleek horses grazed in the fading light. The barn that loomed behind the Tara-like mansion made Rachel's look like a dollhouse version.

Mike parked in front of the huge white Georgian, complete with a circular portico and two-story columns. He expected a butler to answer the bell, but Blake Webb opened the door. His riding clothes bore smudges of dirt, and the high polish of his knee-high boots was dimmed by a few mud splatters. He was the epitome of the well-bred country gentleman. But under the expensive haircut, Webb's eyes were tired. The set of his mouth and the fresh lines on his face suggested he hadn't slept well lately. A tumbler of amber liquid dangled from his fingertips.

"Police Chief O'something, right?" Blake eyed the badge on Mike's chest. "Are you here in a professional or personal capacity?"

"It's O'Connell, and I'd like to ask you a few questions about your relationship with Rachel."

"That isn't an answer." Blake wasn't intimidated by the uniform. Rich people with expensive lawyers rarely were. He stepped back to admit Mike into a foyer flanked by curving staircases. "Well, come in. My father would be appalled to have a policeman in uniform standing on the doorstep."

They passed under a crystal chandelier bigger than a Buick, and Mike followed Blake down a hall of gleaming hardwood into the library. The floor-to-ceiling shelves likely held more books that Westbury's public facility.

"Is your father still active in the business?" Mike took a seat in a leather wing chair, pulled out his notebook, and watched Blake pace.

"No. Unfortunately, my father suffered a stroke a few years ago, and I was forced to take over."

"You didn't want the job?"

"I used to travel with Rachel wherever she was competing. I had to cut back on the globe-trotting after taking the reins, so to speak." He dropped into the opposite chair. Blake sipped his booze and stared out the bank of windows that lined the rear wall. Outside, drizzle spotted a paver patio and disturbed the surface of the lagoon-shaped pool. "Ironically, Fleet was supposed to be my horse. But once Dad saw Rachel ride him, that was the end of that."

Blake glanced over. "I know what you're thinking, but I'm not bitter about Dad's decision. He was right. Anyone with two eyes could see it, and I was already in love with her. I would've given her anything." He paused, swirling the liquid and ice in his glass.

"Did Rachel tell you someone was actively trying to ruin her farm?"

Blake tensed. "No. Except for that one phone call to ask me to buy her horse, we haven't been in contact since we… broke up. I guess I should be glad she still trusts me with her horse."

"It started out with vandalism and property damage, but someone cut the girth to her saddle this morning, and she took a hard fall."

"Is she all right?" Blake's face went paler than the creamy carpet underfoot.

"Yes. Just bruised up."

"I wasn't there when she fell in Tampa. It took me six hours to get to her." Emotion strained Blake's voice. He lurched to his feet and swept a frustrated hand across his blond head. "Dammit. I told her she had no business riding again."

Mike already knew giving Rachel an order was as effectual as bailing out the Titanic with a spoon. "You had nothing to do with it?"

"I would never hurt Rachel."

"Are you sure you don't want her back enough to try to ruin her farm so that she'd come running back to you?"

"You don't know Rachel very well if you think that would work." Blake moved to a rolling cart cluttered with decanters and sparkling crystal. "Drink, Chief O'Connell?"

"No thanks. I'm on duty."

"Ah, a man of principle. You and Rachel have a lot in common." Blake poured three inches of booze into his tumbler. Bitterness swept across his face. He downed half the glass. "Which is probably part of the reason she was never in love with me. Rachel can't love a man she doesn't respect. We were great friends, though, until I fucked *that* up by asking her to marry me."

Mike's pen froze above the page.

Blake capped the decanter with a soft *clink.* "And, to top it off, the night she turned down my proposal, I took comfort in a bottle and a slutty blond I picked up at a nightclub. Rachel came early the next morning to apologize and found us in bed. God, she even thought my disgusting behavior was her fault. Being the coward that I am, I let her."

Blake walked back to the chair and sat down. He leveled his red-rimmed gaze at Mike. "If I could go back in time and undo just one thing in my entire life, it would be that first time I kissed her. She was here, still recuperating from the accident. She'd just learned that her career was over and was at the lowest point in her life. I had no business taking advantage of her. She was vulnerable, but I wanted her so damned much I did it anyway. I am a selfish bastard. I betrayed her and tossed away a ten-year friendship. I knew damned well she didn't feel the way about me that I felt about her."

"That had to hurt, though, that Rachel didn't return your feelings," Mike pressed.

"Rachel isn't capable of falling in love." Which wasn't really an answer. Blake was on his feet again and headed back to the drink cart. Good thing he could afford a new liver.

"I don't understand."

He poured himself a double and refreshed the ice in his glass. "Have you met Rachel's father?"

"No."

"If you do, you'll understand why she is the way she is." Blake swallowed the rest of his drink and refilled, obviously bent on a serious binge. "She wouldn't talk much about her past, but five minutes with her father and any idiot can see that her childhood left some pretty deep scars. Some wounds just don't heal."

"She didn't trust you?"

"It has nothing to do with trusting others. Rachel doesn't trust herself. She's so afraid of hurting people. She'll never let herself fall in love," Blake slurred as he sank into the leather chair. "Her heart has been locked away for so long, she's lost the key."

"Call me if you remember anything else that might help me protect Rachel." Mike tossed a business card on the coffee table. Blake didn't respond, and Mike let himself out.

As he headed back to Westbury, he wondered if Blake were right. Was Rachel too damaged to recover?

Chapter Eighteen

Rachel shoved the truck door open.

"Hold on, there." Sean jogged around the vehicle and took hold of her good elbow. "A face-plant wouldn't help matters."

She slid out of the passenger seat and stared at the silver Mercedes parked a few feet away. Rojas! Wait a minute. Twilight was descending on the farm, which meant it was somewhere around six. Lucia's lesson was hours ago.

Rachel groaned. "I forgot to call my lesson and cancel."

"I think you'll be forgiven." Sean escorted her across the grass.

"Are your workers still here?"

"They'd better be. In fact, the system should be ready to test."

Rachel spotted the two assistants doing something to the back of the house. A power tool was running, but at this point, she was so tired, she didn't really care what was going on. Climbing the back stoop took an enormous amount of energy. Rachel stepped into the kitchen, dreaming of sweatpants and her pillow. She wanted out of her riding boots and into a hot shower. The smells of honest-to-God food hit her nose. Her stomach growled at the thought of her sister's cooking. Maybe food, then bed.

Sean stopped abruptly and whispered in her ear. "Do you know him?"

Rachel looked up. Cristan Rojas sat at her kitchen table. His expensive, tailored clothes were incongruous with her ugly old kitchen. An aristocrat visiting his tenant farmer. Sarah was pouring him a cup of coffee.

He'd never been in her house before. He'd never expressed anything but animosity toward her.

"Mr. Rojas. This is a surprise."

Rojas stood. He and Sean exchanged cold stares, as if they were gunslingers on opposite ends of the street at the OK Corral. As they sized each other up, Rachel gave them a mental eye roll and introduced them.

"Please, call me Cristan." His dark eyes were full of concern and sympathy as they swept her body from head to toe. Hmmm. Maybe he didn't dislike her as much as she thought.

"I'm sorry I didn't call to cancel Lucia's lesson," Rachel said.

"Your omission is understandable under the circumstances." Cristan nodded. "The evening wasn't a total loss. Your sister was gracious enough to offer Lucia and me dinner."

The sound of the older girl's voice was barely audible through the swinging doors. It sounded like she was reading a story.

"It wasn't much. Just pasta." Sarah blushed at Cristan, then faced Rachel. "Can you eat?"

"God, yes." Rachel lowered her aching body into a chair. "I missed lunch."

Sarah went to the stove, removed a lid from a pot, and stirred something. "How about you, Sean?"

He shook his head. "No thanks. I'm going to go check with my men. Excuse me. We'll be testing the system. Don't be alarmed when the siren goes off."

Sarah slid a plate of pasta in front of Rachel, and she concentrated on eating with some semblance of table manners.

"I'd better let the children know about the alarm." Sarah went into the den. Soft giggling drifted into the kitchen as the door opened and closed. Rachel didn't miss the lingering glance from Cristan as her sister left the room.

Interesting.

"I am glad to see that you are all right." Cristan sipped his coffee.

"Omigod." Rachel put a palm on the table and shifted her weight to rise. "Talk about brain fog. I almost forgot to feed the horses."

Cristan leaned across the table and put a hand on her arm. His dark eyes sparkled. "I fed the horses an hour ago according to your *very* detailed chart in the barn."

Was he mocking her? Rachel decided she didn't care. "Thank you."

"You are welcome." His eyes dropped to her feet, still clad in knee-high riding boots. "May I assist you?"

"I can get it. There's a boot pull in the mudroom."

But Cristan merely turned, straddled her legs, and, with a firm hand cupping her heel, eased the boots off one at a time like a pro.

"You've done this before."

"I played much polo in Argentina." He set her boots by the door and returned to his seat.

Argentina was home to the best polo players in the world, and Cristan had the lean, tough body of an athlete. "Then why are you paying me to teach your daughter to ride?"

"Daughters do not always learn well from their fathers." Cristan smiled wearily at the den door. Through it, Rachel could hear Alex and Em giggling. "Lucia's mother died when she was an infant. She needs a strong female role model. It is not easy for a girl to be raised without a woman's influence."

His grief left an indelible print on his face.

"I can understand that. My mother was...very ill."

"I am sorry," he commiserated.

"Me too."

A siren blared, interrupting their touchy-feely moment. The sound ceased as suddenly as it began.

Cristan finished his coffee. He rose and carried the cup and saucer to the sink. Since when did she have saucers? Or decent cups? "Will you be able to manage the stairs on your own?"

She nodded. "It's just a few bruises. I've had worse."

"If there is nothing else that I can do for you, then I will bid you good night." He called gently for his daughter. Sarah and the three children came in. Lucia greeted Rachel politely and followed her father out the door. "Sarah, thank you for dinner. The company and the food were most enjoyable."

Sarah flushed. Again. Well, well. Even after all she'd been through with Troy, her sister wasn't immune to Cristan's Latin looks and charm. Rachel had to admit, the accent was killer.

Two months of giving Lucia's riding lessons, and Rachel knew nothing about this man. Basically, they'd argued twice a week. It appeared as if he wasn't a complete jackass. Under that layer of arrogance, Rojas was smooth—too smooth. Was he attracted to Sarah? Or was there some other reason for his sudden interest in them? The guy was waaaay too good looking for anyone's good.

Sean came back in and went into the pantry. A series of soft beeps sounded. He leaned his head out. "We're done. Can we go over how this all works?"

"Sure," Rachel said.

Sarah gave the girls each a cookie. She gave them a pointed look. "Sit at the table for a few minutes."

The left wall inside of the pantry had been transformed into command central. A digital control panel and a black-and-white monitor had been mounted at eye level. "It's the Bat pantry."

"Oh, look." Sarah pointed over Rachel's shoulder. "We can see the front porch and the back stoop."

"You need to pick a four-digit passcode," Sean explained and demonstrated the basic operations of the system.

"You have a bill for me?" she asked when he had finished.

"I do." He handed her his clipboard, and Rachel read the invoice. The total at the bottom was absurdly low.

"You're kidding, right? Where's the rest of the bill?"

"I gave you everything at cost." Sean ripped the top sheet off and set it on the table. "You don't like it, take it up with Mike." He sauntered out.

She planned to. No matter how much she pushed Mike away, he kept coming back with relentless determination. She balked. He said please. She was rude. He was extra polite. It was annoying. And sweet. Bah!

Rachel went into the pantry and punched the passcode into the alarm panel.

Sarah watched. "Little green light's on."

"Guess that's it, then." She winced. Her shoulder was stiffening by the second. The ibuprofen wasn't making a dent. She went to the freezer for an ice pack.

"You might want to take something stronger for that."

"Maybe. I'll try the ice first."

Sarah steered the girls toward the hall. "Bath time."

Slowly, Rachel trailed her sister, nieces, and the dog down the hall. A shower beckoned. "Hey, where'd we get the saucers?"

"Found them in the attic. Must've been Gram's." Sarah paused on the second-floor landing. "I've been thinking. We should have an antique dealer go through the attic and basement. Some of the stuff looks really old."

"Good idea." China cups and skeletons. What other surprises were lingering?

⌒

Mike spent the hour in his office, signing paperwork and trying to attend to at least a few of the administrative duties stacked up in his bin. Someone knocked on his door. "Come in."

Ethan entered. "No luck on identifying the owner of that Jeep. The VIN number had been removed."

"Probably stolen, then. Back-burner it." Mike's phone signaled that it was time to walk over to the community center, where the council members had established temporarily offices.

He stepped out into the crisp, damp air and scanned the street. Pumpkins adorned doorsteps, blow-up ghosts occupied lawns, and orange lights lighted bushes. Halloween was just two weeks away.

The four councilmen and the mayor were already gathered at a long table in the large meeting room of the community center. Vince and Lee Jenkins, were conspiring with Mayor Fred at one end. Opposite, pharmacist Frank Bent and Herb Duncan, owner of the Main Street Inn, looked worried.

Mike slid into a seat in the center. He opened his notebook and pulled a pair of reading glasses from his chest pocket. He jumped in with his agenda. "All officers are scheduled for both Halloween and Mischief night." Mike quickly reviewed the plans that had been finalized since the last meeting, including extra patrols, parade details, and curfew hours. No one objected.

"The next item on my agenda is potential for flooding this weekend. As you all know, local waterways are already topped out from recent heavy rain. There are several bridges I'm particularly worried about. We should prepare to evacuate flood-prone areas and open shelters as necessary."

"Don't you think that's a little premature?" Vince's condescending tone grated.

"No, I don't," Mike answered. "There are low spots that are already close to flooding, and some of those residents are damned stubborn about leaving. There isn't much we can do to prevent property damage, but loss of life is unacceptable."

"We can't make them leave their homes."

Mike chewed his molars. "No, but we can get the word out."

"But if the rain doesn't pan out, we look like fools." Vince glared at Mike.

"Our public images aren't as important as saving lives," Mike shot back. "And let's not forget our emergency crews.

They risk their lives every single time they respond to a water rescue."

Vince opened his mouth, but across the table, Herb cleared his throat. In a cashmere sweater and casual slacks, the former chef looked every inch the country inn owner. "Do you have an update on the fire, Mike?"

Mike consulted his notes. "I spoke with the state arson investigator. His initial impression is that the fire was arson. There were traces of what appear to be accelerants near the point of origin, which was the basement. Labs tests and the official report, however, will take some time."

"Arson?" Vince smacked the table.

Under his thick white hair, Herb paled. "Someone set that fire? With all those people inside?"

"I'm afraid so." Mike closed his notebook. "On a positive note, the sprinklers kicked in right away. The stuff that was in long-term storage in the basement is trashed. Upstairs, most of the damage is from smoke. Have you checked with the structural engineer, Fred?"

The mayor cleared his throat. "Yes. He said he'll get the inspection done by the end of the week."

"Obviously the fire was an attempt to stop Lawrence Harmon from giving his presentation." Vince jabbed a pencil at Mike. "You should investigate every single protestor. It's clear one of them is behind the fire and the vandalism out at the project site."

"The protestors have stayed well within the requirements of the law. There's no evidence they had anything to do with the fire." Mike tapped a finger on his closed book.

"Do you even have any leads?" Vince sneered. "Did you even have a chance to work on the case at all? I heard you spent most of the day with Rachel Parker, and that she had a body concealed in her basement. She was there last night too. Wasn't she?"

"Yes. Miss Parker was at the municipal building last night. So was half the town, Vince. And we found a skeleton in her basement, not a body. I'm waiting to hear from the medical examiner, but the person was not killed recently."

Vince's face reddened. "You are unable to stop the rampant crime in our town. You don't know anything about the fire. You don't know much about remains in your girlfriend's basement. Why shouldn't we fire you?"

"Hold on there, Vince," Herb interrupted. "No one wants to fire Mike."

"Really?" Vince stood and leaned on the table. "He failed to catch a serial killer operating right under his nose. A woman's death is on his head. Maybe we need a new police chief."

Mike's gut burned. He should have known Vince would try to use that against him.

Herb gave Vince a talk-to-the-hand gesture. "Mike practically works twenty-four hours a day, Vince. What more do you expect? The FBI didn't catch that killer either. Mike is not responsible."

Vince jabbed the table with a forefinger. "I expect him to keep this town safe. To protect businesses. To be professional. To not have personal relationships with those involved in his cases. Like Miss Parker."

Mike opened his mouth to deny it but couldn't. He did have personal feelings for Rachel, and they were messing up everything.

Herb jumped in for him. "Enough, Vince. We all know you hate the Parker woman because she's on the opposite side of your boy's domestic abuse case."

"My daughter-in-law fell down the stairs. Our chief of police is biased against my son. He has a conflict of interest with the case." Seething, Vince clenched his teeth. "Talk to the prosecutor and get the assault charges against Troy dropped or you're fired."

"And I suppose that's not a conflict of interest?" Herb rolled his eyes. "You can't do that without a vote, Vince."

Mike looked around the table. Vince's buddy, Lee, was openly gloating. Fred was studying his notes. Guess Vince had the votes. Mike pressed both palms to the tabletop. Listening to a seventy-year-old guy defend him made something snap inside him. He had to get out of this room before he wrung Vince's neck.

Herb's eyes went wide with shock. He stared at the mayor. "Fred, you can't go along with this. Mike's a damned good cop and you know it. We don't have anyone to replace him."

Fred didn't look up, but his face reddened. It looked like Vince had his majority.

"Thanks, Herb, but I've got this." Mike stood up. Vince leaned back and crossed his arms over his bony chest.

Mike stared at the councilman's smug face, and all his rational arguments floated right out of his head. His mouth started moving without any consultation with his brain. "You know what, Vince? I'm tired of this bullshit. You've been in my face for the past year. But I'm not going to stop doing my job. You want to get rid of me? You're going to have to fire my ass. But keep in mind, the only people you're hurting are the residents of this town."

The five men sitting at the table were staring at Mike, but he kept his eyes on Vince. Cold fury flickered in his beady buzzard eyes.

Mike couldn't stop. "You've been on my ass since you were elected." Sean's question played over and over in Mike's head as he leaned on the table and loomed over Vince. "I can't help but wonder why. Do you have something to hide?"

Chapter Nineteen

Rachel woke from a fitful sleep. The throb in her shoulder echoed her heartbeat. The room was dark, the old house silent, her bed cold. She glanced at the bedside clock. Not even midnight. The long, empty night loomed ahead. Tears burned in her eyes. Though there was no one to see them fall, she blinked them away anyway. Indulging in weakness was as slippery a slope as pain pills.

But despite the fact that three other people were sleeping just down the hall, the loneliness was as discomforting as the bone-deep ache in her shoulder. But if she resorted to medication now, which would she be suppressing?

She rolled to her side, but a comfortable position evaded her. Ice. She'd try a fresh ice pack.

The muffled purr of an engine came through the closed window.

She eased out of bed and shuffled to the window. The sight of Mike's SUV in the driveway opened a flood of yearning. Memories of his arms around her and that single searing kiss flashed, the one that had warmed her chilled soul.

Her head told her to wait, to think things through, not to make one more impulsive decision.

The sound of nails scrambling on hardwood spurred her into action. She hit the stairs just in time to grab an alerted Bandit by the collar. Downstairs, she snapped a leash on the dog and disengaged the alarm before stepping out the door. Her sweatpants, T-shirt, and bare feet were no match for the autumn night air. Shivering, she hugged her arms and hurried toward his vehicle. He was already getting out by the time she reached it.

"What are you doing? It's cold out here." Ignoring the dog pawing at his knee, he shrugged out of his zip-up hoodie, wrapped it around her, and steered her toward the house. "Your teeth are chattering."

"I was j-just going to tell you to come in."

"You could've waved."

In the kitchen, she burrowed into his jacket. It smelled like his aftershave, like him, and carried the heat from his body.

"I didn't wake you, did I?" Mike locked the door.

"No. I was awake." Rachel went into the pantry to reset the alarm. While she was in there, she grabbed a chew and tossed it to Bandit. The dog caught it on the fly. Mike followed her and stood in the doorway. His bigger body crowded her, but she didn't mind.

"Everything working?" He scanned the blinking control panel.

"Seems to be." She turned to face him. The snug T-shirt outlined his heavy chest and shoulder muscles.

"You look tired. How's the shoulder?"

"I was just going to ice it for a while. You aren't exactly fresh as a daisy."

"That isn't an answer." He frowned. He lifted her chin with a finger and turned her face to scrutinize her cheek.

"The plastic surgeon did a nice job. If you take care of that right, it'll barely show."

"I know. Quinn went over the instructions with me twice."

"What am I going to do with you?" He leaned closer and muttered something that sounded like "just a taste" before his lips settled on hers. Warm and soft, his mouth tasted faintly of mint. There was none of the demand of their first kiss, but a gentleness that had her heart begging for more. His hand cupped her face, and his thumb stroked her jaw in a slow arc. Something that had been tightly clenched unfurled inside her, like a fist opening. She didn't have the strength—or the desire—to fight it. She closed her eyes and let him in. A sense of oneness, completion, belonging, flooded into the empty space inside of her.

He lifted his head a few inches. Her eyelids fluttered open. Shock clouded the soft blue of his eyes. She imagined her own gaze was equally stunned.

"Why did you come?" she whispered against his jaw.

"I don't know. Couldn't sleep." He said she looked tired, but purple half circles underscored his gorgeous eyes. He-Man had had a rough day. A surge of protectiveness rushed through her. She was filled with the desire to find out who was responsible and chew him out.

"Did you get fired?"

"Not yet." But his tone suggested termination was imminent.

"Did you eat?"

He shook his head. Rachel reluctantly moved away from him and opened the refrigerator. "You're in luck. Sarah cooks when she's upset. There's some leftover pasta and vegetables in some sort of white, cheesy sauce. It's good.

Want some?" She reached in and pulled out a Tupperware container.

His hip bumped hers. "I can help myself. You get your icepack. Do you want anything?"

"Some milk would be great." She slid her arms into his jacket. Something dropped out of the pocket. Her shoulder protested as she bent down and picked up the roll of antacids. Mint-flavored. Rachel settled in a kitchen chair with a cold pack over her shoulder. She set the antacids in the middle of the table. "Feeling all right?"

Mike sat down across from her with a bowl of cold leftovers and two glasses of milk. He slid a glass in front of her. "Fine."

"Maybe we aren't as different as I'd thought."

Chewing, Mike shot her a wry grin as he forked down the pasta. She let him eat. A comfortable quiet settled over the kitchen. He finished, then rinsed his bowl and placed it in the dishwasher. "Thanks."

Pain stabbed her as she shifted the ice pack, draping it over her shoulder. Numb wasn't cutting it. With a heavy sigh, she went for a pill.

"Not a fan?" Mike sank back into his chair as she stared the medicine down.

"Not really. My mother was manic-depressive. She abused alcohol and prescription drugs." She didn't elaborate, and he didn't press. But those eyes of his… They knew. "But if I don't get some sleep, I'm going to be even crankier than usual."

He didn't react to the quip. His gaze reflected the pain of her confession. "It won't happen to you."

How did he do that? How did he know what was going on in her head?

"Here's hoping." She washed the pill down with the rest of her milk. "Let's go in the den."

"If you're hitting on me," Mike resisted, "drugged women in pain aren't on my list of turn-ons."

"Get your mind out of the gutter, He-Man. You're hot and everything, but sex is the last thing on my mind tonight." She stopped in front of his chair. The thought of being alone again was a ball of unbearable emptiness behind her breastbone.

"You think I'm hot." He grinned up at her.

Her face heated. "Don't let it go to your head."

"Too late."

She took his hand and tugged on it. He hesitated, so she used his own tactic against him. On her empty stomach, the medicine was taking effect quickly—and lowering her inhibitions. She should go to bed before she started blathering. "Please. You can sleep on the couch."

"The couch?"

"Sorry. Kids upstairs."

"Ah, kids." He stood and removed his gun from its holster, then unloaded the weapon and shoved the clip into his pocket. He held up the empty gun. "Do you have something that locks?"

She led him into the den, grabbed the tiny key for her desk, and handed it to him. "Bottom drawer."

She fetched a pillow and blanket from the closet while Mike closed the curtains. He tested the couch. The ice on her shoulder made her shiver, and she zipped up his jacket.

He patted the cushion next to him. "Come here."

"Just for a minute." She eased onto the sofa and leaned into him. His arm wrapped around her. Her face pressed against the hard planes of his chest. Her hand rested against his stomach, the muscles rippled and tight. She'd known he was huge and fit, but the abs under her palm were ripped in a major league man-candy kind of way. What would it feel like to snuggle up against him naked?

Maybe sex wasn't the absolute last thing on her mind.

"How are Sarah and the girls?" he asked.

"Good as can be expected. I'd feel better if they had somewhere else to stay." Though the stalker seemed more interested in her, she hated the thought of her sister or nieces getting in his way or getting hurt because of her.

"No other family to help out?"

Hell no. There was no way Sarah would ever take her children to their father's house. Dad made Troy look like a teetotaler. "Families can be complicated."

"Wouldn't know."

"No family?"

"None close." He let his head fall back. "I'm an only child of two only children."

"Parents?"

"They're both gone." His voice went hoarse.

"I'm sorry." She didn't ask any more questions, and he didn't offer any more explanation. The sadness in his tone was enough.

In the calm silence, Mike's torso relaxed under her. She raised her head. His eyes were closed. His wide chest rose and fell in an even rhythm. Even in sleep, his face was tight with worry. He was that kind of guy. Sleep would be no excuse to relinquish his responsibilities.

She should go to bed. Break this connection that exhaustion and stress made them both unable to deny. But she couldn't do it. She snuggled deeper, her muscles softening, the pain and her defenses sliding away. He made her feel safe, and not just in a physical way. He accepted her for what she was.

Not many people did.

⁓

Predawn mist shrouded the forest. The woods smelled of earth, decaying leaves, and wood smoke. The chilly bite of autumn was cold enough to invigorate without being uncomfortable, which was a good thing. Once he got settled, he'd be sitting still for quite some time. Indian summer was a blessing. The day was forecast to be warm.

Hunting took patience, and just like everything else in life, discipline was the key to success.

The tree, scoped out in advance, was perfect. Medium-sized trunk. The lower section clear of branches. Enough foliage above for concealment. And best of all: a perfect line of sight for today's observation. He had to see Rachel discover the gift he'd left her.

The Watcher raised his knees and drew the lower platform of his climbing stand upward. Pushing down with his feet, he set the platform against the trunk. The rear bar dug into the bark. Repeating the process, he worked his way up the tree foot by foot, like a vertical inchworm.

Twenty feet off the ground, he reached the lower branches and let the autumn foliage settle around him. The clerk at the outdoor store had been right. This camouflage print was perfect for fall hunts. From fifty feet away, he'd be practically invisible. No one could see him at a distance of two hundred yards.

He lifted his camera from his chest and adjusted the focus until he could see the individual stones in the old farmhouse. Rachel was going to have a big surprise, and he was going to catch every frame.

Chapter Twenty

Hot dog breath wafted across Rachel's face. She cracked an eyelid. Tail wagging, tongue lolling, Bandit stood on the bed, his masked muzzle inches from her nose.

Three things occurred to Rachel as she scratched the dog behind the ears. One, her bedroom was fully lit, meaning she'd overslept. Two, she was still wearing Mike's jacket. She pressed the soft fabric against her face and inhaled his comforting scent. He must have carried her up to bed at some point during the night, and dammit, she'd missed it. And three, she didn't hurt nearly as badly as she'd expected. Cotton-mouthed, she squinted at the bedside clock. No wonder. It was ten freaking o'clock. She'd slept for nine hours straight.

She lifted her clock and inspected it. Someone had switched off the alarm. Mike. Grrr. Words would be exchanged on that topic later. But for now, there was work that needed to be done. Cripes, the horses hadn't been fed or watered.

She shuffled into the bathroom. Cold water on her face helped with the pain med hangover, but stiffness made getting dressed a challenge. Something banged from downstairs. Bandit jumped off the bed and trotted off. Dog nails clattered down the wood treads and faded away. By the time her bare feet crossed the duct-taped seam of the kitchen floor, her shoulder had loosened to a tolerable dull ache. As long as she didn't do anything too stupid today, it should continue to improve.

"Oh, you're up. Good timing." Sarah opened the oven. The aged metal door squeaked. Using a dish towel as an oven mitt, she removed a pan of muffins and set them on a stove top burner to cool. At her feet, Bandit stared up hopefully.

The scent made Rachel's mouth water. "Blueberry?"

"Uh-huh."

Snap!

Sarah pulled a mug from the cabinet. "Coffee? I've just made a fresh pot."

Rachel shook her head. "No time. I have to get down to the barn."

"Uhm." Sarah picked at her cast. "No rush on that."

"What do you mean, no rush?" Suspicion flared. "The horses haven't been fed."

"Yeah. Actually they have."

"What?" Rachel shoved her feet into a pair of sneakers by the door. "Who? Mike?"

"Not exactly. He left really early. Was he here all night?" Sarah waggled her eyebrows comically.

"Oh, geez. Nothing happened. He was parked in the driveway around midnight. I thought that was dumb and let him sleep on the couch." Rachel reached for the knob. "What do you mean, not exactly?"

"I'm not getting into this one." Sarah grabbed Bandit's collar.

Rachel closed the door on the comment. The sky was a cloudless azure. The air, unnaturally warm and still for the season, had an eerie buzz that portended a change in the weather pattern. The sun's rays warmed her back as she crossed the back lawn. In contrast, the barn was cool, dim, and empty. All the horses had been turned out. The aisle was freshly raked. She stuck her head into the first stall. Clean and bedded with sweet-smelling straw. Her shoulder practically sang with relief. Feeding wouldn't be too difficult, but she hadn't figured out how she was going to manage a pitchfork one-handed.

"Oh, hi." A lean, wiry young man was pushing her wheelbarrow through the back door. From the hard lines around his eyes, he was probably over eighteen, but with all those freckles the kid would be carded till he was thirty-five.

"Who are you?"

"I'm Brandon." He wiped his hand on his jeans and held it out. "Brandon Sandler."

Rachel shook it. "Who sent you here, Brandon?"

"Chief O'Connell, ma'am. He said I should do everything for you."

"Really?"

"Yes, ma'am. The horses are fed and watered." Brandon parked the wheelbarrow in front of a stall. He picked up the pitchfork leaning against the wall and went inside. A forkful of manure landed in the rusty tray. "I have a couple of more stalls to clean. Then you'll have to tell me what else you need done."

What the hell? How presumptuous was the cop going to get? Even with Lady's sale, Rachel's cash flow didn't warrant hired help. The retainer for Sarah's attorney was due that afternoon. She owned the property free and clear, but there were taxes, insurance, utilities, and operating expenses to pay. Her truck was a MacGyver special. Plus, she had Sarah and the girls to support. Growing kids couldn't live on Pop-Tarts and Ramen noodles. "Brandon, I'm sorry. I can't afford you. I'll pay you for the hours you put in this morning, but you'll have to go home."

"I can't do that, ma'am. Promised the chief I'd stay." More dirty straw hit the wheelbarrow. "He already paid me for the week. You don't have to worry about that."

"Do you do everything the chief says?" Rachel was torn over Mike's meddling. On one hand, he was bossy and presumptuous and controlling, three personality traits she found highly annoying. And yes, she was perfectly aware that she exhibited all three of those behaviors on a regular basis. On the flip side, the knowledge that he cared brought back that melty feeling.

Dammit.

"Yes, ma'am." He stopped, planted the tines of the pitchfork into the dirt at his feet, and leaned on the handle. He leveled warm, honest brown eyes at her. The gaze was too sad and old for his youthful face. "I was in some trouble last year. Totally fu—messed up. Quit school and did some other things I'm not proud of." He stared at his worn Timberlands for a few seconds. "If it weren't for the chief, I'd be in jail right now. So if he asks me to stay here, I'm staying." He went back to cleaning the stall.

Any irritation she'd felt for Mike drained like water from a bathtub.

Brandon pushed the full wheelbarrow out the back of the barn and brought it back empty a minute later. "What should I do after I finish the stalls?"

Rachel's stomach rumbled. Sarah's blueberry muffins and a cup of coffee were calling her name. "Can you ride?"

"Yes, ma'am."

"How well?"

Brandon stopped and wiped sweat from his forehead with the sleeve of his long-sleeved tee. "Well enough." His eyes lit with interest—and regret. "We used to breed quarter horses, before we lost our farm. I did a lot of reining and roping"

"Miss your horses?"

"Every day." He tucked his thumbs into the front pockets of his threadbare jeans.

"Think you can make the switch to an English saddle?"

"Don't see why not. Grew up riding with no saddle at all."

Hot damn. If the kid were going to work his butt off doing all the cruddy farm chores, Rachel was going to make sure his day was balanced. He missed horses? He was going to get his fill of them.

"In that case, I have a couple of horses that need to be exercised. I'm going to grab some breakfast while you finish up here." Rachel grinned. "Then we're going to have some fun."

Sarah wasn't in the kitchen when Rachel poured coffee and grabbed a still-warm muffin. She sank into a chair. Bandit put his shaggy paws on her knee and begged. How long had it been since she didn't have a to-do list a mile long?

Sarah had her purse over her shoulder and her keys in her hand when she walked back into the kitchen. "I have to go."

"Oh, that's right. You're meeting the lawyer this morning. Do you want me to go with you?"

"No. I need to handle it on my own. Blake's lawyer seemed pretty sharp over the phone." Except for the cast on her arm, Sarah looked almost back to normal. The swelling on her face had receded, and she'd covered the fading bruises with makeup. "The girls are still at preschool. Mrs. Holloway will bring them home at noon. Betty from King's Saddle Shop called. That bit you ordered is in. How's your shoulder?"

"Not bad." Nine hours of sleep had worked wonders.

Sarah left. Without all the noise of the alarm installers, the house was uncomfortably quiet. Rachel drank coffee and ate another muffin. She looked down at Bandit, who was licking a crumb off the floor.

"I'm bored."

Unconcerned, Bandit stretched out in a sun patch and closed his eyes. She should emulate the dog, but rest and relaxation weren't her strengths. Brandon wasn't going to be finished for at least an hour. Plenty of time to run down to King's and pick up that bit. She stopped at the barn to let Brandon know she'd be back in half an hour.

"I could do that for you later," he offered.

"No thanks." She turned toward the truck. "I might as well make myself useful."

"But—"

Rachel waved off his protest, drove into town, and cruised down Main Street. She glanced in the rearview mirror. A monster truck was right on her bumper. The sun reflected off the truck's windshield, obscuring her view of the driver. She tapped her brakes, but the truck didn't back off. She made a quick left onto Fourth Street. The truck continued down Main with the roar of a powerful V-8.

Rachel passed the large restored colonials near Westbury's miniscule business section. Houses were less fancy as she drew away from the town center. She made a few more turns onto a deserted side street. The tack shop occupied the first floor of a tall, narrow two-story in need of a complete renovation. In the less affluent outskirts of town, the lots were too small and the houses too close together for driveways. Vehicles lined the street. She parked at the curb half a block down and walked back to the store. Less than ten minutes later, she was back at the pickup, bit in hand.

She dug in her purse for her keys. A hand on her arm spun her around. "Ow." Pain shot through her shoulder.

"Hello, bitch."

Her smart retort never left her lips. Rachel's back slammed into the side of the truck. The breath left her lungs in a hard whoosh. Her leather purse hit the asphalt with a jingle.

"Hey," she yelled. "Get off me."

A hard male body pressed her flat against the cold metal. Will Martin's angry navy blue eyes glared down at her. He pressed his palms against the roof of her truck on either side of her head and used his hips to pin her in place.

A surge of anger helped Rachel recover the ability to breathe. "What do you want?"

"Just conveying a message." Will's upper lip curled like a pissed off, ugly version of Elvis. "You mess with my pal. You mess with me."

"Really?" Rachel squirmed, trying to open up some space to maneuver between their bodies. She glanced around, but the small side street was empty. No one had heard her shout.

"Really." Will ground his erection into her belly. He glared down at her, dark blue eyes full of malice and excitement. "You're going to be sorry for what you did to Troy."

☞

Mike parked his truck outside the county morgue. He squinted against the morning sun that glared off the glass doors of the Lark County Municipal Complex. He really hated visiting the morgue. The place gave him the creeps, taking his phobia of all things medical to an exponential level.

Greg was already in the autopsy suite. Mike donned gown, booties, and mask, then pushed through the glass door. The skeleton was bare bones, but the smell of raw meat lingered in the autopsy suite, mingled with the sharp sting of formalin that never failed to make Mike's stomach dry-heave. He never came here with a full belly. He hadn't even risked water this morning.

Mike kept his eyes off the array of morbid tools behind glass-doored cabinets. The bones were laid out in a disjoined human shape on a stainless steel table. A few gaps represented pieces not recovered. Standing over the remains with a clipboard, Greg looked more mad scientist than doctor behind a plastic face shield.

"Hey, Greg."

"Mike." Greg stepped back and made a notation. "We found about ninety-five percent of him. Missing some of the small bones. That's not bad, considering the evidence of rodent activity in the area."

Mike banished visions of mice stealing fingers and toes from his head. He also made a mental note to put some mousetraps in Rachel's basement. "So, what can you tell me?"

Greg pointed a gloved finger at the pelvic cavity. "The victim is an adult male, as shown by the narrow pelvis and thick skull, no pun intended. The pubic junction straightens with age. From the degree of curvature, I'd cap his age around fifty, probably a bit less." Greg tapped on the skull. "Caucasian. Had a decent amount of dental work, so probably not homeless."

He moved lower, to the femur, and indicated the lower end of the thigh bone. "Growth plates are completely closed, and with the pitting of the ribs, he was at least thirty at time of death. He has one healed fracture of the left tibia."

"He was about five-nine, give or take an inch." The coroner scanned the skeleton. "Bones on the right side are slightly thicker, so he was likely right-handed. Slight to average stature. You probably have femurs the size of tree trunks." Beneath his clear plastic mask, Greg's eyes laughed. "Not that I ever want to find out."

Mike wiped his palms and suppressed the image of himself on Greg's table. "Can you tell me anything else about the remains?"

Greg pointed to a groove in one of the lower ribs. "This nick here could be the fatal injury. Knife to the gut. Or not. It's really impossible to tell. I see no other signs of unhealed trauma on the bones. I'm sending the bones to Dr. McCall, the forensic anthropologist at the university. She'll be able to give you more information and a much better estimate on how long he's been down there. I'll let you know when the report comes in, or if I get any results on the testing of the plastic sheet or the soil and bug samples."

Those reports could come back in a month or a year. Remains this old didn't get top priority at the hopelessly underfunded and overloaded labs. "What about identifying him?"

"I have X-rays on file if you can come up with any dental records to match. Teeth and large bones are in excellent shape, so mitochondrial DNA is another possibility, but again, you have to have something to match. If all else fails, we have facial reconstruction, real and virtual."

"So you dragged me all the way down here to tell me my victim was a middle-aged, average-sized white guy who's been dead an unspecified number of years?"

Greg flashed him a wicked smile. "Well, this might come in handy."

The coroner produced an evidence bag. Nestled inside was a ring. Mike bent closer and squinted at the engraved words surrounding a deep red stone. Well, that narrowed things down significantly. He pulled out his cell phone and snapped a picture of the ring.

Westbury High School. Class of 1973.

His victim was a local.

Chapter Twenty-One

Back in his vehicle, Mike headed back toward Westbury. A few miles outside town, his phone buzzed in his pocket. The number on the display was the disposable cell he'd given Brandon that morning.

"What's up?"

"Chief, I'm sorry." Brandon hesitated, and Mike's heart lurched. "She left."

"What do you mean, she left? I told you to keep her there."

"She kind of does what she wants, sir."

"No kidding." Mike stepped on the gas pedal. "Where did she go?"

Five minutes later he braked in front of the tack shop. Will Martin's oversized ego of a pickup was parked at the curb. Mike cruised down the street and spotted them ahead. Will had Rachel pinned to the side of her truck. His hands caged her in. Her feet were trapped between his widespread cowboy boots. Rachel had something silver and shiny in one hand. Will was rubbing his crotch up and down obscenely against her stomach.

Fury, fresh and hot, gathered in Mike's chest. Finally, he was a witness to the creep's crime. If Will hurt her…

Mike floored his SUV and called for backup. The big ape moved one hairy hand to squeeze Rachel's breast. Mike's red-edged vision tunneled down to the two figures. He reached for the siren just as Rachel swung out with a right hook. Silver flashed in her hand. Will clutched the side of his head and staggered backward two steps. Her front snap kick caught him right between the legs. Will dropped to the ground like a hairy sandbag. His hands fell from his head to his groin.

Mike stomped on the brake and slammed the gearshift into park. He jumped out of the truck. His own testicles crawled up inside his body as he watched a gray-faced Will heaving on the concrete.

"You fucking bitch!" Will made a sick retching sound. "I'll get you. I know where you live."

Rachel leaned on her truck. Freckles stood in stark relief on a face as pale as skimmed milk, but those eyes were brimming with fire.

Mike cuffed the groaning man in the street, then stepped up to Rachel. He wanted to pull her into his arms. But he couldn't, not in public, especially not with Will as an audience. "You all right?"

"Yeah." Despite the jutting chin and fiery glare, her voice shook.

"Did he hurt you?" Mike glanced back at Will, who hadn't moved from his fetal position.

She was going to say she was fine. He knew it. "Let me rephrase that. Do you need to go to the ER?"

She shook her head.

"Would you be willing to press charges against him?"

A fighter through and through, she pushed away from the truck and straightened her spine. "Of course."

Satisfaction welled as he took her statement. Mike had been trying to get Will on sexual assault charges for years. Like a true predator, Will picked his victims well, usually choosing women who were too timid to stand up to him. Until today.

She turned toward her vehicle. Mike couldn't help but admire both the fit of her faded jeans over her muscular legs and the courage with which she'd recovered. With a sigh he turned back to the prostrate Will and hauled him to his feet just as Ethan pulled up in his cruiser.

Mike loaded Will into the back of the police vehicle. "You picked the wrong woman to assault."

"Is that a threat?"

Mike closed the door. "Take him in, Ethan."

Rachel climbed into the driver's seat. Adrenaline ebbed, and her shoulder, forgotten during the moment, throbbed anew. She drove back to the farm on autopilot, cranking up the heat to banish the shakes.

She drove away from town, the isolation and serenity of the green around her soothing. She wasn't meant to live that close to other people. She needed space. Lots of it. Not just the physical kind.

The truck parked itself by the house. Sarah's minivan wasn't back. A glance at her cell told her that the girls weren't due for another hour. Work was the best therapy.

Brandon had finished cleaning stalls and was repairing a broken section of fence.

Rachel pointed out a sleek chestnut gelding grazing in the pasture. "Why don't you start with him?"

The well-tempered chestnut greeted the kid with a friendly nose bump before following him to the gate. Rachel inspected every inch of the tack, then took a seat on a bale of straw in the aisle while Brandon brushed and saddled the horse with practiced efficiency. She followed the pair outside and leaned on a fence rail. Once aboard, Brandon's relaxed posture and balanced seat testified to experience and innate ability. He looked like she felt on the back of a horse. Like that was where he belonged and everything else he did was just passing time. Like climbing on that horse's back made all the misery in his life fade away. A small pang of loss sliced through her. She would never experience that ease again. For her, riding was tainted by pain, guilt, and worry, and for a few seconds she almost wished she'd never sat on her first pony.

Because you couldn't miss what you never had.

Which made her think about Mike and the way his presence and touch made everything easier to bear.

Rachel shook it off. Ninety percent of the good memories in her life were tied to horses. Without them, her youth would've been vastly more miserable.

Rachel sent Brandon off to lap the meadow a few times and adjust to the new saddle. She needn't have bothered. The kid looked like he'd be comfortable upside down or sideways on top of a horse.

She could do something with this kid. So, she would never jump again. The thrill and the rush were a thing of her past. She still knew her stuff. Working with a talented student could be the answer. It wasn't like she could never sit on a horse again. She just had to be sensible about it.

Dammit, she hated being sensible.

Brandon finished with the chestnut and took the gray out for a spin. Rachel had no worries the horse could get away with any of his shenanigans. Shadow Dancer sensed that he'd been bested while he was being groomed on the cross-ties. With Brandon on his back, the normally boisterous horse behaved like a school pony. By the time Rachel left Brandon cooling the horse out, satisfaction had wiped away the memory of Will's attack.

Tomorrow she'd see how the kid handled some low jumps. If he did well, Brandon was going to get a big break.

The sound of an approaching vehicle signaled Sarah's return. Her sister's minivan turned into the drive and parked by the house. Rachel's stomach growled. She checked her cell. Lunchtime had breezed by. Brandon hadn't eaten either.

"When you're finished cooling him out, come up to the house for a sandwich."

"Yes, ma'am."

"And I really appreciate all the help."

Brandon flushed. "I love working with the horses. My schedule is clear until the weekend. The house my family is renting is on low ground. We're going to stay with some family until the flood risk passes."

They both glanced at the darkening horizon. Clouds rolling down from the mountain marked the end of the sunshine. A humid breeze rustled through the surrounding woods. Shivering, Rachel zipped up as she strode down the driveway to the mailbox. She opened the metal flap. Something buzzed, and Rachel froze. A swarm of pissed-off bees poured out of the mailbox and hovered around her.

Mike's butt hadn't even hit his chair before Nancy appeared in the doorway with a whole-grain bagel in one hand and a bottle of water in the other.

"Figured you didn't eat before going to the morgue."

"Thanks." Mike's stomach rumbled, and his head ached from lack of sleep. He kept glancing at the door, expecting to see Fred come in with a pink slip. "Is there coffee?"

"Not for you there isn't." His secretary picked up a pile of signed forms from his outbox. "Think I haven't noticed the gallon of antacid in your drawer?"

Mike sighed and twisted the cap off the water bottle. "Anything important happen this morning?"

"No. There was a minor accident on Main Street, two ten-year-olds set off firecrackers behind the school, and we had a barking dog complaint. You hogged all the excitement. Wish I could've seen Miss Parker lay Will out." She made a punching gesture with one liver-spotted fist.

"It was a sight." But Mike worried that Will's ego could prompt him to seek retribution.

Nancy tilted her head and stared at him like she was working her daily crossword puzzle.

"What?"

"Is Fred right?" she asked. "Do you have something going on with her?"

That was a damned good question, and he didn't ask how she knew about the clandestine council meeting. Nancy knew everything. She'd been secretary to the chief of police for almost thirty years, and Mike was convinced the church ladies' organization she belonged to was more effective than a covert intelligence agency.

"I'm not sure."

"You'd better give it some thought. You're not getting any younger."

"Thanks for pointing that out."

"Oh, stop." She waved off his comment. "You're alone too much. A man your age should have something in his life besides work."

Mike couldn't argue with that. "Rachel is...difficult."

"Easy is boring. Any woman who flattens Will Martin's family jewels gets my vote. Your mother was no pushover."

"No, she wasn't." His mom had hung tough right up till the end.

"Lord, if you're going to have any kids, you'd better get a move on." Nancy punctuated the statement with an emphatic nod. "You are not getting any younger."

Mike choked on his water.

Ethan popped his head in, bright and eager as a puppy with a ball. "It's a good day when we get to arrest Will Martin."

"Don't get too excited. I'm sure he'll be out on bail pretty quick," Mike warned.

Ethan's enthusiasm couldn't be dimmed. "So, what'd the ME say?"

Mike waved Ethan toward a chair and pulled the photo of the high school ring up on his phone. "They found this under the body."

Ethan looked at the picture, then passed the phone back. "That should narrow things down."

"I'm going to need you to start pulling missing person's reports. We'll start with 1980 through 1990. Cross-reference with the graduating class of 1973. Assuming the ring belonged to the victim, this can't be that hard. Westbury High only graduates like a hundred kids a year." Mike lifted the bagel. "Most of our missing persons are runaways. Except for the occasional errant spouse, not many middle-aged adults disappear."

"Ah, Chief?" Ethan interrupted, his zeal visibly diming. "Records before 1990 were stored in the basement of the municipal building."

"Ugh." Mike had forgotten. Everything in town hall's basement was toast. Soggy toast. What the fire hadn't torched, the water had trashed.

"Actually, only closed cases were kept over there," Nancy corrected. "If the body just turned up, this case is technically cold, not closed. We *should* have the file in the back room."

Ethan rose.

"Did you say the 1980s?" Nancy leaned over Mike's shoulder. "What did Greg have to say?"

"Victim was a middle-aged Caucasian male."

Nancy stared at the photo of the ring. "Oh, my goodness. I'll bet you found that missing carpenter."

"Excuse me?"

"His name was…" Nancy put one hand on her hip, the other on her chin, and looked up as if the answer were written on the dropped ceiling tiles. "Boyle. Harry Boyle. He disappeared in the late eighties. Phil Bitten had just been hired as chief. It was his first big case, and the case itself was very strange. Boyle vanished under very unusual circumstances. Phil worked that case for months but got nowhere."

"I'll go look for that file." Ethan headed for the door.

In the outer office, a phone rang. Nancy followed Ethan out. "Files from the eighties are stored in the cabinets on the far left wall. They're clearly labeled."

Of course they were.

Ethan returned minutes later, flapping a manila file folder in one hand. He handed the file to Mike. "Got it."

Mike scanned the initial report. Harry Boyle was a Caucasian male of average height.

"Give the ME a call. Let's see if we can confirm our vic-tim's ID."

Once Ethan was dispatched with his next chore, Mike flipped through pages, his instincts waking to the oddities of the case.

Harry disappeared in February of 1987. The night of his disappearance, his house had burned to the ground. The cause of the fire was listed officially as accidental. Harry had been renovating. The place had been cluttered with con-tainers of flammable chemicals, and Harry Boyle had been a smoker. With no close neighbors, by the time firefighters responded to a call from a passing motorist, the entire place was nearly consumed. It wasn't until the fire investigators went through the rubble that they realized Harry's body wasn't inside.

With no body, murder hadn't been assumed, though the police hadn't found any reason a gainfully employed, reportedly content carpenter would abandon everything he owned and take off. Except for a reasonable mortgage on his house, Harry hadn't been in any debt. Payments on the house were current. No evidence of gambling debts or drug use had been discovered, and his Jeep was missing from the undamaged detached garage.

Could that be the same Jeep they'd pulled from Lost Lake? Mike made a notation to have Ethan find out.

Mike flipped through several pages of notes. The unease burrowing into his gut went ballistic.

There was no way this could be a coincidence.

Chapter Twenty-Two

Mike looked up as Nancy stuck her head through the doorway. Worry thinned her lips, and anger hardened her eyes. Something was up. Something bad. "Fred's here to see you."

She moved aside, and the mayor darkened Mike's doorway. Fred slunk into the office, shutting the door behind him. Mike closed the Boyle file and set it aside.

Fred stood on the opposite side of Mike's desk. "Will Martin claims you roughed him up and threatened him. He's suing you and the town."

"You believe Will Martin?"

"What I believe isn't important. You've already shown your judgment in this case is clouded by your personal feelings for Miss Parker. If you apologize to Will Martin and get her to drop the charges against him, he'll withdraw his lawsuit."

"One, I'm not apologizing to Martin. That would imply guilt, and I haven't done anything." Mike held the mayor's gaze. "Second, this is my department. Not only will we encourage Miss Parker to file charges, we will continue to protect her. She's in danger. The last time we had a violent predator on the loose, a woman died. Remember?"

Fred shifted his eyes to the wall over Mike's head. "Then we have no choice but to suspend you until the council can conduct a thorough review of your actions."

Mike didn't move for a minute, waiting for the news to hit him, but the moment was surreal. Even though he'd known this was coming, he was unable to process the actuality. Mike stood. He reached for his hip, pulling his gun from its hip holster. He unloaded the weapon and set it on the desk. He dropped his badge next to it on the blotter.

"You'd give up your job for her?"

Apparently, he would. Without hesitation. "I'm disappointed in you, Fred."

The mayor flushed. "You're the one who broke the rules."

"Really? Are you sure about that? Or is Vince using you? Have you asked yourself why he wants me out of this office so badly?"

Fred's bony face flushed. He clenched his sagging jaw and stared out the window.

Mike grabbed his jacket and headed for the door. Ignoring the town-issued SUV, he walked the half dozen blocks to his house. The sun still heated his back, but a damp breeze warned of the incoming rain. He walked through the front door directly to the bedroom and shed his uniform in exchange for jeans and a T-shirt. Next he opened the gun vault in his closet. His personal piece, a nine millimeter Glock nearly identical to his service weapon, filled the empty holster on his belt. A loose hoodie concealed the weapon. Just because he'd been suspended didn't mean he wasn't going to protect Rachel. He'd always followed the rules, and look where that had gotten him. He was suspended while the guy who was willing to fight dirty was still sitting on the town council. Vince was up to something. Sean was right. But what? And why was it so important to get Mike out of the picture?

Only one way to find out. The hell with the rules. He typed out a quick text to Sean.

CAN U GET FINANCIALS ON VINCE?

The answer came back almost immediately. NO PROBLEM.

Next question. How was Rachel connected to a twenty-five-year-old murder? If the dates of Harry's disappearance were correct, she was about six when he was killed. If only Mike had had the time to completely review the file.

Mike's phone buzzed. Nancy. Mike put the cell to his ear.

"We just got a call from the Parker farm. Thought you'd want to know. Pete's on duty, but he's doing a drive-by at Lost Lake. Fred's orders. It'll take him a little while to get out there."

"Thanks, Nancy." Mike grabbed a jacket, jogged into the garage, and stopped at the sight of his disassembled Mustang. "Shit!"

"What's wrong?"

"Nancy, I don't want you to do anything that jeopardizes your job."

"I'm thinking of retiring anyway. Might as well start a mutiny on my way out. I'm not working for Fred. That's for sure. What do you need?"

"A car."

"I knew you wouldn't just walk away." Pride came through her voice. "I'll be there in a few."

"Thanks. You're the best."

"I know." Nancy chuckled.

Her white LeSabre pulled up in front of Mike's house in six minutes. Nancy got out. "Don't let anything happen to that girl of yours."

He opened his mouth to deny that she was his, but the words wouldn't come out. Mike slid behind the wheel.

She stepped up onto the sidewalk. "Now go. I'll walk back."

Mike pulled away from the curb. Suspension his ass. He'd be fired before the week was out. He could feel it with the same certainty that the green blotch on the weather map meant flooding was on the way. At the corner, he turned left, away from town and toward Rachel's farm.

Was she really OK? And how would she react when he dropped the bomb about the identity of the skeleton?

☙

Rachel backed away inches at a time. Her heart galloped away at the pace her feet wanted to follow.

"I don't have Mike's number, so I called the police station." Sarah stepped out of the minivan. "Stay inside, girls." She closed the vehicle door.

Rachel didn't respond. She was busy fighting her instinct to run like hell. Her legs were shaking with the effort of going slow. The swarm was circling. Her skin itched as the insane buzzing grew louder. Pulse pounding, she slid a sneaker another two inches backward on the grass. Even with her EpiPen, one sting could send her to the ER.

How many bees were in that swarm? A hundred. More than enough to kill her before she ever got to the hospital, that was for sure.

Rachel continued to backpedal in super slow motion. The bees didn't seem to notice her, but she was sweating by the time she reached her sister's vehicle.

"Are you all right?" Inside the minivan with the door securely closed, Sarah scanned Rachel's face and arms.

"I'm fine."

"No stings?"

Rachel took stock. "Not a single one."

"Thank God," Sarah exhaled.

"Where are you going?"

"I don't know, but you can't be here."

"That's ridiculous. They're not even near the house." Equal parts relief and nausea flooded Rachel. She leaned her head against the window. A faint tap startled her. She jolted upright and turned. On the other side of the glass, two bees hovered inches from her face.

"No way. Too risky." Sarah started the engine.

The insects buzzed around the side mirror, and Rachel wiped her sweaty palms on her jeans.

A white four-door pulled into the drive. Mike was behind the wheel. He lowered his window. Sarah shook her head. Rachel dug her cell out of her pocket and dialed Mike's number.

He answered the call. "What happened?"

Through the minivan's side window, Rachel watched the lines around his mouth deepen as she explained the situation.

"How allergic are you?"

"Allergic enough."

"You're sure you didn't get stung?" Concern creased his face.

"Positive. I'm still breathing."

The worry lines deepened to trenches for a minute before Mike's face smoothed out. "Wonderful. I'll call someone to collect those bees. Any idea how they got there?"

"I assume someone left them for me."

A police cruiser pulled into the drive.

"I'll call you." Mike hung up. The cruiser pulled up next, and both men stepped out of their vehicles. The lieutenant, with his short, square body, was the sidekick to Mike's superhero.

Wait. Mike wasn't in uniform. And why wasn't he driving his township SUV? He must have been fired—because of her.

Sarah turned the minivan toward Mrs. Holloway's house. Rachel sank into the passenger seat with the knowledge that she'd hurt yet another good man. Her life was sinking fast. She had no business dragging him down with her.

⁀

Mike stood next to his lieutenant watching the elderly beekeeper don protective white coveralls a few yards away.

"So you're saying that whoever left this box here did it intentionally, knowing that Miss Parker was allergic to bees." Pete propped his hands on his hips.

"Only thing that makes sense."

"That's creepy." Pete's jowls quivered as he shook his head.

The beekeeper zipped up his suit and walked over to the bees. He had a spray bottle in one hand and a white box in the other. He set the box on the ground, then moved a few feet away and sprayed the air, letting the mist drift over the bees on the wind. A few minutes later, bee guy returned to the driveway. He pulled off the big hood, revealing a sun-spotted, wrinkled face. "It looks like someone broke a chunk of a hive off and stuffed it into the mailbox. What kind of a person would do such a thing?"

"I don't know." Mike's instincts were coiling tighter and tighter.

"A sicko, that's who." Pete adjusted his utility belt under his paunch.

Someone had tried to kill Rachel in a very devious way. What if she'd been stung numerous times? Would she have even survived?

The beekeeper nodded seriously. "It's terrible. This close to winter, the entire hive will probably die. Those bees will have no time to repair the damage."

Mike had no words. Pete coughed.

The beekeeper lowered the mesh screen over his face. "It shouldn't take me too long to capture these bees. They're disoriented and, hopefully, will go for the food right away. I'll save as many as I can."

"We'll leave you to it, then." Mike turned away and took a few steps. The sight of Nancy's Buick, and the emptiness in his chest, reminded him that he wasn't in charge anymore. "I'm sorry, Pete."

"It's all right. I don't like this any more than you do. The mayor better give this some hard thought. Nancy is pissed." Pete scratched his neck. "I'm going to interview Miss Parker now. Will you come along? I read over the file the other day, but you know the situation much better than I do."

Mike grinned. "You sure you want to risk irritating Fred?"

"He can't fire us all."

Pete followed Mike to Mrs. Holloway's farmhouse. They climbed the wide steps to the freshly swept porch. Mrs. Holloway opened the door before Mike could knock.

"Michael, please come in." The older woman stepped aside and ushered them into the hall. At less than five feet tall, she was just as imposing as when she'd taught him in fourth grade. Back then, her curls had been more brown than gray and her frame more substantial.

"Rachel's in the kitchen." Mrs. Holloway's veined hand grasped Mike's forearm. "You're going to keep her safe, right?"

"Yes, ma'am," Mike answered.

The older woman nodded, relieved. "Good." She patted his arm and whispered, "I know she comes off as brusque, but down deep, Rachel is a total softie."

Pete scraped his boots on the mat. They passed the living room, where Sarah and her girls were working a puzzle. In the kitchen, Rachel sat at the long farmhouse table. She clutched a mug in her hands.

"Do either of you want tea?" Mrs. Holloway asked.

"No, ma'am," Mike and Pete answered in unison.

"Then, I'll leave you to it." Mrs. Holloway left the room.

Mike took the seat next to Rachel. "I have to tell you that I've been suspended. Lieutenant Winters is taking over your case."

Clearly uncomfortable, Pete elected to stand behind one of the ladder-back chairs. "Miss Parker."

Rachel looked up, her face bleak as she nodded her acknowledgement.

Pete continued. "Will's bail hasn't been processed yet. He didn't leave the bees in your mailbox."

"What about Troy?" Her voice was distant.

"I don't think it was him either. I called over to the store. A dozen people can place him there all morning. Not just his family. Regular folks."

SHE CAN TELL 241

"Oh." She sipped her drink.

At Pete's glance, Mike jumped in. "Let's talk about your stalker. How many people know you're allergic to bees?"

"I have no idea."

"David?" Mike asked.

She shrugged. "Probably. I've been allergic since I was a kid, and his family lived next door to mine."

"How about Blake Webb?"

"Definitely."

Her quick answer gave Mike a quick jolt of jealousy. She and Blake had been tight. Blake knew personal things about her. Things Mike didn't know. "Cristan Rojas?"

"Unlikely." She wrinkled her nose. "I barely know the man."

But that didn't mean that Rojas hadn't made it his business to learn everything about Rachel. That's what stalkers did.

"Is there anyone else who could hold a grudge against you?"

"No." Of course, she'd said that before and look what had happened. Mike switched tack. "Does the name Harry Boyle ring any bells?"

"Maybe." Rachel's brow wrinkled as she concentrated. "It sounds familiar, but I'm not sure from where."

"Harry Boyle was a carpenter."

"Why should I know his name?"

"Because I think the skeleton in your basement is Harry Boyle, and he used to work for your father."

Rachel paled. "I don't understand."

"I didn't get a chance to read the entire file, but Harry Boyle worked as a carpenter for Parker Construction. In 1987, his house burned down and Harry disappeared."

"Do you know how he died?" Her voiced dropped to a whisper.

"No, but unless he crawled into that room, rolled himself in a plastic tarp, and sealed the entrance from the outside, Harry was murdered."

Chapter Twenty-Three

Phyllis Holloway watched the Buick pull out of her driveway. The sedan hadn't even cleared the stones before she
reached for her address book. Her finger slid down the
alphabetical index along the edge of the book. She flipped
to the letter W. Whelan. Nancy Whelan. Phyllis ran the
Presbyterian Women's Circle. Nancy was her counterpart
at the Catholic church. The two teamed up occasionally to
run a joint food bank or coat collection. Nancy was everything a body could want in a charity drive partner: efficient,
organized, and ruthlessly determined. She could squeeze a
donation from the tightest of wads. She was a veritable jack-
hammer to iron-fisted wallets. Between her job as the police
chief's secretary and her church activities, Nancy knew every
bit of dirt ever shoveled by every family in town.

Rural folks were a churchgoing lot. Between Nancy and
Phyllis, they had the ears of three-quarters of the small town
residents, not to mention one pastor and two priests. Fred
Collins was going to regret firing Michael, as would the rest
of the council members.

The phone rang only once before being answered.

"Phyllis, I was just going to call you," Nancy said. "We need to do something about Fred and Vince."

"We certainly do," Phyllis agreed. "We can't let him get away with this. What did you have in mind?"

☙

"Why am I going with you again?" Not that Rachel minded. She felt safe with Mike in a way she couldn't explain. The episode with the bees had freaked her out more than she'd wanted to admit. Trying to kill her with insects was creepy to the tenth power. Her stalker knew everything about her, things that only someone close to her would know. Goose bumps broke out on her arms, and she wished she'd worn a warmer jacket. Her hoodie wasn't cutting it against the falling temperature.

"Because your place is off-limits until those bees are gone, I have no idea who is trying to hurt you, and Pete doesn't have the personnel to put a guard on you twenty-four-seven." Mike opened the passenger door to the Buick.

"Oh." Rachel slid into the seat, and Mike shut the door. After a brief exchange with Lieutenant Winters, Mike got behind the wheel. "Frankly, you're a hazard to everyone around you."

"Don't you feel scared to be with me?"

He started the engine. "I'm more scared to let you out of my sight."

She tried to stop it, but her insides went all mushy.

"I think there's less of a chance someone will try to kill you while you're with me," he said, dryly.

He had a point.

"Where are we going?"

"My place. Pete is going to drop off a copy of Harry Boyle's file later, and I need to arrange a car. My secretary will need hers back, and mine isn't currently running."

"Why don't we pick up my truck?"

"It might be best to use a vehicle no one recognizes."

Ignoring her raised eyebrow, he took a back road into town. He made a couple of turns and pulled up in front of a neat one-story brick house After getting out to open the overhead door, Mike pulled the car in and closed the garage behind it. Even with an old convertible disassembled on one side on the concrete slab, his garage was neat. Engine parts were lined up on blue tarps. Tools hung on pegboards. They walked through a laundry room into a living and dining room combo. A small country oak pedestal table and four chairs occupied the area next to the kitchen. A flat-screen TV and a pair of huge leather recliners took up most of the remaining space.

Mike stripped off his jacket and tossed it onto a coat tree in the corner. He stopped and glanced around, as if just realizing the Spartan state of his home. "I don't spend much time here."

Rachel shrugged. "At least you don't need duct tape to hold your floor down."

His phone buzzed. He flipped his thumb across the screen, scrolling through messages. "Sean will drop a car here at three, and Pete will drop the file around then too. What time is it?"

"One." She paced his small living room. Her stomach growled. "Sorry. I missed lunch."

"I haven't shopped this week, but I can probably scrounge up some food." He went into the kitchen. The room was too small for a table, but he had a counter with stools tucked under the overhang. The cabinets were oak, the appliances low-end plain vanilla. Outdated, but compared to the butt-ugly stuff her house was sporting, his kitchen was a *House Beautiful* spread.

"I'm not particular about food." She bypassed the stools and followed him in. The muscles of his broad back shifted under his snug navy T-shirt, stirring up a hunger that food alone wouldn't satisfy.

"No kidding." He lit a burner under a skillet and started pulling stuff out of the fridge. A carton of free-range brown chicken eggs. Organic low-fat cheese. A package of frozen something and a loaf of whole wheat bread came out of the freezer. The frozen stuff was green.

"Is that spinach?"

"Yes. Don't look at it like that. It's good for you. Spinach contains vitamins and iron."

"So does a Pop-Tart, and it's not green or slimy."

He added olive oil to the skillet and threw in a handful of the spinach. While the frozen stuff spat, he broke eggs one-handed, then whipped them with practiced efficiency. The eggs went in with an impressive sizzle. He let them bubble while he grated cheese and popped four slices of bread in the toaster. Damn. It actually smelled good.

He did some fancy shaking and rolling with the pan, then added the cheese. A quick flip of a spatula turned out one large and perfect semicircle, which he divided in half. Two slices of toast went on each plate. "Glasses are in there. Help yourself to something from the fridge."

Rachel opened the cabinet. "Let's see, do you take your antacid on the rocks or neat?"

"One cabinet over."

"Are you sure you're all right?" She found the glasses and filled them both with organic milk, skim no less. Ewww. At least he had regular butter.

Mike grabbed forks, and they sat down at the table. "It's nothing."

"You have enough of that white gunk to reglaze a swimming pool."

Mike sighed. "Eat your omelet."

She forked some up to her nose and sniffed it suspiciously. Smelled OK. She took an investigative nibble.

"Oh, for crying out loud, just eat." He covered her hand with his and pushed the egg concoction into her mouth. The eggs were fluffy and the cheese gooey. No slime.

"It's good." She generously buttered a piece of toast and crunched through it. The whole grain bit wasn't her thing, but she was starving. With enough butter, she could disguise the cardboard-like texture. She scooped more butter for slice number two.

"Don't sound so surprised." Mike took a bite. "Oh my God, are you finished already?"

Rachel washed down the second piece of toast with milk. "What? I liked it. Can I have more toast?"

Mike shook his head. "Sure. There's peanut butter, if you want it."

Of course it was that natural junk with the disgusting oily layer on the top. Rachel stirred it with a grimace. Didn't look any more appetizing. She screwed the top back on without tasting it. There were limits. "Do you eat like this all the time?"

"I try."

"Why?" Rooting in the fridge, she found strawberry preserves. All natural, but edible. "Can I eat this?"

"Go ahead." He forked eggs onto his dry toast. Gross. "Habit. I was a wrestler in college. Played some football too. You can't fuel athletic performance on Pop-Tarts. Real food gives you more energy. Except for lately, I'm usually pretty particular about my diet. You should try it out on a regular basis."

"Baby steps." Rachel ate her preserve sandwich. Not as good as a Pop-Tart, but she'd survive. When in Rome and all that. "What now?"

"Now we wait."

Unable to sit still, she loaded the dishwasher while he washed the skillet. The tiny kitchen made for very close proximity. Their hips brushed. His thigh bumped into hers. She closed the dishwasher and turned around. His chest was only a few inches away from her nose. And damn, he smelled good. Good enough to make all her girly parts tingle. That aftershave was making her think of interesting ways to pass the next hour or so.

"I have plenty of energy."

His blue eyes intensified and darkened. "Is that so?"

He was so much bigger than her that he blocked the light from the overhead fixture. She placed one hand on the center of his chest, right over his heart. The thud of its steady beat drew her closer. Rachel stepped forward, until only a few millimeters separated their bodies. The warm and solid muscles beneath her palm made her want to strip the shirt from his body and wrap herself around him. Skin to skin would be blistering.

He covered her hand with his. "We shouldn't."

He was probably right, but she was tired of holding back. Could he really be just an impulse? Her desire for him never abated. She suspected he felt the same way. Despite his protest, the baby blue of his eyes had gone all intense and sexy.

Even guilt wasn't enough to stop the pulse point throbbing between her legs. Was she a terrible person for wanting him regardless of the cost? One time. Just once. She'd get him out of her system and be able to move on. "You got fired because of me?"

"Suspended. But it wasn't because of you. You were a convenient excuse. Vince is up to something. I just haven't figured out what it is yet. Or if it's tied to your stalker."

"You will." She moved toward him, closing the gap between their bodies. Her forefinger traced the neckline of his T-shirt.

"You cloud my judgment."

"Do I?"

"I can't think straight when you touch me."

"Good." She didn't want to think. She didn't want to remember that someone had just tried to kill her or why she shouldn't act on the empty ache deep in her belly. She wanted to feel. She wanted the heat that was under her palm infused through her whole body.

His gaze dropped to her mouth. He leaned over her, the warmth of his breath passing over her cheek. Anticipation buzzed in her blood as his lips hovered. She already knew how the kiss would make everything but their bodies fade into the background.

She couldn't wait. She wanted him now. Before he had a chance to think about all the ways she was lacking. All the reasons they shouldn't do this.

Impatient, she rose onto her toes to meet his mouth. The heat of contact was just as searing as she'd remembered. Her pulse kicked, desire a drug pumping thick through her veins. His hands didn't move, but stayed at his sides while hers roamed over his wide chest. Skin. She wanted no barriers between them.

Mike's hands were quiet, but his lips were doing plenty, traveling in a hungry journey down her jaw to the sensitive flesh of her neck. His tongue traced the hollow of her throat and cruised across her collarbone. Desire speared her to the core. Rachel shuddered, and a deep masculine groan rumbled from his throat.

She lifted the hem of his tee and—

Holy moly.

Why did this man ever wear a shirt? She tugged the cotton over his head and flung it aside. His bare torso was rippled with layers of defined muscle. If somebody were making a Hottest Police Chief's fund-raising calendar, his shirtless photo should be the freaking centerfold. Huge shoulders blended into a broad chest. His abs were hard ridges that tapered in a mouthwatering V to powerful hips. Her fingers traced the valley down the center of his torso to his flat belly. When she stroked the line of hair that disappeared into his slacks, he flinched. His mouth bore down on hers again, his tongue plunging into her mouth, his body vibrating. The hands held at his sides clenched tight enough to turn the knuckles white.

He-Man was holding back, but he was on the brink of losing control. What would it take to drive him over the edge?

☞

Her mouth tasted like strawberries as Mike licked his way inside. God, she was hot and sweet and there was so much more of her he wanted to taste.

Rachel's hands explored the muscles of his chest, those delicate fingertips stroking his skin. He felt like a prized stallion and was a little disturbed at how much of a turn-on that was. But her eager hands and the little noises of appreciation she was making as she undressed him were taking him to the brink.

He wanted to pull her down to the tile floor, strip every stitch of clothing from her body. The sheer violence of his desire held him back. He'd seen her bruises and X-rays. She was half his size. He eyed her slender hand sliding down his belly. Maybe less. "I don't want to hurt you."

She didn't hesitate. "You won't."

His heart leapt at the certainty in her voice.

Her hands were already at the snap on his jeans. Eager for her touch, his hips surged forward. He stilled her hand. "Whoa, slow down."

"Don't wanna." She pressed into him, her soft spots cradling the hand angles of his body in perfect contour.

Heart thrumming, Mike unclenched his fists and took hold of her hips. One hand slid round to splay on her lower back and gently urge her closer, creating more sweet pressure against his erection.

Not that she needed any encouragement. She had one leg up and wrapped around his thigh. She was practically shimmying up his body.

He looked around. Counter, tile, wall. All hard surfaces. *Not in the kitchen, you idiot.*

Mike wrapped his hands around the backs of her thighs and lifted her against him. She wrapped her legs around his waist. He sealed his lips to hers. Mouths fused, he carried her into the bedroom. Daylight filtered through the miniblinds, striping the bed with light.

The second he set her down next to it, her eager hands were at his pants again. Like she couldn't wait to get her hands on him. But he'd like this event to last longer than a breath mint, and she was still wearing all her clothes.

He lifted his head. "Oh no. Your turn."

He unzipped her hoodie, slid it off her shoulders, and tossed it. Mike's fingers went to the buttons of her shirt. He spread the fabric. Underneath she wore a dark fitted tank instead of a bra. The material was thin, and her nipples budded through. He brushed a thumb across her breast but was distracted by the long ropey scars that ran up her biceps and across her shoulder. The pain she must have endured twisted him inside and gave him pause. No wonder she wasn't impressed with mere bruises. He pressed his mouth to the marks, turning her to view the purple patches left by yesterday's fall. She was tough on the outside, but soft and surprisingly vulnerable when those layers were peeled away.

Breathing hard and obviously irritated, she pulled away. "Could you get back with the program here? I'm fine."

She stepped away and, biting back a wince, lifted the tank over her head. It hit the miniblinds with a metallic chink. Her breasts were small but perfectly formed, the rosy tips budded in desire. She wiggled out of her jeans and panties in the next second.

Oh, man.

Getting back with the program, Mike dispatched his own jeans and boxers in record speed and reached for her with the intention of easing her onto the bed, mindful of the purple tie-dye she was sporting. But she was pushing him down and climbed on top of him in all her naked glory. Her mouth was everywhere. In a frenzy of hands and lips and tongue, she moved up his body. Mike had soft skin under his hands and breasts in his face and heat exactly where he wanted it.

Whoa! He slid back a few inches. "Wait…condom."

He rummaged frantically through the nightstand drawer. Oh, shit. When *had* he bought condoms last? *Please don't be expired.*

His hand closed around a box. He pulled out a brand spanking new package. A Post-it note on top read, "You owe me," in Sean's square print.

Mike ripped open the box and dug out a foil square. Rachel was straddling his legs and, oh geez, she took him in her mouth.

Pleasure speared through him and grabbed him by the balls. No, wait. That was her hand. He arched off the bed.

He gave her ponytail a playful tug and pulled the elastic band loose. Dark, silky hair spilled around her shoulder.

"Get up here," he said in a hoarse voice he barely recognized. She lifted her head. A wicked gleam lit those fiery amber eyes as she crawled up his body once again.

She took the foil pack from his hand and ripped it open with her teeth. While she concentrated on rolling it down on him, Mike took her brief moment of stillness to slide a hand between her legs. Slick softness met his touch. Rachel paused to throw her head back and rock against his hand. Mike's sheathed erection twitched.

She was on him in a second.

Part of Mike wanted to say, "Wait. This is too fast." But not the strongest part, obviously, because the protest died in his throat. He was only human, and she was naked and rising over him. His capacity for rational thought had taken off on a distance run. Mike grabbed her hips to steady her as she took him into her body. She paused, their size difference acutely obvious.

Mike fought for control. His arms shook, not from the effort of holding her aloft, but from the strain of holding himself back. His body was screaming to flip her over and take her. The thought of hurting her kept him still.

She shuddered as she focused on lowering her body onto his. Head kicked back, eyes closed, she was the most beautiful thing he'd ever seen. Her body adjusted, and she slid down, closing around him like an almost unbearably tight, hot vise. His vision clouded, and the air left his lungs. Sensation simply swamped him.

Never in his life…

Mike would have savored the moment, but Rachel didn't even take a second to breathe. Gleaming with sweat, she moved in a rhythm that wasn't going to last long for either of them. She moved faster. Way too soon, Mike felt his own release coiling.

He tried to slow the furious pumping of her hips. Mike intended to have more than a quick bang with this woman, but there was no slowing her. Oh well. They'd just have to do it again. Maybe once she'd taken the edge off, he could make love to her properly. Despite the manic pace she was setting, he could still make sure she knew there was more to this than just sex.

"Rachel." He stroked a hand up her sleek flank. His palm slid past her ribcage, over her breast, and cupped her cheek. "Look at me."

Her eyes opened. Their amber depths were glazed with pleasure and an emotion Mike couldn't verbalize but could identify with, a mirror image of the feeling building in his own chest. It filled the empty spaces inside him with frightening speed. Her breath caught. Her eyelids fluttered.

"No. Don't close your eyes." He held her gaze as she bucked with her release and pulled him over with her. Blinding pleasure rushed through him. After his vision cleared and he'd recovered the ability to breathe, he sat up and planted a soft kiss on her mouth, both hands splayed on the small of her back.

Shock clouded her eyes, and pure vulnerability shone from her face. She moved off him. A chill replaced the warmth where their bodies had been joined.

He ran his fingers up her spine. "Hey there."

Something wasn't right. Oh, it had felt amazing. No question. The most intense—albeit quickest—sex of his adult life. Energetic didn't even come close to describing it. But her reaction to it sent a fresh wave of fire through his gut. Her retreat wasn't only physical.

"Can I use your shower?"

"Uhm. Sure. But I wasn't done with you yet." Mike made a grab for her, but she was already off the bed. She scooped up her clothes and bolted into the master bath.

"What's wrong?" Mike lunged after her. The door closed and the lock clicked before he reached it. He banged a fist on the door. "Rachel?"

The shower faucet squeaked and water rushed on tile. Rachel didn't answer.

"Shit." He stepped back. He padded naked into the hall bathroom. A quick shower and fresh clothes didn't make him feel any better. In the kitchen, he swigged directly from the antacid bottle. It didn't, couldn't help either. Because this problem wasn't a medical condition. He was falling in love with Rachel.

He went back into the bedroom and stared at the bathroom door. If she hadn't locked him out, he'd be in that shower with her. Blake Webb's words echoed in Mike's head. *Rachel isn't capable of falling in love.*

The shower turned off. Despite his reservations about her emotional availability, Mike pictured Rachel wet and naked.

A soft rap at the front door severed his train of thought. Mike left the room, pulling the door closed behind him. He glanced through the sidelight before opening the door to Sean. One supersized SUV sat in the driveway, another at the curb. Through the tinted glass, Mike could see one of Sean's men at the wheel. A patrol car was parked at the curb. Behind his friend, Pete was walking up the drive. A file was tucked under his arm.

Pete followed Sean into the house. "I copied the old case file for you." Pete tossed his hat onto the dining table and pulled out a chair.

"Great." Sean held up a bulging gold clasp envelope. "I have that other information you asked for. Maybe among the three of us, we can identify Rachel's stalker and Harry's killer."

The Watcher slid the SD card into the slot on his computer. The new pictures loaded automatically. One by one the images appeared on his screen. Rachel walking across her lawn. Rachel working. Rachel escaping the bees he'd collected for her. How did she avoid getting stung? He scratched a welt on his arm. He hadn't been so lucky.

He loaded photo paper into the printer and clicked the button. With a beep and a soft whir, the printer kicked into action. Images slowly emerged from the machine. He lined them up on his desk. In one shot she was looking directly at the camera. At him. Like she knew.

He opened his drawer, pulled out an old photo album, and opened it. The pictures of Barbara took his breath away. She'd been the only one to understand. The only woman he'd ever loved. The fact that she was gone forever bored a hole through his soul. He lifted a photo of Rachel. The resemblance was uncanny, enough to make the pit of his stomach quiver.

It didn't matter.

Rachel had to go. She was the only one who knew what he'd done.

He turned back to the album. One finger traced Barbara's picture. So beautiful. So vulnerable. And he'd destroyed her. She'd never been the same. Harry had been the one she'd loved. Grief had tipped her precarious hold on life. Like water tipping from the spout of a pitcher, Barbara's interest in living spilled out.

When he'd killed Harry, he'd killed Barbara just as surely as if he'd murdered her with his own hand. His heart wrenched in his chest, his grief raw as a fresh wound. For two and a half decades he'd buried his guilt. Then Rachel had come back and dug it all up.

She knew. She knew everything. She had to be eliminated.

Chapter Twenty-Four

Not even the scalding water pouring from the showerhead could erase the tingling all over Rachel's body. Shit. Shit. Shit. How had she let this happen?

There was no getting him out of her system. If anything, sex had simply entrenched him deeper into her heart. She even smelled like him. She grabbed for the shower gel and lathered up. The scent intensified. She put the bottle to her nose. A familiar aroma infused her nostrils. Mike's musky aftershave wasn't aftershave. It was his damned soap.

She leaned her forehead against the cool tile. She'd just covered her entire body with the very stuff she was trying to wash away. She was going to carry He-Man's scent with her for the rest of the day, and as much as she tried to dislike that fact, she couldn't. If anything, the scented steam rising around her was soothing. It made her heart ache and her body want him again. She'd never intended for their quickie to be anything more than sex, but he'd clearly been making love to her. The emotion in his eyes, the way he touched her with painstaking gentleness, was unmistakable.

Her first impression of him had been right. He was not a casual sex kind of man, and she'd trod all over his heart. As the cabinet full of antacid confirmed, being big and strong as a superhero didn't make him invulnerable.

Five minutes of hot pulsing water didn't loosen the sore muscles of her back. She gave up and turned off the water. Mike's bathroom was as spare as the rest of his house, but she'd found clean towels stacked in the cabinet under the sink. She squeezed the water from her hair, dried off, and dressed. She borrowed Mike's comb. Her search for a hair product of any type came up empty. He obviously didn't have many overnight guests, an observation that shouldn't please her.

How was she going to handle what had happened between them? Running into the bathroom one second after they'd made love had been downright rude. Mike deserved better than that. He deserved better than her. She owed him an apology at minimum. An explanation would be better, but she wasn't sure she could get the words out.

I'm terrified because I feel the same way. But I can't be with you because I'm afraid I'll go crazy any day now.

Sounded lame, at least to someone who hadn't witnessed the debacle of her parents' marriage.

With nothing else to do, she unlocked the door and braced herself to face him. The bedroom was empty. She stepped into the living area and stopped at the sight of Mike, Sean, and Lieutenant Winters huddled around the dining room table. All three men looked up as she walked in.

The lieutenant's face reddened and his mouth opened in shock. He blinked at her for a few seconds, and then anger slid over his stunned face. He swiveled his head to glare at Mike "You *are* involved with her. Vince was right."

Mike turned to the lieutenant. "Pete—"

Still gaping, Pete stood up. "I can't believe it. I went to the council for you. I told them there was no way you'd ever compromise a case or the department. I stood up for you. I stuck my neck out for you."

"It's not what it looks like." Mike stood and took a step toward Pete.

Pete backed away. He jammed his hat onto his head and strode out, giving Rachel a wide berth. The door slammed behind him.

"Mike, you didn't compromise anything," Sean said quietly. "If anything, you worked twice as hard."

Mike dropped back into the chair and scrubbed a hand over his face. "No, he's right. I broke the rules and paid the price."

Rachel's chest tightened. Mike wasn't to blame. She'd selfishly set out to seduce him today, and she'd succeeded. It was one thing to risk her own heart. But had she weighed what deepening their involvement would do to him personally and professionally? No. She hadn't. Once again, she'd acted without thinking. Just like her mother. "This is all my fault."

"So, you're both human. Get over it." Sean tossed a file across the table. "Now let's get to work. My ride's waiting outside."

Avoiding eye contact, Rachel slid into the seat opposite Mike.

"You asked me to dig up dirt on Lawrence Harmon, Vince, Blake Webb, and Cristan Rojas. Let's start with Vince. He's been spending an awful lot of money for a sole proprietor of a small retail establishment. Since he acquired Tanya, Vince has renovated his entire house to the tune of two hundred grand. He's hired a dozen different contractors, including your buddy, David Gunner."

Sean glanced at Rachel. "Though I found nothing incriminating in David Gunner's background, except a couple of speeding tickets."

"David worked for Vince?" Why hadn't he mentioned it?

"It was last year, and half the contractors in town have done work for Vince. Makes you wonder what else David hasn't told you, though, doesn't it?" Sean spread photos across the table. "Like why he was protesting the project at Lost Lake."

The pictures were a little fuzzy, but David, standing a head taller than everyone else, was clear enough to recognize even in the back of the crowd.

"Why would a contractor be opposed to a housing development?" Sean tapped David's face. "It's also interesting that Vince got so cozy with Lawrence Harmon during the same time period. Lawrence Harmon has been investigated multiple times for various shady business practices, but no one has been able make any of the charges stick."

Rachel rubbed her forehead. Vince was up to no good. No shock there. And David had worked for him a couple of years ago. "What could any of this have to do with me?"

"We're not sure." Mike lifted the picture of David and set it aside. "Maybe nothing. But Vince and Harmon are involved in the Lost Lake project, which has been vandalized repeatedly just like your farm."

"Also, Vince has been trying to get Mike fired for the past year. I'd like to pin something on his ass," Sean added. "He's up to something, and he's afraid Mike's going to figure it out."

"But why would he try to kill me?" Rachel asked. "Seems extreme."

"It does," Mike agreed. "What did you find out about Rojas?"

"Absolutely nothing." Sean stabbed a paper on the table with a forefinger. "Which just makes me suspect him more. I don't need a report to tell me he's a killer."

Sean's eyes went Siberian, and Rachel was glad he was on her side.

Could Rojas really be her stalker? They'd had their disagreements, but he'd never frightened her. Goose bumps rose on her arms. She rubbed her biceps. They'd spent many hours together, mostly arguing. Then he'd suddenly changed his attitude. He'd been in her house, with the girls and Sarah.

"Did you find anything on Blake Webb?" Mike asked.

Rachel's answer was a reflex. "Blake would never hurt me."

"He's still in love with you." Mike's tone—and his eyes— turned icy. "How far would he go to get you back?"

Rachel chewed a thumbnail. Blake *had* hurt her, just not physically.

"Spoiled rich boys are used to getting what they want. Plus, he has a sealed juvie record." Sean dug a set of keys out of his pocket and handed it to Mike. "Is there anyone else you need me to check out?"

Blake had a record?

Rachel tipped her head forward onto the heels of hands. Lies and omissions cartwheeled through her head. Was anyone completely honest? Across the table Mike studied his reports. Yeah, He-Man was the last Boy Scout.

"No thanks, Sean." Mike followed Sean to the door.

Sean stepped onto the stoop. "Call me if you need me. Anytime."

Mike closed the door, and silence fell on the house with the subtlety of a fog horn.

"What now?" Rachel's bare toes curled into the carpet.

"Now we go see David and see if he can explain what he was doing at Lost Lake. Then we visit your father." Mike went back to the table, sorted papers and pictures, and slid them all back into the envelope. "In addition to all the people we discussed with Sean, there is one more possibility. Your stalker could be the same person who killed Harry Boyle. I don't like coincidences. This guy tries like hell to run you off the farm, but after the skeleton is discovered, he escalates. Now he wants you dead."

"I don't understand. I was just a child when this guy died. Why would his killer care about me?"

"There's only one reason I can think of." Mike's gaze locked on Rachel's. "Because he thinks you can tie him to the murder."

⁀

The offices of Parker Construction occupied a suite of rented rooms in a converted two-story house on Seventh Street. Mike turned into the narrow alley that led to a small parking lot behind the building. At the back asphalt rectangle, three white commercial vehicles emblazoned with the Parker Construction logo were parked in front of a large detached garage. Mike took a spot close to the house, between a minivan and a sedan.

Rachel stared at the rear entrance. "It looks exactly the same."

From the grim expression on her face, Mike thought that wasn't a good thing. She looked like she was headed in for a root canal. "You all right?"

"Yeah. Fine." She opened the door and climbed out of the SUV. Mike followed her up the steps to the back door, which had been modified as the main entrance. Parker

Construction shared a building with a law firm and an accountant. Rachel led the way down a narrow hall to a half-glass door with the firm's name spelled in black block letters. She rapped her knuckles on the door and opened it.

The office had once been the house's formal parlor. A bay window framed a view of the street. One-by-one tile samples were stacked on the commercial carpet in the corner. A row of cabinet doors in different styles and finishes leaned against the far wall. An old wooden desk occupied the center of the room, its surface littered with stacks of papers and envelopes. Dwarfing the office chair, David looked up from the laptop open on the blotter. Surprise widened his eyes, and he snapped the computer closed. "Rachel, what are you doing here?"

Not the friendliest welcome. Mike wondered what the Hulk had been browsing on his PC. Internet porn?

"Hi, David. You remember Mike?" Rachel hung back, and Mike noticed she stopped just out of arm's reach.

"Sure." David stood and shook Mike's hand with a mitt the size of a bowling ball. "I heard about your suspension. That sucks. Will Martin's an ass."

Ugh. Likely the entire town knew by now. How could this have happened? Mike's gaze was tugged toward Rachel. Oh, yeah. That's how.

"Do you mind answering a few questions for me anyway?" Mike asked, the fact that he was not the police chief anymore settling on his chest like a cinder block. "I'm still trying to find out who's trying to hurt Rachel."

"I guess not. Have a seat." David sat back down in the big leather chair behind the desk.

Mike and Rachel took the metal two chairs opposite the desk.

Rachel craned her neck to peer into the adjoining room. "No secretary?"

"She quit a few weeks ago. I haven't had time to replace her." David straightened. "Do you think Sarah might want the job? I'm getting buried here."

"I don't know. Maybe." Rachel shrugged, her eyes wary as she watched David.

Mike pulled a photo out of his pocket and handed it to David. "Is this you?"

Something flickered in David's eyes before the shutters came down again. Irritation? Or anxiety. "Yeah. Why?"

"I was wondering why a contractor would protest a new development. You specialize in upscale kitchens and baths, right? Wouldn't these new houses mean more work for you?" Mike circled topics. Once he brought up the murder, David might be a lot less cooperative.

"Yeah." David scrutinized the photo again. "I have a hunting cabin on the opposite end of the lake. When I was a kid, me and my dad used to spend weekends fishing and hunting there, before he was paralyzed. I don't use it much now. Don't have a lot of free time, but I guess my attachment to Lost Lake is more sentimental than practical. But I'm not in with those people. I just went over there that morning to see what was going on. I heard they'd been blasting rock. That's hell on the fish."

"Do you have any idea who vandalized the site?"

"No. Sorry." David tossed the photo on the desk in front of Mike. "Is that all?"

"Not quite." Mike tucked the picture back into his pocket. "Did you know Harry Boyle?"

"Sure." David nodded. "He worked for Parker Construction way back when. Just up and split one day."

"Harry didn't leave." Mike paused a second, until he caught David's eye. "He was murdered."

David's face dropped into a confused frown. "How do you—?" His eyes opened. "Oh, skeleton in Rachel's basement."

"We're—the police," Mike corrected, "are waiting for DNA confirmation, but that's who they think it is."

"That's weird." David leaned against the back of the chair. He turned to Rachel. "How the hell did he get in your grandfather's basement?"

"I have no idea. I was little." Her fingers twisted the shoulder strap of her purse.

David crossed his arms over his chest. "You know, the winter Harry disappeared was the same winter your grandfather had a heart attack. He spent a lot of time in the hospital. Rachel's dad kept the farm going. He used to send crews over there to do stuff every day. Shit, everybody had a key. Even me."

$\approx$

"What happened to David's father?" Mike glanced at Rachel, riding shotgun.

"Paralyzed in a car accident. David spent most of his teen years either working or taking care of his father. He didn't get out much."

Mike pulled the truck to the curb and stared at the run-down Cape Cod. An old sedan listed in the driveway. Around its tires, weeds grew in the cracks between the cement slabs, yet the lawn had been mowed. The house needed a coat of paint, but the garbage cans were lined up neatly next to the garage. "This is where you grew up?"

"Yeah." Rachel pointed to a yellow one-story next door. "That was where the Gunners lived. David's mother sold the house after his father died. She moved to Florida to live with her sister."

Rachel made no move to get out of the vehicle. "I had a teen crush on David. He was like twenty something. His room was across the yard from mine. My friends and I used to watch out my window and try to get a glimpse of him."

"Was he always, uhm, odd?"

"He spent way too much time cooped up in that house taking care of his father." She stared out the window.

"Do you want to wait in the truck?"

"He probably won't answer the door." She reached into her purse and pulled out a key ring. "You'd better hope he hasn't changed the locks."

With a resigned breath, she opened the door and hopped down. She flipped her hood up against the drizzle. Mike followed her up the walk. Shrubs were overgrown, shading the walk and allowing moss to coat the concrete wherever the sun's rays couldn't reach. She stood still for a minute in the shadow of an overhang, closed her eyes, and drew in a deep breath. Her posture and jaw stiffened as she reached for the doorbell. Muffled chimes echoed behind the door. The air remained heavy and still with no sound of movement from within. She pressed the bell again. No response.

Rachel stepped off the porch, squeezed behind the ragged shrubs, and peered through a bay window that fronted the house.

Rejoining him on the stoop, she put her key in the lock. The deadbolt clicked open. "Brace yourself."

Mike grabbed her hand. "You don't have to do this."

Apparently, she did. Her jaw tightened enough to crack a filling. Without a word, she pushed the front door open. No chickening out for Rachel. Mike had filled her in on the scant facts of Harry's disappearance on the drive, but her silence had set his instincts off. He wasn't going to like what he found in this house.

The front door opened directly into a small living room. A wide bay window admitted plenty of natural light, but there was no brightening the space. A prevailing sense of gloom sucked up daylight. Mike detoured to a dark pine bookcase. Dust-covered family photographs were lined up like soldiers on the shelves. He picked up a picture of a dark-haired woman who bore a strong resemblance to Rachel. Her mother. Mike scanned the rest of the pictures. A few were Rachel and Sarah as children, all dark haired and forced smiles, but the majority was of their mother. All were more than ten years old. Like time had stopped in this house, and someone had built a shrine.

"Dad," Rachel called.

Mike held back a sneeze. The house had a musty smell, as if it had been closed up for a long period of time. He followed Rachel through a small kitchen. The sink was empty. Mike peeked in the dishwasher. Neatly loaded. The lack of odor told him it had been run recently. The fridge was mostly empty. Mayo, butter, bologna, cheese. On the counter, a quart of cheap gin was sandwiched between a loaf of white bread and a box of corn flakes. Not exactly the breakfast of champions. Mike had expected a disaster, but this was far creepier. Rachel's father was barely going through the daily motions of living. No long-term thoughts here.

Rachel walked toward a dark doorway. Light flickered. Mike hurried after her. She stopped just over the threshold and squinted into the dim space. Her face was a conflicted mask of reluctance and resignation, like a patient waiting for test results when she already knew the tumor was malignant. "Dad?"

"Barbara?" A man's voice, deep and edged with hostility, slurred.

Mike stayed close as they stepped into a small den. A soot-stained fireplace was centered on the far wall. To the right, a door led to the backyard. Wooden blinds over a trio of windows blocked the day's intrusion. The light from the old console TV played over a thin man standing in front of a recliner. His posture was stooped, and one hand reached for the support of the chair's leather arm. Neil Parker was six feet or taller, one-seventy, dressed in baggy-kneed dark blue chinos and a green plaid shirt.

"Barbara?" His voice cracked. Red-rimmed eyes stared in confusion.

Mike glanced at Rachel. She hadn't moved. In the dim, flickering light, she looked remarkably like the woman in the photos.

"No, Dad. It's me, Rachel." She flipped a wall switch. A row of recessed lights illuminated the space.

Her father collapsed back into the chair, blinking at Rachel like a disappointed owl. "I thought you were her."

"This is Mike. He's investigating a murder. He needs to ask you some questions." Rachel turned away and leaned on the wall. She crossed her arms, hugging her midsection, as if she were holding something painful.

Mike perched on the arm of a faded flowered sofa next to the recliner. "Mr. Parker, what do you remember about Harry Boyle?"

Mr. Parker jolted. The remote control slipped from his thigh and landed on the blue shag with a thud. "Harry? Harry's gone. Left. Ran away from something. Only cowards run. And the guilty." Above his leg, his bony fingers clenched like talons.

"No, sir. Harry's remains were found. He didn't disappear. He was murdered."

"You found Harry?" Parker gave Mike a suspicious squint. "Where?"

"In Grandpa's basement," Rachel answered. "I moved into the farmhouse awhile ago. Sarah said she told you."

Parker refused to look at her. He picked up a sweating glass from the table at his elbow. Ice cubes rattled as he downed half of the clear liquid. He wiped his mouth with the back of his hand.

Mike glanced at Rachel. Her face was still as glass, as if one movement would shatter her.

"Harry Boyle worked for your construction company. He was a carpenter, right?"

"Harry's dead." Parker studied the condensation dripping down the outside of his glass.

Was that a statement or a question? Was he thinking or too drunk to remember?

"Do you remember anything about the day he disappeared?" Mike pressed. "It was in February 1987. It snowed that night."

Nothing.

"Harry worked for you. You saw him every day." Mike tried another line of questioning. "Was he depressed? Did he mention anything going on in his life?"

Parker slammed the glass on the table. Rachel jumped. Liquid sloshed.

"I don't give a shit what happened to Harry Boyle." He leapt from his chair with shocking agility. Mike jumped to his feet and stood in front of Rachel. But Parker didn't make a move toward her.

"He deserved whatever he got." He spat out the words, then grabbed his glass and drained it. When he turned back to Mike, fury blazed from bloodshot eyes. "Harry was fucking my wife."

Chapter Twenty-Five

Outside, Rachel leaned on the side of the SUV. The drizzle had progressed to a steady, light rain. By the time Mike came out a minute or so later, her hoodie and sneakers were soaked. He opened the door for her and pretended not to notice that her hands were shaking. Mike rounded the hood, climbed in beside her, and started the engine. He flipped the heat switch to high.

As he pulled away from the curb, Rachel waited for the questions, but Mike remained quiet as they left the blue-collar development behind and turned onto the interstate.

Uncertainty stirred in her belly. Had he given up on her or was he giving her time to get it together? She leaned on the headrest and closed her eyes until the truck stopped at his house. Numbness and cold worked its way through her body. If she were lucky, soon she wouldn't be able to feel anything.

She followed Mike inside, slipping off her wet sneakers in the garage. Standing on the cold cement, the chill seeped through her socks. She shivered. Mike led her into the laundry room. Gentle, efficient hands stripped off her sopping hoodie, then tugged off her jeans and socks. He draped a blanket around her shoulders, nudging her toward the living room. Behind her, she heard Mike moving around. The dryer started up, thudding as if he'd tossed in her sneakers. Rachel wandered into the dark room and dropped into one of the leather recliners. She curled her feet under her and pulled the blanket tighter, but warmth was elusive.

She closed her eyes, but her brain kept replaying her father's angry face and words in an endless, repeating clip.

"Hey."

She looked up. He was squatting next to her. "It's almost dinnertime. Are you hungry?"

With a throat too dry and tight to form words, she shook her head.

His eyes went soft. He slipped his hands under her and picked her up. Turning, he dropped back into the chair with her on his lap. A few tugs pulled the blanket up over her shoulders.

Rachel rested her head on his wide chest, and the most unexpected thing happened. She burst into tears, without preamble or warning, just an outpouring of raw pain. No delicate, ladylike crying for her. These were noisy, messy tears that would leave Mike's shirt soaked and her eyes swollen.

As her lungs heaved and her body quaked, the strong arms wrapped around her were the only things keeping her from flying apart. When the worst had passed and her breath slowed to ragged hiccups, he pressed a kiss to the top of her head. Waiting for humiliation to swamp her, Rachel closed her eyes against his now-damp shirt. But it never came. Instead, peace settled over her. The warmth from his body flowed into hers. Her soul was drained, her body limp down to her bones.

As if the crying hadn't been enough, words began to tumble from her mouth. Things that had been tightly bottled inside her popped out like snakes in a can.

"She used to take off every once in a while, when she was in hyper mode. She'd be gone two, maybe three days. Then she'd come back and fall back into a depression. We never knew how long those would last. Never did I hear him ask her where she'd been. I guess he knew." Rachel hiccupped. "In a way, it was worse when she was normal, especially when it lasted awhile. We'd start to get used to it. Expect it. Which made it even harder when she fell apart again. And she always fell apart again."

A shudder swept through her. Mike didn't say anything, but one big hand stroked her back.

"I'm sorry. I wasn't very useful today."

Mike's hand cupped her jaw. He lifted her chin. Expecting pity, she was surprised by the respect that filled his eyes. "I don't know many people who could've held it together as well as you did."

She stretched up and touched her mouth to his. This time their lips met with a slow sizzle instead of a blast.

He lifted his head. "I don't want to take advantage of you."

Gazing up into those baby blues, something unfurled inside her. Heat. Need. Longing burst forth. Her hands curled in the fabric of his T-shirt. "I need you."

His eyes darkened. He kissed her again, his tongue sliding through her lips to stroke hers. One of his hands slipped under the blanket and stroked her thigh. She suddenly realized all she was wearing was a tank and panties. His palm settled heavily on her hip. His thumb teased the elastic waistband of her bikinis. Heat built rapidly under the blanket.

Her hand found the hem of his T-shirt and tugged the fabric up, displaying his rippled abs. Her fingers traced the valley that led into his pants. With a low groan, Mike stood up with her in his arms and carried her into the bedroom. He set her on her feet. The blanket fell to the floor, and cool air rushed over her hot skin.

Why was he still dressed? She yanked his T-shirt over his head and tossed it aside. Her fingers spread over the heavy muscles of his chest.

Mike captured both her busy hands behind her back. "This isn't a race."

"Hey, let go," she protested.

He put his mouth to work on the sensitive skin of her neck, and she stopped squirming. Thoughts of complaining ceased as his lips trailed down to her collarbone. Rachel's head fell back. Heat and dampness pooled between her legs, where she was empty and aching for him. Only him. This man who could make her muscles tremble, her bones weak, and her heart giddy as a high-schooler. She shifted her hips forward until his erection was lined up in just the right place. All she wanted was to have him inside her. Where he belonged.

A deep groan rumbled through his chest. Panting, he pressed his forehead to hers. "Slow down. You won't regret it. Trust me."

"I do." And she meant it.

He froze for a second, and then his eyes went all sexy and intense, the blue deepening as his eyes darkened with desire.

His hands skimmed up her ribs, taking her tank with them. He eased it over her head and tossed it over his shoulder. When she reached for his pants, he stopped her.

"I want to look at you for a minute. OK?" he asked in a hoarse voice.

"Uhm, sure."

He switched on the bedside lamp. Soft light filled the room. Like a hot caress, his hungry stare swept over her, lingered on her breasts, and then dropped to her hips. No one would ever accuse her of being overly shy, but she flushed in response. Everywhere his gaze landed, her skin tingled, anticipating his touch.

"I want to see you naked." Without waiting for her approval, his thumbs hooked in the sides of her string bikinis. On one knee, he slid them down her legs. Gentle hands circled her ankle, lifting her foot. Her panties dropped to the beige carpet. He pressed his lips to the sensitive skin below her navel. The gesture was as affectionate as sensual. Abruptly, she stopped fighting the love that bloomed in her chest and let it have full rein.

Blue eyes looked up at her, full of masculine desire and passion. Mesmerized, Rachel forgot her hurry. She watched him kiss a path from one hip bone to the other. His tongue dipped into her navel. Then lower. The skin of her belly quivered as his lips slid over it. He inhaled and moaned low and deep in his throat. His hands skimmed up the backs of her calves to her thighs, separating her legs and holding her in place as he licked closer to her aching center. The sight of his huge body kneeling at her feet, his head wedged between her thighs, was the most erotic thing she'd ever seen.

Pleasure speared her as the tip of his tongue hit the money spot. He circled, slowly, deliberately, drawing out the sensations, building the tension until her body screamed for release. Every muscle in her body tightened. Her spine arched.

"Oh, yes. Right there. Please."

The low groan that came from Mike sounded almost like a growl as he obliged. Her hands shot into his hair, the slow caress finally driving her to peak. Instead of an explosion, a chain reaction started deep inside her. Her knees buckled as tension coiled and burst in great waves. His arms wrapped around her thighs, holding her up as the orgasm rolled through her.

He surged to his feet, lifting her limp body as he stood, then laid her gently on the bed. Somewhere between the floor and stretching out on top of her, he'd shed his pants and acquired a condom. Biceps bulged as steely arms supported his body over her. His weight pressed her into the mattress, more comforting than restricting. She wrapped her body around him and let him in. Her breath caught as emotion swelled beneath her ribs and filled the cold, lonely spaces inside her with warmth.

⁀

Moving slowly, Mike eased his way inside her tight but oh-so-ready-for-him body. His limbs trembled with the effort of holding back. He felt the subtle change in her body as it relaxed under him. Her acceptance was more than physical. Her soul-deep trust rocked him even more than the response of her body.

He withdrew and thrust again. Her body bowed, and her legs wrapped around his waist. Pleasure built with electric intensity. He looked down into her eyes and discovered he liked them glassy with pleasure even more than fiery with temper. Her body arched and a moan slipped from her lips.

Every stroke of his body in hers brought them both closer to climax. He wasn't ready for this to be over. Not by a long shot.

But her hands were on his back, the nails digging in, as her body tensed under him. Her spine arched as the climax rolled through her, tightening around him in vibrant pulses. There was nothing Mike could do but go with her. As far as orgasms went, it was nuclear.

Several minutes passed as his heart slowed from all-out sprint to jog, and a few aftershocks passed through the lax body under his. Mike kissed her with all the tenderness that had gathered in his heart. A contented sigh purred in her throat. She stretched, sleek and graceful. Though she seemed content, Mike searched her face for signs of panic.

She raised a brow at him. "Is everything all right?"

"I think so. If I get up to deal with the condom, you're not going to lock yourself in the bathroom, right?"

She cupped the side of his face and kissed him. "You might regret this, but I'm not going anywhere, He-Man. Except maybe to the kitchen. I'm starving."

Laughing, Mike ducked into the bathroom. "What time do you need to be home?"

"What time is it?"

"Six." Sheets rustled in the bedroom, and Mike stifled a pang of regret. He'd like to keep her here, safe—and naked—for the rest of the night.

"No rush, but I can't stay over." Rachel yawned. "Brandon said he'd feed the horses tonight, but then he's leaving with his family. The river is going to crest by morning. Their rental is in the flood zone. They need to stay with relatives for a few days."

"You're not going to have a problem, are you?" Mike cleaned up and brushed his teeth while he was in there. When she didn't answer, he returned to the bedroom.

She was curled up on her side. Her eyes were closed, her face relaxed in a way it never was while she was conscious.

Rachel didn't stop moving long enough to relax. She looked innocent, vulnerable without her usual guarded expression.

He set the bedside alarm for two hours and climbed back into bed with her, easing an arm over her body. She curled into him. Just a couple of hours. Then they'd get back to trying to find her stalker.

⟋

Lt. Pete Winters turned the township SUV into the Lost Lake development project. With a tighter suspension than his cruiser, the unfamiliar vehicle bounced through sloppy ruts. Mud splashed onto the windshield. He turned on the wipers, and a liberal spray of fluid cleared two arches of glass.

Headlights swept the site as he turned into the parking area. Gravel crunched under the truck's tires. Cluttered with chain-link fences, the yellow carcasses of large equipment, and port-a-johns, the bulldozed acreage slashed like a scar through the forest. Beyond the muddy beach, the overfull lake undulated, black and forbidding, in the darkness.

A man came out of the office trailer and picked his way across the sloppy lot. The wind kicked up the tails of the unbuttoned flannel shirt he wore over his jeans and tee. Recognizing one of the job foremen, Pete got out of the truck. "Hey, Ernie. How's it going?" He pointed his flashlight at the ground and switched it on to avoid the puddles.

"Quiet so far." Ernie yawned. "Man, I'm loving the time-and-a-half, but I'm not used to second shift."

"When do you get off?"

Ernie scratched his belly and yawned. "Midnight. Tonight's the last night. Harmon hired some hotshot security company. They start tomorrow."

"Guess they're tired of all the vandalism."

"Can't blame them. The missing dynamite was the last straw." Ernie reached into his chest pocket and pulled a pack of cigarettes.

"Dynamite?"

"Oh yeah." He tapped a Marlboro out of a full pack. "You didn't know? When they said to keep it quiet, I thought they'd told the cops."

"The chief probably knows." But doubt was creeping into Pete's gut. The chief wasn't the kind of guy to let something like missing explosives slide. But then, Pete never thought the chief would compromise a case either. Maybe he'd handled it on his own. There was only one way to find out.

"I'm sure." Ernie cupped a match and lit his smoke. The end flared bright orange as he inhaled. Smoke cut across the scents of pine and wet earth.

Pete fingered the button on his flashlight. "Well, if everything is fine here, I have to get back to the station."

"See ya, Pete." Ernie dragged on his smoke and backed away from the police vehicle.

Pete navigated the exit and turned back onto the rural road. With no moonlight, the darkness was a solid wall that ended at the reach of his headlights. He pushed the pedal down and high-beamed it all the way back to town. In the dark police station lot, he parked behind the brick building and let himself in. The night dispatcher waved as Pete continued to the chief's office. After unlocking the door with the key the mayor had given him, he switched on the light, rounded the desk, and sat behind it. The chief's chair felt too large, and Pete's short, pudgy frame couldn't quite fill it.

He rummaged through drawers and files until he located the Lost Lake folder. He flipped pages and scanned reports.

No mention of stolen explosives. He collapsed against the chair's high leather back. What did it mean?

Had the chief purposefully kept the dynamite theft out of the reports? Doubt lumped in the pit of Pete's belly. His gaze wandered to the window. At the community center across the street, lights glowed in the windows of the main meeting room. The town council was the only group that would be there this late.

Pete locked up and crossed the street to the old building that housed everything from Weeblos to senior fitness classes. In the main meeting area, Vince and Lawrence Harmon sat at the long table that spanned the room. The rest of the council was conspicuously absent.

Pete walked up the aisle that ran between two banks of folding chairs and stopped in front of the councilman. Annoyance flickered in Vince's eyes before he blinked it away. He closed the file in front of him. Next to him, Harmon sat back and crossed his arms over his chest.

Vince gestured to the empty chair opposite him. "Pete, have a seat. What can we do for you?" He rested his elbows on the closed folder and steepled his fingers.

Pete stood behind the chair. He grasped the metal back with both hands, the chair and resolve holding him steady. "Why isn't the missing dynamite in any of the Lost Lake reports?"

Harmon sat up and glanced at Vince. "I told you—"

Vince held up a hand. "Because we don't want to upset the public, that's why." The confident, condescending tone in his voice confirmed everything.

Pete ignored Harmon's angry glare. "Did the chief know about this?"

"Mr. High-and-Mighty?" Vince snorted. "Of course not. He'd never have gone along with it."

Pete's stomach balled up, sick and pathetic as the rest of him. He'd taken Vince's side over the chief's. He'd betrayed the best man he knew. Why? Because the chief was human? Pete's fingers tightened on the chair back.

Vince leaned closer. "Which is why he's gone and you're driving his truck and sitting behind his desk."

Pete's vocal cords wouldn't respond.

"We expect you to play nice, Lieutenant Winters." Vince circled, like a hawk over its prey. "You have three kids and a wife who doesn't work, right? Keep this to yourself. You can be terminated just as easily as Chief O'Connell."

Chapter Twenty-Six

A hooded man stood across the icy ground. A dark blob fell from his glove and stained the snow at his feet. His coat was splotched with dark stains, and though his face was but a blackened hole, she could feel his eyes on her.

He was watching. He knew.

Her legs trembled. The rest of her body was locked in place. Even her scream was frozen, trapped in her throat with no way to escape.

"Rachel, wake up."

She bolted upright. Sweat coated her clammy forehead. Mike's hand splayed on her back, supporting her. "Just a nightmare."

But was it? Something about the dream was familiar, but she couldn't pinpoint it. "I've had this same dream since I was a kid. He's my own personal bogeyman."

Mike's hand moved in a slow circle. "Tell me what you see."

"A man's shadow. He's wearing a hood that shadows his face, but his coat has dark stains on it. I think they're blood."

"Do you remember anything about the first time you saw him?"

Rachel nodded. A shiver crossed her bare shoulders. Mike pulled her close and tugged the blanket over her.

His arms wrapped around her. She rested her head against his solid chest. "I was six and sick with chicken pox. There was a noise outside. I remember being hot, really hot, and itchy. I got out of bed and went to my window. It had snowed since I went to bed. He was out there, standing in the snow, looking at me."

"You're sure this was a nightmare?"

"I assumed."

"Did you call anyone?"

"No." The loneliness in the memory was as clear as the vision. "Sarah was just an infant and my mother was, well, you know. I wasn't allowed out of my room. Couldn't risk getting them sick."

"So, you had a high fever and couldn't go to your parents?" Mike's voice was tinted with anger.

"I guess I could've yelled for my father. Believe it or not, he was the available one back then. Before my mother died, he took care of pretty much everything. But after Sarah was born, the stress level in our house was at an all-time high. It was a downward spiral from there."

Mike stroked her hair for a minute. "So you're not one hundred percent sure your father was in the house that night?"

"I never thought about it. I just assumed he was in their room." She stopped, suddenly realizing what Mike was implying. No. It couldn't be. Or could it? "Do you think I saw my father? Do you think he killed Harry?"

He hugged her closer. "I don't know anything."

"I don't think he would have left her alone with the baby." Sarah was an easy baby. If they were both asleep... Rachel had never thought of her father as a violent man. But the way he'd changed when he'd told them about the affair made her wonder if he had any other skeletons in the closet—or basement.

Rachel nestled her head against Mike's shoulder. "Don't you have any deep, dark secrets, He-Man?"

"I was married once."

"Really?"

"Yeah. It didn't last a year and ended a decade ago. Laura liked the idea of being a Philadelphia detective's wife. The reality was a different story. My mother was diagnosed with stage four stomach cancer. When I took the job as chief here and moved home to take care of her, Laura filed for divorce."

Anger flared in Rachel. "What a bitch—" She covered her mouth. "Oh, I shouldn't have said that."

"No. It was fine." Mike laughed. "Laura liked the city, and she was tired of me anyway. All I ever did was work."

"Plenty of people like their work."

"I did anyway."

"I'm sorry. It's my fault you lost your job." Rachel's hand settled on his abdomen, but she wasn't admiring the rippled muscles. She was thinking about all that antacid He-Man was stocking and the fact that his mother had died of stomach cancer.

"No, it isn't. Whoever is trying to hurt you and Vince Mitchell can share that blame." He covered her hand with his. "Anyway, the divorce was more of a relief. We weren't a good match. Mom was dying, and I was glad to have that year with her. It had been just me and her since I was ten."

"I'm sorry." She didn't miss the catch in his voice. She nodded at their joined hands. "Don't you think you should get that checked out?"

His blue eyes narrowed. "You're not going to start too, are you? God, Quinn is enough of a pest."

Rachel sat up, pulling the sheet to cover her breasts. "So, I'm a pest if I care about you?'

"I didn't say—"

"You get to care about people, but they aren't allowed to care back?'

"I—"

"You *made* me get an X-ray, but you can ignore *this*." She tapped her forefinger on his flat stomach. "This could be serious."

"But—"

"Look, He-Man. That's not the way this works." Rachel gestured between them. "And I totally get that you're afraid of what it is."

Mike looked horrified. He squirmed. "You don't like closed spaces or the sight of blood. I have this phobia about all things medical. Sometimes I freak out." His gaze dropped to her hand, still resting on his rib cage. "My mother's death was pretty ugly. Sometimes, the treatment was worse than the disease."

"Well, you're going to have to man-up and find out what's wrong." She linked her hand with his. "You're not alone if you don't want to be. You have a decision to make. I'm not exactly sure what we have here either, but I don't do things halfway. I'll even go with you."

Mike opened his mouth. Closed it. Cleared his throat. Then he rolled over, tugged her down on the mattress, and took her mouth in a searing kiss.

Rachel put her palm on his forehead and pushed his head up. "No. You will not distract me with sex."

His ducked around her hand. His mouth moved down her neck and found the sensitive hollow under her jaw. Tingles shot deep into her belly as his lips roamed. Her hand strayed to grip his shoulder.

"This is an important discussion, dammit." But as she said it, she tilted her head back to give him more access. Her fingers dug into the heavy muscle of his back. Mike shifted his weight and slid a hand between her legs. His mouth trailed across her collarbone.

"I am making a mental note." Rachel's eyes fluttered shut as callused fingers slid inside her. "Ah. This discussion is not...oooh...ver." *Gasp.*

The nightstand drawer scraped open and shut. Mike nudged her legs farther apart and settled between them.

"You cannot distract me with sex."

With one long and slow thrust, he stroked deep inside her. Rachel arched her back and wrapped her legs around his hips to take all of him. Pleasure burst in a sparkly rainbow behind her eyelids. She opened her eyes. He was staring down at her with complete focus—and as much tenderness as desire. He eased back and thrust again.

And she gave herself up to the sensation, to him. "For more than an hour."

⌒

Will pulled off onto the shoulder and drove onto the grass. He parked his truck behind a stand of trees, flipped up his hood, and tossed back the last of his beer. Drizzle speckled the windshield. Across the field, light shone from the first-floor windows of her big stone house. He couldn't miss it.

He stumbled out of the truck, then leaned back in and pulled the latch to fold the driver's seat forward. His hand curled around the aluminum baseball bat he'd stashed on the floor of the cab. He tested its weight with a trial swing. Perfect.

He headed across the meadow. Tall weeds squished under his boots as he breathed in the isolation. Rachel Parker's closest neighbor was a half mile down the road, and town was a fifteen-minute drive away. Even if he tripped an alarm, he figured he had at least ten minutes before the cops showed up. He only needed five. That bitch was going to pay. His nuts still hurt, and there was no way he was going to jail. She'd be sorry. So sorry she wouldn't testify against him.

The old farmhouse stood in solitary relief against the night sky. Was she home? Circling to the right, he ducked under a wet branch. Water dripped onto his head and into his eyes. He brushed it away.

There. Her pickup was parked near the house. The front of the farmhouse was dark. He looped around to the backyard. Concealed within a stand of pines, he found the kitchen window. A dark-haired woman was in front of it, looking down, probably doing dishes or something. Will's vision blurred, and he rubbed his eyes.

A twig snapped to his left. Will froze for a few seconds and listened to the sounds of insects chirping and rain dropping on dead leaves. He turned back to the window. Excitement swirled in his belly as focused on the brunette.

⌒

The Watcher pulled his boat up onto the muddy bank and tied the bow line to a tree. He strapped on his backpack, full of the necessary supplies, and lifted the extra-large gas cans out onto the muddy creek side. The game trail was sloppy, but the mud thinned out as he headed uphill toward Rachel's farm. Tall, wet stalks of grass slapped at the knees of his black jeans. Though the rain had stopped, water dripped from the canopy. After tonight, he wasn't going to have to worry about Rachel anymore.

Soggy leaves squished under his boots as he climbed the trail. Lights glimmered through the dripping foliage ahead. He circled the property to get a better vantage point. Her truck was parked right where it was supposed to be. But where was the cop's vehicle? The Watcher had the perfect distraction planned. Half of the dynamite he'd stolen from Lost Lake was already in place. He checked the luminous dial of his Timex. Plenty of time.

He continued around until he was directly behind the barn. He stashed the fuel cans in the underbrush and settled in to wait.

Something large rustled in the bushes nearby. His head swiveled. Deer? Too noisy. He crept across the spongy ground. The bulky figure of a large man lumbered noisily through the trees and stepped into the open. With eyes accustomed to the darkness, the Watcher assessed him. The man's purpose and identity were clear. A baseball bat swung from Will Martin's hand.

Will turned suddenly and looked right at him. Recognition crossed Will's intoxicated features. He'd have to die, which was appropriate, considering he'd taken advantage of Tanya just like Harry had with Barbara. Everything really did come full circle.

"Hey." Will stumbled toward him.

Plans were never perfect. He'd have to shift his timetable around to deal with Will.

"What are you doing here?" Will slurred.

The Watcher's hand strayed to the knife in his pocket. He opened the blade. "Same as you, Will. Just cleaning up some loose ends."

The knife-hand slid from his pocket and into Will's abdomen with a sick, wet sound. Will's mouth opened. Blood trickled out as he pitched forward.

The Watcher wrenched the knife free and caught the limp body. Warm blood soaked the sleeves and front of his hooded sweatshirt. Just like another night, long ago. There was no surprise and no panic this time. He ducked and dragged the body across his shoulders. Will was bigger and heavier than Harry had been. Liquid trickled down the Watcher's back.

He hiked down the game trail and deposited Will behind a shrub. He'd deal with the body later. After Rachel was eliminated.

⌒

"Does your property flood?" Running a towel over his wet hair, Mike strode naked into the bedroom. Rachel was bending over and picking up her panties. She put them on. Pity.

"No." She shook her head. "Those old Quaker farmers knew their stuff. The house and barn are on high ground. Flooding shouldn't be an issue, but the roof is questionable. I really do have to get home."

Mike dressed and slid his gun into his holster. A loose rain jacket concealed the weapon. He tossed a duffel bag on the bed and stuffed a couple of changes of clothes in it, then headed to the bathroom for his shaving kit.

She pulled her tank over her head. She eyed his bag. "So, you're staying for a while?"

"You bet." He added socks and underwear. "You're going to make me sleep on the couch, aren't you?"

"Sorry."

"It's OK. You're right," he grumbled.

"Could you get my clothes out of the dryer?"

Mike stepped up to her and wrapped his arms around her waist. "If I don't give you clothes, you'll have to stay."

She laughed, her breath warm against his skin. "Don't worry. You'll get another chance to get me naked."

"It's not just that." He tucked her head to his chest and breathed in the lemon scent of her hair. "Since we've been here, no one's tried to kill you."

Fifteen minutes later, they pulled into Rachel's driveway. Mike's phone buzzed. Pete's cell number appeared in the screen.

"Pete?"

"We have an emergency," Pete shouted.

Sirens in the background made the lieutenant's voice hard to hear. Mike covered his other ear.

"The supports under the bridge on West Drive washed out. I'm en route, so is the rescue squad. Could really use you."

"Are you sure you want me there?"

"Yes. I have two cars in the creek and people trapped inside. Thank God the creek's not that deep, even at flood level, or they'd all be dead already."

Mike's gut twisted with indecision for a few long seconds. But there was only one thing he could do. The rescue squad was mostly volunteers. There wouldn't be enough strong backs to haul people out of flood currents. West Drive was only a mile from Rachel's farm. He could be there before the squad. "I'll be right there."

Mike hung up and dialed Sean. "Can you come and stay with Rachel?"

After securing Sean's promise, Mike explained the situation while hurrying Rachel into the kitchen. "I'm sorry. Stay inside with the alarm on. Sean's on his way."

She scooped up the yapping dog. "Be careful."

"I don't like leaving you." Every muscle in his body was tense, protesting his exit.

"People need you." Rachel kissed him as he opened the door. "Go."

He heard the locks click behind him as he jogged to the truck. The rain had stopped, at least for now, but the damage was already done.

⌒

"What happened? Where's Mike?"

Rachel turned as Sarah walked into the kitchen. A full laundry basket was tucked under her good arm.

"The bridge on West Drive is out. People are trapped in cars in the creek."

"Oh no."

Rachel followed her sister into the laundry room. Sarah dumped the load into the washer, added detergent, and closed the lid. She pressed start. The machine chugged to life with a loud *thunk*. Water rushed into the tub.

They wandered back into the kitchen. Rachel paced to the cabinet and checked the Pop-Tart supply. She pulled out the last box.

"Worried?" Sarah asked.

Rachel took out a foil sleeve. She paused, the unopened pouch in one hand, the box in the other. Nerves swirled in her belly. Mike was a hero by nature. He'd risk his life to save strangers without hesitation. She checked her phone on the counter. The display was blank. "Yeah."

Sarah smiled. "Finally."

"Finally what?" Rachel put the box away. She walked into the den, switched on the TV, and tuned to a local station. Nothing.

Sarah followed her. "You're finally in love."

Rachel's butt dropped to the sofa. Yeah, she *loved* him. But *in love?* It would explain a lot of things. The way she blubbered all over him without shame. The way her heart went all high school every time she saw him. The strange sense of comfort in his touch. "Do you really think I'm in love with him?"

"Why is that such a surprise to you?" Sarah sat next to her.

Rachel offered her sister a Pop-Tart, her hunger dimmed by turbulent thoughts. "Well, you know, Mom."

Sarah pointed at her with a strawberry pastry. "Are you really worried about that? You are not Mom."

Rachel chewed. The Pop-Tart tasted like fruit-filled cardboard.

"If anything, you are the polar opposite of her. Mom didn't take responsibility for anything. I loved her, but she was very selfish. She never put us or Dad before her own desires. You put everyone first."

"I always felt bad for leaving you in that house."

"You shouldn't. You had the chance at a career. Why wouldn't you take it? What would turning down the opportunity have done for either of us? Marrying Troy wasn't a good choice, but it was *my* mistake, not yours. I tried to take the easy way out." Instead of eating it, Sarah stared at her Pop-Tart. "You know, she wouldn't have been able to do what she did if Dad didn't let her."

"I know. She lived to hurt him, and he lived to take care of her." Rachel picked up the remote and checked the other local channels. Nothing. "So, what do we do now?"

"Not repeat their mistakes, I guess. Though I can't see you acting like her *or* putting up with that kind of behavior. I did a lot of excusing stuff with Troy. But no more." Sarah got up and turned toward the kitchen. "Oh my God." She pointed to the window.

Rachel jumped up. Her gaze followed Sarah's finger. A plume of flames and smoke rose from the barn.

Chapter Twenty-Seven

Panic seized Rachel's next breath in her chest. "Call the fire department!"

Sarah jolted into action and grabbed the phone.

Rachel pulled her work boots on her bare feet and tucked in the legs of her jeans. "Stay inside with the girls, no matter what happens. Reset the alarm."

"This could be a trap!" Sarah yelled at her back.

The possibility that the fire had been intentionally set had already occurred to Rachel. The fire at the town hall was still fresh in her mind.

"I know, but I can't let those horses burn to death." She grabbed her jacket, pulled the door open, and ran. Panicked whinnies carried over the cracking of wood burning. Slipping and sliding down the back lawn, she sprinted to the barn. Her foot skidded on the slick grass, but she scrambled back to her feet. On the way past the water trough, she dunked her jacket before tugging it on.

An animal's high-pitched scream lifted the hair on her nape. Visions of trapped animals burning alive played in her mind. Her stomach clenched. She had to save them!

The flames were contained to one front corner of the wooden structure. Recent rains had left the exterior boards wet, hopefully giving her a few precious minutes. She pulled her wet hood over her head and plunged into the aisle. Smoke swirled, hot and acrid, around her face. Her eyes watered. She threw open the door and unlatched the first stall. Wild-eyed and snorting, the big bay plunged through the opening. She chased the horse out of the barn, then moved on to the next.

Smoke thickened as she pulled a chestnut pony out. Rachel blinked through the black smoke and worked methodically through the barn. Her eyes burned and soot clogged her throat as she opened the last stall. Rojas's gray snorted and reared in panic, its eyes rolling wildly back in its head, exposing the whites. As his feet hit the dirt, Rachel moved forward and secured the lead to his halter. She pulled, but he resisted. Rachel slid out of her jacket and tossed it over the animal's head. She dragged him out of the perceived safety of his stall into the increasing heat of the aisle. The blindfolded and terrified horse trembled. His sides bellowed. Rachel wiped a forearm across her eyes. The front exit was engulfed in flames. She'd been afraid to open the back door. More air could fan the flames higher, creating a chimney effect as wind blew through the building. The fire gave her no choice now. The back door was the only way out. She pulled on the handle, ignoring the searing burn of the hot metal on her hand.

As she'd feared, the fire grabbed the fresh air. It licked up into the rafters and caught the hay in the loft. Rachel tripped and went down hard in the dirt. Choking on thick smoke, she struggled to regain her footing as the black cloud thickened around them. The gray, smelling the fresh air just beyond the doorway, staggered forward. Rachel gripped the rope tightly in her fists and let the horse drag her out.

She lay on the grass, gulping cold, wet air into her lungs for a minute before pushing herself to her hands and knees. Coughing and gagging, she looked up at the horse. Black streaks marred the gray's pale coat. His sides heaved, and there were several burns on his back and haunches that would need treatment.

Neither of them would come out of this unscarred, but they were both alive.

Something crashed to her left. The barn was totally engulfed. Flames shot into the black sky. Wood creaked. A piece of the roof caved in with a loud crash and a shower of sparks. Rachel crawled backward, numb with shock, eyes riveted on the burning building as her dreams turned to ash in front of her.

An enormous explosion of sparks sprayed into the air. Tongues of flame licked at the remaining structure, wrapped around rafters and joists, and pulled them to the ground. Embers flew through the air as the walls collapsed, consumed by the raging fire.

Sirens wailed in the distance.

Something squished in the grass behind her. She swiveled her head. A shape loomed over her. The fire reflected over a tall, hooded, and blood-covered form. The shocking image transposed over her nightmares. Doubt paralyzed her for a few seconds. Was it real or was she hallucinating?

Her brush with indecision cost her. He lunged. A blade gleamed in the firelight. One steely arm wrapped around her middle. He pulled her to her feet and pressed the knife to the tender skin of her throat. Something warm trickled down her neck. Before she could react, he lifted her off the ground. She shot a hand over her shoulder to strike his face, but smoke inhalation had left her winded and weak. Her body seized in a fit of coughing. He tossed her over his shoulder in a fireman's carry. Blood rushed to her head as it bounced against his back. He hurried into the woods. Five long minutes later, she heard the rush of water.

"Put me down." She hacked. Her lungs burned as she struggled to inhale sufficient air. She twisted to see where he was taking her. His flashlight beam gleamed on water. The river. A boat was tied to a tree. Her captor whirled, his light sweeping over the riverbank. Half concealed under thick underbrush was a body. She barely recognized the dead-white face of Will Martin. Blood soaked his shirt.

Her head struck wood, and her vision dimmed as her captor dropped her in the bottom of the boat.

∼

She weighed nothing over his shoulder as he settled her into the boat.

He should have killed her. She was the only thing that could tie him to the murder. He was going to do it cleanly. No gutting her. Just a quick slice across the throat.

But when he'd pressed the knife to her soft neck, he hadn't been able to do it. He shined his light on her unconscious face. Her resemblance to Barbara was startling.

Keeping her was like having Barbara back again. Only this time would be different. The Watcher glanced at Rachel. So much like Barbara. This time there would be no husband, no Harry, just the two of them.

Arranging her limp body between the seats, he quickly tied her hands and feet. Sirens drew closer. He jumped back

onto the shore and rolled Will's body deeper into the underbrush. With all the chaos at the fire, there was little chance
anyone would track them all the way to the river. Who would
notice an extra set of boot prints after dozens of cops and
firemen traipsed over the scene? He'd come back and dis-
pose of the body later. He pushed the boat off the bank into
the swirling water and started the engine. From under the
rear seat, he produced a handheld spotlight. He switched
it on, shining it on the water ahead as he headed across
the river. The small vessel bucked on the waves. Neither the
dark nor the rough current alarmed him. He'd been navi-
gating these waters his entire life. Still, attention must be
paid. If he capsized, he'd lose her.

In his mind, Rachel's face blurred into Barbara's. After
all these years, he was finally taking her home.

⤳

Mike surveyed the scene. Two cars were submerged in the
flooded creek. Normally just a few feet deep, the water
surged waist high. Four people, wrapped in blankets, huddled behind an ambulance. The fact that everybody was
all right was a miracle. Creek water rushed past. Its depths
churned dark with sediment. On the surface, foam swirled
and eddied. Despite the height of the creek, this bridge
hadn't been on Mike's short list of trouble spots.

"Mike!" Pete stood on the bank, shining a flashlight on
the water. "I need to talk to you."

"Chief!"

Mike turned.

Behind him, Ethan called from the open door of his
patrol car. "Fire department just got a call out to the Parker
place. Barn's on fire!"

Mike ran for his vehicle.

"It's important," Pete shouted, but Mike kept going. Pete chased him down. Mike paused, one foot in the SUV.

"This could be a setup," Pete gasped. "Explosives went missing from Lost Lake. Vince and Harmon covered it up. I can't see shit, but there was enough dynamite to blow these bridge supports."

The sinking sensation in Mike's stomach went into a free fall. He glanced back at the creek. Inspection of the bridge supports would have to wait until the water receded.

"Thanks." Even with the drop in temperature and soaking wet clothes, Mike's body poured sweat all the way back to Rachel's. Pressure built in his chest, growing tighter as he neared. He saw the glow as he turned down Prescott Road, orange and warm against the storm clouds. Higher up, smoke billowed in a black plume upon the charcoal-gray sky. As he drew closer, the flames became visible, tongues licking around the remaining wood of the structure, eating the barn right down to its skeleton.

Heart slamming, he unlocked his glove box and grabbed his gun and holster before leaping from the SUV. Sean's vehicle was already there. A fire truck pulled into the driveway. Sarah stumbled across the lawn toward him.

Mike caught her by the shoulders. "Where's Rachel?"

Tears streamed down Sarah's face. "I don't know. I can't find her."

Mike faced the barn. A crack split the air. A large rafter fell, taking most of the roof with it. It collapsed with a boom and a roar. Flames and sparks shot into the air like fireworks.

She couldn't be in there. Nothing was alive in there.

Sean was jogging around the back of the burning building, but Mike couldn't tear his eyes off the inferno. Everything around him blurred as the possibility that she was dead sank in, and his insides twisted until his lungs wouldn't expand. His vision blackened at the edges.

"Mike, listen." Sean grabbed him by the shoulders and shook him until Mike looked at him and blinked. "She's *not* in there."

Mike focused on Sean's face.

"She's not in there." Circling wide to avoid the heat and flying embers, Sean led the way around the side of the barn. "I counted all the horses. Eleven. Sarah said that's all of them. So why would she have gone back in?"

A bit of burning debris landed on Mike's arm with a sizzle. He swatted it out. The sharp burn brought him back to reality. He looked over the meadow. Big shapes moved in the dark. Was Sean right?

"Bandit, no," Sarah's voice shrilled over the crackling of the flames.

A small brown missile was heading straight for the fire. Mike rushed forward, but the little dog veered off, circumventing the inferno and heading for the woods behind the property.

Mike looked at Sean. "Right. Follow him."

Sean pulled a flashlight from his pocket and trained it on the ground in front of them. Bandit stopped at the edge of the woods. He ran back and forth on the bank of the creek. Normally, just a few inches of water tumbled over the rock bed. Tonight, the creek was knee-deep and double its typical width. The dog yapped and zoomed off into the trees. Mike and Sean followed at a run. Just beyond a strip of tall grass, a game trail led through the forest, running parallel to the creek.

"Look." Sean illuminated a clear set of footprints in the mud. "Big man wearing boots. And he was carrying something heavy."

The tension in Mike's chest compounded. He pulled his gun from its holster and jogged next to Sean toward Bandit's barks. They slowed when the river sounded ahead of them. Sean held up a hand and ducked behind a tree at the edge of the woods.

Ahead, the river churned and eddied, black and ominous in the dark. The riverbank was empty, except for the furious dog, running back and forth, growling at the water's edge. Mike picked up Bandit. "Hush."

The distant sound of an engine's purr floated over the rushing water. Sean trained his beam on the bank. A furrow in the mud showed where a boat had been pulled onto the riverbank.

"Son of a bitch. He's been coming in by boat." Sean pointed his light at the water, but the boat was long gone.

Nausea rose fresh in Mike's gut. Rachel's stalker had won.

☞

Rachel opened her eyes to a dark and blurry sight. She blinked hard to clear her vision. The cold metal under her head rocked and pitched. Pain ricocheted through her skull as it bounced. Water sloshed over her, the icy cold a cruel slap that sent a shiver coursing through her torso. She tried to raise a hand to her face, but couldn't. Her hands were tied together with rope. Nylon bit into the bare skin of her wrists. Her ankles were similarly bound.

The floor beneath her pitched sharply again. A boat. She was curled in the bottom of a flat-bottomed aluminum boat, wedged between the seats. Whoever was manning the outboard motor at the rear of the boat wasn't in her line of sight.

She debated moving so she could reach her bound ankles. Would he notice in the dark? She was partially concealed between the bench seats. Was he preoccupied handling the boat on the rough water?

The bow lifted and slapped down violently on the water. Rachel's head bounced, and her vision blurred for a few seconds. She closed her eyes against rising nausea. Terror and soot clogged her throat. Slowly, she curled tighter, drawing her knees up until they were close to her chest. Her hands sought the rope binding her ankles. Moving as little as possible, she picked at the wet strands of nylon. Agony shot up her hands. Her burned fingers fumbled. She inched her hand toward her front pocket, where her knife pressed against her hip.

The flat-bottomed hull of the fishing boat was meant for calm lake waters, not the rough chop of the swollen river. The boat rose and slapped on the water rhythmically as the hull hit a series of waves. Rachel's body jarred on the bottom of each trough. Water poured over the side and soaked her jeans.

But she slid the knife between her palms and went to work on the ropes.

The boat turned sharply and then picked up speed. Then the ride abruptly smoothed out.

"We're almost home."

Rachel turned toward the familiar voice. Concealing the knife between her hands, she lifted her head to see over a cushion. He sat at the rear of the boat. One hand steered the outboard motor. The other held a spotlight. He set the light on the seat next to him and flipped a toggle. The light switched from spot to lantern, illuminating a circle around them. He adjusted something on the motor. A gust of wind blew his hood back and revealed his face.

⌒

Mike listened to the engine sound fade. "Who? Who is it?"

"What's your gut tell you?"

"It's someone who knows her very well. Someone who knows she's claustrophobic and faints at the sight of blood and is allergic to bees. Who would know all that and be comfortable taking out a small boat on a flooded river?"

"Will Martin? Troy? They both hunt and fish."

"Maybe." But it didn't feel right. Bandit squirmed in Mike's arms. The dog stared into the underbrush. A growl rose out of the small muzzle.

Someone groaned.

Gun in hand, Sean crept toward the sound. "Oh, shit." He holstered his weapon and pushed through the brush. A few seconds later, he dragged a limp body into the clear.

Will Martin's face was gray as river water. Blood soaked his T-shirt over his belly. Sean pressed two fingers to Will's throat. "He's still alive, but just barely."

Sean ripped the bloody cloth, revealing a gaping knife wound. He tore off a strip of Will's shirt, balled it up, and pressed down hard.

"He can't last long the way he's bleeding." Mike whipped out his cell to call for an ambulance. The 911 operator confirmed what he already suspected. "An ambulance was already dispatched to the fire. They should be at the house. I'll send them back." Mike was already moving back toward the house.

"Don't you go after her without me."

"Gotta go." Mike jogged off. He called over his shoulder, "I'll let you know where I am. You can catch up." He left Sean cursing.

Dialing Nancy's home number, Mike took off through the woods.

Well, that ruled out Will. And Troy. He was a lowlife, but he wouldn't kill his best buddy.

Nancy picked up on the second ring. "What happened?"

Mike summed up the events of the evening. "I need you to access some tax records."

Mike ended the call just as he burst from the trees. An ambulance was parked behind the fire crew. Firefighters trained hoses on the burning pile that had once been Rachel's barn. They were also spraying down the back and roof of the house. The wind had shifted, blowing embers toward the old stone structure. Mike snagged the arm of the first paramedic and gave him quick directions to the spot where Sean tended Will.

Mike looked for Sarah and the girls and found them huddled on the front lawn. He handed Sarah the dog.

Damn. He couldn't just leave them here.

A Ford Explorer bounced up the driveway, drove across the grass to avoid the chaos of emergency vehicles, and parked near the house. Jack slid out, grabbing his cane and limping up the back lawn. "Look, I don't know what I did to piss you off, but Sean called me for help. Where is he?" Jack's gaze scanned the chaos in the yard.

Mike told him. "Look, I don't want to get into…everything right now. Can you take Sarah and the girls back to your place?"

Disappointment crossed Jack's face, but he covered it quickly. He'd been a good cop, but his leg injury kept him out of the action. "No problem. But where are you going?"

Being sidelined sucked, but Mike couldn't risk Jack slowing him down. "Rachel's father knows more than he's saying, and I have someone pulling tax records to see who owns waterfront property."

"Wait for Sean."

Mike shook his head. "It'll take the paramedics too long to get to him. Waiting is too risky. I'm going after her."

"Good luck." Jack nodded, understanding in his eyes. He knew what it was like to have the woman he loved in danger.

Chapter Twenty-Eight

Light played across David's face. Shock immobilized Rachel for a few seconds. "Oh my God." Everything blurred around her as her lungs locked down.

"Surprised?" His smile was cold and feral in the lamplight.

Icy fear restarted Rachel's heartbeat. She sucked in a breath. Then another, until her vision cleared.

The boat bumped into a dock. David shut off the engine and climbed. He gathered the bow line and pulled the boat alongside the dock.

While he was occupied securing the lines, Rachel sawed at the rope around her ankles. David turned to check on her. She froze, though her hands continued to shake. "Why?"

"You look so much like her." David leaned over the boat. Still trussed like a turkey, Rachel cringed at the intensity in his stare. His eyes were too bright, nearly feverish in the yellow light of the lantern. "Do you know what life was like for me? Changing my dad's diapers when everyone else was out having fun? Your mother was the most beautiful woman

I'd ever seen. I couldn't leave my dad alone; watching her was all I had. She got me through those terrible years. *She* understood what I was going through. *She* knew what it was like to be unhappy. Because she was miserable too."

"Did you kill Harry Boyle?"

David grabbed the light and scooped her effortlessly off the bottom of the boat as if she were a child. Her skin crawled where he touched her. He'd been tormenting her for months. Now she was helpless. He could do whatever he wanted.

"Harry had to die for using her like that. She was fragile. He was trying to talk her into leaving me, running away with him. She was going to do it. Betray me because of his manipulation. So I took him out of the picture. And she stayed."

He carried her up the dock.

"Why did you bury him in my basement?"

"It was the only place where the ground wasn't frozen solid. I'd been helping take care of the place while your grandfather was in the hospital. I had a key, and I'd found that room while I was putting some stuff into storage down there." David sighed. "I was just a kid. I panicked. Over the years I thought about moving him but decided it wasn't worth the risk. Even if he was found, no one would tie me to his death. Except you. You were the problem. You saw me that night. Looked right at me. You are the only one who can link me to anything."

"What do I know?"

"You saw me that night. Only you can link me to Harry's murder."

A shiver, part cold, part terror, shook Rachel's bones and lodged in the pit of her stomach. David wasn't thinking straight. He'd just left a murder victim behind. Now he was going to kill her because she could link him to a twenty-five-year-old case? She would never have put her nightmares together with Harry's murder if David hadn't started all this.

"Too bad they found you in that storage bin. If you'd just died then, I wouldn't be in this situation now." David looked down at her, his eyes bright with maniacal intensity. "Too bad another opportunity like that one never popped up over the years."

"Why didn't you kill me years ago? You had plenty of chances."

"As long as the body remained hidden, I figured I was safe. Now that Harry's been found, everything's different. There's no statute of limitations on murder. I tried to make you leave, but you wouldn't go. Now that there's a body and a new investigation, I have to kill you." But the odd light shining in his eyes told Rachel he had other things planned. Whether he was going to rape her and kill her or just kill her didn't matter at the moment. She had to get away. Mike would never find her in time. She was on her own. Thoughts of him sent a pang through her heart. She'd finally found someone who truly understood her—and wanted her anyway. She wasn't going to let David take that away from her. Dammit.

Beyond a sloping and weedy rear lawn, the cabin at the top of the hill was small and dark and isolated. Rachel did not want to be alone in it with David.

She stabbed him in the shoulder.

"You bitch!" He dropped her and the lantern.

The soft, wet earth cushioned her fall. She still clenched the knife. One more flick of the blade freed her feet. Clutching his wounded shoulder, David lifted a boot and tried to stomp on her. She rolled out of the way. When his foot hit the dirt, she slashed at his hamstring. The pocketknife was small, but she kept it sharp. He fell to his knees and grabbed the back of his thigh.

Rachel ran for the darkness of the woods on rubbery legs, her hands still bound.

Cursing and irregular footsteps echoed in the moist air. Even injured, David was right behind her. She plunged into the trees. Her lungs burned as she ran into a pine branch. Needles stung her skin. She was seized by a bout of coughing as she stumbled on a dead bough in the dark. She couldn't run like this for long, not with lungs still filled with smoke and soot. All he had to do was follow the sound of her hacking her lungs up.

David's footfalls drew closer.

⌒

Mike banged on Neil Parker's door. There was no sound or movement in the house. He ran around to the back of the house, where the den was located. Covering his eyes with one hand, Mike peered in the window. Parker was sprawled in his recliner, an empty glass by his elbow. From the looks of him, he'd been there awhile.

He definitely wasn't currently piloting a boat on the river.

But did he know anything? Mike went to the back door and raised a foot to kick it open. His phone buzzed. Nancy.

"I'm here at the tax office now. Edna is at the computer. No waterfront property for Cristan Rojas, Blake Webb, Neil Parker, or David Gunner."

Damn. Mike's eyes drifted to the house next door. *We had a place at Lost Lake when I was a kid,* David Gunner had said. Harry Boyle had owned a Jeep like the one pulled out of Lost Lake. Rachel's voice played in his head. *David's bedroom was across the yard from mine. My friends and I used to try to catch a glimpse of him through the window.*

Mike walked to the side yard. The windows of the houses looked out on each other. Had Rachel seen David covered in blood after he'd killed Harry?

"Mike? Are you there?" Nancy shouted over the line.

"It's Gunner." Mike sprinted for the truck. "What's his address?"

He heard Nancy relaying the information and keys clicking in the background. Nancy read off an address in town.

"Is there a property out by Lost Lake registered to him?"

More keys clicked. "Not that we can find."

"Keep looking." Mike ended the call, pulled away from the curb, and pushed the gas pedal to the floor.

David Gunner owned a small saltbox-style house on a quiet street at the edge of the town proper. The wooden clapboards were white and freshly painted, as was the black trim and shutters. Mike looped the house, peering in all the windows on the floor. As expected, no one was home. This residential street would be a tough place to stash a kidnapping victim. A rural cabin, however, would be just the spot.

If she were still alive. Mike pushed back the panic.

David should have records somewhere in his house. Mike, grateful for the moment that he wasn't acting as the police chief, climbed the front steps and smashed the sidelight with the butt of his flashlight. With gloved hands, he reached in and flipped the lock.

The inside of the house was just as neat as the outside. His boots clumped on the hardwood as he checked each room downstairs and climbed the narrow stairs to the second floor. Bingo. First room was a home office. He booted the computer and searched the desk while it warmed up. A locked drawer on the bottom yielded to a solid kick.

Instead of tax or utility bills, Mike found a stash of photo albums. He lifted them out. No dust, although one was yellowed around the edges. He opened the book. Pictures of Rachel's mother filled every page. They weren't posed shots either, but the kind of photos taken without the subject's knowledge. Many were amateurish, some were shot through a bedroom window.

Other albums contained pictures of women Mike didn't recognize. David's subjects over the years? Mike set them aside. The top drawer held a pile of loose photos. A rubber band held a stack of pictures of Rachel. Rachel working. Rachel looking out her kitchen window. A blurry shot of Rachel passing her bedroom window in a towel. Another group of photos were of Tanya Mitchell, all equally personal and private and sick.

Mike suppressed his rage and disgust as he moved to the computer. Getting through the password protection would take too much time.

Mike kept moving through the office until he found a stack of current bills tucked in a ledger for Parker Construction. There it was. A utility bill for a property at Lost Lake. The house was owned by David's mother and listed under her maiden name. He dialed Sean's number. "Where are you?"

"Just getting in my truck. What did you find?"

"It's David Gunner. He has a cabin out at Lost Lake." Mike read off the address. "I'll meet you there." Sean was on the opposite side of the township. Mike would get there first.

He dialed Nancy while he sped out to Lost Lake.

☞

Rachel stopped beneath a huge pine to breathe. She leaned a hand on the rough bark, turned her mouth into her shoulder, and muffled a cough. Her damaged lungs constricted. The path ran parallel to the water. Below, the lake shifted in the dark. She turned her knife backward and sawed awkwardly at the rope binding her wrists. The clouds parted and the moon glimmered on the water. The rope dropped away from her hands. She picked it up and shoved it into her pocket. He might find her, but she wasn't going to make it easy.

She continued her climb, aiming for an outcropping that rose from the slope above. A twig snapped behind her, and she quickened her strides. The trail flattened out into a small clearing. A narrow crevice separated two enormous boulders. She stuck her head inside; the crevice continued, but it was too dark to see how far. If she couldn't see the end, then David couldn't either. Sweat broke out on her freezing skin at the thought of wiggling into that small space. The fit would be tight for her. David would never be able to squeeze through.

She glanced behind her again. What choice did she have? Even injured, David was closing in on her. She couldn't outrun him. She wasn't exactly in prime condition.

Something rustled.

Options? Chicken out because of an irrational fear or die.

She turned sideways and eased into the crevice. The rock walls scraped her back through her the soft cotton of her shirt. The space tightened. She pushed forward. She was going to get stuck. She'd be trapped. He'd find her and kill her while she was helpless and unable to defend herself.

Her heart beat loudly enough that David would surely hear it if he passed. She exhaled and sidled a few more inches into the crevice. Almost there.

Underbrush rustled. Closer.

Tucked three feet into the fissure, Rachel peered out into the darkness. She heard him before she saw him, the snap of pine needles that could've been an animal but wasn't. David limped into the clearing, his bulk casting a long shadow across the ground. He passed her hiding spot and kept going, moving out of her narrow field of vision.

She breathed shallowly through her mouth, her fear of the tight space momentarily overridden by the terror of discovery.

Light illuminated the crevice.

"There you are." An arm reached for her.

Rachel's heart went ballistic as she pulled backward as far as possible. She was trapped. Her hiding place had just become her grave.

⤨

Headlights off, Mike eased to the side of the road. David's cabin was ahead. A small timber structure with a wooden front porch. The forest closed in so tightly around the building that the canopy met over its steeply pitched roof. Sunlight wouldn't touch its cedar shakes, not even at high noon. Even with the moonlight that had broken through the clouds, David's place was dark as sin.

"I'm here," Mike whispered into his cell.

"Wait for me," Sean demanded. "I'm ten minutes away."

"Can't. She could be dead in ten minutes." Fear clamped down on Mike's chest. "She could be dead already."

"He snatched her for a reason," Sean reasoned. "Wait for me."

"If it were your wife, would you wait?"

"Fu—"

Mike snapped the cell closed and switched it to silent. Glock in hand, he slipped out of the SUV and approached the dark cabin from the deep shadows of the trees. Pine needles and wet moss underfoot silenced his steps. The cabin was dark and still. Mike eased up to a side window and strained his ears for sounds. All he heard was the wind rustling through the pines.

"You bitch!" The male shout came from the rear of the house.

Staying in the cover of the woods, Mike circled around. Fifty yards away, at the rear of the cleared area between the house and the lake, David was climbing to his feet. Too far away for a clean shot. David hobbled into the darkness of the nearby woods. Beyond, the terrain rose sharply.

Mike followed the tree line to the spot where David disappeared. A clump of thick trees gave way to a rough path cut into the steep slope. Mike climbed the narrow trail. The woods opened up, more rock, fewer trees. A section of wet earth gave way under Mike's foot. He slid sideways and lost his grip on his gun. Dirt and stones tumbled down the incline. One hand shot out and grabbed a tree branch, stopping his descent. He righted himself as the gun bounced down the slope and into the lake below with a small, final splash.

His gut clenched as he moved on without it.

Mike climbed up to a small, flat clearing around a clump of rock and boulders. A form shifted within the shadow of the rocks.

"There you are." David was reaching into a crack between two huge boulders, where Mike assumed Rachel was hiding.

Mike closed in. David's head whipped around. His eyes widened. He raised his hands to his chin and threw a hard right. Mike ducked and slipped left, then dropped and shot in at David's hips. Mike caught the bigger man around the thighs, turned, and took him to the ground. David hit the ground like a felled oak. But he moved fast for his size and managed to kick and roll out of Mike's grasp. His heel caught Mike's lip. Blood seeped into his mouth.

In his peripheral vision, he saw Rachel emerging from the rock crevice. "Rachel, get out of here!"

Jumping to his feet, David's gaze darted in Rachel's direction. His face tightened as his eyes tracked her movement. He circled the clearing, his intent clearly to intercept her escape.

Mike maneuvered between them. "Oh no you don't."

With an angry hiss, David swung out with a looping left hook. Mike blocked the punch and drilled him in the jaw. David's head snapped back, and he stumbled to the side. Crazed fury lit his eyes.

David was no trained fighter. He dove in for a sloppy tackle. Mike sprawled his legs backward to block the takedown. He wrapped his arms around the larger man's shoulders. David threw him off, staggered back, and pulled a knife from his jacket pocket. Leading with the knife, he lunged forward.

The blade swiped through the air at Mike's midsection. He tried to move left, but the uneven, sloped ground under his feet shifted. But David came in again with a low thrust. Mike grabbed the wrist of the knife-hand and cocked his other arm to punch David in the face.

The ground slid out from under them. Both men slipped sideways in a miniature avalanche of loose mud and rock. David fell to his hands and knees. Mike tumbled backward.

White-hot agony burst through his leg as David plunged the knife into Mike's thigh.

He grabbed David's wrist and the hilt with both hands to keep the knife in his leg. If the blade came free, Mike would bleed like a slaughtered deer.

Chapter Twenty-Nine

Mike held on to the knife, but his strength was fading. David would win and they both knew it. His eyes gleamed with excitement as he pulled. The movement of the blade in his leg sent waves of pain surging through Mike and pumped more blood from the wound.

Thwack.

David's hold on the weapon loosened. His eyes went wide, then rolled into the back of his head. His fingers opened.

Thwack.

The huge man fell sideways. Rachel stood over him, red faced, panting, and wielding a thick branch. She nudged David's body with a foot. Apparently satisfied he was no longer a threat, she dropped to her knees beside Mike and looked down at his leg. Blood welled around the protruding knife.

"Don't pull it out." The pain dimmed Mike's vision, and a cool sensation drifted over him. "But you need to apply pressure..." Mike sucked in a deep breath, "around it. Can you do it?"

Her face paled as she stared down at the wound. With a quick shake of her head, she stripped off her shirt and wadded it up around the knife.

"Cell. In pocket." He wasn't going to stay conscious for long. And at the rate he was bleeding out, he might not wake up. "Love you."

She hesitated for a second. "I love you too." She packed her shirt around the blade. "You're going to be fine."

He knew better. The way he was leaking, both his leg and life were iffy.

"Christ, I told you to wait for me." Sean's voice boomed over the clearing. "Son of a bitch. You had to go get yourself stabbed." He nudged Rachel aside. "Let me in here."

Mike's body trembled violently. Sean spread his jacket over Mike's chest. Cold washed over him like floodwater. He could barely feel Rachel's fingers gripping his, but the tears streaming down her soot-streaked face said it all. Unfortunately, the numbness spreading though his body didn't extend to the knife sticking out of his leg.

Sirens approached. Sean was working on the wound. He looked away for a second. "Rachel, take my gun." Sean nodded at David's prone body. "If he moves, shoot him."

"He's not dead?" Mike croaked.

"Unfortunately not. At least not yet. Remind me to never piss off your girlfriend." Despite the joke, his friend's eyes were serious—and worried—as he whipped out a cell and punched a key. Blood coated his fingers. He handed Rachel the phone. "Put it on speaker. I need both hands here." Then he leaned over Mike's face. "Hold tight. This is gonna hurt."

The searing pain in his leg exploded until, mercifully, everything faded to a blissful nothing.

⟣

Curled into a ball on an armchair in the surgical waiting room, Rachel shivered in a state of numb disbelief. On the pale yellow wall next to her, a plaque read *In loving memory of Robert Taylor.* Death had funded the room. Death had bought the upholstered chair in which she sat waiting to learn Mike's fate. Death owned this place.

Sean paced the navy carpet, as he had for the past two hours. The blood splatters on his clothes had dried to a dark, rusty red that matched the stains on the tank and jeans she still wore. Though the room was crowded with cops and some other people Rachel didn't recognize, she was very much alone. The only empty chairs were the ones on either side of her. The group overflowed the small room into the hallway, but the silence was more crushing than the crowd.

Mike had filled the spaces inside her she hadn't known were empty. If he didn't make it, she felt like she'd wither and die. And wouldn't care very much. In fact, right now she didn't feel much at all. Her overloaded system had shut down, as if the overwhelming events of the night had tripped her circuit breaker.

A tall man with a cane entered. Sarah was right behind him. Wiping tears from her face, Sarah rushed to Rachel's side and enveloped her in a desperate hug. "Oh my God. I've been looking for you."

The tall man pulled out a phone. "We found her." He touched Sean's shoulder. "You didn't answer your cell."

Sean pulled his phone from his pocket and looked at it blankly. "Sorry, Jack. I didn't feel it vibrate."

Sarah pushed Rachel back to arm's length. "Are you all right? Did a doctor look at you?"

Two women came through the door. Sean took the slim brunette in his arms and held her tightly. Or maybe she held him tightly. It was hard to tell who was supporting whom. Watching them, Rachel's heart hurt more than the raw burns on her hands.

"There you are." The other woman, a tall blond, took the empty seat at Rachel's side. "I'm Claire, Quinn's wife."

Rachel nodded.

Shrewd but kind eyes sized her up, and obviously, didn't like what they saw. Claire took a stethoscope from her pocket and pressed it against Rachel's back. A minute later she produced a blood pressure cuff from another pocket. She took Rachel's pulse, then turned her hand over and frowned at the burns that Rachel was ignoring. "Sean, didn't it occur to you that she needed treatment?"

Sean shrugged. "Figured she needed to be here."

Claire disappeared and returned a few minutes later with a blanket. She wrapped it around Rachel's bare shoulders. Heat enveloped her. She didn't realize how cold she'd been.

A shadow filled the doorway. Quinn stepped into the room. He walked over to Rachel and squatted down in front of her. "The surgery went well. He's going to intensive care for the night, but it looks good."

All the air left her lungs. Had she been holding her breath? Tiny pinpoints of light speckled her vision.

Quinn's frown matched his wife's. "I was looking for you in the ER. Why aren't you there?"

Standing next to him, Claire crossed her arms over her chest. "Small second-degree burns on her hand. She's hypothermic and dehydrated."

Quinn uttered what sounded like a curse under his breath. "Here's the deal. I will get you in to see him for a couple of minutes *if* you agree to go back downstairs and get treated afterward." It wasn't a question, and Quinn didn't wait for an answer.

In short order she was gowned and standing in an ICU cubicle surrounded by a host of medical equipment she knew all too well. Is this how Sarah had felt? Afraid to believe what her eyes were seeing? Hope crushed was worse than no hope at all. Rachel moved closer. Mike's face was white as the hospital linens. Tubes and wires snaked across and under the sheets. But his massive chest rose in an even rhythm, and the bank of monitors assured her that his heart was beating regularly too. Tears trickled down her face as she watched, as it sank in.

He wasn't dead.

After the past few hours of mentally replaying the sight of his blood draining into the earth, the relief buckled her knees. Quinn's hand subtly supported her elbow.

"He won't be alone, will he? No offense, but he doesn't like hospitals much."

"I know all about Mike's, uhm, issue." Quinn smiled. "I'll be right here all night. Go with Jack. Mike isn't going to wake up tonight. But tomorrow, the first thing he's going to want to see is you. He'll feel better if you don't look half-dead or have blood in your hair."

Her hand strayed to her head. Her hair was stiff and sticky. Ugh. But still she hesitated, not used to seeing the big and capable man she loved so vulnerable.

"You and Mike are a lot alike. Yeah, I know, you seem like opposites because he's so calm all the time, and you're, well, not. Besides the fact that much of his calm is an act, you both spend a lot of time taking care of other people,"

Quinn said quietly. "It's OK to let those others take care of you occasionally."

"You'll really stay with him?"

"All night."

Downstairs, the ER staff wrapped her in heated blankets, then cleaned and bandaged the burns on her hand. Rachel passed on an IV, chugging a bottle of water instead. She'd rather be upstairs with Mike, but she had to admit she was as tired as she'd ever been in her life. Having other people like Quinn to rely on wasn't half bad. Maybe she could adjust.

Rachel stiffened in the backseat of Jack's SUV. Now that she was assured that Mike would be all right, her brain cells were rebooting. She tapped Jack on the shoulder. "Oh my God. The horses. Jack, I have to go home."

"No, you don't," Sarah said from the passenger seat. "Cristan rounded them all up, and Blake took them back to his place."

Rachel fell back into the seat. This having friends thing was pretty nice so far.

Jack's place was a freaking mansion behind a huge set of black wrought iron gates no less. Blazing lights illuminated scaffolding along the stone façade where repairs were in progress. Jack drove around to the back of the house.

He parked as close to the house as possible and led Rachel and Sarah to a set of French doors. "Everybody's probably asleep—"

Yap, yap, yap. Bandit's high-pitched alert was followed up with the deep *woof* of a much bigger dog.

A delicate, petite woman with long brown hair opened the door for them. Bandit and a giant German shepherd vied for the opening. Bandit won. The woman stuck a foot in front of the little dog to block his exit. "Quiet."

Jack hustled through the doorway, pushing the big dog out of the way. "Back up, Henry." The shepherd head-butted Jack's bad leg. "Ooof."

Beth pointed. "Henry, sit."

The German shepherd dropped his butt to the floor.

Rachel followed Sarah into a huge and comfortable old kitchen. Despite the grandeur of the house's exterior, the outdated interior had a homey, broken-in feel. Sarah scooped up Bandit.

"I'm Beth," the small woman said. She gestured to a tall, fit-looking older woman hustling around the kitchen. A whipcord-lean man of about seventy leaned against the counter. "This is Mrs. Harris and my Uncle James." Beth's uncle was watching Rachel with blue eyes too sharp and piercing for a man of his age.

Frowning, Jack kissed Beth. "You should be in bed."

The top of Beth's head barely reached Jack's shoulder. "I'm fine."

The way Jack's broad hand kept straying to Beth's barely discernible baby bump gave Rachel an acute case of the warm and fuzzies. What would it feel like to carry Mike's child? To have him touch her with that tender joy? And she suddenly needed to sit down.

A chair was under her butt as her legs jellied. Uncle James moved faster than she expected. Mrs. Harris was right behind him. She set a steaming mug on the table. "You look done in, dear. Here's some tea. Let's give her some space." Mrs. Harris tugged on James's arm. "If there's anything you need, my door is just beyond the kitchen. Knock anytime. Are you hungry?"

Rachel shook her head.

"Feel free to root through the kitchen," Beth said as Jack steered her through the doorway. "Sarah, the room next to yours is ready." Beth tapped her thigh. Henry fell into step behind her.

James hesitated at the door. "You need help getting upstairs?"

"We'll be fine. Thank you for everything." Sarah sat down next to Rachel and rubbed her back. Quiet settled over them.

"I feel like I'm having an out-of-brain experience. The thoughts going through my head can't be mine." Like those about marriage, babies, and other terrifying events she'd never before contemplated. "I just found him, and I almost lost him."

"I almost lost you." Sarah draped an arm over her shoulder. "Again."

"I'm sorry I put you through that." Rachel was going to start thinking about others before she just did stuff from now on. Really.

"Not your fault." Sarah stood and set Bandit on the floor. "Come on. Getting cleaned up will help loads. You want a shower or bath?"

Rachel stood and looked down at her blood-crusted clothes. What she really wanted was to be with Mike. "Both."

᷾

Mike opened his eyes to a hazy, dim room. Something beeped softly next to his head.

"You're awake? Amazing. We gave you enough juice to put an elephant to sleep." Quinn was leaning over him and pressing a hand to his shoulder. "Don't move and don't freak."

Mike opened cracked lips. His throat was scratchy and dry, and his mind too hazy to even contemplate freaking. Not to mention the fact that his body weighed about a zillion pounds. He probably couldn't lift his pinkie finger if he tried. Whatever was chugging through his veins was making him feel very Zen with the whole hospital deal.

Quinn put a plastic spoonful of ice chips in his mouth. The cold liquid in Mike's mouth was heaven. Quinn moved down to the foot of the bed and lifted the sheet. Panic gave Mike a surge of energy. He struggled to raise his head. "Is it...?"

"It's OK. Leg's still here. I'm not going to lie though. It was close. The knife hit a branch of the femoral instead of the main artery. That bit of luck and Sean's combat first aid training saved your life and your leg." Quinn's hand closed around Mike's foot. "Can you feel that?"

Mike nodded.

"Wiggle your toes."

The effort was Herculean.

"Good." Quinn tossed the sheet back over his leg. "And now for the other bit of good news. While you were out, you had your gut scoped."

"Dammit, Quinn. You can't just—"

"Normally, I would agree, but you are an extenuating circumstance. I watched the whole thing, by the way. You were very cooperative."

"I was unconscious." And the creepy-crawly feeling that gave him was one of the many, many reasons he hated hospitals.

"Exactly." Quinn nodded. "I thought it might be my only chance."

Quinn would've been right if Mike hadn't fallen in love with Rachel. While he'd been lying in mud, bleeding, he'd been more afraid of dying than anything else. He would have done anything to stay alive—to stay with Rachel. Now he understood now why his mother had fought hard and endured so much.

"Anyway, you are the proud owner of an Olympic-sized, but perfectly ordinary ulcer, easily treatable with medication. Aren't you relieved?"

"Yes," Mike grumbled, but relief coursed through him like the morphine drip. "How's Rachel?"

"She's fine. Treated for minor burns and released a couple of hours ago. I wouldn't let her in to see you unless she agreed to go home with Jack and get some rest. I also told her there was no way you'd wake up until morning. So it'd be good if you didn't mention this discussion."

Mike's face pulled into a weak smile. "I won't tell her if you won't."

When he opened his eyes again, Sean had taken Quinn's place in the chair by the bed.

"I'm not going to freak out."

"So you say." Sean scooted closer. "But we all remember that panic attack in the ER a few years back. You broke stuff."

Mike cringed. "Seriously, I can barely lift my head. I don't need a babysitter." But having someone by his side didn't hurt. He was so, so happy to be here instead of dead, but the place still gave him the willies.

"Jack called. He's bringing Rachel over now. She's been driving him up the wall since dawn and being a general pain in his ass."

"So she's all right."

"That she is." Sean snorted. "That is some woman. She literally bashed Gunner's brains in to protect you. You'd better marry that one ASAP."

"Plan to."

Sean laughed. "Those must be good drugs. You didn't even break a sweat when you said that."

"Any woman who defends my wounded body with a tree branch is a keeper."

"Amen."

"Did Gunner make it?"

"So far." Sean sounded disgusted. "But he has a serious head injury. Rachel has quite a swing. The doctors don't know if he's going to come out of it. The state police detective has been sniffing around. Quinn chased him off, but you'll have to give a statement."

"I know." Worry wormed its way through the drugs. Even if David died, Rachel's actions were clearly defensive. He'd kidnapped her. He'd tried to kill Mike. There was a clear record of stalking and escalating violence. David was a killer. But Mike wasn't working the case. He was flat on his back and useless.

Well, damn. Just when he thought he didn't have anything else to worry about.

Rachel walked in a few minutes later, and Sean ducked out. Watching her cross the room, Mike's heart doubled in size. Except for a bandaged hand, a few bruises, and a general air of exhaustion, she looked great. Safe. Alive.

His.

Her eyes were misty, and she swiped a hand across her cheek. "I swore I wasn't going to cry anymore. I don't think I've cried this much in my entire life."

"Come here." The tears in her eyes were making him choke up. Mike held out a hand.

She took it gingerly. "I don't want to hurt you."

"Everything but the leg is fine." Mike tugged her closer.

She leaned down and kissed him, then laid her head on his hospital-gowned chest. "I was so afraid."

Mike untangled his IV line from her hair and wrapped his arms around her. "It's over. He can't hurt you again."

"No, I meant I was afraid I was going to lose you." She shuddered against him. "I love you."

Mike stroked her hair. "I love you too. When David had you, I could barely function."

"But you did, and you found me. But let's not do any more of that, OK?" she said against his throat. "Let's just be nice and boring from now on."

"Good idea." But Mike honestly didn't think life with Rachel would ever be boring. He kissed the top of her head. "Are you going to be able to live with what you did?"

"You mean if he dies?"

"Yeah."

"I watched him stab you. He tried to burn my horses alive." She picked up her head. Anger lit her eyes. "Yeah, I'm good with it. Though I might have nightmares that I didn't hit him hard enough."

Mike coughed. Pain shot through his leg. The drugs were wearing thin. "The state police detective is going to want a statement. When he does, you might want to express that a little differently. Remorse would be good. Feel free to cry some more."

She made a disgusted noise that sounded disturbingly like Sean. "Jack already lectured me at breakfast. Then he arranged for his lawyer to go with me at ten."

Thank you, Jack.

"I'm sorry I wasn't here when you woke up." She sniffed and straightened. "I didn't want to leave last night, but I was handily manipulated by Quinn."

"It's a sign of affection. He only bullies people he cares about."

She smoothed the thin blanket over his chest. "Did Sean tell you my house isn't habitable?"

"No. But I saw the firemen hosing it down last night."

"The roof needs to be replaced, among other things. It's going to take a few weeks to get it repaired."

"Move in with me," Mike said with no hesitation.

"With my sister and her girls?"

"Would be kind of tight." Besides, he was done with the *sleeping on the couch* thing. But he also noticed she hadn't turned him down. He was lying in a hospital bed, the pain growing in his leg was enough to drop a rhino, and he was happier than he'd ever been in his life. "We'll work something out."

Jack stuck his head in the door. "Can I talk to Mike for a minute?"

Rachel slipped out into the hall. The tightening of Mike's chest had nothing to do with his injury.

Jack approached the bed, arms crossed over his chest. "OK, now that you can't run away, tell me why you've been avoiding me."

Mike looked down at the waffle weave white blanket. "It was my fault Beth was nearly killed."

Jack's face scrunched into a what-the-hell expression. "Your fault? Why would you think that?"

"I should've known. He was murdering women right under my nose. How did I miss that? How could I talk to him and not know what he was?"

"Mike, you can't blame yourself." Jack put a hand on Mike's shoulder. "None of us knew. In the twenty years I worked homicide, do you think I caught every killer? Not even close. So get that thought right out of your head. That's too much responsibility for anyone to carry."

Tension eased out of Mike. "Thanks for taking care of Rachel and her sister and the girls. It has to be bedlam over there."

"Yeah, but it's a comfortable sort of chaos. Last year I was a cranky bachelor who lived for the job. Today, I'm living with two seniors, three women, four kids, and two dogs— *and* I'm getting married next week." Jack's face stretched into a wide grin. "You're all welcome to stay as long as you need to. We have plenty of room." He glanced at his watch. "I'd better get Rachel over to the state police station so she can get this statement out of the way."

"I'm a little worried about that."

Jack nodded in understanding. "I talked with the state detective who's handling the case. Seems Gunner's place is quite the treasure trove. He's been spying on people since he was just a kid. Started with stills, thousands of them. Recently he progressed to video surveillance. He installed hidden webcams inside the vents of Vince and Tanya Mitchell's house, with live streaming. In addition to videos of Tanya showering and doing the nasty with old Vince, Gunner had some audios that sure sound like Vince making deals with Lawrence Harmon. Mitchell and Harmon are both under investigation right now. Plus, Gunner's facing kidnapping charges and two counts of murder. Will Martin died overnight."

A nurse hustled into the room, checked Mike's wristband, and injected something into his IV.

Relief ebbed through Mike, or maybe it was just the pain medicine. Whatever it was, he was too tired to fight it. "I appreciate this, Jack."

"She'll be fine," Jack continued. "She didn't do anything wrong, and my lawyer's going to be there."

"Thanks for that. She can be…difficult."

"You got a live one, that's for sure."

☞

A week later, Mike eased his bulk out of the passenger seat of Sean's SUV. Pain shot up his leg as he hopped onto the concrete apron in front of the community center. He winced and leaned on the open door.

Sean was already at the curb with a pair of metal crutches. "Are you sure you're up for this? You've only been out of the hospital for two days."

Which Mike had spent sleeping and hobbling around Jack's place. Rachel was recuperating there as well. "Nancy said I should be here. Something must be up."

"If Quinn finds out I brought you here, he's gonna kill me."

Mike tucked the crutches under his arms. "He's working tonight."

"Yeah, but he has spies everywhere. It's not healthy to piss off my brother. He's liable to misplace the lidocaine just when I need it." Sean scanned the overflowing parking lot and vehicle-lined street. People were pouring into the community center from every direction. "Something's definitely up."

Rachel and Sarah got out of the back and joined them on the sidewalk. Rachel took her place at his side as they started up the walk.

"I'll go park." But as Sean turned to his SUV, Troy Mitchell came out of the building. Wide-eyed, he stopped dead and stared at the group on the sidewalk.

"Shit." Troy pivoted and took a running step in the opposite direction.

Sean grabbed him by the back of the collar. "What did you do?"

Troy stiffened. "Nothing. Let go of me."

"Why did you try to run away?" Sean lifted him onto his toes.

"Get your hands off me." Troy pointed at Sarah. "I haven't been anywhere near her. You can railroad my old man, but I am *not* going to prison."

Mike looked closer. Troy's eyes were clear. His clothes were clean. Most importantly, he didn't stink like booze.

"I haven't missed a single AA meeting or been to the bar or done anything else my lawyer says I shouldn't," Troy bristled. "Whatever Will did, he did on his own. I had nothing to do with it, and you can't prove otherwise."

Sean pulled him closer. "Troy, if you ever bother her again, prison will be the least of your worries."

Sean let go, and Troy race-walked away.

"He's sober." Rachel's eyes narrowed with distrust as she watched Troy's departure. "I hope he stays that way."

"Me too." Sarah was smiling.

Rachel grabbed her sister's arm. "You're not—"

"Definitely not," Sarah blurted out. "But it would be better for the girls if their father weren't a drunk."

"I'll be back as soon as I can find a place to park." Sean stepped into his vehicle.

Mike moved toward the entrance. Rachel opened the door for him. Inside, town residents packed the main meeting room to standing-room-only.

"Chief! Over here." Three men vacated their seats in the back row. Mike's face heated at the attention, but he let people herd him toward a seat. More tired than he wanted to be, he eased into it gratefully. Somebody took his crutches. Someone else pushed a chair in front of him. "Better get that leg up."

Rachel slid into the chair next to him, with Sarah on her other side.

A gavel banged at the front of the room. Chairs scraped on the wood floor, and voices hushed as the crowd took their seats, giving Mike his first view of the front of the room. Fred was at the podium. Behind him, three members of the town council sat at the long table. Vince's seat was conspicuously empty. Herb and Frank were grinning. Lee slouched miserably over a piece of paper.

A hand landed on Mike's shoulder. He glanced up to see Sean standing behind him.

Up front, the mayor cleared his throat. "I'm distressed to report that Councilman Mitchell was arrested this morning on multiple counts of fraud and accepting bribes."

Excited murmurs rose from the audience.

"Tell us something we don't know," someone yelled over the noise.

"Yeah, Fred. Like what's going to happen with the Lost Lake project?"

People went silent. All eyes turned back to the mayor.

Mike rubbed his aching thigh, just above the thick bandage. Quinn was right again. Mike should be taking it easy, not sitting in on a long-winded town meeting. On the bright side, his gut was burn-free. His ulcer had already responded to the lack of stress and the handful of pills he was swallowing twice a day.

Fred sagged. "Lawrence Harmon was also arrested this morning. I have no idea what's going to happen to the development project at this time."

The din swelled to a crescendo.

Fred banged his gavel again, but the crown ignored him. Two people pushed their way through the crowd to the front of the room. Mike grinned as Nancy and Phyllis nudged Fred out of the way.

Nancy plucked the gavel out of Fred's hands and brought it down on the podium with authority.

Phyllis took the microphone. "Settle down." She waited for the crowd to quiet. "Fred can't be expected to know what's going to happen with the project yet, but there are several matters that he should be addressing." She paused for effect, scanning the crowd with clear gray eyes. "Like why he suspended the police chief who has served this town for more than a decade."

Mike's hand froze on his leg. Did he hear what he thought he heard?

Nancy pulled a sheaf of papers from a portfolio and raised her glasses from where they rested at the end of their chain. She leaned over the mic. "We have here a petition signed by over five hundred residents, calling for town council to rescind Chief O'Connell's suspension."

Applause and whistles broke out. Phyllis tapped on the microphone. The noise level dropped. "We'd have more names if we weren't in such a rush."

Stunned, Mike shut his gaping mouth. Rachel squeezed his hand and wiped a tear from her eye. He glanced over his shoulder and gave Sean a questioning look. Sean shook his head, as if he had no idea what was going on either.

Nancy held the microphone toward the mayor. Fred's mouth opened and closed like a skinny trout. "There will be an immediate inquiry—"

"Can it, Fred." Nancy straightened her cardigan. "The whole thing was obviously orchestrated by Vince so he could get away with the very things he was just arrested for doing."

Phyllis tapped her sensible, low-heeled shoe on the worn wood floor. "We need Michael, Fred, much more than we need you."

Fred's face reddened, but he didn't attempt to argue the point. He walked around to the back of the table, where the three remaining council members had their heads together. A minute later, Herb Duncan jumped out of his chair and practically soft-shoed to the podium. He hugged Nancy and Phyllis. "The town council unanimously votes to offer Chief O'Connell both our profound apologies and his job."

The crowd surged to its feet. People around Mike turned and offered hands and congratulations. Sean planted himself next to Mike's injured leg.

Herb's voice boomed over the speakers. "Mike, you take as long as you need to heal up. Your job'll be waiting whenever you're ready."

Chapter Thirty

A few days later, Rachel sat next to Mike on the sloping back lawn of Jack's estate. Their joined hands rested on her thigh, their fingers interlaced. Mike's leg was propped on a cushioned chair. A cool breeze rustled through the trees and sent fallen leaves tumbling across the rolling green grass.

Jack and Beth exchanged vows in a quiet ceremony. Rachel highly approved of the lack of froufrou. Beth was lovely in an ivory dress that skimmed her barely rounded belly and fell to just above her knees, Jack tall and handsome in a dark suit with Quinn at his side. Their I-dos were punctuated by the pop of corks from bottles of sparkling apple cider and champagne.

Everyone moved toward the paver patio, where the caterers were passing glasses around.

"I'm sorry. I'm so sappy lately." Rachel wiped her eyes and held Mike's crutches while he got to his feet. He didn't say anything, but his face tensed with pain. "Do you want to go inside and rest for a while?"

"No, I'm tired of lying around, especially when all I can do is lie around."

"I know. The whole recovery process stinks." She slowed her steps to match his pace. "But you need the rest."

He leaned down, whispering in her ear, "Come with me, just for a couple of minutes."

She followed him past a horde of screaming kids and barking dogs. "You shouldn't be on that leg for long. Quinn will have your hide."

"Quinn will be fine with it. The therapist said I could start putting some weight on it." At the rear of the house, Mike gestured to the golf cart Jack used to get around the huge property. Rachel hiked up the skirt of her black fancy all-occasion dress and hopped into the driver's seat.

"Move over." Mike nudged her. "I can manage a golf cart."

"But *should* you?"

"Just move over. We're not going far."

She slid across the bench seat. Mike stowed his crutches and climbed behind the wheel. He drove down the path to the barn. Horses grazed in the pasture, placidly swatting flies in the warmth of the autumn sun.

"It's pretty here." She sighed.

"So is your place." Mike got out and repositioned the crutches.

"My barn is a pile of rubble and my house needs a complete renovation."

"That can be done." He swung toward the barn.

Walking on her toes so her heels didn't sink into the soft dirt, she followed him. "The insurance money should cover the barn. I'll be lucky to get a new roof on the house. But it'll do."

Mike led her inside the cool building.

"Why are we here?"

"I wanted to get you alone, and I wanted to show you something." Mike stopped in front of a stall. Straw rustled inside.

Rachel took a tentative step forward. "Beth's horses are outside."

"They are."

It couldn't be. He didn't.

Lady stuck her graceful head over the half-door and nickered.

He did.

The waterworks started up again as Rachel stroked the mare's forehead. "How did you—?"

"Wasn't easy. Blake refused to sell her to me." Were Mike's blue eyes misty? "The bill of sale is actually in your name."

Rachel threw her arms around his neck. He nearly lost his balance returning her hug. His crutches fell to the ground with a clatter.

She pulled back, cognizant of his injury. "I'm sorry. Did I hurt you?"

"No." Laughing, he turned and put his back against the wall for support. Strong arms wrapped around her, pulling her tight. "Will you marry me?"

"Yes. Definitely, yes." She breathed in the scent of him. Lady nudged her shoulder. Rachel lifted her head and patted the long nose.

"So, here's the plan. I move in with you, and Sarah and the girls can have my house in town. It's only a couple of blocks from the elementary school. We'll rebuild the barn and fix up the house."

"Wait." Rachel stopped him. "That's a great plan, but I don't have the money for a renovation."

Mike kissed her. "I have some put aside. I inherited my house free and clear ten years ago. The township provides me with a vehicle, and I don't remember my last vacation. I've been banking most of my salary for ten years."

"Old houses can be a pain in the butt."

"I know, but they're worth it." Mike pulled her hard against him. She was careful not to touch his injured thigh. Certain parts of him had recovered just fine. "You just have to promise me you'll try to be less reckless."

Rachel tapped the center of his wide chest with her forefinger. "That goes both ways, He-Man. You have to take care of yourself too."

He grinned. "It's a deal."

"Are you sure?" Rachel. "I can be a real pain in the butt too. No matter how hard I try, that's not likely to change."

Mike kissed her again. "God help me, but I sure hope not."

THE END

About the Author

John Tannock Photography, 2012

Melinda Leigh abandoned her career in banking to raise her kids and never looked back. She started writing as a hobby and became addicted to creating characters and stories. Since then, she has won numerous writing awards for her paranormal romance and romantic-suspense fiction. Nominated for an International Thriller Award for Best First Novel, her debut book, *She Can Run*, sold over 100,000 copies within six months and was the number one bestseller in both Kindle Romantic Suspense and Mystery/Thriller. When she isn't writing, Melinda is an avid martial artist: she holds a second-degree black belt in Kenpo karate and teaches women's self-defense. She lives in a messy house with her husband, two teenagers, a couple of dogs, and two rescue cats.